E B

The Green Bay Tree

ALEXANDRA CONNOR

The Green Bay Tree

HEINEMANN: LONDON

First published in Great Britain 1993
by William Heinemann Ltd
an imprint of Reed Consumer Books Ltd
Michelin House, 81 Fulham Road, London sw3 6rb
and Auckland, Melbourne, Singapore and Toronto

Copyright © Alexandra Connor 1993
The author has asserted her moral rights

A CIP catalogue record for this book is available at the
British Library
ISBN 0 434 14222 0

Typeset by ROM-Data Corporation, Falmouth,
Cornwall, England
Printed and bound in Great Britain by
St Edmundsbury Press Limited, Bury St Edmunds, Suffolk

This book is dedicated to Dr Nicola Binns, a true and constant friend.

The green bay tree is the tree of Apollo – the god of love. It comes from the fable that tells of Daphne, a very beautiful goddess who swore to remain a virgin. But Apollo fell in love with her and pursued her relentlessly, so that, in despair, she fled to her father for protection and he turned her into the bay tree. From then onwards, Apollo wore a crown of bay leaves in memory of his undying love.

Traditional Fable

… flourishing like a green bay tree … I went by, and lo, he was gone; I sought him but his place could nowhere be found …

The Book of Common Prayer

Prologue

Yorkshire

Let me out, the voice said from somewhere beneath her feet, low toned, almost muffled, but urgent. *Let me out.* Startled, Freddie's eyes fixed on the ground, fear scratching like glass splinters in her stomach. No, she thought, Bart is dead, he is definitely dead … The wind nudged at her, making its own dark cries. Perhaps it had just been the wind she heard, mistaking it for the sound of her dead husband calling. An image darted in front of her eyes – a man in a coffin, struggling to escape as the heavy weight of earth pressed down on him.

The day was unwelcoming. A blackthorn winter in York-shire, the second week in May as cold as December, the buildings ringed with frost, the whole dark green slide of the moors whitened. When dawn had finally broken, the cold had crept shivering over stone walls and vigilant hedges, the chill picking at the locks of the house and making rushes through briefly opened doors. By nine o'clock everyone felt the cold's unwelcome presence, shuddering as it passed by them and curled malevolently up the stairs.

No clothes gave sufficient protection against such weather, and as Freddie stood by the grave her toes and fingers were bloodless, the pain of cold and grief making her eyes water as they fixed on the heap of earth at her feet. Only a sonorous bell made any noise, ringing down from the dour country church, its tolls winging over a passing flock of birds flying silent and black against the light.

To present a united family front, Greville and Sarah Clements

1

accompanied their daughter, her mother silly with compassion, her father silent. Yet once, when she looked up, Freddie caught him watching her as he had done so often when she was a child. He was still a glamorous, handsome man, betraying some hint of foreign blood, his clothes sombre but well-cut, and his beautiful hands kept warm in the pigskin gloves, his smooth skin smelling faintly of lemon cologne. It was so simple for Freddie to remember the fear he had instilled in her as a child and even though distance had dulled much of her recall, one incident always remained.

She had been playing, her voice high with excitement, and, disturbed, he had come into the playroom to quieten her. His hand had gripped her arm and, softly, almost as though it was to be a secret between them, he had told her of the Ice Saints. He had said that because she had been naughty, that night, when it was dark, she would hear a scratching, then a tapping on her window as the Ice Saints from over the moors came looking for her. Wicked children had to be taught a lesson, he said, and so the Ice Saints would crawl out of their graves on the moors to punish her.

The ground was hard under her feet as Freddie remembered the words and shuddered.

Let me out.

She stared at the earth and shook her head disbelievingly. Sleep, darling, sleep, she urged him. Sleep.

Under the earth lay her husband, far under, where the Ice Saints could never reach him, and there he would lie, as she had last seen him, hands across his breast, a dark business suit replacing the finality of a shroud. Bart Wallace, an American born in New York, but laid to rest in Yorkshire, under a blackthorn sky.

A sudden, violent gust of wind pushed a scattering of snow over the grave and for an instant there was a definite noise from below. Maybe the earth shifting, Freddie thought frantically, or maybe the sound of someone knocking and calling out for her. Stiff with horror, she stared at the interrupted earth. *I know you are dead*, she thought, *I know ...*

But what if he had woken and was still angry, she thought

2

suddenly. What if he was now clawing with blackened fingernails, breathless and frantic, to get out from under the packed earth? What if he wanted his revenge so urgently that he would come back from the dead to punish her?

A thin moan escaped her lips as Freddie stepped back quickly, almost losing her footing as she stumbled across the graveyard to the waiting car. Urgently she wrenched open the door and climbed in, only glancing back once as they drove through the cemetery gates. A circle of wreaths bordered her husband's grave, the red of the flowers bright like new blood, the leaves burned black with the frost.

Surely so far beneath the earth he was safe, she thought desperately. So far below he must sleep and forget ... Another thought followed on immediately. Maybe he would not sleep. Maybe instead he would be wakened by the sound of feet passing over, the heavy feet which came at night, making their way across his body and across the dark moors towards a light in a bedroom window.

Let me out.

For nearly a year after Bart's death, Freddie slept with the lamp on by her bed. Sometimes she slept, but at other times she would wake quickly, imagining the quick scratch of cold fingers on the windows as the Ice Saints came for her.

PART ONE

By a route obscure and lonely
haunted by ill angels only

Dreamland Edgar Allan Poe

Chapter One

'Cambuscan'
Tydale Brook
Yorkshire

Over the crumpled copy of *The Times* a dragonfly passed. Iridescent winged, it threw a shadow over the fading print before the quick sun forced it back into the shade. The newspaper lay open, half read and then dismissed, wedged under a porcelain cup and saucer, the colour of winter skin. An inch of dark coffee cooled, the sunlight skimming round the cup's rim, an unused lump of brown sugar enticing a scavenging bee.

Without moving, tucked in the house's shadow, a child watched silently. Her eyes, the colour of May lilac, followed the insect's movements as the bee hovered over the sugar, humming uncertainly. Carefully the child copied the sound, the buzzing noise vibrating against her lips as she repeated in her head the words: *I will not cry. I will not cry* ... The insect hummed in unison with her. The late spring sun crept towards the child, looping over the grass towards her feet so that she drew her legs up towards her body to avoid it, her chin resting on her knees.

The rabbit had been an Easter present, an early Easter bunny bought by her mother, a pink ribbon tied around its neck, an ideal gift for a seven-year-old girl. Freddie had been delighted with the animal, large and docile, not overly affectionate but willing to be handled. She called it Mrs Gilly after the village postmistress – amused that the animal had the

woman's same resigned look – and the two became inseparable. For days Mrs Gilly had been carried around, pushed in a
doll's pram, or simply laid on the grass beside Freddie, its
thick white hair warm to the touch, its eyes the colour of
magenta.

A hutch had been bought for Mrs Gilly, but she was never
left in it for long, and every random dropping was quickly
removed to prevent irritation, her father having taken a strong
dislike to the rabbit. He watched it, his dark eyes returning its
magenta stare, his long-digited hands twirling a piece of limp
salad in front of the furred face ... Freddie blinked, repeating
the litany, *I will not cry*, and then suddenly sniffed the cool
shadowed air. From out of the open window came the smell
and sounds of baking, a hot oven, water boiling on a gas flame,
an old fan wheezing as it turned overhead. Cooking smells
made their escape to the garden, gravy smells, potatoes steaming in their jackets, and a quick hiss of cold water dropped on
a hot plate.

Suddenly Freddie wanted to move, to escape the aromas
creeping over her. Only yesterday they had sat down to their
Easter lunch, her mother, her father and herself in the dining
room, being served in silence. Behind Freddie, on the sideboard, lay a selection of toys as impersonal as a layout for a
magazine catalogue. All from her father, all expensive but
imposing, the doll and bear regarding their new owner without interest or sympathy. Soon Freddie found herself longing
for the end of the meal and an escape to the garden with Mrs
Gilly, but the first course was idled over, her father chewing
thoughtfully as she glanced at him.

He fascinated her almost as much as he frightened her.
Cutting his food, his head was inclined slightly downwards,
the full marvel of his looks not apparent. His knife see-sawed
into the pâté, then dipped into the thick ochre butter on his
plate. With sensuous strokes his smoothed it over a small
knuckle of bread and then smeared the pâté on top, slipping
it into his mouth and then glancing over to his wife.

She smiled, partially with relief and partially with desire;
he was in a good mood, his eyes long-lashed and luminous

8

promising after-lunch sex. Freddie continued to watch her father, noticing how his hair rested against his collar, its length and thickness unusual, as was his luminous skin.

Suddenly he glanced over to her, his eyes clicking as he blinked, then glanced away. Chilled, Freddie felt suddenly exposed, as though he had stolen something from her without permission, and in order to steady herself she gazed longingly out of the window. In just a little while she would be outside with Mrs Gilly, all she had to do was to get through the meal, that was all … As had happened so many times before, her father lingered, his wife making no effort to hurry him.

Finally, he leaned back and waited for the next course to be served.

'So what do you think of your presents, Frederica?'

She smiled warily as a large baked pie was laid in front of her father, a hot plate placed in front of her. She could feel the heat rise and warm her face.

'They're lovely.'

'They *are* lovely,' he corrected her, looking at his wife for approval.

Sarah smiled encouragement.

'They are lovely,' Freddie replied obediently. 'Thank you.'

'*They are lovely, thank you*,' he parroted. 'Who?' he said more loudly, a knife poised above the baked pie, ready to strike into the browned crust.

Freddie faltered. 'Pardon?'

The knife remained in the air. '*Who* am I?'

Her face reddened, 'My father.'

'So what do you say?'

Sarah watched her daughter, willing her not to antagonise him further.

'Thank you, father … ' Freddie said quietly, her voice trailing off.

The knife still hesitated. 'You've been very surly lately, Frederica,' he went on, 'and you're not doing well at school, are you?'

Her head hummed. The room seemed suffocatingly hot, the pie steaming defiantly on the table. She felt for an instant

9

that when he plunged the knife into the pastry, it would be full of maggots and bats would fly out, tangling in her hair.

She moaned quietly to herself.

'What did you say?'

'Nothing.'

The knife finally began its descent and severed the dark crust.

'Pass me your plate.'

Freddie did so, holding it with her napkin, the heat still burning her fingers. But she wouldn't drop it, even if it made her fingers bleed. He ladled some meat onto the plate, then some crust, then some vegetables.

'Now eat.'

Freddie regained her seat, her knife and fork poised over the steaming food. The gravy was thick, rich in aroma and shiny like wood as she dipped her fork into it.

'You have to be a little more responsible. Show a little more control,' her father went on, watching her. His own plate was still empty. 'Is that good?'

She glanced up, hesitated and then nodded.

'So why aren't you eating it?'

Suddenly suspicious, Freddie dared to ask, 'What is it?'

'Taste it and see.'

Her eyes fixed on his. She felt an overwhelming sensation of panic and shook her head.

'What is it?'

He had waited for this, and smiled. 'Rabbit.'

Freddie ran out of the room and vomited in the cloakroom, a foaming of acrid bubbles coming down her nose as she rinsed out her mouth. Shivering with shock, she made her way to the kitchen, Meg Kershaw glancing up as she arrived.

'All finished?' she asked smiling and wiping her hands. 'I never heard the bell ring.'

Her husband, sitting by the Aga with the afternoon paper, looked at Freddie carefully. 'You all right, pet?'

Freddie's mouth opened and closed soundlessly, but her body shook as though someone was jerking her on strings. Alarmed, Mike Kershaw put his arms around her.

'Whatever is it?'

'Mrs Gilly … ' she stammered, her eyes unfocused.

He glanced at his wife and then gestured as the dining room bell rang. 'Go on, you see what's up in there. I'll look after the little one.' He lifted her easily onto his lap. A few scatterings of tobacco lay on his jacket, a half-smoked hand-rolled cigarette burning in an ashtray beside him.

'What about Mrs Gilly?'

'He's eating her.'

Mike frowned. *'Eating her? Who?'*

'My f … father,' Freddie stammered.

Mike smiled disbelievingly. 'Your father didn't eat your rabbit,' he said, then paused, remembering the hutch being empty earlier when he had gone to clean it out. Oh, for God's sake, he thought to himself. His wife had cooked rabbit, but she would hardly cook the child's rabbit, would she? 'Listen, pet, no one's eaten Mrs Gilly,' he paused, not wanting to ask the next question. 'Who told you such silliness?'

'My f … father,' Freddie said, again stuttering on the word.

Mike Kershaw said nothing – his anger was too violent to trust speech – instead he gripped the child tightly and laid her head against his chest. For years he had watched trivial acts, petty unkindnesses inflicted on Freddie; birthdays supposedly forgotten, the child heart-broken until lunchtime when a mound of impressive gifts would be left on the table for her. He remembered too how he had watched father and daughter in the garden, and how Greville Clements had told Freddie to jump off the orchard wall.

'Don't be afraid, I'll catch you.'

He did too; swinging her high in the air, smiling as she laughed. Twice she repeated the process, squealing with pleasure, but the third time Greville had stepped back, leaving Freddie to land heavily on the earth by his feet.

'That will teach you never to trust anyone,' Greville had told the shaken child, picking her up again and smiling that unearthly smile of his.

After a few such incidents, Freddie had become withdrawn, afraid of her father and quiet in his company; but she

11

knew better than to ask for protection from her mother. Sarah was too devoted to her husband to risk siding with her child. So Freddie had turned to the Kershaws for affection instead and they, childless and willing, became her surrogate parents. Every time some new cruelty was extended to Freddie, Mike had to fight the impulse to redress the balance a little. As a middle-weight boxing champion in the Army he wondered how brave Greville Clements would be if he had to face up to him. Oh, he was taller and younger, but Mike was certain that he could lay him out cold. And besides, he would have right and God on his side.

' ... if you ever laid a finger on him we would be fired, and who would look out for Freddie then?' his wife had reasoned.

'But Meg ... '

'No, I don't want to hear it, Mike!' she replied firmly. 'You keep your fists in your pockets and I'll keep my thoughts to myself. It's the best way to help that child, believe me.'

But it became harder and harder to resist challenging Greville and now Mike felt all the old anger smouldering as he held the distraught child.

'He said that the rabbit in the pie was Mrs Gilly,' Mike said as soon as his wife walked back into the kitchen.

She touched her finger to her lips, glancing at Freddie who lay silent against her husband's chest.

'Mr Clements wants her back in the dining room.'

Mike's hands gripped Freddie; her eyes were open, but registered nothing. 'No, never! If he wants her, he'll have to come down here and face me.'

Meg stroked Freddie's hair, avoiding her husband's eyes. 'Darling, listen to me,' she said softly, kneeling by the chair, her highly coloured face bent towards the child. 'Are you listening?'

Freddie nodded absently.

'You have to go and talk to your father, my love,' she said, adding quickly. 'You know how Mike and I love you, don't you?' Freddie's eyes flickered. 'And you know that we've never told you a lie ... ?' Again, the flicker of life. 'Well, Mrs Gilly wasn't in that pie, silly one.' Meg said lightly, as though

12

the thought was too absurd even to consider. 'Do you think I would have done anything to harm her?'

'But w ... where is she?' Freddie asked softly.

Meg took in her breath. 'I don't know.'

A skimming of tears pooled over Freddie's eyes, but stayed under the lids.

'She's gone, wandered off somewhere,' Meg continued, adding emphatically. 'But she *wasn't* in that pie. Honestly, sweetheart, she wasn't.'

The tears floated, seemed almost to fall and then dried in the corners of Freddie's eyes as a change came over her. She knew that Meg was telling her the truth and yet Mrs Gilly, the first living thing she had possessed and loved, was gone. No more early mornings going down to the hutch and lifting the cold latch to pick up that warm body; no more painful secrets whispered into furred ears, no rubbing her face in the dense ivory coat. Gone. Mrs Gilly, gone ...

'Can we d ... do something?' Freddie said carefully.

Mike glanced away, heartsick.

'Like what, pet?' Meg asked.

Freddie thought for an instant. 'Make her a cross or something? Just to put her n ... name on.'

That night Mike smashed up the empty hutch and buried it at the bottom of the garden where the lawn ended by the stone wall. He then cut out a small cross, painted it white and added the name, *Mrs Gilly* in black copperplate writing, adding underneath, 'Gone Missing, April 4th 1966.'

As usual, Freddie woke early and crept down to the kitchen, taking Meg's hand as she was lead out into the garden. Across the misted lawn they walked towards Mike, who was watching and waiting for them, smoke curling skyward from his cigarette.

In solemn silence Freddie regarded the cross and read the words. They seemed to please her, but her speech was hesitant and she stumbled on simple words. Meg glanced at her husband, frowning as the child knelt to pat the chilled earth, her hand the colour of stone. Freddie had slept badly, her memory replaying the traumas she had endured, her father's actions stomping through the early hours of her sleep, as did her mother's selective affection, and ultimate betrayal. She knew nothing of their real motives; she was, after all, only a child, but she knew that Mrs Gilly had gone and with her, all hope of childhood.

Chapter Two

The house had been built for privacy, pushed deep into the countryside, a few miles from Ripon. Access was only afforded by an lengthy drive barred by double gates, the surrounding hedges grown high enough to keep out intruders and prevent any sight of the house from the road. Only a sign fixed on the gates implied habitation, the name 'Cambuscan' striking an irregular note in the pragmatic Yorkshire surroundings.

If admittance was allowed, the meandering drive offered only unsatisfying glimpses of the house. Cushioned by azaleas the drive was banked with trees whose branches joined overhead, making a mushy shadowland in summer. Blood-coloured roses, generations old, loomed like bell towers, their stems thick with age, their perfume musky and dark. Below them smaller vegetation struggled for life, heathers pooling in violet smudges as they spread and nuzzled at the lawn edges. Rounding a final bend, a small lake shone deep, cold and still, its surface undisturbed by birds. A single bay tree stood darkly alone.

When the house finally emerged it seemed faded, the voyage through the garden overworking the senses so that the building seemed an anti-climax, its perfect symmetry dull. High windows looked out from all floors, the front door a little narrow and out of proportion, a pair of antique statues flanking the entrance like hesitant guests. Unkindly aged by the elements, the bronze male and female figures had developed a green patina, their faces streaked unflatteringly by Yorkshire rain.

15

Inside, the house seemed more certain of itself and opened out confidently from a gloomy hallway. Rooms led off into other rooms, passages running busily to the kitchen, a walnut staircase leading into a collection of bedrooms, some with recently added *en suite* bathrooms, others, on the top floor, converted long ago into a nursery, playroom and staff quarters. Everywhere there was evidence of old money – furniture in a wide variety of styles – Georgian, Victorian, Edwardian – each generation contributing their own taste. Some rooms had not changed at all. The billiards room was as pointedly masculine as it always had been, Sarah Clement's great grandfather having had the table and matching oak mantelpiece carved to his own design. Above the fireplace was the faded head of a stag which Sarah's grandfather had shot on one of his yearly stalking holidays in Argyle; the gun which had hastened its end hanging beneath the trophy.

When Sarah's father inherited the house there were alterations, a conservatory hastily added at the back for his wife. A fretful woman, much prone to illness, she was an argumentative wife and an unlikeable mistress whom the staff resented for her continual and critical interference. Her purpose in marrying Gordon Clough had been political. Coming from a wealthy family herself, both sets of parents had thought it expedient to combine the family fortunes and so enable the Clough carpet business to continue to thrive in the capable hands of the next generation. Regrettably, the best laid plans can fail through over-confidence and although the money was assured, the continuation of the Clough line was not. Sarah was their first and only child and although a frisson of disappointment ran throughout the entire family at her birth, her parents soon rallied and little Sarah Clough was, quite simply, adored.

Toys were ordered from Hamleys, dresses from Peter Jones and The White House; trips abroad were marked by a succession of ever more glorious presents including a doll's house made in Paris, the ultimate culmination of every seven-year-old's dreams. Ever the doting father, Gordon Clough had had it made as a replica of Cambuscan. Its diminutive beds were covered with embroidered sheets and the dining room was a perfect copy of the original, correct in every detail, with its table set for three. In the miniature library were the same books as were available in the real house and on the writing desk was a minute pen and ink-stand and a selection of headed paper. For Sarah, the doll's house became a place of enchantment, her imagination providing her with a whole world in miniature, the rooms populated with invisible playmates.

She needed them too, because no real children came through the gates, or played in the grounds, or stood by the the bay tree and peered at their reflections in the lake. No toy boats scuttled across the water, no kites flew up in the summer air and no dogs left their footprints in the snow when winter came. Sarah Clough was isolated, her doll's house as separate from the world as her parents' house was separated from the rest of humanity. The three of them existed in a humming cocoon of devotion, and as Sarah grew and was taught by tutors, her personality did not develop the kind of curiosity usual in children.

It was natural therefore, that after a while, excursions into the outside world were no longer thought of as treats, but threats, although Sarah's yearning to remain at home was seen by her parents as a tribute to their upbringing, not as a peculiarity in her development. Cambuscan provided her with everything she needed and as she became a young woman her character did not change. She remained as uncomplicated as she had always been, her voice actually retaining a child's light immaturity of tone.

To some, Sarah's simplicity of nature was fascinating, if surprising. The Second World War had changed many women, forcing them into taking more responsibility for themselves and for their children. Whilst the men had been away fighting, the women had worked in their place, had found companionship amongst other women and had waited for the telegram which confirmed that another father, brother, boyfriend or husband had been killed. But in Cambuscan Sarah knew nothing of such ructions in the world outside, and it was her mother's sudden illness when she was twenty which marked the final ending of her childhood.

Throughout the summer months of 1955 Irene Clough suffered the agonies of stomach cancer and, afraid and uncertain of her mother's condition, Sarah confronted her father.

'How bad is she?' she asked, her voice lowered, her eyes averted.

He glanced up, seemingly surprised by the question. 'Your mother will get over it. She's always been sickly, you know that.'

The answer was inadequate and Sarah felt cheated by him. He glanced away from her, smiling an all-encompassing smile and turned back to business. A scattering of square offcuts of carpet lay on the floor beside his feet, a spread of dyed fabric on the desk. Bent over a set of figures he was frequently preoccupied, his work absorbing him so much that concern for his wife was secondary.

'I think we should get a second opinion,' Sarah said bravely, her high voice firm.

Surprised, her father glanced up. He felt suddenly diminished in her eyes, and was reminded of the time when he had been caught lying at school. 'Listen, my love, I trust Dr Hackworth and I think we should do what he says. Just give your mother the medicine and keep an eye on her … '

Sarah was not in the mood for appeasement. 'But if she's really ill, we should be doing more.'

Gordon Clough blinked and fielded the suggestion, feeling the unwelcome rush of colour to his face as he resorted to parental superiority. 'I think I know what's best,' he replied, then added gently. 'I'll call in and see her later.' Having always trusted her father implicitly, Sarah acquiesced.

Irene Clough did not recover, but she did not decline. Meanwhile September came, bringing an Indian summer, the days sultry and heavy with the scent of late roses; whilst in the conservatory bird-song sometimes filtered into the invalid's aching dreams.

It was late one afternoon when Irene came awake slowly, the drugs making her listless as she pulled herself upright with difficulty. Glancing towards the white Grecian summer house at the rise of the lawn, she saw her daughter, Sarah, sitting on the top step of the pavilion, her head lifted up, the sun falling between the high trees and striking her upturned face like a sword blade. Altered by the light, she no longer looked like a child and Irene felt a cold shudder of panic. She tried to rise to her feet and call out, the rug falling from her lap as she did so. Overhead bird-song juddered in the cooling air, the ferns brushing at the back of her hands, a fine beading of sweat breaking out under her eyes as she moved to the door and clutched at the wood for support. Her gaze focused, then blurred, and the last thing she saw was her daughter sitting in the little white pavilion with the sun on her upturned face.

The funeral was a sad affair, and not well attended by friends, although many of Gordon Clough's business colleagues came to pay their respects. Sarah was desolated by her mother's death and found little comfort from her father who turned to his business and spent more time at the factory in an attempt to blot out his grief. Dinners were eaten in silence, Gordon Clough failing to notice the drop in standards or Sarah's humiliation as the staff took more and more advantage of their inexperienced mistress. Food was delivered to the table cold, or indifferently cooked, and Sarah's hesitant complaints were met with hostility or immediate threats of resignation.

Hopelessly unsuited to the job of running such a massive house and still grieving for her mother, Sarah withdrew into herself totally, her time spent reading or visiting the playroom on the top floor where the doll's house from Paris still stood, a defiant reminder of her childhood. But it was obvious that the domestic arrangements would have to be attended to, and matters came to a head after one particularly disorganised meal when Sarah went down to the kitchens and tackled the cook – who promptly served notice and packed her bags. The times had changed without the Cloughs realising it and people no longer wanted to be servants when they could go and work in the factories in Leeds, or earn their living as shop staff in Harrogate or Ripon.

19

Stoically, Sarah set about trying to make the next meal herself, but soon gave up and in desperation rang the only person she could think of – her father's solicitor, Mr Peter Threlfall.

'I don't think I can help you, dear,' the old man replied patiently. Having a practical wife and two competent daughters of his own, Sarah's dilemma was a mystery to him.

'But where do I get a cook?' Sarah pleaded.

'Advertise,' Mr Threlfall replied confidently.

'Where?'

The old man sighed, but remembering that Gordon Clough was one of his best clients, he offered the only help he could think of. 'My colleague, Mr Greville Clements, is going to be passing your house this afternoon. I'll ask him to drop by and leave some information for you.' He smiled as she thanked him profusely. 'It's nothing really, my dear, I know how difficult things have been for you lately.'

Greville Clements knew about the difficulties of his colleague's most prominent client too; he had made it his business to do so. Great beauty in a woman is regarded with awe; in a man it is often seen as a character defect – and Greville Clements was handsome in a way which was undeniable and intimidating. Tall, erect and strongly built, he was well-spoken and in his dark business suit, appeared to be the archetypal English professional gentleman. Only on closer examination did his background emerge, his wavy black hair betraying a Middle Eastern grandfather, his aristocratic nose the legacy of a Jewish grandmother. Intellectually precocious, he had worked hard at school and developed considerable arrogance to hide his inferiority complex. Taunts like 'Yid' and 'Pretty Boy' did little to help his violent temperament and when he won a place at university, Greville Clements soon earned the rare distinction of being the most intelligent, yet most despised, undergraduate.

Nevertheless, using his brains and ruthless drive, he learned to control his temper and adapted. Shaving twice a day prevented the tell-tale shadow of the heavy beard peculiar to foreigners, and by affecting a very English manner of

20

dress he avoided any flashiness. Yet he did retain one personal idiosyncrasy – the application of too much lemon cologne which soon faded from his cheeks but lingered on his hands for hours afterwards.

Not that cologne was his greatest weakness. Women soon played an obsessive part in his life, and he had little trouble attracting them. Then, in his early twenties, he met a woman who was much older than he was, and in her, he tried to find his mother – to disastrous effect. He idolised her, asked her advice, relied on her, and made love to her almost reverently. She in return found his attention at first flattering and then cloying, and when the affair lost all attraction, she humiliated him. All his love turned instantly to hatred. Greville struck out at her and found only a fleeting relief when he left her badly beaten. Guilt soon cornered him and he attempted to make amends with other women, but never trusted anyone again. The more they promised love and offered affection, the more he expected rejection, and waited for the inevitable.

Then after a few years of doomed relationships, he discovered that he could only find sexual gratification in humiliating, and later, hurting women. The gratification was intense, but left a feeling of such self-loathing that he turned to others to punish him. The pattern of his life was then set; he could only find fulfillment in violence, and he could only find absolution in punishment.

Seriously disturbed and unable to sustain an emotional relationship, Greville still managed to shine in his professional life. After qualifying as a solicitor in London, his impressive progress was only halted by a scandal when he was discovered to be having an affair with a partner's wife. In exchange for a promise of being given a good reference, Greville told the firm he would leave at once and turned his eyes to a faraway location where he could sink into obscurity for a while to plan his future.

The town he chose for his exile was Harrogate, a smart spa town with little glamour. Greville Clements was greeted with interest and considerable curiosity by the firm to whom he applied.

21

'You have an excellent degree,' Peter Threlfall said, regarding the handsome man in front of him carefully, 'and you soon found a position in a highly respectable firm. So what made you leave London?'

Greville frowned as though he was concentrating. 'I didn't feel at home in the capital,' he said, 'London is not a place I would want to settle.'

Peter Threlfall was surprised. The man in front of him seemed altogether too talented and too glossy to fit into a neat town in the middle of Yorkshire. London seemed exactly the place for him.

'Am I to take it that you have no ambition then?'

Take it how you want, you stupid old bugger, Greville thought, although his face and voice remained impassive. 'I have ambitions, but I want to become more involved with a family firm. In London everything was so impersonal,' he said, his confident voice full of conviction.

It was exactly what Peter Threlfall had wanted to hear and after only a few more minutes, he offered Greville Clements a job.

Any sub-conscious misgivings Threlfall might have had were quickly dismissed. Greville impressed the male clients, and he was popular with the female ones. On the strength of his considerable intelligence and charm, a goodly amount of new work came to the firm of Threlfall, Dulwich and Hall and Greville made sure that old man Threlfall was well aware of it.

For a year Greville managed to keep himself in control, not getting involved with any of his clients and keeping his sexual activities secret. But his natural aggressiveness soon surfaced and his arrogance began to show in small ways. Arriving late one morning he was tackled by Peter Threlfall who had watched a succession of long lunches and overtaxed expense accounts. Although the old man's rebuke was mild, Greville responded violently.

'What the hell has it got to do with you?' he said savagely.

The old man stepped back, startled. 'I like the firm to be run a certain way ... '

'You get enough clients from me – why don't you just count your blessings and stop the bloody moans?' Greville snapped belligerently. 'I can't stand people checking up on me all the time. If you want a bloody clerk go out and hire one.'

Slamming the door of the office behind him, he stormed off down Montpelier Place, leaving a shaken Peter Threlfall. Never in all his fifty years as a solicitor had he met with such behaviour, or such language. It was indefensible – what if there had been a lady client waiting outside? He sat down, unnerved, his attention so distracted that when Greville walked in a few minutes later and offered his hand, he was too surprised to take it.

'Go on, shake hands with me. I was wrong, I admit it,' Greville said easily. 'I've a quick temper and I behaved un-forgivably. Sorry.'

Reluctantly, Peter took his hand.

'You see, it was easy. We should let bygones be bygones,' Greville said amicably, smiling and walking off into his own office.

But Peter Threlfall was not reassured and sat immobile for another few minutes. When he finally did move he sighed and raised a hand to his forehead, surprised by the smell of lemon cologne which clung resolutely to his skin.

From then onwards, he encouraged Greville to be out of the office as much as possible as his presence disturbed him. So when Sarah Clough phoned, he was only too pleased to give his colleague the small envelope to drop off at Cambuscan that afternoon.

'I thought you could do it after you've seen Mrs Fitzroy.'

'Certainly,' Greville replied, aware that he had seriously jeopardised his standing in Threlfall's eyes and anxious to repair the damage. Besides, a drive in the country would be pleasant on a day like this. 'I know the place.' He weighed the package in his hand. 'Is there any message?'

'No,' Peter replied, 'it's just some information to help Sarah out. I want you to assist her all you can,' he said innocently. 'Her family has considerable local standing, and besides, they're our wealthiest clients.'

23

The gardener watched with interest as Greville Clements drove up that day, asking his name before unlocking the gates and standing back to let him pass. Pulling up outside the front door, Greville screwed his eyes up against the glare of sunlight and smoothed down the waistcoat of his three piece suit.

From her sitting room window on the first floor Sarah Clough looked out – and stared, stunned by the darkly handsome man who waited outside. As she watched, he leaned down and checked his reflection in the wing mirror, straightening his tie as she giggled softly from her hiding place. Some vague presentiment warned her as she ran downstairs but she had neither the inclination nor the experience to question it and, fascinated and curious, Sarah Clough opened the door.

The sun magnified him and for an instant the stranger appeared ethereal, almost too perfect for the world. For his part Greville saw a very young woman who seemed familiar. He scratched at his memory and tried to place her, realising finally that some echo of the woman he had first loved was repeated in Sarah Clough. A wave of such longing overtook him that he almost touched his chest to guard his heart, but in the instant he felt it, a sense of unavoidable suspicion settled in him instead.

Slowly he walked into the dark hall, blinking from the dazzling sunlight, and smiling. He realised at once that Sarah Clough's prettiness relied on her extreme youth. Instinct told him that by the age of thirty she would be in decline, her jawline already giving her away, the soft skin suggesting a double chin and the tops of her arms fleshy beneath the voile sleeves. Unaware of his thoughts, his smile reassured her as he continued his examination and decided that she was obviously a virgin. The thought excited him and yet he felt also a sense of unexpected pity.

'Sarah Clough?' he asked, offering his hand.

She smiled. 'Yes … would you like to come in?'

'I am in,' he replied, laughing, and making her laugh too. The light sound surprised him almost as much as her high-pitched voice. His first lover had laughed in that way. 'What a beautiful home you have,' he continued, looking about him. 'Perhaps you could show me around?'

24

It seemed to Sarah that fate had smiled on her. After her mother's death she had been powerless and confused and now here was a man who might help her. She glanced over to him shyly. But why would he help? Someone like him would have a wife already, and even if he wasn't married, she asked herself, what would he see in her?

Memory was what Greville saw in her, and a way to ensure a luxurious lifestyle without having to work for it. In his mind's eye he could already see a Jaguar in the drive and imagine the delight of winter holidays abroad. Not for him the steady drag of the law, not for him the slow climb up the ladder until old man Threlfall died. No, he wanted money and he wanted it *now*. That same fate which Sarah thought was working on her behalf, he believed to be working for him. Fortune was presenting him with an opportunity in the shape of a hesitant, soft-fleshed virgin, and it seemed only right for him to take advantage of such a chance.

His approach was simple and its success lay in speed. Sarah was vulnerable *now*, and so now was the time to make himself indispensable. His tactics worked perfectly. Soon Sarah depended on him utterly and since he was obviously indispensable to his trusted law firm, Gordon Clough had no reason to suspect Greville's motives and actually came to rely on him as he spent more time at Cambuscan. Left to pursue his own business, Gordon was grateful to be freed from domestic worries and allowed Greville Clements a free hand. To the Cloughs delight, he soon found a new cook and gardener from Harrogate, Mike and Meg Kershaw. Of course, he asked Sarah to report back to him on their progress.

Feeling protective of their inexperienced mistress, the Kershaws were wary of Greville, and although he tried valiantly, his charm had little effect on Meg Kershaw and even less on Mike. Both treated him with respect to his face and caution behind his back. They instinctively suspected him, and quickly noticed a variety of little details which gave him away, for, having worked for real gentlemen before, they knew the genuine article ... and it wasn't Greville Clements. They soon realised, however, that as Greville was intent on becoming a part of the Clough family and inheritance, they had better keep on the right side of him.

Sarah was as foolish as Meg and Mike were astute. Lulled into a false feeling of security by Greville Clements, she became more adventurous. She began to take care of her appearance and ventured out more, visiting Binns in Harrogate to buy the latest fashions and having her hair restyled. Each innovation Greville greeted with enthusiasm, smiling as she paraded her finery self-consciously in front of him, trying, with only partial success, to avoid seeing her as a younger version of his first love. His bad temper was concealed from her, his arrogance transformed into tenderness, his charm at times genuine enough to disturb even him. Not that he made love to her. In the 1950s any deflowering would have lowered him in her father's estimation and as the future heir to the carpet fortune Greville wanted to remain irreproachable in Gordon Clough's eyes.

Throughout the autumn of 1955 he courted Sarah and by winter she thought only what he told her to think. Her expressions were his, her opinions were formed by him, his dislikes and loves became hers. A moment apart from him was worthless, a touch from this glorious man total contentment; whilst Greville felt only amusement at her devotion and fixed his eyes on the fortune which was coming closer to him every day. When he finally asked her to marry him she accepted without a pause, rushing to tell her father the news.

As they knew only a few people socially, there was little celebration, but the ones who did hear of the engagement greeted it with a mixed response. At Cambuscan, the chauffeur, the maid and the Kershaws raised their eyes in unison and said they had expected it for a long time, but when old Peter Threlfall read the announcement in the *Harrogate Gazette*, he shook his head in amazement.

'Are you really going to marry Sarah Clough?' he asked when Greville arrived at work that morning.

What the hell has it got to do with you, Greville thought. Before long I'll be telling you what to do with your dreary little law firm. 'Yes, I am,' he said cheerfully, 'and no man was ever more happy.'

'Well … I wish you luck,' Peter Threlfall replied awkwardly. 'Give Sarah my best wishes and tell her I wish her every happiness.'

The words were well meant, but they sounded hollow in both men's ears. Greville smiled in the sunny office but his eyes flickered as Peter Threlfall glanced back to the entry in the paper. As he read it, he remembered the little girl who had played with the doll's house from Paris, and sighed.

That winter Peter Threlfall retired at last and soon afterwards Greville found himself promoted to partner in the legal firm, then, two months later, in the February of 1956, Gordon Clough caught influenza and, after fighting for his life for three weeks in the local hospital, died with Sarah at his bedside. At his father-in-law's funeral, suitably grieving, Greville's thoughts turned rapidly to Sarah's inheritance and his further advancement.

Naturally Greville attended the funeral with Sarah, their car pulling up outside the church gates, their feet slipping on the hard snow underfoot. Around the open grave barely a dozen mourners stood in the savage cold, the vicar stamping his feet surreptitiously under cover of his vestements. Bitter March wind chilled the group as they listened to the church bell tolling ominously in the frozen air. As the coffin was lowered into the ground Sarah sobbed, and Greville instinctively put his arm around her.

Only they knew that she stiffened and pulled away, his touch reminding her all too vividly of his hands on their wedding night. He had waited for Sarah in their hotel bedroom, drinking, and humming under his breath, his confidence soaring. Timidly she had come to him, eager to please, and he had been so moved by her that he was tender and coaxing, making love gently as she lay beneath him. But soon he found himself unable to become aroused and began to whisper to her to stimulate himself. The words were familiar to him, but shocking to her, and Sarah's expression soon altered from devotion to disbelief as she listened to him.

'Do it for me, please … please, darling … ' he urged her.

She moaned, repelled suddenly. 'I can't … '

He raised himself on his elbows, irritated. 'For God's sake!' he hissed, overcome with anger at her prudishness and his own inadequate performance. 'What's the matter with you? Don't you love me?'

She touched his face, awed by its perfection, and tried to cajole him, but he was angry and slapped her hand away.

A shot of fear glinted in her eyes. Immediately aroused, Greville felt the welcome rush of excitement and began to make love to her roughly, coarsely, as Sarah lay shocked and unmoving under him. When she did finally cry out, he struck her across the face twice to silence her. Inexperienced and frightened, Sarah lay rigid on the bed as he pulled and fondled her, the warm blood spilling from her mouth as it did between her legs.

When, later, Greville slept, Sarah looked in the bathroom mirror and then glanced away, repulsed yet oddly fascinated. Her instincts warned her, but her own sexuality had been unexpectedly satisfied and she felt a bizarre mixture of desire and loathing for her husband. Whatever happened she knew she was committed to him, partnered to this violent and beautiful creature for life. The very thought alarmed her. But even if she wanted to, who could she go to for help? Who could tell her if this was the way things were supposed to be? Bewildered and self-conscious, Sarah stumbled back to bed, where Greville's heavy figure lay asleep, the back of his right hand bruised along the knuckles.

In the deep night he slept, dreaming of his first love, then of his wife, only to wake suddenly, guilt making him sweat. Without waking Sarah, he watched her and then passed his hand slowly over her face, its shadow darkening her features momentarily like a thunder cloud moving over a ruined house.

Frederica Clements was born on November 14 1958 in the main bedroom at Cambuscan. Mr Flowers, a Harley Street consultant, was in attendance, assisted by a midwife called in from Ripon. In labour for nearly twenty hours, Sarah, as so often in her life, was totally unprepared and found herself clinging helplessly to the midwife. Meg Kershaw, who had developed a protective instinct for her mistress, ran around obeying every command from the redoubtable Mr Flowers, whilst still managing to return downstairs frequently to attend to a fractious Greville.

In the months preceding Frederica's birth Greville had succeeded in taking over the Clough carpet business, citing his experience and his position as a prominent solicitor as a recommendation for running a factory. With his typical high-handed manner he called on the manager, Mr Doddersley, and demanded immediate changes in the organisation. Doddersley, a softly-spoken man who had worked his way up through the company over a period of twenty years, agreed with all of Greville's suggestions, but altered little, trying to restrict his new master's radical ideas. It was a vain hope. When he realised what Doddersley had done, Greville threatened him with the sack unless he carried out his orders. As a result, fifteen men were immediately laid off, the reason given that not only did such cuts in manpower reduce unnecessary wages and increase efficiency, but they also served as a warning to any dissatisfied employees.

Greville's attitude and ideas outraged everyone. It was not that Gordon Clough had been popular – he had been too aloof to be well loved – but he had visited the mills and factory, had known all his employees by name and had taken a personal interest in each carpet pattern and dye. Nothing was done at the Clough factory without Gordon Clough approving it. Carpet samples were scrapped if they were imperfect, and all salesmen were seen personally and never turned away. With the energy and enthusiasm which had made the Clough business so successful, Gordon had travelled to Europe and the Far East, testing new dyes for colour and bringing home patterns from India, Egypt and Turkey, his ideas kept constantly up to date by his own diligence.

It was not so with Greville Clements. Within months of Gordon Clough's death he had bought the Jaguar he craved and a small flat in London, and joining a selection of clubs, spent as much as three nights a week away from Yorkshire. Already bewildered by his actions, Sarah was further confused by an unexpected visit from Mr Doddersley.

29

'I know it's difficult,' he began, accepting the chair and the afternoon tea she offered, 'what with Mr Clements being your husband and all, but ... '

She paused in the act of pouring his tea. 'Yes?'

'He's making himself unpopular.'

Her face was turned away from him, but there was something in her actions which indicated that the news was not a total surprise.

'Why don't you have a talk with him?' she suggested in her strange, high voice. 'I'm sure he'll listen to you. After all, I know my father always thought very well of you.'

'It's not that simple,' Doddersley said, balancing a teacup and saucer on one knee, a plate of cake on the other. 'I can't seem to make him realise just how the business works.'

'But if you tried,' Sarah insisted, her agitation apparent suddenly, as she topped up her already full cup.

'I have. But I wondered if *you* could have a word.'

She spilled the tea immediately and then began to dab at the polished surface of the table with her napkin. 'I really can't ... I really can't.' She smiled briefly and Doddersley felt a faint jolt of pity as he watched her. 'My husband doesn't listen to me either you see.'

Greville didn't listen to anyone, but fortunately his interest in the business soon waned. Unable to sustain his enthusiasm, his natural idleness emerged and his visits to the factory decreased. He was surprised at his lack of interest – apparently even making good money lost its appeal – and his thoughts wandered back to London. Sarah could never satisfy him sexually, and he knew that he could only demand so much of her. The type of sex he wanted and missed soon called him back to the capital, and there he remained, neglecting the legal and family business in an increasingly fruitless search for sexual satisfaction.

Soon all business enquiries were passed back to Doddersley. The innovations which Greville had so vigorously pursued were left as unread memos collecting dust in the files.

The office in which Gordon Clough had spent so much of his time was left unoccupied for weeks. Letters went unanswered, phone messages unreturned, lists of complaints building into an aggressive little pile as the days passed. Quickly realising the state of affairs, Doddersley took over and caught up with the backlog – a collective sigh of relief running from Leeds to Bradford when everyone knew he was in charge again – the upstart Clements was out and all was well.

The upstart was not totally oblivious to the anxiety he had caused, but saddled with a remorse and frustration he could not control, he merely indulged himself. As a man of consequence, he joined the golf club of his choice, dined in the finest restaurants and wore the best tailoring, attracting hangers-on whom he despised but understood, seeing in them some mirror image of himself. Not needing to answer to anyone, he slowly discarded the very refinements which had made him acceptable in legal circles and although his appearance was, at first glance, immaculate, his conversation could be crude at times and his clothes a little too flamboyant. The social circles Greville had tried to court in Yorkshire remained solidly aloof, whilst in London he was fêted and admired by profligates who lived off inherited wealth, and by society women who had made their way to the dining rooms of the Savoy via the bedrooms upstairs.

Greville flirted with the theatre too, acting as an 'angel' and putting up money for a production which folded after only six weeks. The financial loss did not matter to him for the thriving carpet business was easily able to cope with his excesses, but in an attempt to gain something from the situation he made the ex-leading lady his mistress. Unfortunately he was as easily bored with her as he was with everything else and soon looked elsewhere – the bosomy wife of a Tory politician providing a brief but welcome distraction from his pregnant wife.

Greville's feeling of guilt over his frequent absences from Sarah, made him kind when he was home. Knowing that her money provided him with his pleasant lifestyle, he decided that the only way to continue his good fortune and secure his name and bloodline was to have an heir, a son to whom the Clough fortune would pass. In this one area he acted nobly.

He had love enough for Sarah to resist tainting her; he had already seen her change and had felt an unaccustomed sense of shock. Unstable as he was, Greville did not want to inflict his sexual deviances on his wife; that much goodness remained in him because in Sarah he still saw his first lover, and the lost shadow of what might have been. Instinctively, he sensed that by protecting his wife from himself he could also safeguard that pure part of himself, that tiny iota of goodness that she held in trust for him.

Deeply obsessed by her husband, Sarah was unaware that she was about to be forced into the role of protector. Relying on Greville so much, she did not see that he relied morally on her. When his son was born, he had decided that he would no longer make love to his wife. Instead, he would raise Sarah to role of mother – asexual, and all-forgiving, the woman to whom he could always return and be absolved.

Unaware of her husband's future plans, Sarah clutched onto the midwife's hand and with one final exhausted push, spilled her child into the world. The baby cried lustily, angrily, as Mr Flowers laid it carefully in Sarah's arms.

'It's a little girl,' he said.

'Oh, look,' Sarah replied, her voice filled with tears, 'she's so beautiful.'

Dark and fierce, the baby cried for nearly ten minutes. Then after feeding, she lapsed suddenly into sleep, her black eyelashes resting on her cheek, her mouth slightly open and her lips moist. She smelt of new life and her skin was so transparent her veins shone beneath. Even as a newborn baby, there was a quality which marked out the adult Frederica Clements, something unique in the long strength of her limbs and the shape of her hands. As Sarah leaned back against the pillows holding her daughter, Meg Kershaw opened the curtains and a fine smudging of Yorkshire mist peered in at the window, a blurry sun falling across the sleeping child's eyes.

When Mr Flowers had washed, he walked downstairs to congratulate the father, looking round the empty hall and then calling out. Almost immediately Greville walked out of the drawing room, an expectant look on his face.

'Well?'

'Congratulations,' Mr Flowers said, offering his hand.

Greville took it with little enthusiasm. 'It's over then?' he asked, glancing upwards. 'How is he?'

'The child,' Mr Flowers said evenly, 'is a girl.'

Greville's facial expression never altered, but the look in his eyes became the same one Peter Threlfall had seen one late summer afternoon a year before.

'I wanted a boy.'

The doctor hesitated. Such sentiments were not unknown – it was not unnatural, merely sad. 'You mustn't worry, your wife is fit and healthy. There will be other children.'

Greville nodded listlessly. His dream of emotional salvation was gone, destroyed – and by whom? By a daughter. He was cheated, and cold with bitterness.

'What are you going to call her?'

Having prepared for a boy, Greville had already picked out the name Frederick. Frederick Clements sounded perfect for an heir, he had thought, writing the name repeatedly on a piece of paper, his handwriting underlined with a flourish of black ink. So when his daughter was born he had no interest in other names, especially female ones, and when Sarah pressed him later that day, he was offhand.

'Call her Frederica ... it's the female version of Frederick, so it'll do.'

Defiantly proud of her child, Sarah ignored the tone in his voice and looked down at her daughter.

'Frederica is a very special name,' she said gently, 'but then you are going to be a very special person, aren't you?'

The child looked up at her mistily.

'Frederica Clements,' Sarah crooned, rocking the cradle with her left hand. 'I love you.'

Frederica grew up with an excess of affection from one parent and a lack of attention from the other. Intelligent and aware, she soon recognised her father's indifference and resented it, longing for the times when he was away and she lived happily with her mother and the Kershaws. In this way Frederica's world, like her mother's before her, was encompassed by the borders of Cambuscan. She found sanctuary in the same pavilion where Sarah had been sitting the day her mother died, and was also captivated by the doll's house with which Sarah had played so often as a child. Each year she too saw the lake freeze at the first onset of winter, and saw the same solitary bay tree standing silently on guard.

Frederica soon became known as Freddie, her character more suited to the informal version of her name, although her father would never shorten it. Even in the first years of her life Freddie was aware of the tension between her parents. Birthdays, holidays and Christmases were spent between hostile parents; Greville quick to be irritated, Sarah making allowances for his temper, her high voice perpetually soothing him.

'Greville, do calm down,' she said, turning to her daughter and smiling. 'Freddie, darling, look what Daddy brought you from London.'

Freddie smiled automatically in response, quick to realise that gifts were the only affection her father could offer her. For weeks before Christmas, parcels would arrive from Hamleys, dolls from Italy, a fir tree delivered by the local greengrocer in Ripon. There was always considerable thought behind the presents, but there was no communication beyond the wrapped packages which seemed repeatedly to deliver the message *Your father must love you; after all, look at all these lovely things he gives you.* Always willing to make allowances for Greville's parental detachment, Sarah would coo over the gifts as if each had been for her, and spend hours dressing the Christmas tree, waiting for her husband to telephone and tell her when he was coming home.

Sarah's feelings for Greville remained contradictory. Whilst he was away she dreamed of the sexual excitement he could offer her, although he had shown little interest in her over the last few years. His indifference worried her, not only because she missed his lovemaking, but because she wondered where she had failed him. Embarrassed attempts to instigate sex left Sarah humiliated, but as time went on she found herself more and more willing to look foolish in an attempt to try and please her husband.

34

Many complex seductions were planned whilst Greville was away, but most were discarded when he returned to Cambuscan. The paradox of Sarah's love meant that when his car drove up and his voice sounded in the hall, her longing was quickly supplanted by unease and late night arguments in the bedroom after failed lovemaking were commonplace. Sarah, finding some relief in the violence of their verbal abuse, never realised that Greville rejected her to protect her. Yet whatever Greville had sought to do, it was too late, for his sexual violence had satisfied some quirk in Sarah's personality and a strange need, quite separate from love, developed in her.

Complicated as their relationship was, Greville only continued with their intermittent lovemaking to produce an heir. Seven years after the birth of Freddie however, there were still no further children. Two miscarriages and a stillborn son were the sum of their failure. Greville by now expected disappointment and Sarah was confounded by grief. As their marriage grew more unsteady, she gravitated towards the one security in her life – her child – and as each year passed and further pregnancies seemed unlikely, she clung ever more resolutely to her daughter and slowly adjusted to Greville's prolonged absences.

And meanwhile, what of Freddie? After her seventh birthday, and the Easter which tore her out of childhood, she never referred to Mrs Gilly again. She was inarticulate in her grief – and soon, too, in speech. Almost overnight she developed a stammer, stumbling over words and finding conversation so difficult that she became withdrawn and silent when her father was at home. Turning inwards in an effort to escape unhappiness, she developed a curious behaviour pattern. At night she wandered and was found in various places – in the playroom, in one of the spare bedrooms of Cambuscan, or curled up behind the curtains in the drawing room.

Meg Kershaw discovered Freddie the first time, the little girl's hand pressed against her mouth in a gesture which suggested silence, her bare feet tucked under her nightdress. She had wandered up into the playroom and had obviously been looking out of the window when she dozed off, her head resting against the pane. Gently Meg lifted her and carried her back to bed, shuddering as the child's cold skin touched hers. But Freddie never settled for long. One or two nights would pass, but soon she would be wandering again, leaving her own room and sleeping in one of the hiding places she had made for herself.

'I can't understand it,' Meg said to her husband, pulling on the nylon housecoat she wore whilst cooking. 'I found her in the laundry last night.' She fastened the buttons irritably. 'There's something wrong with that child.'

'Are you surprised?' Mike answered angrily. 'That business with the rabbit could have turned any kid's mind. That bloody man's got a lot to answer for.'

Meg had heard it all before, but the conversation led nowhere. There was nothing they could do, except be there for Freddie when she needed them. Timidly Meg pulled a small notebook out from behind the clock on the fireplace.

'Look, Mike, I've been making a few notes about Freddie, and there's something – a pattern like – which might be important.' She suddenly felt embarrassed, an uneducated woman making suggestions about things only her betters could understand. But her husband was interested and prompted her.

'Well, go on.'

Meg glanced at the scruffy notebook in her hands.

'You see Freddie only wanders when her father's home ... '

'Hah!'

'Mike, hear me out!' she said impatiently. 'The wandering isn't the only thing. She only stutters around him and the stammering only came about after Mrs Gilly went.' Mike's eyes fixed on hers. 'You know what I'm referring to, don't look so blank!'

'I'll never forget it as long as I live,' he said coldly. He gestured at the notebook. 'But what does it all mean?' Keeping notes was one thing, trying to suggest a meaning was another.

'I'm not sure ... ' Meg faltered. 'Maybe Freddie feels unsafe when her father's home ... and maybe that's why she wanders.'

36

It seemed reasonable. 'But what do we do about it, Meg?' Mike asked. 'Tell him?'

She shook her head vehemently. 'No, not Mr Clements, but maybe her mother.'

'If she was anything like a good mother she would have noticed for herself!' Mike snapped. 'Haven't you seen how Freddie hardly says a word when her father's home? I bet Sarah Clements hasn't even noticed that her kid stammers.'

Meg sighed impatiently. 'Should I tell her about Freddie wandering about at night?'

'No!'

'Why not?'

'Because she would only tell her husband and that might mean trouble for Freddie. You know how it goes, Meg. He would punish her in some way – and for what? Let the child be, for God's sake, she's not doing anyone any harm.' Mike paused, filled with misgivings. 'Freddie doesn't sleep-walk and from what I understand it's only sleep-walkers who can harm themselves because they don't know what they're doing.' He marshalled his thoughts. 'That child *knows* what she's doing – just because we don't understand it, we shouldn't go running off to her parents.' He paused, then added softly. 'It would be like betraying her.'

His wife nodded. 'Should I talk to Freddie then, and ask her what's wrong?' she asked, tucking the book back behind the clock.

'Talk to her and watch her,' Mike agreed, suddenly aware that they were taking on the responsibility of someone else's child. 'But that's all we do ... for now.'

Yet whatever prompted Freddie to her nocturnal wanderings, in the daytime, when the sun was high, she found plenty to keep her happy. If her father was home, she spent nearly all her time with the Kershaws, helping Meg in the kitchen, and following Mike around in the garden, or going with him into town for supplies. In the front of the old Land Rover he sang to her 'Ten Green Bottles,' making her shout out the lines, not stammering once.

She sang out loudly, her face creased into laughter when

Mike pretended to get the lines wrong, her hands clapping together as they bumped along the uneven country roads. Many times he would park the Land Rover and lift Freddie out, sitting her on a fence and pointing out the new foals in the fields, the dragonflies skitting overhead and the flies humming in the dry air.

Once he surprised her with a picnic that Meg had made for them. Grinning broadly, he lifted Freddie over a fence and walked her to a stream, tying a string around the neck of a bottle of milk and dipping it into the water to cool it. Laying out sandwiches, he told her stories of the Army and of his boxing matches.

'You hit him!' Freddie cried delightedly, flicking a wasp away with her hand.

'On the chin,' Mike answered, pretending to knock himself out and falling back into the high grass, his legs in the air.

Freddie screeched with laughter, her skin lightly tanned by the summer sun. Laughing, Mike handed her the cool milk and watched as she drank from the bottle. It tasted of chilled cream, the yellow head of the milk clinging to her upper lip.

'Mike, what will happen when I grow up?'

He glanced at her, surprised by the question. 'You'll be beautiful and get married and have lots of children.'

Freddie considered his words and smiled. 'No ... I don't think so.'

'Why not?' Mike asked, chewing thoughtfully.

She ignored the question, pursuing her own thoughts. 'Mike?'

He smiled, glancing at her. 'Yes?'

'What's love?'

He took in his breath, watching as a small twig floated downstream and jammed behind the roots of an overhanging tree. 'Love is ... goodness,' he said, embarrassed. 'Love is wanting good for the person you care for.' He smiled at her again, his face creased with effort. 'Love is ... protecting someone from harm.'

'Oh ... ' Freddie said quietly, 'then no one will love me.'

38

Mike had bitten into a sandwich, but stopped chewing immediately, the food balling up in his throat. Freddie had spoken without self-pity, but as though she knew something, some inescapable fate towards which she walked. The damage Greville Clements had inflicted was already forming his daughter's opinion of the world and of herself. Because he did not love her, she believed herself worthless and unworthy of any love at any time. It was the future she saw for herself.

'Listen, little one,' Mike said softly. 'I love you, and Meg loves you. Your mother does too.'

Freddie's eyes were screwed up against the sun. 'But not my father?'

'In his way he loves you.'

She nodded as though satisfied and glanced away but Mike was aware that he had disappointed her and felt a crushing sense of inadequacy.

For a minute he said nothing else, then asked suddenly. 'Why do you wander around at night, Freddie? Why don't you stay in your room?'

She glanced back to him, surprised. 'I feel … safer.'

Mike's heart began to beat too fast. He knew the feeling, the rush of adrenalin before a fight, the heat of anger. 'Freddie, no one has ever hit you, have they?' He thought of Greville Clements and his fists tightened. Just give me enough of a reason and I'll kill him, he thought.

'No,' she said simply, closing the conversation, her eyes turning towards the stream.

Mike relaxed, feeling suddenly stupid. What right had he even to put the idea into her head? It might frighten her and God knows, she had enough fear in her life.

They ate their picnic in easy silence for a few minutes longer. Quick fish darted under a rock and on the far bank a duck groomed its feathers diligently.

'I'm sorry about your little boy,' Freddie said without warning.

Again, Mike's heart raced. Who had told her about their child, the child who had died of meningitis when he was only three? The child Meg still mourned, but about whom she

39

never spoke. Or *had* she talked about him? Refusing to discuss the topic with him, had Meg confided in this child instead?

Freddie's eyes turned back to Mike for a response and he felt a sudden jolt of understanding. Oh God, he thought, she's fey, this child knows things that others don't. She's different.

'He was very sick ... ' Mike said finally. ' ... we were very, very unhappy when he died.'

Freddie's eyes never left his face. In them he saw the sympathy of a woman, not a child. Her eyes were older than her years and steady as she listened to him.

When they returned to Cambuscan, Freddie stayed in the kitchen a while and then left to keep her mother company as her father was away for the week. Mike watched her run off, childlike again, and for an instant he wondered if he had imagined something in the field by the stream. Perhaps the heat had overworked his senses and made him susceptible to wild notions. But much as he tried to deny it, he had seen something in Freddie which was extraordinary, an understanding beyond childhood, and a sympathy rare in anyone.

'What's the matter with you?' Meg asked, watching her husband with fascinated amusement as he stared at the door through which Freddie had passed moments earlier.

He turned to her, his expression serious. 'Meg, did you tell Freddie about our boy?'

She blinked, startled, then shook her head. 'No, you know I never talk about him,' she said finally.

'Well, she knew,' Mike said wonderingly to himself. 'She knew.'

Chapter Three

The signs of Greville's return were everywhere: the dark overcoat on the rack in the cloak-room, the copy of *The Times* on the hall table, a glass of his favourite liqueur from from Fortnum & Mason. He sat in his own dressing room in silence, his legs stretched out before him, summoning up the energy to go down for dinner. Already Sarah and Freddie were waiting for him, both beautifully dressed, and perfectly displayed to please him. After another long moment, Greville rose to his feet and undressed, pulling off his shirt and catching sight of his back reflected in the cheval-glass. He frowned at the cross hatching of weals and cuts and found himself repelled by the abuse to his body – seeing it as though he looked at the torso of another man.

A knock on the door made him jump and he pulled on an evening shirt quickly.

'Who is it?'

'Sheila, sir,' the maid answered. 'Mrs Clements said that dinner is ready.'

He didn't reply, just waited until he heard the woman's footsteps retreat and then he slid the shirt off again and regarded his back thoughtfully. Such a lot of money to pay for blood, he thought, feeling suddenly aroused, his fingers touching the marks gently then falling away as the sexual excitement faded in his genitals.

Stooping, he pulled on his shoes and then paused for a final glance in the mirror. For once, his own face angered him.

Scrutinising the ideal features he almost wished that some of his self-loathing and deviation showed. His face no longer seemed to him a useful disguise but appeared to be mocking him, and for an instant he felt that he only looked out through the bone and skin of his head, and that his body was not his. He was trapped inside, a person apart, not living as a part of his body, but merely *in* his body, unable to find release or relief.

Freddie smiled obediently as her father walked into the dining room, then turned away, watching him instead through an elaborate mirror, fly blown in one antique corner. His image was reflected there, but for an instant the damage in the glass became superimposed on his face and he looked diseased. Startled, Freddie glanced away, catching her mother's eye and smiling reassuringly. Instinct told her that Sarah was weak-willed, experience told her she was silly, but time had brought out Freddie's protective instinct. By the age of ten, she understood the looks of pity which passed between the servants; and by the age of eleven, she felt all the burden of her mother's hopelessness when another false pregnancy was declared by Mr Flowers.

Desperation had driven her mother to such lengths; desperation and bleak optimism. Time without number she told Freddie about her birth, pulling baby clothes out of the cupboard and stroking them, a wistful expression on her face. 'When I have a son your father will stay home more, you'll see.'

The thought winded Freddie. 'Why?'

Sarah's eyes widened ingenuously. 'Because he wants a son,' she said, watching as Freddie folded the baby clothes and laid them back in the drawer. With her head down and her eyes averted she seemed suddenly unrecognisable.

'I love you, Freddie.'

The girl looked up and smiled warmly. Too many confidences had passed between mother and daughter for there to be any awkwardness at a sudden show of emotion.

'Do you love Father?'

Sarah's hand went to her throat and she laughed lightly. 'Of course, he's my husband.'

'Oh,' was all Freddie said.

Greville didn't know what was passing through Freddie's mind, but he found himself surprised by the change in his eleven-year-old daughter. She was too thin, and too light skinned for her dark hair, he thought, but her eyes were familiar and he saw in her a less spectacular version of himself. Not that it troubled him; his feelings for his daughter went much deeper than surface appearances and his initial resentment was now compounded by some inner quality in her which inflamed him. Her stillness and her calmness defied all his attempts to intimidate her, and after the incident with Mrs Gilly, Freddie had never cried again – whatever he did.

Watching Freddie now, Greville felt a new sensation, one so totally unexpected that he found himself unable to continue eating. *He was afraid of her.* The thought galvanised him, belittled him and outraged him, but it remained. Hearing the clatter of his knife and fork on the plate as he dropped them, Freddie glanced over to her father. It is in her eyes, he thought, and a soft sound escaped his lips.

'Are you all right?' Sarah asked, concerned.

'Fine,' he said, unable to look away from his child. She was *judging* him, he thought. She knew all his secrets and she was judging him. A film of sweat broke out on his forehead. Her eyes bored into him. He felt that she could see his back and the marks there, that her mind could imagine him as he had been the night before, kneeling, on all fours, in sexual heat, every injury taken and paid for, only the one restraining order remaining. 'Not my face. Don't mark my face.'

For agonising seconds, Greville felt such terror that he put his hands to his face, seeing in this child the goodness he had abused in himself and had tried to destroy in her. Sarah was stupid and could be duped and protected up to a point, but this girl, this daughter, could see into his soul.

'What are you staring at?' he shouted at Freddie finally.

She blinked, breaking the spell. 'N … nothing … ' The stammer was back. He heard it, felt momentary relief, and realised she had no power over him after all. He had imagined it, that was all. She couldn't do anything to him; she was just a child.

'Stop stammering!' he snapped.

'I … can't h … help it,' Freddie said, staggering over her words.

'I don't want an idiot child who stammers,' he continued, back in control. 'People will think you're stupid.'

She glanced at him bleakly.

'Freddie's not stupid, she's doing very well at school.' Sarah chimed in eagerly, trying to break the deadlock between her husband and daughter. 'She's very good at history, aren't you, darling?'

Greville turned back to Freddie. 'Do you stammer at school?'

'No, only with you,' Sarah replied, her hand flying up to her mouth as the words left her lips.

Greville raised his eyebrows. 'I was talking to my daughter!' he said, mulling over what he had heard as he turned back to Freddie. 'So you only stammer when I'm around?'

She said nothing. Defying him.

'Talk to me!'

Her eyes held his in a steady gaze and his thoughts tumbled uneasily under the stare.

'Freddie, I don't ever want to hear you stammer again. Do you understand?'

She understood.

'There is no reason for it. You only do it to draw attention to yourself. If you stammer, you must be punished,' he paused, savouring the moment. 'Now, tell me what's been going on whilst I've been away.'

Freddie hesitated. To stammer would mean punishment, but she couldn't control it. Her eyes smarted but she didn't cry; she *wouldn't* cry. Sarah watched her from the other end of the table, willing her on. But still Freddie did not speak.

Greville repeated the question. 'What's been happening here?'

Freddie's lungs felt as though they were filled with water. Breathing became difficult, the room swimming in front of her. Then her lips moved as he leaned towards her.

'Nothing,' she said quietly. 'Nothing happened.'

Sarah smiled, then sighed with relief. Greville glanced at her and then turned back to his daughter, infuriated. 'Surely something happened? This can't be the only place in England in a time lock.'

Freddie flinched, but stood her ground. 'Nothing *important* happened.'

With a grunt of impatience, her father turned and pointed to her head with the blade of the knife he was holding. 'Do something with that hair.'

Instinctively Freddie touched her head. 'I went swimming,' she said slowly, to keep the stammer under control. 'That's why it looks untidy.'

'I don't care what you did, just smarten yourself up. I don't want people to think my daughter looks like an orphan.' Having started he was unable to stop his criticism. The pain he was inflicting produced just the response he wanted and he watched with grim satisfaction as Freddie glanced down, her face reddening with embarrassment.

'You watch your step, my girl, or you'll find out just how difficult I can make life for you.'

Throughout that summer, in the idyllic days when they were alone, Sarah and Freddie talked. Every detail of her mother's childhood was related so vividly that Freddie could imagine the happy childhood she had had, and as Sarah talked, Irene Clough walked again in the garden, becoming real in the late summer afternoon whilst mother and daughter had tea beside the lake.

'She was very beautiful,' Sarah said lightly, and Freddie nodded although she had seen the photographs and knew Irene to have had a doughty face. 'My father was handsome too, and very kind.'

That was nearer to the truth, Freddie thought.

'And he was very successful, you know. The firm had not done too well under my grandfather, but he really got it going again.' She smiled, as though the triumph was a recent one.

'Is father good at business?' Freddie asked Sarah.

'He's a solicitor,' Sarah said, by way of explanation.

'But he never goes to work here.'

'Maybe he does in London.'

'Where?'

'I'm not sure.' Sarah dropped her voice conspiratorially. 'You mustn't ever question him about his business, Freddie. He doesn't like it.'

'I know, but does he go to the factory?'

'Mr Doddersley sees to that.'

'But it's our factory, not his.'

Sarah was flustered. 'People are all different, Freddie, and your father is very ... creative, so he gets bored with all the irritating details.'

'So what does he do instead?'

The question caught Sarah off guard and she shrugged. 'I think he does some business with the theatre ... '

'An actor?'

'Oh, Freddie!' her mother said, laughing. 'He's not an actor, but he lends money to put on plays.'

'Do they make money?'

'Well ... no, not really.'

Sarah shifted in her seat, having never really thought of the matter before. This sudden interest in the family finances unnerved her and she changed the subject.

'You should bring home some children from the school,' she said lightly. Freddie turned away, sighing and reaching out to run her hand along the grass by the lakeside.

'Why don't you bring friends home?'

'I don't want to.'

'Oh, darling,' Sarah said meekly. 'Why ever not?'

Freddie rolled onto her back and looked up at her mother. Under her scrutiny, Sarah smiled self-consciously, one hand fluttering around the table, the sleeve of her dress transparent in the sunlight.

'Wasps! Oh, dear, I do hate wasps.'

'I'm happy the way I am,' Freddie said simply.

Sarah paused and then leaned towards her child. Her face was luminous, her blue eyes wide with sheer delight. 'Oh, are you? Are you?'

Freddie nodded briefly and sat up. Smiling gently, she laid her head in her mother's lap. 'I'm the happiest girl in all the world.'

Sarah's small hands stroked her daughter's hair, her eyes gazing far off to the little pavilion. 'I'm so glad, Freddie, because that's all I shall ever ask. For you to stay happy ... and for you to stay with me.'

Chapter Four

Harold Bexenhall Fox Avery was standing in deep contemplation looking at a locked gate. He calculated that it was no more than four feet three inches high, and that, given a good run up to it, he should clear it with an inch or so to spare. The thought pleased him, and a premature feeling of achievement rushed to his head as he stepped back. The sun fell full on the old gate, casting a long dark shadow behind it on the high grass as he stood, rocking backwards and forwards on his heels, mentally preparing himself for the leap. Then, full of confidence, he bounded forwards, taking several long looping steps before leaping upwards. His face had already taken on a smile of triumph when his left foot caught on the top rung of the gate and he plunged ignominiously to earth, a bump the size of a farm egg rising almost instantaneously on his flushed forehead.

Stunned and more than a little surprised, he lay motionless, every thought concentrated on the pain in his head.

'Are you all right?' someone asked.

Painfully slowly Harold opened his eyes. A head bent towards him, the features indecipherable against the sun.

'I should have cleared it, you know,' he said, without a trace of embarrassment as he sat up and glanced back at the gate. 'I was almost over.'

Freddie followed his gaze, and then looked back at the boy. He was fair haired and fair skinned, with slightly protruding blue eyes and a narrow face. Good humour was apparent in his voice and in his expression, even though she knew that the lump on his forehead must have been throbbing with pain.

Harold got to his feet, brushed down his clothes and extended his hand. 'I'm Harold Bexenhall Fox Avery.'

'Oh,' Freddie said simply, taking his hand.

'But you can call me Harry,' he said, eager to put her at her ease. Now that he was no longer lying flat on his back, he could see her clearly and recognised her at once. 'Good Lord, you're the heir to the gate I just jumped.'

'Tried to,' Freddie corrected him, smiling at her own bravery.

'Tried to jump,' he agreed without rancour. 'You are Frederica Clements?'

'Freddie,' she said, shaking his hand warmly.

'Freddie,' he repeated as though it was important that he should get the name right. Though only a boy, his mannerisms were curiously gallant and mature, almost old-fashioned.

'Where do you come from?' Freddie asked shyly.

'Where? We're neighbours.'

She frowned. 'You can't be. The Hall's been empty since the fire.'

'Not any more,' he said happily. 'It's ours now. "Now that the bloody lawyers have stopped fighting over the carcass."'

Freddie's eyebrows rose with surprise. 'What?'

'That's what my father said,' Harry explained patiently, breaking off two long blades of grass and handing one to Freddie. The other he chewed half-heartedly. 'My father – Farley Bexenhall Fox Avery, known to all as Avery – has now inherited the Hall from his aunt. We moved in yesterday.'

Freddie digested the information thoughtfully. She liked the idea of this boy as a neighbour, and knew instinctively that they would be friends.

'Is the house repaired then?' she asked, remembering how Mike had told her about the fire years ago which had ruined much of the old building.

'Oh no, we haven't the money for that kind of thing,' Harry said easily, touching the impressive lump on his forehead and wincing. 'But my father has plenty of brilliant ideas to raise

49

funds. "Lots of cash," ' he said suddenly, his voice altering and startling Freddie until she realised that he was apparently mimicking his father. ' "Lots and lots of bloody cash, that'll sort us out." ' Obviously pleased with his performance, he smiled as he waited for her response. Freddie bit her lip, trying not to laugh.

'How ... ' she asked finally, ' ... how old are you?'

He blinked, suddenly ill at ease. 'Sixteen – how old are you?'

'Thirteen,' she replied honestly.

He considered the information, surprised, because he had thought that she was the same age as him. 'You look older,' he said, changing the subject. 'And you're really quite famous. At least, your father is.'

Freddie chewed hard on the grass stalk. 'Really?'

Harry nodded. 'My father knows him in London. They've been friends for a while.' He glanced back at the gate thoughtfully. ' "The Handsomest Man in England." '

'Who is?'

'Your father,' Harry said, surprised. 'Tatler said so, in their last issue, so it must be true. There was a big black and white photograph of him all over the cover, didn't you see it? Father was bloody outraged.'

Freddie shook her head. 'No.'

Harry studied her, incredulous. 'If it had been my father we would never have heard the last of it. "The Handsomest Man in England," ' he repeated, awestruck. 'Can you imagine being called that?'

' "Handsome is as handsome does." ' Freddie replied enigmatically.

'What does that mean?'

'It's something Meg told me; it means that you're only handsome if you do good things.'

Harry frowned. 'I do good things all the time,' he said impressively, 'but I'm not a bit handsome. I don't think I agree with Meg at all.' His thoughts wandered suddenly and throwing aside the half-chewed grass stalk he eyed the gate fiercely.

'I wouldn't try it again,' Freddie said, warningly.

But Harry was deaf to reason and stood rocking backwards and forwards on his heels, his gaze unwavering on the gate. He made a move to run forwards, then stopped. He retraced his steps, made another run – and stopped. Then he made another – and jumped. In hazy slow motion Freddie saw Harry leap upwards into the summer air, and whoop with delight as he cleared the gate, landing soundly on the other side.

Harry's face was transformed with pride as he turned to her and called out. 'I did it! I did it! I knew I would.'

'You did it,' Freddie agreed, suddenly disappointed now that the gate separated them. For an instant they looked at each other, both wanting to stay longer, then awkwardly Harry glanced at his watch.

'I have to go,' he said, turning away, then he turned back suddenly. 'Come for tea tomorrow. Over at the Hall.' Freddie smiled brilliantly with relief and nodded. 'Come at four,' he called, running over the field, his voice fading. 'I'll see you tomorrow.'

At four precisely Freddie walked up to the entrance of the Hall, her footsteps flagging a little as she approached the front doors. The red brickwork was in urgent need of pointing, damp rose ignominiously from the base of the building and the great oak doors were rotting at the top of the chipped steps. Overgrown Virginia creeper obliterated half the windows and crept stealthily up to the barley sugar chimneys like a thief making an escape over the roof. A brass door-knocker, dulled by age and neglect, felt sticky under her touch as Freddie tapped nervously.

A balding middle-aged man in a jumper opened the door and stood back to let her in. 'Mr Avery?' she asked timidly.

He jerked his head towards the back of the hall. 'Lord Avery's over there.'

Lord Avery jumped to his feet in the shadows and rushed over to Freddie. He was thin, shabby and blond, with the same slightly bulbous eyes as Harry. His hands were buckled with arthritis, and his handshake was clumsy.

'Lovely, lovely, bloody girl,' he said, his voice matching

51

exactly Harry's impersonation. 'My boy can certainly pick his girlfriends.'

Freddie stood uncertainly, not knowing what to say.

'Don't embarrass her,' said the middle-aged man who had let her in. Avery glanced towards him and pulled a face. His gestures, voice and mischievous eyes made him seem younger than he was.

'This is Bill Ketch. My friend,' Avery said with a mock sneer. 'He's in Public Relations and he's supposed to help me raise funds.' He bent towards Freddie conspiratorially. 'Actually he's my cousin, so I don't have to pay him – just keep him in food and booze.' He smiled wickedly. 'Isn't that right, Bill?'

Bill winked at Freddie. 'Actually I'm just waiting for him to die, and then after I've murdered Harry, my wife and I can inherit this palace, and live like royalty in all this luxury.'

They both laughed, Freddie looking from one to the other, smiling uncertainly, until Avery guided her over to the far side of the hall. Pushing aside a broken chair with his foot, Avery pointed to a collection of boxes, and demanded. 'Well, what do you think?'

Freddie kneeled down to get a better look. The packages were full of broken tiles and chippings of coloured glass. Mystified, she glanced up at Avery. 'What are they for?'

'Mosaics!' he said, grinning hugely. 'I've had a brainwave, you see, and bought up all this stuff for a song. Can you imagine how much money I can make, selling this to people so they can make their own mosaics – in bathrooms, swimming pools?' The bizarre idea was becoming almost feasible, such was his enthusiasm. 'I'll make a fortune, and then we can repair this place properly.'

'It's a bloody silly idea,' a voice said suddenly. Freddie rose to her feet as Harry came in.

'It's a winner!' Lord Avery said defiantly. 'And don't swear at your father.'

Harry approached Freddie and smiled, obviously pleased to see her. Then, with a wicked look, he pushed a magazine into her hands, the front cover emblazoned with a photograph of Greville.

Avery peered over her shoulder and snorted. 'A man should be fined for looking like that.'

Harry cast a sly look at Freddie and grinned as his father went on. ' "The Handsomest Man in England" – hah! I saw him only yesterday and he looked tired. After all, the cover's touched up – everyone knows what a good photographer can do.' He waved his clumsy fingers over the page. 'It's so unfair, good looks aren't earned. Not that you should complain, Freddie,' he said, gazing into her face critically. 'You're going to make a beauty one day.'

Freddie blushed furiously, unable to respond. No one had ever referred to her looks before. People were so amazed by her father that anyone following was an anticlimax. Now, for the first time, Freddie felt a pride in her own appearance – and a rush of grateful affection for Avery.

'I invited Freddie over for tea,' Harry explained, suddenly jealous of the attention his father was paying to his guest.

Avery frowned. 'I've got some sandwiches left over from lunch, and half a pork pie,' he offered helpfully.

Harry sighed. 'Didn't you ask Mrs Gibbons to come over?'

His father looked sheepish. 'I asked, but she said she hadn't been paid for last week, so … ' He raised his eyebrows at Freddie. 'You can't get the staff these days.'

Behind him, Bill Ketch began to laugh. 'Give me five minutes and I'll get something together,' he said simply, wandering off into a gloomy back passage. 'Why don't you show the young lady round in the meantime?'

Harry had wanted to take Freddie on a tour by himself, but his father was bored and, having second thoughts about the mosaics, decided to accompany them. They began in the hallway, hurried through the library which was being used as a box room, hardly paused for breath in the dining room, study and kitchen and then lingered in the drawing room. The paper had peeled off in listless strips and several lighter patches of wall showed gaps where paintings had once hung, the curtains crumbling at the touch where sun and moths had withered them. One broken window was boarded with hardboard, the others grimy with dust, and as they walked around,

Freddie felt her heel catch momentarily in one of the carpet's many holes. The whole room smelled of damp and when Avery sat down on a faded settee, an impressive dust cloud obliterated him for an instant.

'I thought we could have tea in here,' he said, as though the idea was irresistible,

'Only if we dust the sandwiches first,' Harry said cheerfully, turning to Freddie. 'I know what you're thinking. The place is a dump ... '

'Not when we've restored it,' Avery chimed in.

' ... but the garden's not bad.' Harry pressed on, 'd'you want to see it?'

The garden showed the same signs of neglect that the house did, but it was living, and if it was overrun with weeds, there were still some dogged flowers which bloomed defiantly amongst the chaos. An old herb garden, badly in need of pruning, led up to the kitchen window, Bill waving to them as they passed. Harry chatted easily, but Freddie could sense his embarrassment under the bravura, and was saddened by it.

'Mosaics! Can you believe it! Last week he was going to have a car rally here.' Harry shook his head disbelievingly. 'Bill helps to keep him on the straight and narrow, but he's no idea about business, never had.' He glanced over to Freddie. 'Your family's rich, isn't it?'

She nodded. 'The money came from carpets. Clough carpets.'

Harry whistled, impressed. 'I'm going to make money one day, then I'll come back here and do this place over.' He paused. In his dark blazer he looked older. 'She could be a real beauty, you know.'

Freddie glanced up, trying to see the house through his eyes. But she saw only an exhausted building, crumbling through neglect, and turned away, her eyes fixing elsewhere. She shivered unexpectedly.

'What is it?' Harry asked, following her gaze. 'Oh, that's where the fire was. D'you want to see?'

Freddie nodded, not trusting her voice, and together they

walked around the side of the house. The full impact of the burned ruin rose up in front of them, blackened timbers out of place against the summer sky, a few crows cawing irritably as they were disturbed. Freddie experienced a coldness washing over her and the same sense of threat that she felt in her father's presence left her rigid with unease.

'W ... when did this h ... happen?'

Harry glanced at her. 'I didn't know you stammered.'

She winced, unaware that she had betrayed herself. Slowly, she repeated her question, without juddering on the words.

'It happened about fifteen years ago,' Harry answered, surprised by the look on her face. 'There was a gas explosion.'

'Was anyone hurt?' she asked, speaking more slowly to prevent the damning stammer.

'No.' Harry said, already tired of the subject. To him, the burned part of the house held no magic or fear, it was simply something else to repair and restore. Nothing more.

But Freddie stood fixed to the spot. She stared at the building, at the piles of neglected rubble. A bird had made a nest in the ruins and now flew backwards and forwards, feeding its young. The ground was marked with summer puddles and a burnt table lay twisted on its side. Above it a distorted window frame swayed as the breeze plucked at it. Freddie's eyes flickered over the scene and she imagined the smell of burning, the crackling of things destroyed – and sensing not the past, but the future, she rocked uneasily on her feet.

In the next two years the friendship between Freddie and Harry deepened. He continued at Eton (a trust fund having secured his education), whilst Freddie remained at her private school in Harrogate, and Avery relentlessly embarked on more fantastic schemes to raise money to save the Hall. Now and again (generally due to the intervention of Bill Ketch) a few ideas were translated into workable money-spinners – a film company partially restored the facade in order to film a Martini advert there, and a jeans manufacturer paid well to hold a fashion show in the Great Hall. But the repairs always outran the money and before long Avery's ideas became a local joke. Not that he wasn't popular; he was too easy going to be disliked – and besides, he was a Lord.

That fact was not lost on anyone, least of all Harry, who, though never a snob, was well aware of what he would inherit one day. At the age of eighteen he was tall and elegant, his manners always impeccable, his appearance singled out by a certain eccentricity in his dress – red braces with a dark suit and a woman's watch. Not that he appeared effeminate, simply strange, and besides he was too good a sportsman to be the butt of anyone's jokes.

Meanwhile Freddie, too, was growing up. The fear of her father was always there, but Greville spent so much time away from Cambuscan that she saw little of him. When she knew he was coming home, Freddie went out with Mike or whiled away her days at the Hall with Avery, or with Harry if he was home. Her father seldom asked for her – although the tortuous family dinners usually took place once a week – and generally Sarah and Freddie were left alone.

In this way, Freddie moved between three worlds, comparing them, and weighing the differences between the happy Kershaw marriage, her parent's wretched relationship, and the bizarre all-male household at the Hall.

'Harry, do you miss your mother?' Freddie asked him one day when he was home for the holidays. He had been studying hard for his exams and had seen little of her, but when he did call at Cambuscan he was surprised to realise how much he had missed her.

Freddie had come running out of the front door to greet him, just as she had done so many times before, only on this occasion she was different – or maybe he was. Catching hold of him, she hugged him as a sister might, but her heavy dark hair smelled of perfume and her face had filled out, replacing the pinched look of her childhood. Only the eyes remained the same, steady under dark brows, and yet … and yet … wasn't there a sensuality there? Harry thought disbelievingly, reluctant to let go of her as she moved away.

'Do you miss her?' Freddie asked again.

Harry's thoughts turned back to the present as he glanced

at Freddie, suddenly confused and awkward. Why had he never noticed her hands before? Such fine hands ...

'Harry?'

He swallowed, fiercely confused. 'Sorry, Freddie. I don't miss my mother because I don't remember her.'

She thought for a moment. 'What about your father? He must miss her.'

Harry shrugged. He had never considered the matter. 'He's too involved with his schemes.'

Freddie nudged him with her elbow, teasing him. His stomach fluttered unexpectedly at her touch. 'Oh, Harry, how can you say that? Your poor father's probably terribly lonely.'

Harry glanced away. Freddie's presence, seated on the garden bench beside him, seemed so overpowering that he imagined heat radiating out from her and for the first time wondered what it would be like to kiss her. The thought made him blush furiously and he kicked at the gravel under his feet.

Freddie misread his reaction and thought she had been tactless. 'Oh, I'm sorry, Harry, I didn't mean to imply that your father was lonely, I just said he *might* be.'

Bloody hell, Harry thought violently, why does she have to keep rattling on and on about my blasted father?

'I won the boxing prize. Middle-weight.' He said suddenly, throwing down the fact to impress her. It did.

'Oh, Harry, that's great!' Freddie said, beaming with pride. His heart swelled like a sponge filled with warm water. 'Mike was a champion in the Army, you know.'

Harry groaned inwardly. 'Middle-weight?' he asked, reluctantly polite.

'Yes, same as you,' Freddie agreed, getting to her feet and calling across the lawn. 'Mike! Mike!'

Mike glanced up, waved and walked towards them. For a fleeting instant Harry hoped that Mike would be struck by a bolt of lightening, or some other freak accident of nature which would stop him disturbing them. But Mike made his way over in perfect health and nodded towards Harry.

''Lo there.'

'Hello.'

Freddie was triumphant. 'Harry's just won a prize – he's the best middle-weight boxer at Eton.'

Mike grinned, showing his uneven teeth as he extended one thick, dirt-encrusted hand. Harry took it like a gentleman. 'Well done, young man, well done. It brings back old memories talking about boxing. I was champion for five years.'

'Five years!' Freddie said delightedly, beaming at Mike.

Five bloody years! Harry repeated to himself, and with a stab of jealousy, tried to bring Freddie's attention back to himself. 'I hope I can match that.'

Mike grinned. 'Oh, you'll do just as well.'

'Five years is incredible,' Freddie said thoughtfully.

'Maybe we could have a bout sometime,' Harry said recklessly. 'A friendly match.'

Surprised by the suggestion, Mike beamed with pleasure and pride. Lord Avery's son sparring with him – just wait until they hear about that at the pub.

Freddie frowned darkly. 'Oh, Harry, do you think you should?'

Desperate to impress, Harry blundered on. 'Of course we should. I can probably pick up a few good tips from Mike.' He said it, but didn't believe it. Instead in his mind's eye, he could see Mike Kershaw out cold, a towel being waved over his unconscious face as Freddie ran into his conquering arms.

'When?'

'What?' Harry said, looking into Mike's face.

'When shall we have a bout?'

'Whenever you like.'

'Friday?'

Harry nodded.

'Where?'

Harry thought of the Hall, and then dismissed the idea. He wanted a classy backdrop to his triumph. 'Could we do it here, Freddie?'

'It is just a friendly match, isn't it?' she asked, anxious that no one should get hurt.

Mike raised his eyebrows. 'Of course, pet. I can show Harry

what made me a champion for five years, and he can show me what he's made of.'

Pure steel, Harry thought bleakly as they shook hands.

Harry felt anxious on Wednesday, worried on Thursday and by Friday was well aware that he was about to behave like a heel. Mike Kershaw was forty odd and although in good shape, was obviously out of practice. How could he seriously fight him, Harry wondered, weighing his doubts against the seductive image of his victory – Freddie in his arms, planting a winning kiss on his lips …

Groaning, Harry pushed the books he was studying away from him.

'Miniature ponies!' his father said, bursting into the room with a sheaf of photographs. 'That's a winner. We could buy a string of them, then hire them out for rides.'

Harry's eyes flickered with impatience. 'For who? Dwarfs?'

Avery was unmoved. 'They're small animals, they won't eat much.' He touched his son's forehead with one misshapen hand. 'Are you all right? You've been piquey for a few days.'

'Do you miss my mother?' Harry asked suddenly, repeating Freddie's earlier question.

Without hesitation, Avery shook his head. 'No, I never liked her much.'

'Is that it?'

Avery seemed surprised that more was required. 'Yes, that's it.'

'Well,' Harry persisted, 'don't you sometimes wish there was a woman around?'

'We've got Mrs Gibbons.'

Harry sighed. 'Not a cleaner, a wife.'

Avery crossed himself dramatically. 'Don't ever use that bloody word again, even in jest.' He raised his eyebrows. 'Funny you should ask though, because my sister's coming on a visit.'

Harry was riveted to his seat. 'Dione?'

Avery nodded, his fair hair falling over his forehead. Clumsily, he knocked it away from his eyes and leaned against his

59

son's desk. 'She's bored with travelling so she's going to come and see us – intent on improving us, I suppose. Bloody silly old bag.'

An image of Dione came into Harry's head. Immaculate and well-read, his aunt spoke three languages and had the force of personality to make an impact anywhere. 'How long is she going to stay?'

'Who knows,' Avery said, getting to his feet again. 'Dione once told me she would kill herself if she was ever left for more than a weekend in an English country house – we can only pray she hasn't changed her mind.'

Friday dawned misty, the sky clearing around eleven, a thin September sun curling over Cambuscan. Mike, resplendent in his old army shorts and vest, pulled on his boxing gloves in the kitchen whilst Meg looked on.

'Now you're not going to hurt the boy, are you?'

Mike looked at her reprovingly. 'Ah, come on, Meg, it's just a friendly sparring match.'

She was unconvinced. 'Whose idea was it? Yours?'

'His!' Mike replied sharply. 'He's a fine boy, and I'll do what I can to help him.'

'He's Lord Avery's son.'

'So what?' Mike snapped. 'I'm going to spar with him, not kill him.'

Meg shook her head. 'Many a true word is spoken in jest,' she said darkly. 'What's it all in aid of, anyway?'

Whistling softly, Freddie walked into the kitchen. 'Are you ready?' she asked, her voice light with excitement.

A look of indulgent understanding came into Meg's eyes. Of course, that was it! Mike was going to show his beloved Freddie that he was better than her rich young friend. He was going to give the Eton boy a showing up. Oh God, she thought, don't men ever grow up?

'Well,' Meg said, folding her arms. 'Are you ready?'

Mike flushed slightly and walked to the door. 'I'll be back soon.'

'Oh, that's all right, there's no hurry,' Meg said, taking off her apron and winking at Freddie. 'We're both coming to watch.'

The three of them stood on the cool back lawn at Cambuscan, the bay tree throwing its dark shadow across the grass. They waited for Harry, Mike jabbing fiercely at an imaginary partner, whilst Freddie glanced repeatedly towards the gate. Where was Harry? she wondered, looking around, then turning to scan the dark little copse behind the pavilion. At any minute she expected to see him appear, but as the moments passed she became anxious and began to chew the nail of her first finger.

Mike kept lunging at his imaginary foe, his head down, his face carrying an expression of determined ruthlessness. A horrible suspicion overtook Freddie. Perhaps Harry was afraid, she thought. She dismissed the idea immediately, although it wouldn't entirely dislodge itself from her mind. Perhaps he was lying in bed under the covers even now, trying to avoid facing Mike. Oh, where are you, Freddie thought with lurid shame. Where are you, Harry?

He rounded the drive at that precise moment, luminous in a white towelling robe, his boxing gloves swinging by his side, his blond hair glowing like an angel's in the sunlight.

Freddie turned to Meg, beaming. 'Look, there he is.'

'So I see.'

Mike, also saw him, stopped sparring and waved, Harry walking across the wet grass with a confident gait.

'Morning everyone,' he said brightly. 'Lovely day.'

'Oh, you both look wonderful,' Freddie said, beaming with pleasure.

'Ready?' Harry asked Mike.

'Ready,' he agreed, smiling.

They shook hands, and then Harry signalled to Freddie and Meg that they should stand back. Obediently they did so, watching as Mike laid out some white tape on the grass to indicate the limits of the boxing ring.

'Well, he's thorough, I'll give him that,' Meg said, watching the preparations with amusement and smiling as Harry took off his towelling robe to expose his white shorts and white vest. 'I hope there's no blood spilt though,' she said slyly. 'Those whites will be a devil to clean.'

Freddie ignored the remark and clapped. Harry bowed, Mike nodded in her direction, and then they squared up to each other. Mike was the first to throw a punch. Harry ducked to one side, Mike followed up, and Harry's foot just clipped the white tape which marked the limit of the ring. A few words were exchanged between the two men, friendly words, although Freddie couldn't hear them from where she stood. A moment later they began again. Mike was fast, but Harry was quick to learn and when he landed a punch squarely on Mike's chest, the hit thudded in the morning air.

Another quick exchange occurred, then Mike demonstrated a clever combination of punches and Harry laughed, walking back to his corner and coming out as though a bell had rung. Mike swung up his glove and caught Harry on the cheek. The impact forced the younger man to his knees. Freddie and Meg were silent, watching, listening to the accusing sound of the blow echoing in the sharp air. Seeing Harry struggle to get back on his feet, Mike immediately walked over to help, but Harry, humiliated and ashamed, jerked his fist upwards and struck out at Mike. Dodging the punch, Mike frowned and warily moved out of Harry's reach as the younger man came at him again.

Cool headed, Mike held back deliberately, knowing that he could hurt Harry, and that the supposedly friendly sparring match had turned into something altogether different. Harry wanted to win in order to impress Freddie, Mike realised, and as he moved around the makeshift ring, he wondered if he should throw the fight. He aimed a few half-hearted punches at his opponent's shoulders and Harry hesitated, knowing that Mike wasn't trying. For an instant both men waited to see what would happen. They could have stopped it then and made a joke out of it, exchanging a few words to take the sting out of the fight. But it had gone too far. Mike might be older, but Harry had more to lose – and besides both men wanted to win.

The punch hit Mike on the forehead, sending him backwards onto the grass. It had come from out of nowhere, with all the force of Harry's hand, arm, shoulder and head behind it, and it came viciously with all the speed and force of a thwarted eighteen-year-old. Defeated, Mike lay on the damp grass, the white tape around him, his limp hands by his sides as the women ran over to him.

A trickle of guilt ran through Harry as he looked at the fallen man. He had put all his strength into the punch, using more than was necessary to send Mike spinning to ground. Because he had been so desperate to win, Harry had taken advantage of the older man's kindness and his years, and he had given in to his temper. He could only pray that Freddie did not realise what he had done.

But she did, and when she turned to him she didn't hug him in a victory caress, or kiss him as he had dreamed she would; she simply swung back her own strong right hand and slapped him just as hard as she could.

Chapter Five

The wind blew down from Piccadilly, catching at Greville as he came down St James's, pulling out the key to his flat and hurrying in. From the ground floor came the sounds of a Bach toccata, and he shivered as he moved quickly into his flat and closed the door.

Greville had bought the place reasonably cheaply soon after he had married Sarah, and had been pleased to see its value increase steadily over the years. Now it not only provided him with considerable financial collateral but also served as a convenient watering hole in London. Walking into the lounge, he pulled off his coat, pushed some papers off the settee and sat down heavily. The magnificent lunch with Lord Avery had exhausted him, but it been intriguing. Who would have thought that Frederica would have caught Avery's eye? Oh yes, she was obviously being considered as Harry's future wife. The thought made Greville chuckle softly to himself. Avery needed money to prop up his mausoleum, and Greville wanted the stamp of respectability *Lord* Avery could offer. By allying their children, Avery would secure his finances and Greville would be accepted socially.

The taunts from Greville's childhood came back to haunt him savagely, the words 'Yid' and 'Jewboy' resounding in his head. Greville closed his eyes as all the old agonies seeped out, his mind blurring; then almost as suddenly as they had come, they disappeared and he sighed, his hands relaxing their frantic grip on the arm of the settee.

*

In a little house in Eaton Mews North, not too far away, Madelaine Glauvert was buzzing with energy. In fact, she was sitting bolt upright by the window looking out, the table beside her laid for an intimate dinner for two. Swiss born, she had dark blonde hair which had recently been highlighted, and a boyish figure and face, her gamine appeal heightened by a short haircut which was flicked back from her ears.

A failed actress, Madelaine had moved to London three years previously, at the age of nineteen, when she had won a part in a musical. Unfortunately the production had closed and when no other offers had materialised Madelaine looked for employment elsewhere. With no experience she decided to open a flower shop off Grosvenor Square. A wealthy lover who foolishly thought it might turn out to be a good investment had financed her, only to withdraw his support unconditionally when Madelaine visited his wife to demand they divorce. With hindsight Madelaine had to admit that the gesture had been a stupid one as she had not loved the man, but her jealousy had got in the way of her sense and the result had been catastrophic.

From that day onwards Madelaine had decided she would never be so sentimental again. Courting the company of several divorced women of a certain age, she became one of the many London ladies who moved in a certain circle of society and attended parties and dinners with any unattached male who required a partner for the evening. Sometimes there were compensations, a love affair could develop, even a trip to Venice on a business account, but often the men were tedious and unreliable.

'I think I love you,' one had said to her only the previous evening. She had smiled and touched his face. The gesture had almost passed for tenderness, but both of them had known it for what it was.

'That's nice, maybe I could love you too. You are a very attractive man.'

He had returned her smile, his hand moving onto her leg, his wedding ring gleaming in the candlelight.

Her lifestyle was erratic. The rent of the house in Eaton

Mews North was paid for by lovers, or by the odd job as a film extra. If necessary, Madelaine could always find work to raise the money, but she was basically indolent and preferred to earn extra cash by renting out the flat to friends when she was away, turning a blind eye to the screwed up pieces of tin foil in the bathroom bin. And after sordid parties, the beds were left unmade, the sheets scattered, even torn, when she returned. The chaos made little impression on Madelaine for there was always enough money to pay for a cleaner to tidy everything up.

Once, many years earlier, Madelaine had had a baby, but believing that her acting career was finally about to take off, she had left the girl with her parents in Geneva, and now thought of her as a sister, rather than as her own child. Without ties, Madelaine had been free to go where she chose, each whim gratified immediately, each disappointment stifled in a haze of drugs and booze. It was only after she caught an infection from a transient lover that Madelaine sobered up and looked at her life. She did not like what she saw and so, with a dedication which surprised her, she set about recreating herself.

Innumerable trips to gyms tightened up her figure, visits to Michaeljohn resulted in a new hairstyle, and a shopping binge at Chlöe and at Browns provided a new wardrobe. At the end of two months, Madelaine Glauvert was in peak condition and back in circulation, her mercenary eyes scanning the dinner party to which she had been invited, and her gaze finally coming to rest on Greville Clements ... Immediately they recognised something in each other, a mirror image of souls which was not spiritual. Across the table their mutual attraction seemed reflected in everything they saw: the heavy-lipped orchids in their bulbous glass bowl; the round bellied peaches, whose colour darkened in their amorous clefts; and the cheese, runny and potent, sticking to knives and fingers.

Greville watched her and wiped his mouth with his napkin. 'Who are you?' he asked finally.

Her expression was amused, cynical. 'Madelaine Glauvert.'

Her accent interested him. 'Are you French?'

'Swiss.'

'And what else should I know about you?'

She sipped her wine; the underside of her arm, unlit by candlelight, was shaded and secret. 'I am a healthy ex-actress, and a good Catholic girl.'

'I don't doubt you are a Catholic, but good?'

She shrugged. 'It depends. I am also very weak-willed, and can be persuaded to do virtually anything … My religion thinks highly of obedience.'

He smiled his understanding.

Their affair began that night and quickly developed into a frenetic passion, filled with violent arguments which frequently disturbed the peace in Eaton Mews North. The neighbours turned a deaf ear, but when a fight broke out one morning at four o'clock and Madelaine threw a decanter through the window, a passing milkman took exception and banged on the door.

Drunkenly Madelaine opened the upstairs window and looked out. 'What the hell d'you want?'

'That bloody thing nearly hit me!' The man snapped. 'What are you playing at?'

Clumsily, Madelaine rubbed her eyes. 'It wasn't aimed at you, I was throwing it at someone else.' There was a commotion below her and the front door opened, Greville pushing past the milkman.

'Hey, watch it!'

'Get out of my way!' Greville snapped, as Madelaine screamed out from the window above.

'You bastard! I hate you … ' Her words were hard to decipher. 'If you come back here I'll kill you, I swear it.'

Greville opened his car door and then turned, his voice raised as lights went on in several houses. 'Look at yourself in the mirror, Madelaine. You're a fucking hag! There's no way I'm coming back.'

Drunkenly she leaned forwards on the window ledge, appealing to the milkman. 'He's the one I wanted to hit … '

'Oh, go and sleep it off!' Greville shouted, starting up the engine and jerking the car into gear. 'You're an embarrass-ment, you stupid cow.'

The milkman looked from Greville to the woman in the upstairs window, who was sobbing quietly.

'I hate him! He's a bastard.' She said miserably. 'I'm sorry I'm such a lousy shot, I wanted to kill him.' She peered down blearily at the shattered glass, ' ... And now it's broken.'

The milkman raised his eyebrows and moved back to his cart. 'Next time stick to a bottle of pasturised. It'll be cheaper.'

Harry felt the slap long after Freddie hit him. Shame gagged in his throat and he was wretched with misery. On that same afternoon he had returned to Cambuscan and apologised to Mike, who merely shook his offered hand and made a joke about the bruise over his eye, saying worse things had hap-pened to him in the Army. But when Harry asked to see Freddie he was told that she had gone into Harrogate and was not expected back for some time.

His feet dragged over the lawn as he returned to the Hall, cursing himself for his stupidity, his whole body weighed down with the realisation that he had disappointed Freddie. Her face appeared in front of him constantly, with that look of disgust he had never seen before. It burned him fiercely – but not as fiercely as his own shame.

'Jesus!' Dione said as she walked into the Hall and glanced around. 'This place gets no better – where are the bodies buried?'

Avery kissed her lightly on both cheeks. 'I'm so glad you like my little changes, darling,' he said guiding her into the drawing room.

Her elegant features froze into disbelief. 'If I had ever thought that my brother – *my* brother – would enjoy living here.' She shot him a quick look and then grasped his hands, scrutinising them. 'Your arthritis is getting worse, you should be getting treatment for that. Anti-inflammatory drugs.'

Avery shrugged. 'They don't agree with me.'

'They aren't supposed to *agree* with you – they're drugs, not bosom pals.' She tugged at a piece of the peeling wallpaper. It came way in her hand. 'I thought you said you'd made improvements,' she said, wiping her fingers on a handkerchief. 'What was it before? An abattoir?'

'You will have your little joke, Dione,' Avery said patiently, steering her upstairs to the guest bedroom – the one bedroom that had been fully restored. She glanced round, trying to look disapproving but obviously relieved.

'Not bad.' Her manicured figure glided towards the window. 'Oh, Harry's coming,' she said, peering down to scrutinise her nephew's face. 'I think the strain of living here has caught up with him. He looks middle-aged.'

Avery joined her by the window. 'He's sick with love,' he said, laughing not unkindly. 'Poor bloody silly boy.'

'No!'

'Oh, yes,' Avery said ruefully. 'Frederica Clements has laid siege to his heart. In short, Dione, he's smitten.'

She raised two carefully pencilled eyebrows. 'Frederica Clements? Not Greville Clements's daughter?'

Avery nodded.' "The Handsomest Man in England," no less.'

'He's a foreigner,' Dione said bluntly, 'and he has a mistress.'

'With looks like his I'm surprised he isn't beating the women off with sticks.'

Dione's attention turned back to her nephew. 'Really, I'm surprised that you're encouraging the relationship ... '

'I've known Greville for years,' Avery said, sitting down on the ottoman at the end of the bed and rubbing the knuckles of his left hand. 'He's not as bad as some people make out. He's generous when he wants to be, and he's good company.' He paused, 'I think he's an unhappy man at heart.'

'Be that as it may,' Dione persisted, 'he's suspect.'

'But his daughter isn't.' Avery interjected firmly.

Dione's curiosity was aroused. 'Is she special?'

'She could be,' Avery answered. 'She *could* be a beauty, and she's intelligent, but no one seems to expect anything from her, so she's never been pushed. She goes to school in Harrogate and seems to spend much of her time with her mother ...'

'Well, that's fatal for a start.'

Avery grinned. 'Freddie could be a remarkable woman,' he said, throwing down the gauntlet to his sister. 'With the right help.'

The object of Harry's affections was soon under intense scrutiny, for Dione called at Cambuscan that weekend on the pretence of inviting the Clements to dine at the Hall.

'The dining room is almost habitable,' she explained, 'and the food is remarkably good now that Avery's found a cook at last.'

Sarah smiled uneasily. 'Another piece of cake?' she said, offering her visitor the plate of sponge.

'Oh, no thank you. I watch my weight like a pointer watches a pheasant.'

Sarah shifted her position on the settee in an effort to make herself look smaller.

'You have exquisite taste,' Dione said admiringly, glancing around. Indeed, she was impressed, the furniture was obviously inherited, the mirrors bevelled French glass and the lamps Venetian. In an Adam fireplace a log fire glowed cheerily, and the windows which flanked it were hung with Belgian silk. Cambuscan was not simply a beautiful house, it was a showplace.

'My parents were collectors,' Sarah offered happily, her high voice quick with pleasure. 'They took great pleasure in their home.'

'And they travelled a great deal?'

'Only my father,' Sarah replied. 'He was always bringing back things. My mother was happier at home, like me.'

'And you, Freddie? Are you happier at home?' Dione asked, turning to the girl sitting in the chair beside her.

'I love Cambuscan,' she said simply.

Dione nodded. 'But don't you want to travel? To broaden your interests?'

She smiled easily. 'In time. But it doesn't worry me.'

Sarah smiled at her daughter. 'She's such good company – my best friend.'

Freddie smiled at her mother; a kind, secret, protective smile which was older than her fifteen years. Her dark hair, falling around her face, was thick, and her eyes were well shaped, as was her mouth. Avery was right, Dione thought, she could be incredible if she knew how to present herself.

Such matters were familiar to Dione. As a child with ash blonde hair, she had resented her pale eyelashes and eyebrows and only came into her own in the Elizabeth Arden Salon in 1947. Make-up did not make her a beauty, but it gave her confidence and with that she found her own style. A year later she was being referred to as 'the elegant Dione Avery' and two years later she married a wealthy Milanese banker, Caesar Salari.

Stories of her wealth and style travelled back to London. She was fêted for her friends and her chef, for her clothes and her cars, for her furs and her intelligence. Devouring the classics, she talked to intellectuals and scholars and although she had little natural aptitude, she mastered French and Russian in order to read Proust and Turgenev in the original.

On matters of style she was impeccable. She knew not only the background of everyone, but also the bank accounts of most. Formidable and quick-witted, she saved her Italian husband from ruin when his bank was under threat and then opened her own gallery in Milan, selling 16th century furniture to her rich friends and contacts. What would have been a disaster for anyone else was seen as challenge by Dione, and she triumphed.

The only disappointment in her life was her lack of children. With her usual thoroughness she had sought out every doctor from Milan to Rome, from New York to London, but none could help. So instead she turned her attention to her husband, her business, her travels – and her nephew.

'There is so much to see abroad, Freddie,' Dione continued. 'You would be amazed at the difference in cultures.' She extended the invitation without thinking. 'Perhaps you would like to come to Florence with me next week? I'm going there for a few days on business, and I think it might be nice for you.'

Sarah took in her breath as Freddie hesitated. She had only just met Dione Salari and was as surprised to receive the

71

invitation as Dione was to offer it. But she accepted nevertheless. 'Thank you,' she said wonderingly, and then smiled at Dione, as though to seal their pact.

The news of their trip offered hope to Harry, although he had still not yet spoken to Freddie, either to apologise or explain. He took the fast friendship between his aunt and Freddie as a good sign, and then began to suspect Dione's motives. Perhaps she was simply giving Freddie a good looking over, scrutinising her whilst she was away from home. The thought that his love was going to be judged was abhorrent to him and he considered tackling his aunt, until his father stopped him.

'Well, thank God my bloody sister's off tomorrow,' he said, staring hard at a package which had been delivered two days ago and still stood in the middle of the hall. 'Taking Freddie too – that was nice of her. She must like the girl.'

'Father ... '

'What *is* that box?' Avery asked, interrupting his son. He walked over to the package. 'I can't remember ordering anything.'

'Why do you think Dione's taking Freddie to Florence?'

Avery's eyes widened. 'Company?'

Harry sighed with relief. Of course, it was that simple. Caesar Salari was busy in Milan and Dione wanted company – why hadn't he thought of that?

'Do you think they'll like each other?' Avery asked his son innocently, one hand resting on top of the mystery box.

'No one could help liking Freddie,' Harry said quietly, not noticing his father smile and turn away.

Although she had been nervous before the trip, Freddie found herself too excited to be anxious once they were under way. Besides, as she had repeatedly reassured her mother, the journey was only to be for five days. Sweeping all before her, Dione organised everyone at the airport and at the hotel in Florence, her bedroom already sprayed with her favourite perfume, a bowl of welcoming gardenias on the table beside the bed. Used to luxury, Freddie was not surprised by the hotel, but she was impressed by the detail with which Dione ran her life and decided to watch her hostess and learn from her. Acutely intelligent, Dione had already noticed how her young companion observed her, and decided on the second day to discover if Freddie had the style she suspected.

'Would you be very offended ... ' she said to Freddie as they had breakfast on her terrace the following morning. ' ... if I asked how old you were?'

'Fifteen – well, sixteen next month.' Freddie replied, biting into a piece of brioche.

'Your father is known as "The Handsomest ... " '

' ... "Man in England," ' Freddie finished for her. 'Yes, I know.'

'So why don't you make the most of your own good looks?'

Freddie wiped her lips on her napkin and glanced out of the window. The huge golden dome of the *duomo* shone under a pale sun. Traffic horns sounded hollowly in the streets below.

'I've never been very interested in my appearance,' Freddie said simply, without explaining that she had a suspicion that good looks were a curse, a cover for the truth.

'I see. Well, Freddie, I want you to trust me,' Dione said, leaning forwards, her face animated. 'I want to take you to meet someone.'

The someone they went to see was Signora Guardi. Obviously delighted to see her friend, the celebrated Dione Salari, the old woman ushered them both into a small dark room off the main beauty salon and then leaned towards Dione.

'You have the skin of a twenty-year-old,' she said, her own smooth face betrayed by her old, liver-spotted hands. 'You look after it like I say?'

Dione nodded obediently. 'But it's not for me today, Signora Guardi. This time it's for my young friend.'

'Ahhh,' the old woman replied, scrutinising Freddie's face without speaking. After a minute she moved out of the room and called to someone. A pale man appeared and Signora Guardi spoke quickly to him in Italian, Dione smiling reassuringly at Freddie who was gazing anxiously into the mirror.

'Good face. Bad hair,' Signora Guardi said emphatically,

picking up Freddie's hands. 'Lovely.' She then touched her visitor's ears and nodded. 'We pierce them.'

'No!' Freddie said bluntly.

Dione rested her hands on her shoulders and looked at Freddie firmly. 'Oh, yes.'

For three hours they worked on Freddie without letting her look in the mirror. Her over-thick, over-long hair was tied back, her eyebrows plucked slightly to shape them, her skin pummelled with a variety of creams and oils. Slowly and painstakingly Signora Guardi prepared and then made up Freddie's face, talking all the time to Dione in Italian.

Then the pale young man worked on Freddie's hair, cutting it to shoulder length and lifting it back from her face to give emphasis to her eyes. Finally, satisfied, he pierced her ears quickly and slipped in a pair of fine gold hoops before pushing her under a hair drier with a frothing *cappuccino* to drink. Unable to read the Italian magazines, Freddie sat impatiently under the heater, her feet jiggling in front of her, her newly varnished nails rigid in her lap. Three quarters of an hour later Freddie was pulled out and her hair was subjected to a vicious brushing and styling. Then her make-up was touched up and perfected before the new Frederica Clements was presented to Dione.

'So!' was all Signora Guardi said when she had finished.

Gingerly, Freddie turned to look into the mirror.

A sleek beauty looked back at her. The hair, now lifted away from her face made her dark eyes seem larger, and the make-up gave them a look both challenging and seductive. Her skin, which Freddie had never really noticed before, glowed a perfect pale olive, betraying just a hint of her father's ancestors; but her full mouth, darkened faintly with lipstick, was her own.

Dione gazed in astonishment at her and for once found herself unable to speak, her eyes filling with tears.

'*Bella!*' Signora Guardi snapped, clapping her hands and speaking for them both.

The transformation begun, Freddie did not want it to stop, and she begged Dione to help her choose some new clothes.

Knowing full well that this would happen, Dione pleaded tiredness and then relented, taking her charge to the myriad boutiques along the Ponte Vecchio.

'Put that down! You look like a whore!' Dione snapped, snatching the clothes from Freddie and hurling them back at the patient salesgirls. Out went the Chanel and the Dior and in came the Valentino.

'Try it on.'

'But ... '

'No buts!' Dione ordered, forcing Freddie into the red dress and zipping up the back. She then turned the girl to look in the mirror. 'Don't ever wear patterns again. You have a good figure – mind you, you'll always have to watch your weight – so show it off.' She paused, watching with amusement as Freddie studied her own reflection.

'I look ... '

'Expensive. Classy – but young,' Dione said, walking out of the changing booth, Freddie trailing behind her.

An hour later they were exhausted. Laden with Valentino dresses, a few pairs of perfectly cut jeans, several silk shirts and four pairs of shoes, they collapsed onto Dione's bed.

'I never thought ... '

' ... that you could look so stunning?' Dione finished off the sentence for her and grinned. 'I know how it feels, believe me.'

Freddie rolled onto her stomach. 'Do you know, Dione, suddenly I want to do so much. I feel as though I've never really lived ... ' She paused, but her companion was listening carefully. 'I want to go everywhere, and do everything.'

Dione heard an echo of herself in Freddie's words, and pressed her, 'What about books, Freddie? What do you read?'

'Dickens, and the usual paperbacks.'

'And what do you want to do with your life?'

Freddie frowned. 'You mean a career?'

'Yes, a career.'

'I've never thought about it,' Freddie admitted. 'I suppose I just thought I would get married.' She paused. 'I like history though, and I know something about furniture from what my mother's told me. Maybe I'll go into antiques ... '

75

Dear Lord, thought Dione to herself, how little we travel in the end, simply to return to where it all began.

'You're not serious!' Sarah said, for once standing up to Greville. Her face was white with indignation, her voice shrill. 'I won't let you do this.'

'I know what's best,' he replied, glancing over to his daughter, his admiration intense. Dear God, who was this creature, this spectacular girl who had materialised in Italy? No wonder Avery wanted his son to have her.

'Frederica will make more progress at boarding school. She could be an intelligent girl if she was kept away from distractions.'

'I don't want her to go away.'

'No, I don't suppose you do, after all you've made her what she is,' he said. 'Spoilt.'

'She's not spoilt!' Sarah said, glaring defiantly at her husband. 'And you can't send her away. You're never home, so what difference does it make to you whether she's here or not? You're just being spiteful.' She broke off and turned to Freddie. 'You don't want to go away, do you?'

Freddie's eyes were wide with anxiety. 'No, of course I don't ... '

Ignoring his daughter completely, Greville was adamant. 'What she wants does not concern me. I know what's best for her, that's all.' Yes, and I want her to be prepared to be Harry's wife, he thought. 'You've seen how she's come on since she went to Florence. She needs to see the world and she needs to be well educated.'

Freddie said nothing, but her father's sudden interest in her welfare made her suspicious.

'Where is this school?' Sarah asked blindly.

'London.'

'London!' she repeated. 'Why so far away? Why?' Her high-pitched voice was pleading, defeated. 'Who will I talk to when she's gone? She's everything to me.' Desperately she tried to reason with her husband. 'Greville, darling, don't do this. I can't stay up here on my own now that you're away so much.'

'Oh, act your age, Sarah,' he replied wearily. 'Take up a hobby or make some friends. Besides, you won't get lonely, I'll be spending more time at home soon.'

They all knew that was a lie.

Chapter Six

On 4 September, Freddie arrived at the boarding school near Hampstead. Although unwilling to leave her mother, she did not entirely resent her father's action. Her curiosity had been aroused by her trip to Italy and she felt the need to extend herself, Dione's example galvanising her into action. Freddie had no real idea of what she wanted to do with her life, she only knew that the world extended beyond Cambuscan, and that she wanted to explore it. But leaving home had been difficult. For days, Sarah had followed her daughter around, stroking her hair and then hugging her tightly, her eyes filling with tears. Already anxious, Freddie found herself alternating between pity for her mother and a guilty longing to be gone.

When she did finally arrive at the school however, she felt such a hollow loneliness inside that she could speak to no one. Trying to keep her nervousness hidden, she unpacked, hanging her uniform in a locker exactly the same as a hundred others. Constant reminders of home gnawed at her: the smell of Meg's ironing still clinging to her clothes, a piece of one of the rushes from the lake that Mike had pressed into her prayer book, a note her mother had written and slipped into her wash-bag.

As the sounds of a hundred pairs of feet and the shouts of as many unknown schoolgirls echoed round her, Freddie propped up a photograph case by her bed. A picture of her mother stood on one side, facing a photograph of Cambuscan. Under a fall of snow, the house loomed wide and high against the sky, the statues by the door sheeted in white, the bay tree solemn in the bleak garden. Beside the case she placed another photograph of Mike and Meg Kershaw – but none of her father.

'Are you homesick?'

'What?' Freddie asked, turning round to face an ethereally thin girl.

'I asked if you were homesick,' the girl repeated. 'I was, the first term I came here.' Leaning forwards she peered at the photograph. 'Is that where you live?'

Freddie nodded. 'That's Cambuscan, up in Tydale Brook.' There was no response. 'That's in Yorkshire.'

'You're a long way from home then, aren't you?' The girl replied, extending one bony hand to introduce herself. 'I'm Jao Wilkie.'

'I'm Freddie Clements.'

Jao grinned delightedly. 'So *you're* Frederica Clements. I heard someone talking about you. Your father's ... '

' ... "The Handsomest Man in England," ' Freddie said wearily. 'Did everyone in the world read that copy of the *Tatler*?'

'Well, everyone here did. Besides, you can't expect us not to be interested. He is rather dishy, isn't he?'

'I don't really know,' Freddie said stiffly. 'You can't tell if your own mother or father are good-looking.'

'Oh, I can,' Jao said blithely, passing a worn photograph over to Freddie. 'This is my mother, and she's stunning. We live in London, Dorman Square.' She put her head on one side. 'Do you know it?'

'No ... no, I don't,' Freddie said, staring at the colour print. Three women sat in a large, untidy kitchen. The woman nearest to the camera was full-breasted and smiling, her arm flung over the back of her chair. Purely on instinct, Freddie liked her. 'Who's this?' she asked.

'That's Bea,' Jao said, pleased with Freddie's response. 'My mother ... and that,' she said, indicating a smaller woman, 'is my aunt Trisha, and this one ... ' She peered at the photograph, ' ... you can hardly see her because she's turning away,

79

but that's my other aunt, Pam. She has bad feet and a bad temper. Aunt Acid, or Antacid, if you prefer!' She laughed noisily, enjoying her own joke.

Freddie studied the photograph carefully. 'Where's your father?'

'I don't have one.'

'Oh, I'm sorry.'

'Oh, don't worry, I don't miss him,' Jao replied happily. 'Bea says he was a villain and she should know. She says he used to eat oranges in bed.'

Freddie was nonplussed. 'Is that bad?'

Jao laughed, a surprisingly dirty laugh from such a wistful little face. 'I suppose that depends on whether you like oranges or not. Bea said he used to try and spit the pips into the waste-paper bin. Can you imagine? From the bed to the bin? That must be nearly ten feet!'

Freddie was fascinated. 'What happened to him?'

'Oh, they got divorced,' Jao replied easily.

'On what grounds? Pip spitting?'

Jao burst out laughing. 'What does your father do for a living?'

'He's a solicitor.'

'He should be in the movies, looking like that,' Jao said wistfully, dropping her voice. 'Listen, you won't laugh, will you? But I actually cut that picture out of *Tatler*.' Freddie was at a loss to know what to say. 'Silly, isn't it?' Jao continued, then changed the subject. 'I could go home at night, but Bea thinks boarding is good for me. It's supposed to make me independent. Anyway, I go home most weekends.' She paused. 'Have you got a boyfriend?'

Freddie thought of Harry and a wave of homesickness rose in her stomach. 'There is someone ... '

'What's he like?' Jao asked avidly.

'Harold Bexenhall Fox Avery.'

Jao grinned. 'Aviary? Isn't that where they keep birds?'

Freddie laughed loudly, then added, hoping to impress. 'His father is Lord Avery.'

Jao pulled a face. 'That'll cut no ice here – half the girls are

80

lady this, or lady that, and all their mothers have the horse-faced look of our beloved aristocracy.'

'That's unkind.'

'Nope, that's a fact,' Jao responded unabashed. She studied the new girl next to her. Even on such a short acquaintance Jao found herself drawn towards Freddie, and not at all jealous of her ripe good looks. Jao was as delicate as Freddie was strong and their contrasting physiques prevented either from feeling jealous.

'Do you have any sisters or brothers?' Jao asked finally.

Freddie shook her head. 'No, only me.'

'I'm an only child too. When my father left, Bea and my aunts brought me up,' Jao said, getting to her feet and peering at her profile in the mirror on the back of the wardrobe door. 'Bea keeps promising me that I'll get a bust any day now, but there's not even a bump.' She glanced over to Freddie. 'I thought that once I'd got my periods, I'd be off, bursting the buttons off my blouses overnight and flattening all before me with my rogue breasts … but no such luck,' she said wistfully, turning away from the mirror and folding her arms over her flat chest.

'I always wanted one of those low, sexy voices,' Freddie confided suddenly.

'Oh, but you can fake that,' Jao said, dropping her voice a pitch.

'So? You can fake a bust too. Get a couple of socks stuffed into your bra.'

'It wouldn't be the same,' Jao insisted. 'Besides, what happens when a boy touches you? He would hardly be impressed when he found he was mauling a pair of hockey socks, would he?'

Freddie grinned, but was secretly embarrassed by the turn the conversation had taken. At home, sex had never been referred to directly, although at times the sheer potency of her father's physical presence was uncomfortably apparent, and the desire her mother felt for him all too obvious.

'Homesick again?' Jao asked sympathetically, misreading the look on her companion's face.

Freddie lied, too careful to risk confiding all her secrets at once. 'Yes,' she said gently. 'I was thinking of home.'

Harry wasn't going to give up on Freddie easily and he soon pressed Dione for advice. Her reply, after listening to his story of the boxing match, was a loud snort of laughter.

'Good for her!' she said, imagining Freddie's face as she slapped her nephew. 'You were in the wrong and she let you know it. Good girl.'

'But she won't have anything to do with me any more,' Harry said miserably, kicking the boot scraper by the front door. 'She hates me.'

'Oh, I think that's a little extreme. She probably just wishes you were dead, that's all.'

Harry threw her an agonised look and Dione laughed again. 'Oh God, Harry, write her a letter.'

'She returns them as soon as she recognises my handwriting.'

'In that case, you write the letter, and I'll write the envelope,' Dione said wearily, getting to her feet. 'And please, Harry, get it sorted out soon. You haven't done a stroke of work for days and you have to pass your exams if you want to go to university.'

Harry nodded, dumbly miserable, but that afternoon he screwed up all his courage and wrote to Freddie again.

Dear Freddie,
I know you're angry with me and you have every
reason because I behaved badly. Not like a gentleman
at all. This is not supposed to be an excuse, but I
wanted to win that boxing match to impress you. I
don't know what to say now, only that it would be
terrible if our friendship ended like this. Or in any
other way.
   Write back and say I'm forgiven, Freddie. After all,
you're in the right, so what have you got to lose by
being magnanimouse? (That was supposed to be a
joke.) Remember when I tripped over the gate the first

82

day we met? Well, that bump on the head didn't hurt half as much as your silence is hurting now.
Please write,

Harry

Freddie received the letter, together with another one from Dione, both enclosed in the same envelope. Dione's read:

> Harry's pining,
> I'm declining
> He'll get no better
> 'Til you send a letter.

Freddie burst out laughing and slowly opened Harry's note, reading it twice. She then folded it and tucked it into her pocket, thinking of him, of his guileless expression and over-large eyes, his charm and easy manners, the odd little eccentricities in the way he dressed. It was so easy to remember him and to miss him – and it was even easier to write.

Harry responded immediately and the lines of communication reopened like a floodgate, correspondence winging its way from Hampstead to Eton, and from Eton to Yorkshire again. Avery found the whole experience thoroughly amusing, although he was well aware that Greville was following every twist and turn of the romance with compulsive interest. Indeed, Greville had even taken to calling at the Hall on his trips home, inviting Avery over for dinner and pressing him for news of the romance. His voice was casual, but it was apparent even to the naïve Avery, that his interest was profound.

Dione met Greville only once and disliked him on sight, much to Avery's amusement.

'He gives me the bloody creeps,' she said, slamming down a copy of *Harper's* onto the settee in the drawing room and waiting for the cloud of dust to rise. When it didn't, she smiled with satisfaction. 'So Mrs Gibbons finally managed to beat the grime of centuries out of the cushions, did she? Well done, Mrs Gibbons.'

Avery glanced over to his sister. 'I was wondering if I could do something with the burned out part of the house – make it into a horror chamber ... '

'No!'

Avery frowned, preoccupied, and rubbed his left hand, the thumb twisting at an odd angle to his palm.

'Is your arthritis bothering you again?' Dione asked, genuinely concerned. 'Listen, I could easily get someone to see you in London ... '

'Yes, and it would cost me a fortune.'

'Don't be absurd, Avery!' Dione snapped. 'You know I would pay for it.'

'That's the point, old girl. I don't want you to.'

'Well, then move away from here for a while! It might be summer but the heat never gets through these walls. Come and stay with me in Milan, the warmth will do you good.'

Avery glanced around the room. It was his inheritance, and his responsibility. As an easygoing man who had never had a real occupation, he had little idea how to run a business, but he did have that inbred respect for tradition. To desert the Hall would be to fail his ancestors. Besides, he never felt really depressed about the state of the building, and never saw the destruction without seeing the possibility of reconstruction. To restore the Hall was his life's work – but quite how he was going to do it was another matter.

'Bill said we could approach some more film companies and rent the place to them for their shoots.'

'Pah!'

Avery smiled wickedly. 'It's amazing just how much they loath the aristocracy,' he said, remembering the film director who had been unable to exchange two words with him. 'They come here, see this massive place and the title, and their envy rises faster than a helium balloon. You can see it in their bloody eyes, "Why should this twit inherit all this, when I have to work like a dog?" ' he mimicked. 'Actually people should be grateful to the gentry. People like me serve a very useful purpose in the scheme of things. We, my love,' he said, pointing to his sister, 'are here to be despised. That is our lot in life.'

'Speak for yourself, Avery,' she replied coolly.

'Oh, but I am,' her brother responded, teasing her. 'Some day, not far away now, when there is anarchy in our land, the tumbrils will roll up the driveway and I will find my head decorating the end of a spike in Whitehall.'

Dione smiled, but the conversation, although light-hearted, had taken a grim turn and was out of character for her brother. 'Are you all right?' she asked.

Avery continued to rub the knuckles of his hand and then smiled, his fine hair slipping over his forehead. For an instant she saw him as a boy again, not as a middle-aged man with too many problems and too much pain.

'I am aware of my own mortality all at once,' Avery replied, then smiled engagingly. 'I fear the house is taking me into decline with it.'

'Bloody fool!' Dione said brusquely. 'You just need a change of scene, that's all.' She made her mind up quickly, seeing a chance to kill two birds with one elegant stone. 'You and I, and Harry and Freddie, are all going on holiday,' she announced. The relief in her brother's eyes was touching. 'A week in Paris.'

'The money ... '

She put up her hands to stop him continuing. 'Avery, when I die I shall leave my money to Harry, so why can't he have some a little prematurely and benefit us all? Especially when I can enjoy it with him.'

The school holidays were always a difficult time for Freddie. Long trips by train returned her to Yorkshire and her mother would greet her at the station, waving giddily, full of excitement and news of Cambuscan and the Kershaws. But within hours of Freddie's arrival Sarah would be regaling her with every tiny detail of Greville's awful behaviour since Freddie had last been home. What he had said, what he had done, what he had not done. Everything saved up in the previous weeks was duly served, piping hot, for her daughter's homecoming. So when Dione wrote to Freddie suggesting the week's holiday in Paris, Freddie was eager to accept, especially as Harry and Avery were going too.

'But … but I thought you were coming home,' Sarah said over the phone, her voice plaintive.

'I am, Mummy. It's only for a week and I have a month's holiday.'

To Freddie's surprise, her father suddenly came onto the line. 'I think it's a good idea,' he said firmly. 'You should get out and about with these people, Frederica – broaden your horizons.'

Greville was the ally Freddie least expected, but it was due to his intervention that Sarah's doubts were crushed and Freddie went to Paris. Freed from the strictures of school, she applied her make-up and styled her hair as Signora Guardi had taught her, wriggling into her jeans and silk shirt and walking transformed into the lobby of the George V the following day. Harry glanced up, literally dazzled by her.

'Freddie … you look marvellous.'

She returned his smiled, noting his casual clothes and the ease with which he fitted into the plush surroundings.

'Avery's sleeping in, and Dione was out late dining at La Tour d'Argent last night,' he explained, 'I thought we could go for a walk.'

They walked for over an hour and then paused for a coffee on the Avenue Montagne. Harry talked of his ideas and plans for the future, inspired by the architecture of the city. Freddie listened carefully, realising for the first time just how much the Hall meant to him. She had always known that he felt a sense of responsibility for both the title and the property he would inherit, but this time as he talked she had the feeling that he had finally passed from boyhood to manhood, and was trying valiantly to plot out the structure of his future.

She sipped her coffee, her eyes shielded with sunglasses, watching him.

'At least we've got the west wing restored. OK, that's not bad, but there's so much else to do, Freddie.' He paused, pushed back the sleeves of his open necked shirt. His arms were lightly tanned, covered with a dusting of fine hair and Freddie felt an almost painful impulse to touch him. 'The Hall will be a showplace one day, you'll see. Like Cambuscan.' He stopped suddenly.

'Go on, Harry, I was listening.'

'I just wonder sometimes ... Oh hell, what's the use!'

Surprised by his show of irritation, Freddie fell silent.

Surreptitiously, Harry watched her, feeling the familiar sense of longing. 'When I've finished university,' he said, 'I'll come and live at the Hall all the time.' He hesitated. He had done well in his exams, despite the emotional turmoil of his fight with Freddie, and he wanted to carry on with his education. But another part of him wanted to stay in Yorkshire, to work the land ... and to be within walking distance of Cambuscan.

'It won't be for long – only three years – until I get my degree.'

Freddie smiled behind her glasses.

Harry couldn't see her eyes and thinking for a fleeting moment that he was losing her, panicked. 'Freddie?'

'Yes?'

'After university ... ' he faltered, 'after I finish university I'll be twenty-two and I'll have come of age.' He felt stupid, ill at ease, and fiddled with the cube of untouched sugar in his saucer. Freddie was only sixteen, only a girl. How could he ask her now? And ask her what exactly? Ask her to be always at Cambuscan? Always just over the gate where he had fallen at her feet that first day?

'Freddie, I just wanted to say ... '

'Well, I wondered just how far you would walk before stopping for refreshment,' Dione said, interrupting Harry's imminent declaration and sitting down beside Freddie. 'I had an appalling night, the bed was chilled, my dear. *Chilled.*' She shuddered at the memory. 'I phoned down to reception and told them that I did not expect such treatment at the George V, and they rushed upstairs with all manner of hot water bottles and electric blankets.' She gestured to the waiter for fresh coffee. Harry watched her in wretched silence; Freddie was remote behind her dark glasses.

Dione continued, 'It's not that I mind the occasional bout of cryogenic suspension – freezing is supposed to refresh the skin – but I just kept wondering if Avery was all right. I mean, with his arthritis ... ' She turned to her nephew. 'Did your father sleep well?'

Harry was rigid with frustration. 'Fine.'

'Good,' Dione replied, sipping her coffee and then frantically signalling to the waiter again. 'What is this?' She asked in superb French. 'I ordered coffee, not hair dye.'

They each returned from Paris in a different condition. Freddie was excited, bearing new clothes, presents for her mother and a number of books on architecture; Avery was rested, almost louche; Dione was triumphant that her brother's health had improved; but Harry, poor Harry, was frustrated beyond endurance. His one moment of emotional bravura had passed. He had the sensation of having run a race from the front and then having tripped just before the finishing line. Everything he desired had been within his grasp, and he had flunked it.

The rest of the holidays came and went, Freddie returning to London for the autumn term and Harry going up to Cambridge. They wrote to each other constantly, Harry sending drawings of the alterations he wanted to make at the Hall, Freddie teasing him about studying Classics when he should be reading Home Maintenance instead. And all the time Greville was watching, and waiting.

Freddie's curiosity was not confined to the Averys. Much as she enjoyed their company, she found that when she was away from home, other people in other places interested her. People who were totally dissimilar from her elegant Yorkshire neighbours – people like the Wilkies.

'You must come and stay with us – even if it's only for the weekend,' Jao urged Freddie. 'It'll be a change for you.'

Freddie hesitated, but only for a moment. 'You're on,' she said, smiling at Jao, knowing instinctively that this was to be the first of many trips to the Wilkie women in Dorman Square.

'Oh, my God! Where's the bloody soda siphon?' Bea called out, looking down by the side of her chair in the sitting room. 'Pam! Where's the siphon?'

'I don't know,' her sister replied, walking into the room and sniffing. 'It smells smokey in here.'

'Probably because of all the cigarettes smoked last night,' Bea replied evenly, her hands on her hips, her voice husky. 'I know I saw it. The dog's peed on the hall carpet so I have to find it.'

Pam sighed and bent down to look, her lanky frame tight with ill humour. 'I could hardly sleep for all the noise last night, Bea. God knows what the neighbours thought.'

'They probably wished they were here enjoying themselves,' Bea replied, shrieking with pleasure and holding the siphon aloft. 'Got it!' she said, rushing out and squirting the dog's urine stain on the carpet before turning back to her sister. 'Why didn't you join us last night?'

Immediately Pam stiffened. 'I don't like parties. Besides, I'd feel out of place. I knew you didn't want me there.'

Bea sighed. 'That's not true. You're always more than welcome.'

'I'm not!' Pam said, her voice shrill. 'I don't fit in anywhere. You just put up with me – you and Trisha.' Her eyes filled with self pity. 'No one ever really wants me.'

Bea laid down the soda siphon on the hall table and put one arm around her sister. Under the hall light, Bea's hair was the colour of liquorice, her face sensual, yet sympathetic. 'You do go on, Pam,' she said softly. 'You should relax more and stop worrying about what people think. You could make friends ... '

'I can't!' Pam replied instantly. 'You know I can't. I never could at school, or at work. No one likes me.' She blew her nose, her face reddening. 'It's so easy for everyone else. Look at Jao, for instance – she's bringing a friend home tonight.'

Bea dropped her arm from her sister's shoulder. 'Bloody hell, so she is!' she said, moving towards the bathroom. Quickly she wrenched open the door of the airing cupboard and piled sheets and blankets into Pam's outstretched arms. 'I'd completely forgotten!' she moaned, rushing into the spare bedroom and turning up the radiator. A steady thumping noise sounded in the pipes as she shook the sheets and began to make up the bed. 'Pull open the curtains, Pam, and give this place a dust.'

'She's not royalty. She's just a school girl ... '

'Get the flaming duster!' Bea said impatiently, tucking in the blankets and pulling over the bedspread. 'Oh, and turn the soup off on the cooker or it'll boil over.'

Looking round, Bea dug her hands in her hair and sighed. The room was cold and uninviting and a stack of magazines stood in one corner besides a selection of Christmas decorations half-heartedly packed in boxes. Usually the spare bedroom was used as a storeroom, which meant that everything in the free world ended up – and remained – there. Hurriedly Bea pushed the boxes of decorations into the cupboard under the stairs, threw the magazines and a stray tennis racquet on top of the boxes and slammed the door closed before the whole lot fell out onto the damp patch on the hall carpet. Then she moved into the lounge and groaned. The room was in semi-darkness, the daylight blurred behind still closed curtains, an empty bottle rattling underfoot as Bea flicked on the light.

Pam walked in behind her. 'What a mess.'

Bea sighed. 'We have two alternatives. We can either buckle down and clean it up, or set fire to it and claim the insurance.'

To the accompaniment of Pam's persistent moans, the room was tidied. Bottles and cigarette stubs were deposited in the bin on the fire escape, glasses left to soak in hot soapy water, the dust pan and brush pressed into service, a dis-guarded cocktail stick piercing Pam's thumb as she swept under a chair. Ignoring the plaintive yelp, Bea plumped up the cushions and straightened the lampshade, pictures and curtains, whilst a liberal spraying of polish made the surfaces look reasonably shiny. The dog sat unmoving in its messy bed in front of the Hoover, growling every time anyone came close.

'I hate that dog!' Pam hissed under her breath, her hand hovering over the wicker basket as the peke eyed her.

'Stop playing with him,' Bea said wickedly. 'We've got to do the kitchen now.'

Moan as she might, Pam was a quick worker and they were just complimenting themselves on the transformation when Bea looked at her sister and said. 'What about the bathroom?'

Pam had no time to answer because at that moment the doorbell rang.

Bea Wilkie's first impression of Freddie was indelible. She saw a graceful, composed young woman who was already stunning. Thick dark hair hung down to Freddie's shoulders, and her blue eyes, haloed with back brows, looked clearly back at her, steady over her easy smile.

'This ... ' Jao said happily to her mother, ' ... is the daughter of ... '

' " ... The Handsomest Man in England!" ' Bea chorused in unison with Jao. Laughing, she stood back for her guest to enter. 'Sorry, Freddie, it's a family joke. Jao had something of a crush on your old Dad,' she explained, winking and closing the door. 'It's wonderful to meet you at last. You don't know how much she rattles on and on about you.' She turned to her daughter, 'Did you have a good journey?'

'Fine,' Jao replied, sniffing the air. 'God, it smells like a pub in here.'

Bea gave her a warning look.

'And I think we've got another leak,' Jao went on, spotting the damp patch on the carpet. Then she suddenly stopped talking and grinned.

'The leak is being attended to,' Bea replied deftly.

Laughing, Jao turned to Freddie. 'It's the dog,' she explained. 'Miku's always peeing on the carpet and Bea sprays soda water on it to take out the stain!'

Folding her arms in resignation, Bea glanced over to Freddie and said calmly. 'My daughter thinks it's a big deal that the dog pees on the carpet, although I suppose she failed to mention that she was in nappies until she was *three*!'

'That's not fair!' Jao replied hotly.

'Who the hell are you to talk about fair?' Bea countered. 'You said you'd be home about five, so how am I supposed to have everything ready when you come home early? The meal's not even started.'

Jao shifted her feet. 'It's not a problem. Freddie can freshen up first.'

'No, she can't,' Bea said simply.

'Why not?'

'Because,' her mother continued quietly, 'the bathroom's

not fit for use.'

'Oh, Bea!'

With a look of abject apology, Bea walked down the hall-way, avoiding the damp patch, and flung open the bathroom door, her eyes fixed ruefully on Freddie.

'I would like to have hidden the ghastly truth from you for a little while longer, but I had a party last night and there was a lot of mess.' She pointed to several empty bottles in the basin and a collection of wet underwear and tights hanging on a string over the bath. 'Terrible housekeeper that I am, I've not got around to cleaning it up yet and because you came early you caught me out.' She sighed. 'I can't cook, can't keep house, and I can't resist a party. Everything my daughter says about me is true, and she was probably hiding the worst bits. I can't pretend to be anything I'm not. I know you come from a rich family, but you won't find any fuss here. We don't have the money or the inclination. People come and go as they please. As *you* please … ' She smiled, her eyes warm. 'Now, tell me, do you think we're going to get on?'

Freddie returned the smiled and glanced over Bea's shoulder into the devastated bathroom.

'Where do you want me to put the empty bottles?' she asked.

Chapter Seven

Over the next few years Freddie was a frequent visitor at Dorman Square and spent many weekends with the Wilkies. In the long school holidays she divided her time between Cambuscan and frequent trips abroad with Dione and by the time she was eighteen Freddie was able to speak French and Italian. She knew how to dress, and to converse with anyone; she was as comfortable at the George V in Paris as she was in the Hard Rock Café with Jao, or visiting Harry at Cambridge. Self-composed, she found a confidence in her looks and yet remained free from vanity. She was secure in herself, moved in enviable social circles, but had no snobbery. As many people remarked, Freddie Clements had the makings of a remarkable woman.

But the *makings* Dione realised, were not enough. There was that inescapable, incomparable quality which made people remarkable, and Freddie had not yet discovered it within herself. Surely it was just a matter of time, Dione thought, just a question of maturity, and then Freddie would make that jump from charming to charismatic. Just a matter of time ... or was it?

Over the years Dione had grown to love Freddie, seeing in her the child she never had. She loved to teach her about style and clothes, to hear her master a language, and to watch how people stared at her. But where is the fire in you, Freddie, she wondered. Where are the guts, the fight? Did you have it too easy? Were you too indulged and spoiled as a child to develop any real strength of character?

93

Dione mused over the matter at length, wondering if Sarah Clements's upbringing had constricted Freddie, but she didn't really believe that. Instead her intuition told her that the problem lay not with the mother, but with the father. Yet much as she pressed her, Freddie never confided a word about Greville Clements and refused to criticise him in any way. To all intents and purposes she had had an idyllic childhood, and even Harry found her reluctant to be drawn on the topic.

The reason that Freddie remained silent was simple. She did not want her childhood to be exposed to the gaze of others, neither did she want it to taint her present life. As each day passed she walked further away from the memories – the temper and the verbal cruelties, the fall from the wall, the taunts about the Ice Saints, and the day Mrs Gilly disappeared. Not that the memories were easy to control. Certain smells would always remind her of the past – the aroma of hot gravy on a plate, the smell of warm straw in a rabbit hutch, and the scent of lemon cologne. Sounds, too, returned to inflict their own damage – Sarah pleading with her father, cajoling him in the night, and the sound of footsteps in the hallway pausing by her bedroom door.

Too many memories flickered in Freddie's head to allow her ever to fully relax and there was always that tiny portion of control which remained, although she had mastered her speech and now only felt the threat of her stammer when her father talked to her. Otherwise she developed an easy manner and could be funny at times, wanting people to like her and think her fun. No one was to suspect the dark side of her childhood. *She* might have to live with it, but she had no desire to inflict it on other people – so she held her tongue.

But in doing so Freddie limited herself, and like Dione, Bea Wilkie pushed her. 'You should want to make your mark in the world,' she said, her voice rich and without censure. 'I know I made a cock-up of my life, and I know I'm only a singer in a second-rate hotel, but at least I'm happy.'

Bea was sitting at the kitchen table in Dorman Square, peeling an apple. A low sun poured in from the open window onto a pot of herbs which Trisha had planted, the leaves

94

mottled with light. Outside, the fire escape provided a landing place for several London pigeons, the sound of an afternoon TV show swinging across the empty street.

As part of the divorce settlement of her second marriage, Bea had been conveniently left the house on Dorman Square, and as she had two unmarried sisters, it seemed only practical that they should they all live together. Practical, but not perfect. Surrounded by women, Jao was treated like a toy and her upbringing was erratic. Bea's opinions on childcare were countered by Pam and Trisha never voiced any opinion at all, which the numerous men who sauntered in and out of their lives never stayed long enough to make any lasting impression.

At first the house seemed a generous settlement, but it soon proved to be a costly luxury. After one hard winter the white stucco walls needed painting and the heating bills were astronomical. When Ted Wilkie realised that his golden egg had turned out to be a turkey, he kept his distance, and refused to contribute to the upkeep of the house although he did pay for the education of his daughter.

So it fell on Bea and her sisters to make money – and that proved to be a problem. During her first marriage, Bea had never worked and during her second, when boredom set in, she began her flirtation with show business. With a singing voice as husky as her speech, Bea specialised in torch-songs and was soon performing in the lounge of a Park Lane hotel. Ted thoroughly approved of his wife's career, but when he fell in love with a PR agent half his age and asked Bea for a divorce, ignominy followed. Having thought she had a firm place in show business, Bea was shaken to discover that her success had been due to a contact of Ted's and within a month of their separation her act moved downmarket – from Park Lane to Bayswater in one fell swoop.

The humiliation might have crucified a lesser woman, but Bea knuckled down and sang like Milton's fallen Gabriel from nine to midnight every night. She had to, for neither of her sisters were successful at earning money. Trisha, a devotee of the alternative health brigade, tried her hand at journalism, but she was always late for deadlines and wittered on repeatedly about the moral ethics of her pieces. Pam, on the other hand, staggered manfully through a teacher's training course only to find that she couldn't control the pupils at the comprehensive where she won a post. Later her attempt to run a health food shop with Trisha faltered after only weeks and Pam found herself working as a telephonist for a property company in Highgate. The work was boring, and the pay was poor, but she stuck to the job like a martyr to the cause.

Bea stretched in her seat and glanced over at Freddie. 'You've got to sort out what you want to do when you leave school. I'll help if I can. I could always read the cards for you.'

Freddie smiled. 'Oh, Bea, you're not still doing that, are you?'

She was unrepentant. 'It's good money, Freddie,' she said, dropping her voice. 'Only don't tell Jao I've started reading fortunes again, will you? You know how she goes on about it.' She changed the subject deftly. 'What does your mother want you to do?'

'Mummy doesn't want me to do anything except go home and live with her.' Freddie replied. 'She wants me to be a companion, someone to talk to. That's all she ever wanted.'

Bea grunted. 'What about your father?'

Freddie stood up. Careful not to knock over Trisha's herbs, she leaned out of the window. Even with the sunlight falling on her hair it was still dark, her brows shiny and black. Due to a long summer, her skin was tanned and the evening light threw a walnut coloured shadow under her chin and turned her arm the colour of wild honey under a light down of hair.

'He wants me to marry well,' she replied truthfully. Her father's hopes for the future were obvious to her, even though they had never discussed the matter. Over the years he had carefully cultivated Avery, and easily convinced him that the marriage of their children would benefit both families.

'I wouldn't rush into marriage, Freddie,' Bea said, her thoughts turning to Harry. She had met him a number of times and found him genuinely charming, but although she realised he loved Freddie, she wondered often if he was the right man for her. 'Look at this flaming plant,' she said suddenly, her attention wandering to the herbs again. 'Trisha never uses the kitchen, but it's fine to fill it up with her rubbish and then leave it for me to look after.' She filled a cup with water and poured it onto the dry soil. 'I'll tell you something, Freddie,' she said, 'I was shattered when Ted left me, but I learned to get on with life. Take a chance with your own life, Freddie, or you'll end up like Pam, disappointed and frustrated. Do you know, when we were young, she was the best looking of the three of us.'

Freddie raised her eyebrows in surprise. 'Pam?'

Bea nodded. 'Yes, Pam, it's incredible to think of it now. She was such a fabulous looking girl, but she never buckled down to anything and soon she got so bloody miserable that her face caught up with her attitude and now she looks … well, she doesn't look too great.' Bea opened the door onto the fire escape and fanned herself with one hand. 'Get out there in the world and have a go, Freddie. It doesn't take brains, just guts. There are enough opportunities and love affairs for everyone, it's just that most of the time people either give up, or daren't try in the first place.'

Freddie glanced down at her bare feet. Her toe-nails, painted with Bea's fuchsia pink polish, twinkled cheerfully. 'I don't want to get married yet,' she said quietly. 'I'd like to have some adventures first.'

'Quite right!' Bea said firmly.

'Dione's got a friend in London, an antiques dealer who wants some research doing for his book. When I get my A level results, he said he wanted to meet me,' Freddie said, finally putting her thoughts into words. 'I'd like to live in London, Bea, and I'd like to do something before I settle down and have a family.' Her mind was suddenly made up. 'I could do it, I just know I could.'

'Of course you could, Freddie,' Bea said proudly, hugging her. ' "Men can make your life, or mar it," my mother used to say and I'd go along with that. Only I'd put it a little stronger. I've married two men, and had a few bloody hot affairs, and I'll tell you this – men are great to have around, but don't ever rely on them. If you get sick, they leave; if you get old, they leave; and if you've got money, they generally spend it.'

Freddie thought of her father, but said nothing.

'But despite that,' Bea continued, 'in order for a woman to feel really fulfilled she has to have a man, temporarily or permanently. Buggers they might be, but they make you whole, and that's what I'm trying to tell you. Don't make the mistake of making them the centre of your life, make them part of your life, Freddie, then whatever happens you'll still get by. And that applies to all men – lovers, husbands … and fathers.'

The white walls of Cambuscan flickered under the sleepy summer heat, the lake a motionless blue, the water rushes vividly green and unmoving. As Freddie walked up the drive she smiled to Mike who waved happily in response. Overhead a blackbird sung in the still air, it's mate answering from the copse behind the pavilion. Beneath Freddie's feet, the dry gravel rasped against her shoes and as she walked round to the back of the house, a plane droned lazily overhead.

Through the open conservatory doors, Freddie could see her mother fast asleep in a sun lounger, her hands laid protectively across her stomach. For the last few weeks Sarah's letters to Freddie had been ecstatic, full of news of her pregnancy which was already absorbing her totally. Freddie had greeted the news with mixed feelings; a sense of relief coupled with an unexpected jealousy. For too long she had been the sole confidante of her mother. She had comforted her, listened to her, commiserated with her, and put her own needs secondary to those of the neglected wife.

After the miscarriages, the still birth and the pathetic phantom pregnancies, no one expected that Sarah would ever bear another child. But if everyone else had doubted, Sarah's own unshakable, blind optimism had never faltered. She wanted a son to keep her husband; and by God, she was going to have that child.

Freddie leaned against the door frame of the conservatory and looked at her mother. Sarah had become plump, her feet slightly puffy in their fashionable shoes and her hands small and soft fleshed, the wedding ring digging into the soft skin on her fourth finger. A large straw hat threw a deep shadow across her closed eyes, her mouth relaxed above her rounded chin. For an instant Freddie saw her as a photograph taken out of focus, each feature slightly blurred – apart from the hump of her stomach in which the child rested.

The ferns and falls of ivy hung motionless behind her, the dark masses of living plants attracting indolent, drowsy bees and the occasional wasp which hummed angrily by the open doors before moving on again. Freddie glanced upwards through the glass ceiling of the conservatory, her gaze travelled along the white painted framework and came to rest on the small table beside her mother's chair. Carefully she tiptoed in and looked at the cover of the book lying there – *Motherhood Made Easy* it proclaimed, the picture of a young mother and baby emblazoned on its cover.

At thirty-eight Sarah was hardly a young mother, but a kind of youthful serenity was apparent in her features and it fascinated her daughter, so much so that she did not hear the approaching footsteps and only glanced up when a shadow fell across the floor of the conservatory.

'Your mother's asleep,' Greville said, his voice lowered, his hand beckoning his daughter to follow him. When they reached his study, he closed the door and turned to Freddie.

'I thought you were going to ring us when you got to the station? Mike Kershaw would have picked you up.'

Freddie felt uneasy in her father's presence as she always did. She had read somewhere that when you grew up people who had frightened you shrunk to their proper size. But it wasn't true, Greville seemed larger, not smaller.

'It was a lovely d ... day,' Freddie heard herself stammer and slowed down her speech, 'so I thought I'd walk home.'

He smiled, trying to be pleasant. Uncertainly, Freddie smiled back. 'You've come a long way,' he began. 'You look very pretty, and Avery tells me you've become quite a scholar.' His effort to be light-hearted grated on both of them and he glanced away, looking out of the window.

God, why did his daughter always have this effect on him? Even looking at her was enough to make him feel guilty. The memories of his own cruelties flickered in him like hot coals.

He had meant to be kind to her when she came home – and yet when he saw her all the old feelings curled into life and he wanted her away from him; wanted to avoid the expression in her eyes, and the judgement there. Besides, he reasoned to himself, now that the new baby was on the way, their lives would all change. When the child was born Sarah would put all her energies into its upbringing, so what purpose would Freddie serve? After all, Sarah would no longer need a confidante now that the biggest problem in her life was solved.

'Avery told me that his sister – ' Greville avoided using Dione's name as their dislike was mutual ' – had an aquaintance who was interested in offering you a job.'

'As a researcher for his book, yes,' Freddie replied, growing uncomfortably hot in the stuffy room.

Greville rubbed his hands together. Freddie could almost imagine the scent of lemon cologne drifting over to her on the hot air.

'Well, I think it's a good idea. You have friends in London, and it's about time you went out in the world. I'll give you an allowance, and pay the rental on a flat for you – and you can come home at the weekends, of course.' He smiled, his handsome face showing only a trace of ageing. 'You see, Frederica ... '

She winced, anticipating what he was about to say.

'Now that there is a new child on the way, I don't want your mother being upset. It would be nice for her to know that you're settled in your work and that your relationship with Harry is going well.'

Freddie felt a roar in her ears and for an instant was so angry that she nearly walked out. So everything was decided, was it? After everything you have done to me, bygones must be bygones. Rage balled up in her throat. All her years of patient attendance on her mother had resulted in this civilised banishment, with all affection passed over to the blessed son and heir. *Son and heir*, Freddie winced, remembering how Sarah's letters had emphasised the sex of the baby, the amniocentesis ascertaining that the embryo was male and that the Clements empire would continue for ever.

For nearly thirty seconds Freddie regarded her father steadily and with her eyes she damned him so fiercely that he drew in a deep breath and left the room. Quickly Freddie crossed to the window and looked out in time to see her father pause by her mother's chair and touch her face. Waking instantly, Sarah reached for his hand, all anguish forgotten, all darkness bleached into purity under the absolving sun. As she watched them, Freddie felt her mouth dry and, without realising, took hold of her father's letter opener and scored a deep bloodless gash into the leather top of his antique desk.

Under the sunlight Sarah dozed. When she wakened she called for Freddie, but when her daughter didn't come she fell back to sleep or day-dreamed. The afternoon shadows length-ened in front of her, creeping across the little pavilion and over the face of the lake.

Happily Sarah thought of Mr Flowers' words. 'It's a boy, Mrs Clements,' he said, and she had begun to cry.

'I'm so sorry … I know it's silly,' Sarah stammered, 'but this child means so much to my husband.'

Mr Flowers had looked after Sarah since she had conceived Freddie and was astute enough to realise that this baby meant more than most. This son would secure the fortune and marriage.

'Now you mustn't get upset, and you must rest a great deal.'

'Oh, yes, I intend to,' Sarah replied, glowing with happiness.

'Well, as I said, you look after yourself. If there are any problems, just give me a call.'

Sarah walked to the door, a small, plump woman with a high-pitched voice. 'I will, Mr Flowers, and thank you. Thank you so much.'

As she remembered the conversation, Sarah's eyes flick-ered under her closed lids. She was finally having another child, and it was a boy, she thought triumphantly. Greville would spend more time at home now. He would stop staying away in London and come back to her. She frowned suddenly, trying to forget the smell of perfume on his clothes and all the other careless betrayals of his adultery which she had so long ignored. No one could pity her any more, she thought, not now that she was pregnant and her husband was so pleased with her. No, that would stop Meg Kershaw's sympathetic looks, and Sheila the maid's sly glances. Sarah moved in her seat, her hands firmly clasped over her stomach. Five months to go until the birth and already Greville was being thoughtful, bringing her little presents from London and buying toys for the baby. He'd even arranged for the nursery to be repainted and decorated with paper fit for a boy.

It was a shame that the doll's house had to be moved, Sarah thought, but it wasn't suitable for a son and although she had loved it and so had Freddie, no one could hang onto the past. Unceremoniously it had been relegated to the attic, a toy train set taking pride of place instead, all trace of Freddie's childhood suppressed under the overwhelming presence of the coming son.

In the pavilion Freddie watched her mother until the daylight faded and Sarah moved reluctantly indoors.

Something burned inside Freddie which she hardly recognised, something stronger than rage, a jealousy which frightened her. Much as she tried to deny it, Freddie bitterly resented the child her mother was carrying, because in him she saw the last remnants of her security threatened, her tenuous position at Cambuscan destroyed. Silent and shaken, she laid her head down on her arms, her eyes fixed on the house. All her childhood she had loved the place. She had explored and come to know every inch of it. The old clock beneath the weather vane over the stables; the dark curtain of ivy on the back wall; the french doors in the drawing room which were opened on summer evenings; and the drip of the outside tap when Mike drew water there. She had survived her initial homesickness at school because every night she had thought of Cambuscan, and had slept soundly as she dreamed of trailing her hand among the water rushes, or opening the doors of the doll's house where she had played so often as a child. She knew the sweet scent of earth in Meg's vegetable garden and the stagnant smell of water coming from the lake in late August before the fresh Yorkshire autumn blew in from the truculent moors.

Throughout her childhood when her father had terrorised her, Freddie had found comfort at Cambuscan. When her mother had depended so much on her, she had listened and then found her own peace in the little pavilion. Now she sat, her eyes dry, her mind conjuring up images of the past. Pictures of Sarah and her father; of Irene Clough, ill-tempered and sick, dying in the conservatory; of the diffident Gordon Clough. And soon another heir would take his place at Cambuscan. Another heir, already loved, already forgiven for any sins he had yet to commit, already welcomed before his arrival.

'Don't come,' Freddie said helplessly. 'You have no right to come here. You have no right to be born. Not now, not now.'

No one answered, or even reproached her. No one even missed her.

Safe behind the protective high walls of the house, Sarah hummed happily under her breath.

Dione met Freddie for afternoon tea in Claridges in order to prepare her young charge for the interview to come. She noticed no difference in Freddie because there was no external change in her manner. As always, Freddie kept her injuries to herself.

'His name is Pennsylvania Parry ... '

'What!' Freddie cried, disbelievingly.

'I know what you're thinking, but his mother was an American and came from that state, so what can you expect?'

'I suppose we should be grateful she wasn't born in the Bronx,' Freddie replied. 'Bronx Parry would have been even worse.'

Dione let out a shout of laughter.

'He's called Penn for short,' she went on, tossing her Persian lamb jacket over the chair next to her. 'And he's a little strange.' She raised her eyebrows. 'His mother, apart from having an aberration over his name, was also besotted with Dickens and she brought Penn up in what she thought was a typically English way.'

103

Freddie was intrigued and more than a little grateful for this welcome diversion.

'So Penn has turned out to be a bit of an odd ball,' Dione concluded succinctly. 'But he's clever. Listen to him Freddie and you'll learn a lot.'

Freddie was prepared to learn, but nothing prepared her for Mr Parry. His shop, just off Belgrave Square, had a large square window in which a Japanese vase large enough to hide a body in, resided. On the door was a card emblazoned with the words.

I Will Return in Ten Minutes

Freddie read the card and was just about to walk off when a lumbering, corseted, redheaded figure came towards her. Pennsylvania Parry was waving frantically, much of his face hidden behind a red beard and a pair of oversized tortoiseshell glasses.

'Freddie! Freddie Clements!' he shouted, arriving by her side and fumbling with the door lock. 'I thought I was going to miss you.'

He stood back to let her enter. 'Mind the ... '

She tripped over a raised floorboard and he shrugged. 'Floorboard. I've got a man coming to see about it tomorrow. I had a leak, you see.' He leaned down, jutting his face towards hers. 'Well, what do you think?'

'Get it fixed,' Freddie said firmly.

Penn frowned. 'What?'

'The leak.'

Penn's eyes flicked away as he wheezed impressively and then waved one arm around, indicating the assortment of wall hangings, rugs, resplendent bronzes and hideous Chinese vases.

'I meant the shop – what do you think of the shop?'

Freddie bit her lip. 'You've got some pretty exciting things.'

'And what about colours?'

'Yes,' she said emphatically, 'they're pretty exciting too.'

'I mean ... What colour do you like?' Penn asked, his forehead creased with concentration.

'Oh, colours,' Freddie said eagerly. 'I like green.'

'Good! And green is the colour of ... ?'

104

'Green is the colour of … ' Freddie faltered as he stared at her, holding his breath, ' … of drowned sailors.'

'Fantastic!' Penn exclaimed, picking up Freddie's hand and kissing the back of it noisily. 'Dione said I should see you and she was right. You're just what I'm looking for,' he gushed, scratching his beard. 'What about this?' he asked, hurrying over to a lacquered screen and resting against it. 'What does a screen like this mean in the context of your life?'

Freddie suppressed a desire to laugh but instead assumed an air of careful deliberation. 'I would have to say that it has a feeling of … well, a tragic quality.' She smiled confidently. 'Only a strong person could live with it.'

Pennsylvania nodded, his eyes glistening. 'You'll have to forgive me, dear, but it's so infrequent that anyone *feels*.' He thumped his chest with his right fist. '*Feels*, as I do. You are a wonder.' He sniffed. 'You see, I am an emotional man. I make no excuses, I live by my emotions. Emotion makes me buy well.' He swept one arm around his display. 'It makes me feel alive. I was an emotional child,' he confided, leaning towards Freddie again, 'and I had an emotional childhood. Tragedies. That's what I had. Tragedies. Of all kinds. My father died young, and my mother was an American.'

Freddie nodded sympathetically.

'She loved me very much though and understood that I was emotional. I make money and I give it away … all away … What's the point of it, if you can't give it away?' He lifted his glasses and dabbed at his eyes. 'I'm sorry, I hope I don't embarrass you, I'm just emotional, that's all. Not that some people don't take advantage of my kind heart.'

'They do?' Freddie asked with mock wonder.

'They do. One woman I supplied with such pretty things at a reduced price because she had the sweetest ankles in London,' he sighed. 'And what happened? No sooner had I furnished her house than a long haired yob moved in with her. I should have spoken up sooner,' he said, slumping beside a gigantic Eastern urn. 'What's the point of living without love? For a man as emotional as I am, it's killing.'

'Things will cheer up,' Freddie said firmly. 'They always do.'

Penn smiled, instantly restored. 'You're right! And you've got the job. Now, let's go out.'

Freddie smiled, baffled. 'But I've only just arrived. Who's going to look after the shop?'

'No one.' Penn said simply. 'We'll close for the morning,' he waved his hand magnanimously, 'and clear off.'

'Where?'

'Madame Tussauds. To celebrate.'

Talking incessantly, Penn hailed a taxi and hussled Freddie out at Baker Street. His eyes brightened at the sight of the waxworks and Freddie had to run to keep up with him as he rushed to the entrance. Once inside, he made for the Chamber of Horrors with Freddie in hot pursuit. His considerable bulk blocked the view for smaller customers.

'Can't you move over?'

Penn glanced over his shoulder at a woman with a punk hairstyle standing with a small boy at her side.

'I beg your pardon, madam?'

'My son can't see because of you.'

Penn looked wounded. 'I'm so sorry, but you'll have to wait your turn.'

'Why?' she countered aggressively, her Cockney accent reverberating around the room. 'If you'd just move your great backside we could all see.'

'Madam,' Penn hissed, mortified, 'I have paid for my ticket and I intend to have a full view of this show.'

'And I paid for two tickets and all I've got is a view of your bloody arse.'

'I can't see!' the child began to wail. His mother looked down at him and then back to the towering Pennsylvania. 'How can you be so bloody minded?' she snapped, and leaned back towards her snivelling boy. 'Don't worry, luv, Mummy will sort it out.'

'Why don't you look at the other exhibits and then come back here?' Penn said not unreasonably, Freddie thought.

'Because my son wants to see *this* one, that's why.'

'So do I!' Penn said childishly. 'And anyway, an infant shouldn't be in the Chamber of Horrors. If you were a good mother you wouldn't allow it. Good Lord, what he sees in here might upset him for life. Children are so sensitive.'

Immune to Penn's concern for his welfare, the child was fast losing patience and after failing to get his mother's attention by pulling on her jacket, finally shouted up to her. 'Why won't the fat man move over?'

Cut to the quick, Penn reeled back and the child pushed into his place immediately.

'Well ... I'll be damned,' Penn stammered to Freddie, as the mother looked at him with an expression of undisguised triumph.

Chapter Eight

Freddie was delighted with her job. She wrote to Harry and told him all about Pennsylvania, promising to tell him more when they met that weekend.

By now it was deep November and the weather was bitterly cold. At the Hall Avery was only heating the study and kitchen constantly, whilst his bedroom was intermittently warmed by a portable gas heater. The effect the cold was having on his arthritis worried both his sister and his son. Harry begged his father to spend some time with Dione abroad, but Avery would have none of it. Committed to one of Bill Ketch's fund-raising schemes, he was determined to sit the winter out in Yorkshire.

So whilst Cambuscan snuggled comfortably under the first snows and Sarah's bulk grew, only acres away Avery shivered and as the sun went down he took to pushing the gas heater from room to room, the eerie light flickering along the corridors as he moved it around with him. His hands, already clumsy and buckled with arthritis, stiffened, and he was forced to wear gloves constantly. Yet he never complained about the Hall; it was, for all its discomforts, the only place he wanted to be.

Each morning he rose early and washed quickly in the old-fashioned bathroom before going down to the kitchen and making himself some tea. His movements were awkward but he managed, and when the chore was completed he would carry the full beaker to the window and look out. A fresh fall of snow, dazzlingly white, was banked up to the front doors. A few wild pheasants scratched around the frozen lawn. Avery sighed contentedly and sipped at his tea, waiting for the film company to arrive. Bill had done well – for only one day's work they would pay him enough to repair much of the upper floor. Life was good, Avery thought suddenly, and although chilled to the bone, he felt nothing but optimism. His heart soared like a summer bird.

Harry came to London and collected Freddie at the shop, driving her up to Yorkshire on the Friday evening. He talked of his friends and she laughed when he said that her photograph was the envy of everyone. In the warm car she felt secure, her anxiety about visiting Cambuscan fading as they talked. Occasionally she glanced at Harry and he would turn his head and smile. With his twenty first birthday only a few weeks away, Harry had filled out but still retained the slimness of limb which he had inherited from Avery. His old eccentricities, the woman's watch and the red braces, were as much a part of him as ever, but his eyes had altered, his guileless expression maturing into one of warm intelligence.

The years had changed Harry from the boy who leapt over the gate to a young man with prospects, and Freddie, suddenly overcome with fondness, touched his hand. He smiled warmly, but said nothing. In his own mind he was certain of his future. Freddie would marry him and they would restore the Hall. No more than that. He wanted no other girl. His heart was hers as surely now as it had been on the day of the fateful boxing match. Their lives, he believed, were already mapped out and whatever befell them, they would share together.

When they finally reached the outskirts of Ripon, Harry nudged Freddie gently to awaken her.

She moaned softly and stretched out her arms.

'Are we home already?'

'Nearly,' he said.

Outside the car the night was still, save for the gentle humming of the engine as they waited at the traffic lights. Yet, for some unaccountable reason, Freddie shivered suddenly.

'Do you want the heating turned up?' Harry asked her.

She shook her head and smiled, but the chill remained in her bones and nudged her peevishly.

'I'll drop you off at Cambuscan.'

'No!' she said sharply. 'No, Harry, let's go straight to the Hall. Please.'

He was startled by her tone and drove on quickly in silence. Between them both something loomed and although neither knew what was to come, both felt and shared the same fear.

They had hardly rounded the bend in the road when Harry saw the blaze at the Hall, the flames rising towards the night sky. In panic, Harry slammed his foot on the brake and leapt out of the car, running towards the Hall, Freddie rushed after him.

'My father's in there!' Harry screamed, pushing his way through a small gathering of people on the lawn. 'My father's in there!' he repeated frantically as he ran towards the blaze.

Freddie continued to follow him, but was suddenly jerked to a halt as someone caught hold of her arm.

'Stop!' Greville said. 'You can't do anything. I've rung for the fire brigade.'

Her father was the last person Freddie wanted to see. 'Let me go!' she shouted violently. 'Let me go!'

Surprised by her own strength, Freddie shook off Greville's grip and continued to run towards the burning building, her eyes still fixed on Harry whose figure was silhouetted against the fire as he passed beyond the front doors and disappeared into the blazing hall. Freddie screamed his name as she followed after him.

But as she reached the front steps the heat caught at her throat and she jumped back suddenly as part of the Hall ceiling crashed down beside her. Her eyes burned in the acrid smoke. Unable to make herself heard over the roar of the fire, Freddie looked around helplessly for Harry, then saw him slumped against the main window, bent over something as he dragged it towards the front doors.

Sobbing with relief, Freddie hurried over to him and then stopped in horror. The thing he pulled was Avery, horribly disfigured. Without thinking she caught hold of Avery's burned jacket. Harry turned, saw her, and tried to push her away but Freddie shook her head violently. Harry looked at the rapidly encroaching flames, and realising that Freddie wasn't going to leave him, nodded quickly and together they pulled his father to the doors, reaching them just as the fire engine arrived. Immediately two firemen rushed into help them and a bank of water hoses shot up into the flaming sky and onto the burning Hall.

Avery lay unmoving, blind and silent on the snow-covered lawn whilst Harry kneeled beside him, his hands badly burned, the palms blistered and peeling. He had found his father trapped in the library, and without realising that Avery was already dead, had pulled off the burning timbers which had fallen on him, and dragged him out.

Freddie knelt beside the men, her throat raw with smoke. She said nothing, just watched as Harry took off his jacket and covered his father's face.

They bandaged Harry's hands at the hospital and let Freddie take him back with her to Cambuscan. He said nothing, the loss of his father taking all words away from him as he lay sleepless, staring upwards, well into the night. Cambuscan was silent, whilst across the way the old Hall still smouldered, fulfilling the premonition Freddie had felt the first day she visited it.

When the clock struck three, Freddie rose and made her way to the guest bedroom, situated away from the main body of the house. She found Harry awake, his burned hands painful, his eyes dry, too shocked to weep. She was about to turn on the lamp and then paused and instead opened the curtains so that a softer light entered the room. Sitting beside Harry on the bed, she stroked his arm above the bandages, not trusting her voice to speak.

Freddie had no words to comfort the man she loved. Nothing she could say could make up for the loss of a father and a dream. All she could do was keep him company in the silence. Tenderly, Freddie leaned towards him and kissed Harry's forehead. He did not move, but closed his eyes. She then kissed his eyelids, then his cheeks, and when she kissed his mouth she tasted the first tears, salty against her lips. With infinite tenderness she lay beside him on the bed and then began to make love to him, her own tears mingling with his.

In hopeless and desperate need, they clung to each other and when Harry climaxed he cried out for the love of her and the loss of his father. He cried for all the hopes which had been burned that night, and for the death of a man he had idolised.

PART TWO

The beauty coming and the beauty gone.

Most Sweet It Is, William Wordsworth

Chapter Nine

The cold continued relentlessly, snow falling every day so that by the beginning of December, Yorkshire was in the grip of what promised to be a cruel winter. Trees were stiff under dark frost and the lake at Cambuscan lay frozen, the green bay tree staunchly keeping its lonely vigil. Across the whitened fields, the Hall stood like a burned fossil, crouching defiantly over its patch of earth. Against all the odds it was not destroyed entirely, one wing remaining intact as a callous reminder of what had once been.

Deaf to advice, Harry returned to live at the Hall, unable to mourn properly away from the place where his father had died. With the help of Bill Ketch, the surveyors assessed the damage and the dangerous areas were roped off leaving only four rooms habitable. When the appalling news reached Dione, she rushed up to Yorkshire with her husband and tried to persuade Harry to return to Cambridge.

'You have to finish your studies, Harry. It's what Avery would have wanted.'

Harry was implacable. He sat in the drawing room, and gazed out of the window. The smell of smoke still hung around the room.

'My father loved this place.'

'I know he did, darling.'

'And now it's mine,' Harry said firmly, encouraging no arguments. 'What is the good of my reading Classics at Cambridge when I could be here, rebuilding this place?'

'To what end?' Dione asked with exasperation. 'You've inherited the title, but why inherit the problems? Listen, Harry, think of what you really want to do with your life. Avery spent every hour God sent thinking up ludicrous schemes to raise money ... '

'He wanted to do it!' Harry said angrily, rising to his dead father's defence. 'And now I want to do it. I've always been interested in the Hall and the land. I can farm here, this is some of the best grazing land in the country.'

Dione took in her breath. She could see that Harry was not going to be as reasonable as Avery had been. With all the idealism of youth, and as a tribute to his father, Harry was going to throw away his time at Cambridge as easily as she would have sent back a badly cooked meal.

'Listen, Harry,' she said carefully. 'I can give you all the money you need to restore the Hall – if you'll just stay on at Cambridge and take your degree.'

Harry turned and for an instant seemed to look through Dione before he replied. 'Dione, my life is here. *Here*. In this house and on this land.' His voice was steady. 'I will never leave. My whole life is here.'

Dione shrugged, then wondered briefly about Freddie. The feeling between the two had deepened, she could see that, and unless she was much mistaken they were now lovers. The plan laid so carefully and supported so willingly by Avery, was already in motion. The thought should have pleased her. She loved Freddie after all, but a change had come over her nephew which was alarming. The blond boy who had once leaped over gates was now Lord Avery, bearing all his father's obsessions as surely as he carried the family name. The timing was unlucky, she realised. Freddie was just moving out into the world as Harry was reining himself in. Their lives, steered in the same direction for so long, had suddenly taken different courses. Their spectacular future had seemed so certain – and now, Dione thought angrily, who had any idea what was to come?

Freddie's thoughts were at that precise moment in unison with Dione's. As she stood outside her mother's room at the hospital she also wondered about fate and the sour tricks life played on people. On defensive, helpless people in particular. The pity was not for herself, nor even for Harry. Three weeks had passed since the fire, during which time they had quietly celebrated Harry's twenty-first birthday and his inheritance of Avery's title. Only twenty-one days, Freddie thought, remembering how they had made love a number of times, their affection for each other deepening as they sought mutual comfort.

Freddie hadn't been surprised at the depth of Harry's commitment to the Hall. After all, he had never made a secret of his love for the place and she herself loved Cambuscan profoundly. But his intentions did alarm her. At first she believed his obsession was due to shock and that it was his way of grieving, but daily his absorption with the house grew and she found herself trying hard to reason with him when he told her he was leaving Cambridge.

'But you're not a farmer, Harry. Be reasonable.'

'I can learn how to be one!' he said stubbornly. 'Bill Ketch will help, and besides, I can make money with a farm.'

'It will take years to get established,' Freddie went on. 'You can't just walk in and start a farm up overnight.'

'I can do it, and I will,' Harry said defiantly, then took her in his arms. 'I can do anything with you.'

Her thoughts returning to the present, Freddie took a deep breath and then pushed open her mother's door, a smile on her lips and her arms full of flowers. Sarah glanced up at her from her hospital bed, bewildered still, the full impact of her situation not yet apparent.

'Hello,' Freddie said softly, kissing her mother's cheek. 'How are you feeling?'

Sarah's eyes were not properly focused. The sedation made her slow to respond. Her voice was childlike when she finally spoke. 'What happened?'

Freddie hesitated. The miscarriage had been dangerous and the doctors had had to perform an immediate hysterectomy, Sarah Clements's chances of motherhood ending on a surgical table in the London Clinic. The child, so long wanted

117

and waited for, had been a boy – but he was stillborn. Perfect, but without life.

'The doctor told you what happened, Mummy,' Freddie said gently. 'You'll be all right.'

'The baby?'

The baby is dead, Freddie thought. An image of Avery, lying burned on the snow covered lawn, rose up in front of her. Two deaths in a few short weeks, and both of them so pointless.

'The baby didn't live,' Freddie said softly, clasping her mother's hand, her eyes filling with tears. 'But I saw him, and he was beautiful,' she went on, talking and trying to explain. 'I took a picture of him, Mummy, so that you could keep it.' She swallowed, remembering how she had arranged the blanket around the little body and then photographed the baby. He looked as though he was sleeping, that was all. 'He was so handsome.'

Sarah said nothing but tears filled her eyes and she turned her head away, her hand slipping from Freddie's, her heart closing inwards.

Bea was waiting in the reception hall of the hospital, and rose to her feet when she saw Freddie walking down the corridor.

'Oh, love, I'm so sorry,' she said.

'My mother lost the baby, Bea, … ' Freddie said helplessly. 'I feel so bad for her, and I feel guilty too because I was jealous.' She wiped her nose with a piece of scrumpled tissue. 'She looks so lost, in there, and I kept talking to her and telling her about the baby … but it's no good, is it?' Freddie shook her head. 'I just hope it never knew how I felt about it,' she said, sobbing suddenly and laying her head on Bea's shoulder. 'Do you think it did? In the womb they say children know everything that goes on around them … ' Bea stroked her hair gently. 'I was so jealous of it. After all those years I spent with Mum, and all that time she relied on me – and then she forgot me as soon as she was pregnant. I hated her for that,' Freddie said disbelievingly, 'and I hated the baby too.' Her voice was so faint Bea had to struggle to hear her. 'But it didn't deserve to be hated and now I keep thinking that if I hadn't felt that way, it would still be alive.' She looked at Bea, her expression haunted. 'I feel as though I killed him. As though I killed my own brother.'

'Sssh.'

'But I can't stop seeing my mother's face!' Freddie continued blindly. 'She's almost out of her mind with grief and she knows that my father won't stay with her now. Not now. Her one chance was with that baby. And it's gone.'

Bea shook her head. 'It's not your fault.'

'If you say that to me every day for the next fifty years,' Freddie said quietly, 'I'll never believe it.'

In the weeks that followed, Greville spent little time at Cambuscan. Freddie took on the responsibility of the house and arranged the redecoration of the nursery with Mike, giving all the toys to the school in the village. Down from the attic came the doll's house which was returned to the play-room window, and Meg took back the pram to the shop in Harrogate.

Sarah recovered slowly and uncertainly, her tears frequent and hysterical, and Freddie comforted her throughout the long nights, sleeping in a bed made up for her in her mother's room. Both dozed only intermittently. In the early mornings Freddie would phone the Hall, and Harry would answer immediately, their mutual grief making them almost telepathic. Later Freddie would make her way over to the ruined house to find Harry standing by the back door, waiting for her.

'Behold, the mighty landowner,' she would call out with fragile humour.

'Behold, the beauty of the Shires,' he would respond, pulling her to him.

And as they kissed all memory of death was forgotten and in the shabby little bedroom over the kitchen they made love out of their shared grief. Afterwards he would pull the blankets around her and make her some strong tea.

'It's so cold here, Harry,' Freddie said, cupping her hands around the mug. Pricked by the same uneasy memory, both of them thought of the gas heater which Avery had used; the heater he had tried to light with his stiff fingers, fumbling with the match in his arthritic hands.

'I was talking to the farmer down at Crookes,' Harry said, changing the subject rapidly. 'He's going to help me out, and Dione sent some money.' He grasped Freddie's hand. 'It's only a loan, that's all, just until I make this place profitable, then when we're up and running we'll get married.'

He said the words quickly, committing them to the cold air, and Freddie, stunned, didn't respond at first, she merely laughed as he jumped onto the bed beside her and lifted her hair in his hands, his rough palms still marked from the fire. Tenderly, he began to quote a poem by Edgar Allan Poe:

' "I was a child and she was a child
In this Kingdom by the sea ... " '
He pulled a quick face.
' " ... But we loved with a love that was more than love –
I and my Annabel Lee." '

Harry paused again, burying his face in her hair. 'Or in this case, I and my Freddie.'

Harry's love and support helped Freddie to be endlessly patient with her mother's pain, and her guilt made her listen as Sarah constantly relived the loss of her son.

'He was everything your father wanted,' she would say, unaware of the pain her words inflicted on her daughter. 'I thought that when he was born everything would be all right between us.'

'Go to sleep, Mummy. It's OK,' Freddie urged, knowing that nothing would ever really be right again.

'Perhaps I should have been more careful,' Sarah said, turning over in bed and switching on the lamp beside her. She looked pale without make-up and older than her years, and when she picked up the pills beside her, her hand shook.

'You don't need those,' Freddie said reproachfully.

Her mother looked at her with eyes which were close to

120

tears. 'Oh, darling, let me take a couple, please. I can sleep then … Please don't make me lie awake. I won't take any tomorrow, I promise, but tonight I have to. You understand, don't you?'

Reluctantly, Freddie nodded and passed her a glass of water, watching as Sarah swallowed the pills and then leaned back against the pillows. When she spoke, her mother's voice had a plaintive quality. 'Your father will come home at the weekend, you'll see.'

Freddie smiled weakly, although she doubted that he would come home that weekend or any other in the near future. In his eyes, his wife had failed him for the last time. After this debacle, he would keep the marriage going only as long as it suited him. And as long as Sarah's money continued to support his extravagant lifestyle.

Stroking her mother's hand, Freddie watched as Sarah slipped off to sleep. Then her thoughts wandered to the entry she had found in Penn's accounts a few weeks previously. It was for a purchase her father had made, and being naturally curious when she saw his name on the bill she had tried to picture the lacquered cabinet which he had apparently bought. When she couldn't bring it to mind she tackled Penn.

'Oh yes, Freddie, I remember it well. It was a lovely piece,' he said, enthusiastically, 'I wanted to keep it myself, but where? I have to be practical sometimes, and stop letting myself get so emotional.'

'Are you sure my father bought it?'

'Yes,' Penn replied emphatically. 'Absolutely. It was for the little house in Eaton Mews North.'

Freddie was about to open her mouth to contradict him, when she suddenly stopped and listened carefully.

'Your father has a few nice pieces there now. He's got quite a good eye. Rather a cosmopolitan taste actually.'

It had not been difficult for Freddie to discover the address and the following day she had visited the sparse little mews house in time to see Madelaine Glauvert leaving, dressed in a tracksuit. It looked as though she was about to go for a run in the park, but instead she climbed into a small sports car and

121

drove off. Freddie walked over to the house and peered in through the front window.

It was an ordinary sitting room, not remarkable like Cambuscan, or welcoming like the Wilkie house. In fact, it was curiously characterless. Craning her neck, Freddie could just make out the lacquered cabinet in a far corner and one of her father's scarves lying on a table next to a bottle of gin. When she had finished her scrutiny she paused and leaned against the outside wall, shaking. Thoughts of the Clough carpet factory came into her mind; the business whose profits allowed her father to have a mistress and enjoy a life apart from the wife he despised but whose money supported him. Her protective instinct for her mother aroused, Freddie began carefully to calculate the extent of her father's avarice. Not only had he a flat in St James's, but cars, holidays, and now a little love nest. And yet what had he ever given Sarah in return? For all her generosity and tolerance, what had *she* received? Nothing, Freddie thought bitterly, except the trauma of a lost child and the prospect of an empty life.

Freddie had left Eaton Mews North soon afterwards, but she remembered the incident as she sat beside her sleeping mother and remembered the guilty little house and the brittle face of the woman who lived there – and she swore that if it was within her power her mother would never learn of their existence.

At eleven thirty, Jao walked into the hotel lounge in Bayswater and sat down. She waved at her mother across the room and ordered a glass of white wine. Having finally secured a job as a receptionist in a hotel across the road, Jao felt giddy with good fortune. Bea was quick to notice Jao's good mood as she slid into a seat next to her daughter. 'Have you had a stroke or luck, or are you taking something?' she said drily.

'You won't believe it,' Jao said excitedly. 'I've got a job!'

Bea clasped her hands together in an extravagant gesture. 'You mean we can eat again?'

'Ho, bloody, ho!' Jao responded, glancing round the hotel lounge and then turning back to her mother. 'Freddie's back in town. I called at her flat just now. You know, Bea, it's a relief, I can tell you, I had a horrible suspicion that she was going to get trapped up in Yorkshire forever.' She sipped her wine. 'God knows what it must be like there now – what with Harry's father dying and then the baby … '

'Freddie's had a rough time of it lately,' Bea agreed, thinking over the last few weeks. 'And she feels so responsible for her mother.'

' … who was very quick to forget Freddie when she thought there was another baby on the way,' Jao interrupted.

Bea sighed. 'Yeah, I know. But unfortunately Freddie's inherited her mother's short memory – only it's her injuries she forgets too quickly.'

'Which is more than I would do,' Jao said, draining her glass. 'Incidentally, I called by to see Penn and tell him that Freddie was back and he was so *emotional*,' she said gleefully. 'I tell you, I was nearly in tears by the time I left.' She mimicked him mercilessly. ' "It's not that I miss Freddie's work, I just miss her – she's such a sweet girl, *so* understanding … and I'm such a fool about pretty women." ' Jao paused, her voice returning to normal. 'So I tried to look like a pretty woman, and opened my eyes so wide I looked hypothyroid – but it had no effect.'

Bea burst out laughing, amused as ever by her daughter whose slender features were as sharp as her wit.

'Listen, love, I'm on now, but I'll be back in about twenty minutes. Will you wait for me?' Bea asked.

Jao nodded, and turned to watch Bea cross the lounge, her eyes fixed firmly on the raised dais where her mother curtsied, the spotlight picking her out as the pianist struck up the first bars of the song. With her eyes closed, Bea crooned the old standards and took her applause like a pro, then hurried back to the table with her coat over her arm.

Jao and Bea arrived back at Dorman Square soon after midnight and crept in, trying not to wake Pam and Trisha. Bea made two cups of coffee, raising her eyes in exasperation when the taps clanged noisily as she filled the kettle. Then she crept into her bedroom, her daughter following after her.

123

'You looked good tonight,' Jao said, sitting on her mother's bed and biting into a biscuit.

Bea looked at the woman's face on the biscuit tin and frowned. 'Why don't they ever have crow's-feet?'

'What?'

'The women they put on biscuit boxes,' she replied, walking over to the mirror in her bedroom and scrutinising her face. 'I've got crow's-feet and so has every other woman past thirty, but they never get them. I've had that bloody box for nearly twenty years and whilst I'm dropping apart, she doesn't look a day older. It's unnerving.'

Jao sighed. 'It's all a con. They touch all the photos up to blot out the wrinkles.'

'In that case,' Bea replied, helping herself to another biscuit, 'maybe I should forget the foundation and use an air brush instead.'

Jao yawned, then her eyes flashed as she spotted a pack of tarot cards by Bea's bed. 'Oh no, not that again.'

'Shut it!' Bea said warningly, leaning back against the pillows and fiddling with the ornate silver bracelets on her arm. 'I can get ten quid for a reading.'

'Yeah, and a brick through the window when it doesn't come true.'

Bea pursed her lips and changed the subject. 'Someone said I sang like Peggy Lee tonight. It made me wonder what I'd look like with blonde hair.'

Jao stared at her mother in disbelief. 'Ridiculous. And going blonde wouldn't affect your vocal chords.'

'I have a good voice ... '

'Which dyeing your hair wouldn't alter,' Jao persisted. 'God! Next week you'll be thinking of blacking up your face because someone says you sound like Ella Fitzgerald.'

Immune to sarcasm, Bea merely pulled the biscuit tin onto her lap and dug around for a chocolate digestive. The bedroom was warm, heated by a gas fire which hummed gently in the Victorian fireplace. A selection of Bea's costume jewellery hung from brass hooks behind the dressing table. As Bea ate her biscuit in thoughtful silence, she could hear the stamp

124

of Pam's feet as she moved across the floor to the bathroom.

'Listen, she's awake,' Jao said, jerking her head towards the wall. 'You know, she has the only angry feet I've ever heard.'

'She's not happy ... '

'She's not the only one.'

'Jao! Have a heart. Pam hates her job and she's terrified she'll end up an old maid.'

'That's not my problem,' Jao said, always unsympathetic towards her self-pitying aunt. 'She should get out more.'

Bea pushed her daughter sharply with her foot. 'Listen to who's talking! I can remember when you were shy, so don't pretend you've always been so flaming worldly.'

Jao shrugged, her thoughts turning back to Freddie. 'D'you think Freddie'll get married to Harry? He's a Lord now. She'd be a Lady if they did get hitched. Gawd, I'd marry a frog to be a Lady.'

Bea's eyes lit up. 'Do you know what you get if you kiss a frog?'

'No, what *do* you get?' Jao replied patiently.

'Warts on your lips!' Bea shrieked.

Jao raised her eyes heavenwards and reverted to her original train of thought. '*Do* you think Freddie will marry him?'

Bea frowned, suddenly serious. 'To tell you honestly, even though I like Harry, I'm not sure that he would be right for her. In fact, I think that getting married to anyone now might the very worst thing for Freddie. She should learn to stand on her own two feet and then find herself a man ... otherwise there could be a real tragedy.'

'Oh, Bea, you do go on sometimes!' Jao said, heaving herself off the bed and smoothing down her skirt. 'Life's not that dramatic.'

'You don't think so?' Bea asked, brushing the biscuit crumbs off the bed. 'Well don't be too sure, Jao. Don't be too sure.'

Chapter Ten

The flat in which Freddie spent so little of her time consisted of only a bed-sitting-room, a kitchen and a bathroom tucked away in what appeared to be cupboards. Looking out over Albemarle Street, it was however in one of the most prestigious areas of London, and although others would have found its size claustrophobic, to Freddie, who was used to the formidable expanse of Cambuscan, it was surprisingly comforting. Besides, after Penn had furnished it with some incredible pieces of Balinese furniture and Freddie had added her own individual touches in the wallpaper and fabrics, the flat had a peculiar charm of its own. A wide throw of crimson raw silk disguised the bed, a scatter of deep Turkish cushions lay along the Empire settee, and a few ornate masks were displayed on the walls. Masks had become a passion of Freddie's and she now collected them, mixing African tribal masks with the animalistic creations worn at the Venice Carnival.

Demonstrating the artistic flair she had inherited from the Cloughs, Freddie had made a highly individual home for herself – a fact not lost on Dione when she came to visit.

'My God, dear, you've done wonders with this little place. You are clever,' she said, plumping down on the settee. 'What does Harry think of it?'

The question was supposed to be innocent, but Freddie was automatically on her guard.

'He hasn't seen it,' she said, flicking some imaginary dust off a small carved coffee table. 'He's ... busy at the Hall.'

'Leaving Cambridge for that place was the stupidest thing he ever did,' Dione said sharply, her mouth tight with disapproval as she smoothed her Chanel skirt. 'I can't tell you how worried I am about him. He should be enjoying himself – he's only twenty-two, after all – but no, he's obsessed by that bloody heap of stones.'

'He's trying to do what Avery wanted to do,' Freddie said, rising to Harry's defence, although her voice was curiously listless.

'But you can't approve?'

'*I have no choice!*' Freddie snapped suddenly, then shrugged. 'I'm sorry, Dione, but things have been a bit strained between us lately.'

'I'm sorry, sweetheart, I didn't know.'

Freddie frowned, trying to put her thoughts into words. 'I knew how much Harry was shaken by Avery's death and I could understand, in a way, that he wanted to rebuild the Hall as a kind of memorial to his father. After all, he inherited the title, it seems reasonable that he should want to have a home to go with it. But ... ' she paused, ' ... nothing seems to interest him any more *except* the Hall. Only a few months ago he used to come down to London to visit me and get a break from Yorkshire, but now ... ' Freddie thought of Harry's endless excuses. ' ... He's turning inwards. All that sweetness and optimism, all his fun – it's gone.'

Dione took Freddie's hand in hers. She had been expecting a conversation like this for months, ever since she had visited Yorkshire in the spring. Alarmed by the change in Harry, she had deserted the sober Caesar for several weeks, staying at the Hall and trying valiantly to make her nephew see some sense. But angry as she was with Harry, she also admired him. With complete dedication he had built up the farm he wanted, using several discarded outbuildings in the yard next to the Hall. Taking advice from Bill, and enlisting help from some of the surrounding farmers, Harry had taken on a small flock of hardy sheep and had sowed several fields, renting out two others for goodly sums. Impressed by his unexpected grasp of the business, Bill Ketch had helped Harry all he could, taking no money, but using one of the smaller fields, rent free, for his daughter's pony. Bill had always been fond of Avery, and he wanted Harry to succeed. But even he was not prepared for the price success would demand of him.

All through the first bitingly cold winter Harry tended the sheep with an old man from the village. Over snow laden fields, in terrible conditions, he went out day and night, digging out snowed-in animals and making sure that food was taken up to the high pastures. His fine skin became roughened under the harsh conditions; his hair, usually the colour of bleached oak, darkened, its sheen fading. All the little eccentric touches – his woman's watch, and the flashy braces – were replaced by heavy cords and a Barbour jacket and cap. He even traded in his sports car and bought a second-hand Land Rover, explaining to Freddie that he had no need of status symbols any longer.

The only thing that did not change was Harry's love for Freddie. That was the one constant in his life and on that he depended for his stability. Many times, often in howling gales, Freddie watched for the Land Rover coming down the drive at Cambuscan. She would make her way downstairs and clamber in beside him, Harry clasping her hand quickly, as though to make sure she was real. Full of excitment, he would drive her back to the Hall and show her what he had done, pointing out all the improvements and waiting anxiously for her response.

And over the months, as the winter thawed and the spring started over the Yorkshire moors, the Hall began to take shape again. She seemed to Freddie almost like a woman who had been asleep and had been woken unexpectedly, getting to her feet and making herself presentable and welcoming. All her charm came to life under the early sun; all her faults were obliterated by the kind weather. The fire damage to the main part of the house had been restored on the outside, although the left wing remained as it had been since the first blaze. Next to the aged magnificence which had survived the painstakingly new restoration snuggled, the conflagration which had taken Avery's life obliterated under new stonework.

'Isn't she beautiful?' Harry said, pulling off his cap as though in respect.

Freddie nodded, but her voice was quiet. 'She is beautiful, Harry. You must be very proud.'

Harry smiled secretly, and for an instant Freddie felt the same sense of rejection she had endured so often as a child. The Hall obviously enchanted Harry and it seemed to her that he was under its spell, that a form of love had built up between Harry and the place which had killed his father. Avery's love for the Hall had been the reason why he remained there, and in the end, the reason for his death – and that same love, although destructive and terrible, was so powerful that it had survived to be passed down to his son.

A sense of unexpected fear tugged at Freddie as she realised she might soon be relegated to second place. Fleetingly she wondered whether she should put her anxiety into words, and then paused, knowing that Harry would never understand.

'Two years should do it,' Harry said proudly. 'In two years I'll have all the fire damage repaired inside and out.' He glanced towards the fields around the house. The spring morning smelled good to him, the sounds of a few early lambs travelling clearly through the sharp air.

'Harry,' Freddie said quietly, linking arms with him, 'Dione's having a ball next week. I thought we could go.'

'She never mentioned it to me. Where is it?'

'Milan,' Freddie said, smiling widely. She clung onto Harry's arm, feeling the muscles under his heavy jacket. I love you, she thought, you are my heart.

'Milan!' he said, bursting out laughing. 'How on earth can I go to Milan? I've got the lambing to look after. I can't go away now.'

'It would only be for one night,' Freddie said persuasively. 'Oh, think Harry, what it would be like. She's going to have fireworks, and an orchestra, and people are flying in from all around the world – '

'Good for her!' Harry said, suddenly irritated. 'Listen, Freddie, I grew up in that world, with Dione's parties and all the glamorous friends she's accumulated over the years. I don't want it any more.'

'But I didn't grow up like that!' Freddie said angrily. 'I grew up surrounded by money and luxury, but not life. I want a life now!' she said, letting go of his arm and stepping back. 'I want to go to Milan and see these people. I like travelling with Dione. Before she took any interest in me, I was shy, I'd never been anywhere or done anything. She changed my life, Harry, and I owe her something for that. And besides, I don't want to go back to the way I was.' Freddie paused, dropping her voice. 'I wonder sometimes what would have happened if I had never met her. I would have carried on at Cambuscan, cut off like my mother … Well, I want more than a house, Harry, even the most beautiful house – I want to go out and see what I can do in the world.'

Harry took in his breath, surprised. In the years he had known Freddie, she had never once articulated her feelings and her hopes for the future. She had gone along with his plans instead, and he had always thought that was what she wanted to do. The Hall was being repaired so that they could live there together one day. At least, that was what he believed. Wasn't that what she wanted too, he thought helplessly. How could she want to leave Yorkshire, how could she want more than this place?

'I thought you were happy,' he said stupidly.

'I am happy – with you,' Freddie said, walking over to him and kissing him on the mouth. His lips were cold.

'Harry, I love what you're doing, and I love your house – but there is more, my darling, there *is* more.'

Harry looked into her eyes and smiled, but he was shaken by her words and wondered about that other world she talked about. *There is more*, she had said, *there is more*. The phrase repeated itself over and over in his mind as he looked at the Hall in front of him and wondered.

It was a torrid day in early April only a few weeks after Dione had visited Freddie, and freak weather was making the London streets steam, the sun riding high over the roof tops and curling over the Spiritualist Association of Great Britain at No. 33 Belgrave Square. Whistling tunelessly, Penn paused to buy a red carnation from the flower seller at the corner of Belgrave Square, and was struggling to fasten it onto his lapel as he pushed open the shop door and called out for Freddie.

'It's ghastly out there!' he said despairingly, allowing her to fix the buttonhole as he mopped his face with a huge handkerchief. 'I'm sweating so much that it feels as though every pore on my body is sobbing its heart out.'

'You should walk more slowly and conserve your energy,' Freddie said calmly. 'The weather will break soon.'

'So will my all my chances of a romance with Sophie Maas,' he sighed. 'No woman likes a man who squelches.'

'You can't hear a thing from where I'm standing,' Freddie said, with an effort not to laugh. 'Anyway, in this heat she might be doing a fair amount of squelching herself.'

'Sophie doesn't squelch,' Penn said emphatically. 'She merely glows with the heat.'

'Lucky Sophie,' Freddie said drily, pulling a face.

Listlessly, Pennsylvania wandered around the shop, his heavy body bound up in its corset like a child swaddled in a Georges de la Tour painting. Every exertion required superhuman effort. Even shaking out a piece of hand-painted Venetian silk and draping it over a bronze urn left him panting, as he tipped his head over to one side, his eyes thoughtful behind tortoiseshell glasses.

'I was wondering,' he gasped, 'if Dione might like this silk. She has marvellous taste, although that foreign dolt of a husband knows nothing.'

Freddie yawned listlessly, trying to put her notes in order. The research which she had been hired to do was endless, although Penn never actually got down to the process of writing. The idea of the book was obviously little more than a pipe dream.

'Penn, you've got to start writing soon,' Freddie said, frowning as she filed the voluminous notes. 'You've got more research here than they have at the British Museum.' She glanced over her shoulder. 'Stop putting it off and put pen to paper.' She burst out laughing. 'That's exactly it! You've got to get Penn to paper.'

Penn threw up his hands in a defensive gesture. 'Now, Freddie, you know how nervous I get when I'm pressurised.' She moved towards him with a determined look in her eye.

'Freddie! Don't!' he squealed, backing into an urn.

'Penn, I'm not letting you do another thing until you promise you'll begin that flaming book today!'

'I can't!' he screeched. His red beard looked fiery under the sunlight.

Freddie's eyes fixed on Penn's. 'Are you going to start this book?'

'I'm an emotional man,' Penn wailed, 'so naturally I can only put forward an emotional answer. It's the way I think, you see, emotionally.' He tapped his chest around the area of his heart. 'And my emotions tell me that now is *not* an auspicious time. It's not in the stars ... '

'Bullshit!'

'Oh, Freddie!' Penn said, his voice wavering. 'Don't swear.'

Freddie assumed a mischevious look. 'Very well, if you want to play dirty, Penn, I shall *swear* you into submission.' She paused, drawing in her breath. 'Bloody ... '

'Oh, dear,' Penn said desperately.

'Bastard ... '

Penn's eyes exploded with horror as he nodded frantically. 'Enough! I'll start this afternoon! I promise, Freddie, really, I promise.'

'You see,' she said sweetly, passing him the sheaf of notes. 'That wasn't too difficult, was it?'

The heat continued throughout the day, culminating in a fiercesome thunderstorm which rocked the capital at around three in the afternoon. The rain pelted down and then stopped abruptly, the late sun making saunas out of the London streets. People fanned themselves with copies of the *Evening Standard* and drank tepid drinks in cramped pubs, waiting for the sun to go down. Exhausted by the effort to keep cool, Penn left the shop early and retired to his flat above, writing one page of his book before he let his trembling fingers phone the sumptuous Sophie Maas. Downstairs, Freddie pulled the door behind her as she left and then turned quickly as her name was called. From an upstairs window, Penn's bearded face beamed like a sunset. 'Sophie's agreed to go out to dinner tonight!' he bellowed, the handkerchief in his top pocket drooping in the still air.

Freddie gave a whoop of victory.

'Oh, Lord,' he continued, 'I'm so happy.'

A couple of tourists paused and looked up at the monumental figure bellowing from the upstairs window.

'She likes me!' he called out, his voice ringing out in the stagnant air.

Freddie smiled and waved. 'Of course she likes you! What's not to like?' she said, walking off.

At the corner she turned, still smiling, but the figure had gone from the window and the street was empty again.

Darkness fell, bringing little relief. Although the sun had gone, the heat lingered, making restaurants sticky and the bins smell fetid in the alleyways outside, a few opportunist cats stalking the doors of W1 eating houses. Not wanting to go back to her flat, Freddie called in at the Wilkie house feeling uncomfortably hot. The thin summer dress she was wearing clutched at her skin and the dark mess of her hair felt damp against her neck.

'Hi,' she said cheerfully, walking into the kitchen.

Trisha glanced up. 'Oh, hi,' she said simply, turning back to her copy of *Here's Health*. 'There's chicken in the fridge if you want it. Jao's on her way home.'

Freddie tugged open the fridge door and was just pulling out some milk when Pam walked in from the hallway. 'Don't drink all of it, or there won't be enough for everyone else,' she moaned.

'I was just going to have a bit,' Freddie replied, returning the milk to the fridge and running some water instead. The pipes banged violently in protest.

'I see Jao's not home yet,' Pam said, the criticism implicit. Her plimsolled feet made no noise on the kitchen floor as she moved around. 'She's always out ... '

'Well, why shouldn't she be?' Trisha asked idly, her pale eyes directed towards her disapproving sister. 'Why shouldn't she have a good time?'

'I'm not saying she shouldn't … '

'Yes, you are, that's exactly what you're saying.'

'I'm not … '

'Oh, for God's sake, Pam!' Trisha said wearily.

Recognising the beginnings of an argument in which she had no desire to take part, Freddie was relieved to see Jao walk in the front door.

'Boy, am I glad to see you,' she said, rolling her eyes.

Jao glanced over her shoulder. 'Another dog fight?' she asked, grimacing and walking down the hallway to her room. She motioned Freddie to follow.

'So how was your day?' Jao asked, kicking off her shoes.

Freddie's expression was wicked. 'I molested Penn to get him to write his book.'

'That's nice,' Jao said blithely. 'When does your case come up?'

Smiling, Freddie sat down on the chair next to Jao's unmade bed. The glass felt warm in her hand and she could hear the faint sound of voices coming from the lounge.

'Bea's got company,' she said simply.

Jao cocked her head to listen and then nodded. 'I just bet it's some airhead come for a tarot reading.' She mimicked her mother's deep voice. ' "I can see a tall dark stranger that you're going to meet in surprising circumstances." ' Jao's voice returned to normal. 'The poor cretin will be all cock-a-hoop – until he gets mugged on the way home.'

Laughing loudly, Freddie curled her feet under her and leaned her head back against the chair. 'You're too hard on Bea. She must be good, or people wouldn't keep coming back to see her.'

'People come back because they want to be reassured,' Jao said pragmatically, staring at her left foot. 'Christ, look at that corn! I was wondering why I was limping all day – some silly sod actually gave me his seat on the Tube. Can you believe it? Probably thought I was lame.'

'That could be very useful,' Freddie said wryly. 'I would cultivate that corn to ensure future stress-free travelling.'

'How would you like a kick on the shin?'

'No thanks,' Freddie replied deftly, 'I've already eaten.'

The door opened suddenly and Bea popped her head around, smiling. Dressed in a black top and trousers she looked radiant, her make-up perfectly applied, her hair newly washed, two large silver hoops swinging in her ears.

'Dear God,' Jao said wonderingly. 'Who have you got in there? Richard Gere?'

Pulling a face, Bea replied. 'It's Bart. You remember, Jao, Bart from America.'

'Oh sure, American Bart!' Jao said cheerfully – then shook her head, 'No, I don't remember him.'

'Well, allow me to refresh your memory,' Bea said coldly, beckoning for both Jao and Freddie to follow her into the lounge.

Bart was sitting with a drink in his hand and the Pekinese at his feet, snuffling loudly and as the women walked in, he rose to his feet, smiling.

Freddie's first impression of Bart, which would remain with her for the rest of her life, was one of warmth. His smile, set above a heavy jawline, was so welcoming that she smiled back and thought him handsome, although his patrician features had little to do with good looks and more with a good heart. He was over forty then but his well-built body was kept fit by competitive games of tennis and his brown hair had only the faintest smudging of grey. His hazel eyes were large, and their gaze honest. Dressed in a business suit, he was like any of the prosperous middle-aged men one saw hailing taxis on Kensington Gore, his wallet comfortably full of money and photographs of his wife and children.

Bea gestured proudly to him. 'This is Bart, Bart Wallace.'

'Good old American Bart,' Jao said wickedly, taking on a Southern drawl as she extended her hand. 'So how you doing there, son?'

'Forgive her. She's adopted,' Bea said smartly, turning Bart's attention to Freddie.

135

'Hello,' he said warmly.

'Hi,' she replied, adding inanely, 'It's hot today.'

Jao snorted next to her, but Bart nodded. 'I know what you mean, the Intercontinental's like a sauna. In England,' he said, smiling so as to imply no real criticism, 'no one's prepared for the heat.'

Bea laughed. 'Bart's a New Yorker. They have air conditioning there.'

'And hot and cold running water,' Jao added sarcastically. 'Ain't civilisation great?'

Infuriated, Bea shot her daughter a violent look, but Freddie glided smoothly to the rescue.

'You don't sound very American,' she said.

'That's probably because I spend so much time in London and do plenty of business here. When I realised that the English can be very suspicious of loud Yanks, I moderated – ' he paused to give full emphasis to the word ' – my tone.'

'When I first knew him,' Bea said, raising her eyes heavenwards, 'fifteen years ago, he had a Bronx accent which could skin a cooked chicken at ten paces.'

Bart laughed and glanced at Jao. 'She won't allow me any pretence,' he said, 'and it's not that I haven't tried to impress her over the years.'

'Like hell!' Bea replied. 'You've never tried to impress me, you just keep popping up to haunt me and remind me of my youth.'

'You look better now than you ever did,' he said, brushing away Bea's protestations with his hand. 'Some women look good when they're very young, others when they get some maturity, but only a few pass forty and then take your breath away.'

Jao groaned.

'Oh God, if I believed it, I'd ask you to marry me,' Bea said, laughing happily.

Bart smiled and turned to Freddie. 'If I thought she was serious, I'd say yes.'

Bart Wallace had been truthful about the Intercontinental. It had been stuffy and oppressive, but by the time he returned

136

that night his room was aired and refreshed, the bed turned down and the sheets cool to his touch. Locking the door, he took off his jacket, tie and shoes and padded into the bathroom, glancing into the mirror with more than his usual casual interest.

The bathroom light was phosphorescent and unflattering, bleaching his complexion and making him unfairly pale. With an absorption which surprised him, he tapped his stomach with the palm of his hand and was pleased by its flatness. He wondered for a moment if it was obvious to an onlooker that his hair was thinning. Bearing his teeth, he leaned towards the mirror and examined them. He studied the lines around his eyes, and then, in a fit of exasperation, grabbed hold of the cord by the door and jerked off the light.

In her bedroom in Dorman Square Bea also leaned towards the mirror and studied her reflection. She sighed deeply, then stopped chewing the end of her eyeliner and began to apply it instead. On the bed Miku snuffled in his sleep. The gas heater in the Victorian fireplace hummed a harmonious duet with the dog as it sighed wistfully. Tipping up the shade on the lamp beside her, Bea carefully outlined her eyes with shadow, and then re-applied her lipstick, Bart Wallace's voice echoing eerily in her head as she sprayed on a goodly quantity of Shalimar.

Women over forty do not take people's breath away unless they're undergoing mouth to mouth resuscitation, Bea thought wryly, zipping up her long skirt and reaching for her evening bag. Thoughtfully, she rubbed a dirty mark off the leather and then glanced around sternly, surprised to find that for once the bedroom depressed her. However much she tried to fool herself, the dim light did not fully disguise the damp patch which ran from the ceiling to the bed, and neither did it make the costume jewellery look real. Bea had merely persuaded herself that it did because ... Why? she asked herself suddenly. Because she knew things would never get any better? Because there would never be a man to make things right again? The thought upset her usual equilibrium and only when the peke snored suddenly did Bea's irritation

137

lift. Smiling, she leant down and kissed the side of its head tenderly. Any kind of love was love, after all.

Later that night, whilst Bea sang at the Bayswater hotel and Bart lay unsleeping on top of his bed at the Intercontinental, Freddie stood under the shower in her flat with the cold tap turned on full. The water pelted her, pounding her skin and reddening it, making her hair wet and sleek to her head, her eyelashes plastered to her cheeks.

She too heard Bart Wallace's voice even though her ears were full of water; just as she saw him clearly although her eyes were shut. The warmth he exuded seemed to burn her; his kindness compelling. In Bart Wallace, Freddie saw a man who had every quality she admired and understood; his success was familiar to a woman whose family was also successful; and his confidence she recognised as the confidence of money. But one thing she did not fully comprehend and that was his simplicity. Bart's speech and manner were uncomplicated, he was comfortable with himself and with others – and that part of his nature intrigued Freddie.

Having grown up with a father whose personality was complex and unstable, it was not surprising that Freddie had been attracted to the easygoing Harry. For a while she had thought herself in love, but time had altered Harry, and his personality had developed dark corners which threatened her. Under the shower Freddie stood naked and thoughtful. She did not see a future lover in Bart, but she saw a peace in him that she envied, and a security she could only admire.

The early heat-wave continued unrelentingly and Bart often took Bea out, Jao crying off with all manner of excuses, although Freddie was often invited to accompany them.

'Isn't Harry coming down to London this weekend?' Bea asked uneasily. 'Honestly, Freddie, I don't know what's got into that boy.'

'He's working on the Hall.'

'He's always working on the Hall!' Bea responded brusquely. 'He should pay you more attention.'

'I wondered if I shouldn't spend more time up there,' Freddie murmured idly. She had considered it, but could see only difficulties. She was working during the week, and at weekends in Yorkshire she was monopolised by her mother. It had not always been this way. Before Harry would take her everywhere with him – but now he came over to Cambuscan less often, the hours they spent together restricted to meal-times. The easy love-making they had previously enjoyed had taken on all the numbing coolness of a duty.

'I love him,' Freddie said simply.

Bea sat down beside her in the kitchen at Dorman Square. 'Well if you do, you'll have to chose what kind of life you really want. If you get married to Harry you'll be chained to that damn house. He's had his look at the world and he's not interested in seeing much more of it. Everything he wants he has. The Hall, the name, even the status.'

'Harry's not a snob!' Freddie said sharply.

'No, he's not a snob, but he is very aware of his duties,' Bea said softly.'And if you want him, you have to be prepared to take on those duties too.' She thought of Freddie's trips abroad and wondered how she could seriously consider giving up all the excitement for a restricted rural existence. But then again, Bea thought, if Harry was the right man for her, perhaps Freddie would not need anything else.

'I can't think straight these days,' Freddie said. 'Maybe I'm selfish to want more. Most people would think they had everything in Harry ... '

'You're not most people,' Bea said firmly, 'and you're not marrying to please your father either.'

Freddie flinched. Her father had hinted many times that he expected 'developments'. Each time he passed the Hall he wondered when Harry would propose; each time he glanced at Freddie he wondered when his daughter would settle her future and please him for once. If only Avery had still been alive, Greville thought angrily, all this would have been sorted out by now. Instead Freddie was dithering and jeopardising the best offer she would ever have.

Bea had enough sense to change the subject. 'Listen, what you really need is something to take your mind off things. Come to the theatre with me and Bart tomorrow. It'll do you good.'

A couple of feeble excuses cut no ice with Bea, and finally Freddie agreed to go. Sitting between the two of them, her mind wandered from the play frequently, chilled by home-sickness and anxiety about Harry. Unaware of her distress, Bart's attention was fixed on the actors, his body warmth oddly soothing, his expression kind when he turned to her and smiled, or leaned over to catch what she said.

'What was that, Freddie?'

'I said that the actor playing Molière is a friend of Harry's.'

'Really?' he replied, glancing at the man in question. 'He's good.'

'Harry says he'll go far,' Freddie said.

Bart nodded. 'Well, I think he's right.' He turned back to the play.

Harry this and Harry that, Bart thought with amusement, wondering how long it had been since a woman had had such an effect on him. He might be wrong, of course, but despite what Bea said, he thought Freddie was still very much in love with her Harry. Why else would she talk about him so much? Bart stretched out his legs and let his mind wander. What did this Harry have, he mused, to make a girl like Freddie Clements love him? An image of a typical English gentleman came into his mind – a squire from the Shires, young, blond and tall with an impeccable background. Bart smiled good-naturedly – what girl could resist? He stole a surreptitious glance at Freddie, and unexpectedly thought of his dead wife.

Bart was a successful and respected architect who had been a widower a long time – but not too long to forget how he had once loved. After Gill's early death from cancer, he had sorted out the house and found all their old love letters. He had read them in chronological order, his to her, hers to him, and then had wept for the loss of a love which was as strong when Gill died as it had been when he had penned the first lines to her. Without warning, in that dark theatre, memories came back to him. He remembered how Gill used to borrow his socks, the way she parked the car at a slant in the garage, little, inconsequential things which mattered to no one but himself, but for him they were potent and still painful ...

'Are you all right?' Freddie asked him suddenly.

He was startled and embarrassed by the question, but when he looked at Freddie he saw what Mike Kershaw had seen all those years ago by the river at Cambuscan; a dark well of almost psychic understanding towards which he found himself irresistibly drawn. For an instant Bart could not reply and floundered like a teenager before glancing hurriedly away.

Freddie had felt the exchange between them too and frowned, not fully understanding it.

The three of them sat silently throughout the remainder of the play.

Much later that night Bart was still haunted by the expression in Freddie's eyes and he realised that she had begun to obsess him, slipping into his dreams like a bookmark slid into an unopened book. Valiantly he tried to dismiss her from his mind, aware that she was too young and that for years there had been a form of understanding between him and Bea; but against all logic the power of Freddie's image was becoming daily more compelling. Bart sensed in Freddie a vulnerability which appealed to him, and an innate kindness, together with a sensuality which was only half explored. Her beauty was obvious but her injuries were not, and although others might never have guessed at them, Bart knew that Freddie was still suffering from old wounds.

His patience snapped inside him. God, what was the use of even thinking about her? There was not, nor ever could there be, a relationship. He was being foolish in imagining things, nothing more. Yet when he had taken Bea out that night, he was sure that she had noticed the change in him, but he did not dare to ask her advice. He knew he should have done, that she would have laughed him out of his confusion and things would have returned to normal. But he said nothing, even though he knew that she was waiting for him to speak ...

Bart shifted in his car seat and navigated Hyde Park Corner recklessly. He didn't want to hurt Bea. After all, they had known each other for years. He felt suddenly cornered and bewildered. Why hadn't Bea and he done something about their feelings before? Why hadn't they made a commitment he asked himself. Bea was divorced and he was widowed, so what had stopped them? Or maybe he was wrong about Bea too … A car blasted its horn behind him and Bart jammed down his foot on the accelerator, pulling away quickly.

The previous night was still fresh in his mind; but hadn't Freddie's laugh been too quick? Her smile too eager when he told her about his architectural practice in New York? Was she interested in him, or was she laughing at him, he wondered suddenly. But he dismissed the idea immediately. There was no cruelty in Freddie. None at all. Unable to concentrate, Bart pulled out of the traffic and parked, his hands resting heavily on the steering wheel. Oh, Gill, he thought, suddenly missing his dead wife and talking to her as if she was with him in the car. If you had lived, none of this would have happened. We would still be together, you would still be leaving notes under the milk jug, or forgetting your lipstick when we went out. You would be past your first beauty and onto your second. He closed his eyes, almost wearily. It was wrong for you to die, you had hardly got into your stride, and I never got used to Christmas cards with just my name written on the envelope … No one replaced you, did they Gill? Bea might have done when I was newly widowed, but after a while I became used to being alone. Until Freddie … Bart opened his eyes and thought of her longingly. He felt a particular safety with her and believed that, like a good angel, she had some sway over his future. He knew beyond any doubt that he wanted to hand over his life and heart to her keeping, and in return, would stand between her and the world.

It had been a long time since Bea Wilkie had cried, and the last time hadn't been in a ladies' toilet outside a Sainsbury's supermarket. She sat on the toilet seat and hung her head, her fingers clutching a wedge of damp paper tissues, her nose running. Her hands seemed older as she looked at them, the veins raised, the skin dried and wrinkling slightly. Not that it was apparent at the hotel when she sang; the spotlight blasted away shadows and took years off her ... but no one lived in the spotlight forever, did they?

A woman rattled the door outside and then slammed into the next cubicle. Bea tried to move, but the tears came again quickly and forced her back, each bitter sob of disappointment muffled in a disposable Kleenex. She had tried to convince herself that she was imagining things – she, of all people, who usually faced up to everything. But this had been too much to admit, even for good old Bea Wilkie, everyone's confidante. Bea Wilkie – mother, sister, provider, friend – you're a stupid cow, she thought bitterly. You're a fool, a bloody old fool.

Bea's hands gripped the tissues so tightly that she could feel her palms grow hot. She made herself relax and then gently touched her thighs. Covered with a wool skirt no one could see the fine broken veins, or the cellulite. Freddie wouldn't have cellulite, she thought, not at her age. Despair welled up in her – if she had stayed married to either of her husbands it wouldn't have mattered. People get old together, men get paunches, women get veins – so what, if you loved each other, it didn't matter, did it? But what chance was there of finding someone now, at her age? What chance? Who would willingly pick a woman with a weight problem, too old to have children? Too old to make a man feel proud? Bea sighed brokenly, and the sigh shuddered through her as she stared ahead. She was tired of dating and of the effort of making new relationships. It was so embarrassing to have to breathe in when a man caressed her, or to make sure she was lying on her back when they made love because that was the only way her stomach looked flat. She had dreaded the tyranny of an ageing body, knowing that sexual freedom died the night she first asked for the light to be put out, and struggled, hot with embarrassment, to get undressed in the dark.

When young, Bea's body had been admired, touched, wanted. Her face had been, if not beautiful at least striking. And now what was there left? Who would tell her she was beautiful in her old age? Who would whisper those loving lies? Who would choose to sleep with her now, and stay with her? Young men looking for experience? Bea shook her head. No, that was not for her. If they want experience, they can seduce their own age group, or buy a bloody manual, she thought grimly.

There had been one chance left for her and now that had gone. Bart Wallace, I waited for you, she thought, tears running down her face again. I waited and believed that one day you would tell me you loved me. The loss struck her again and she doubled up, the pain almost as strong as childbirth. But this time the child will be stillborn, she thought agonisingly. Dead, gone, lost.

For a further ten minutes Bea sat on the toilet seat and then slowly she pulled herself to her feet. There was no point staying there, nothing would change. Bart would want Freddie, and in the end, Freddie would go to him. It was unavoidable.

Bea's hand hovered over the lock, unable to leave, afraid of having to join the world again. Then as she glanced up, Bea noticed a few lines of graffiti and began to read. The top line said simply: *I wish I was dead,* and underneath someone had added, *If only I felt so good.*

Bea read the lines and smiled, began to giggle, and then finally left the ladies' toilets laughing, the rich deep sound dancing round the car park and tapping on the windows of the Sainsbury's store.

Chapter Eleven

Three weeks passed. The reason for Bart's continued stay in London was his involvement in the building of a block of offices in Chelsea Harbour. The London based architect who had originally been assigned to the building had had a heart attack and Bart had been called in to take over. Initially Bart welcomed the decision and had been pleased to stay, but as time progressed he became more and more unsettled.

Always a kind man, Bart felt guilty about his fascination with Freddie and began to make excuses for refusing invitations to Dorman Square. He said the office building was proving to be troublesome and the crew needed more supervision. The look in Bea's eyes was obvious; she knew he was lying, and yet she did not dare to confront him. For his own part, Bart felt that he was caught between a rock and a hard place. If he told Bea he was fascinated by Freddie, she would be terribly hurt, and he didn't want that – especially if the infatuation burned out – for then he would have no relationship with Freddie and would most certainly have lost Bea forever. No, he reasoned, it was better to remain silent. Torn between wanting to stay and yet wanting to leave, Bart found that what had begun as a short business trip to London had turned into complicated and extended confusion.

Before Bart had come over to London, he had thought that this time he would have a few meals with Bea and generally test the water to see if the temperature was still warm enough to confirm some feeling between them. On his first night in

London he had discovered that it was. The atmosphere was good at Dorman Square, even though he was surprised by Jao's antagonism. Naturally over the years they had encountered each other before, but he was baffled at her continued dislike of him. Suddenly he wondered if she had some intuition and was protecting her mother. After all, he realised with a jolt, his behaviour over the years had been more than a little selfish.

Bart had needed to know that he was loved – even if he was only prepared to return that love on his terms. A sudden rush of shame made him uncomfortable. His own actions, now confronted, began to look horribly dishonourable. He had been fooling himself in believing that he was different from other men, that he was more caring. The truth told a different story. For fifteen years Bart Wallace had been alone, ever since Gill had died from cancer. The shock of her illness and death had affected him so deeply that he had found it difficult to form close attachments afterwards. There had been no comfort of children, and that had been his greatest sorrow. Throughout their marriage, he and Gill had tried to start a family, but as the years passed, it became apparent that she would not conceive; so they had consoled themselves with each other's company, making the most of their marriage and believing in the security of a shared old age.

Which never came. At thirty, Gill had died in New York and was buried on Long Island. Her parents kept in touch with Bart until time distanced them and reduced all communication to a Christmas card. Bart couldn't help thinking that if there had been children it would have been different, but there were no offspring and he found no comfort in other women.

In the first years after Gill's death, Bart told himself that he was still grieving and that time would bring someone into his life. But it didn't. He dated, but although women were attracted to him, he was never truly at ease with them. Sex divorced from love held no meaning for him and his actions remained mechanical, not tender. Affectionate by nature, Bart found such love-making distressing, and after he climaxed a sense of savage depression always overtook him, as he lay with his arms folded across his chest, longing for his wife and for the familiarity of her.

After a while Bart earned the reputation of a man not able to commit himself emotionally. Nevertheless he remained much in demand socially; a useful and charming man to invite to a dinner party, a marvellous escort who would always say and do the right thing. Alone, and often lonely, Bart Wallace's heart was committed to his dead wife, and no woman could usurp her place in his soul. When he finally faced up to the truth, Bart's first reaction was despair, followed by a kind of animal relief, and the only woman for whom he retained any lasting affection was Bea Wilkie.

They had met due to a strange coincidence. Bart had been staying at the Park Lane Hotel where Bea used to sing, and was introduced to her by one of his partners – who also turned out to have been one of Bea's early lovers. Bart had liked Bea immediately and although they were totally different in temperament, Bea and Gill had also had an instant rapport. After that, every time the Wallaces came over to London, Bea would meet up with them, and after her ignominious fall from grace they still came to give her moral support at the hotel in Bayswater. Gill's death affected Bea deeply and it was natural for her to offer comfort to Bart, taking many late night calls from New York when he couldn't sleep, and writing letters which jolted him out of many an imminent depression. Following the initial shock of Gill's loss, the telephone calls were frequent, then reduced gradually as Bart adjusted, their tone changing too. Instead of bewilderment, he began to talk of his work again, and told Bea about the new apartment he had bought on Fifth Avenue, whilst she teased him about his money and warned him of gold diggers, both of them vaguely aware that if time brought any woman into his life, that woman would be her.

So when Bart was called into help with the project in London, he accepted with alacrity, his mind almost settled about his future with Bea. During the trip from New York to London he watched a film on the plane but remembered nothing of it, his thoughts turning repeatedly to Bea. At the airport he phoned her and made arrangements to see her that night, a fabulous sense of well-being buoying him up throughout the day. Maybe this was the end of all his loneliness, maybe at last he was coming home ...

Then he met Freddie and although she was unaware of it, she obliterated Bea and blurred the giant memory of Gill. In Freddie, Bart saw all the energy of his late wife's youth and all the promise of her sexuality. He wanted her absurdly and completely. His mind was freeze-framed on her, his nights invaded. He felt foolish and out of control, knowing that Freddie was involved with Harry – a young man of her class and age.

Meanwhile Bea went through her own torments and although she was not hopeful, she invited Bart round for lunch one afternoon, desperate to effect some kind of reconciliation.

'We'll have the place to ourselves,' she said lightly, 'Pam's at work and Trisha's interviewing some Greenpeace convert, so it'll be quiet for once.'

Bart hesitated, and then accepted the invitation. 'I'd love it,' he replied easily. 'I'll come round about one.'

The meal was friendly, but the ease which had been between them for over fifteen years was gone. It seemed to Bea that it was like listening to a familiar piece of music which you had known and loved, and suddenly discovering that you had been playing it at the wrong speed all the time. They ate willingly, but with little appetite, Bea relating amusing anecdotes about the Bayswater hotel, Bart countering with tales of his niece who had come to New York and moved in with him.

'She said she was only staying until she found an apartment, but the way things look she seems set to stay for a while.'

'Is she nice?' Bea asked, her interest forced.

'She's young,' he replied, 'only twenty.'

'Like Freddie.'

The name came down between them like a guillotine, chopping the last remaining bonds.

' ... she's doing well.'

148

Bea looked up, 'Freddie?'

'No … my niece,' Bart replied, glancing over to her.

The daylight was cold, banished under a smudge of drizzle. On the fire escape a single pigeon pecked at crumbs. A steady stream of water ran down the steamed up window.

'She's going in for marketing … ' he said.

Bea blinked, her tongue running over her dry lips. This was harder than she had imagined.

'Bart, listen … '

' … and she's going to be good,' he continued, almost panicking when he read the hurt look in Bea's eyes.

'Bart, stop it, for Christ's sake!' she snapped suddenly. 'I'm not a complete fool. I know what's going on … '

'Nothing's going on.'

For an instant she almost pitied him. 'I think you know what I mean, Bart. You're in love with Freddie, aren't you?'

He faltered, loathing his own weakness and wondering why he couldn't answer her directly. 'I've only known her for a month … '

Bea laughed shortly. 'What the hell has that got to do with it?'

Bart fiddled with the knot of his tie, mortified. Whatever he said would hurt her now. 'Bea, I can't talk about it.' He shook his head. 'Freddie is only a girl – and she's involved with Harry. You said yourself that they'll probably get married.'

Bea didn't seem to hear what he said. 'Do you love her?'

He closed his eyes to the answer he had to give and for several moments remained silent, hearing the clock ticking in the hall outside and a child shouting in the street below.

'I love her,' he said simply, opening his eyes again. It was done, he thought, grimly relieved. The thought was finally committed to speech.

Shakily, Bea got to her feet and returned to the table with a bottle of vodka, pouring a measure into two glasses and pushing one over to Bart. 'Shit,' was all she said.

'It'll come to nothing! I'm a middle-aged man,' he said quickly, his whole being struggling against the enormity of

149

what he wanted and the impossibility of it all. 'What the hell would she see in me anyway?'

'Safety,' Bea said quietly, swallowing the vodka in one gulp, her voice husky. 'She's never had any real security in her life and you represent everything she wants – even though she doesn't know it yet.' Suddenly Bea banged the glass down on the table. 'Shit!' she repeated, blindly distressed.

Bart extended his hand, but she withdrew hers immediately.

'God, I'd like to hate you!' Bea said fiercely, then glanced down at her empty glass, all anger gone, ' … but I can't.'

'Nothing may come of it,' Bart said, almost hopefully.

Bea's eyes were momentarily bitter as she raised her glass. 'Shall we drink to that, Bart?' she said.

If there was one thing Dione loathed, it was stupidity. Her own brains, hard work and style had earned her a reputation and a sound antiques business – she knew what application and intelligence could do, and she hated to see people behaving foolishly. She particularly hated it when she saw such behaviour in her own family. For years she had been exasperated by Avery. Since their parents died and he had inherited the title, Dione had been constantly mortified by his naivety and dumb optimisim. The eccentric schemes, the lack of money, and the appalling living conditions her brother had endured were an anathema to her. But as time passed and Avery had become more obdurate she had finally stopped trying to change him.

But that was Avery, and Avery was dead. Harry, on the other hand, was not. He was, however, living apart from the rest of the world, and Dione was not prepared to allow him to slip into the life of a recluse without putting up a fight.

After visiting various cities in Europe and attending numerous sales, she sent the furniture she had purchased to Milan and made a stopover visit to Yorkshire. Arriving after nine at night, she asked the taxi to wait for her and got out of the warm car. The Hall was in darkness apart from one light burning in the kitchen and another in the small bedroom above. Sighing, she rang the front door bell.

A moment later the door was opened by Mrs Gibbons. Widowed for the last year she now lived at the Hall, looking after Harry and acting as his general factotum.

'Oh, hello, Mrs Salari,' she said pleasantly, standing back as Dione walked in. 'I'll get Lord Avery for you.'

The Hall was considerably renovated, and even in the half-light it looked impressive. The wooden barrelled ceiling had been restored and the white roses of Yorkshire had been painted on the edges of the carved cornice. The marble floor, no longer bearing any signs of the fire, was polished and a set of fine 17th-century chairs had been arranged along the walls, an indifferent Cornelius Johnson portrait hanging over the stout stone fireplace.

Dione turned when she heard footsteps coming quickly down the staircase.

Harry looked older and for an instant it could have been Avery standing in front of her.

'Dione! How lovely to see you. Have you come to stay?'

'I've come for an argument,' she replied deftly, taking off her coat and glancing around. 'You've done well – with the Hall anyway.'

Harry frowned. 'Do you want a drink?'

'I've had several on the way here,' she replied coolly. 'Any more would render me senseless – much like you, in fact.'

Harry dug his hands deep into his pockets, refusing to rise to the bait. Patiently he asked, 'What is it, Dione?'

'I saw Freddie the other day,' she said, sitting down by the fireplace and crossing her legs. 'When I first met that girl I knew she was special but I wondered if she would ever be remarkable.' She paused. 'She proved to me that not only could she be beautiful, but brave. When she ran after you into that fire I realised she was even more remarkable than I had hoped.' Dione raised her eyebrows. 'I am so proud of her, Harry,' she said, smiling and getting to her feet. 'Avery wanted you two to get married. You know that, don't you?'

Harry nodded. 'I know.'

'He loved Freddie almost as much as I do. He wanted you to have a good wife and be happy. I wanted Freddie to have a good husband and be happy. You do see how we both thought along similar lines?' Her tone was coated with sarcasm.

'Go on,' Harry said calmly,

'I saw Freddie the other day, as I just said. She was in perfect health, enjoying her work, and utterly, utterly, bloody baffled.'

Harry blinked. 'Why?'

'She loves you and she can't understand why you've rejected her.'

'Rejected her!' Harry said, running his hands through his hair in exasperation. 'I've *never* rejected Freddie ... '

'You don't go to London to see her. You don't take her out. You don't come to my parties. You don't *live!*' Dione was blazing with anger. 'You expect a young woman of twenty to want to spend all her time in this Hall? You expect that is enough for someone like Freddie?' Dione moved towards her nephew and jabbed a finger into his chest. 'You are a fool! Freddie has fabulous potential and by God, Harry, unless you are very careful, you'll lose her.'

Harry paled suddenly. 'Did she tell you this?'

Dione pointed to her eyes. 'I used these!' she snapped. 'And I suggest that you start following my example.'

For a moment Harry studied her and then moved away, leaning against the window-ledge and looking out. It was dark and Harry saw nothing other than his own reflection looking back at him. Although he was afraid of what his aunt said, he was also faintly angry. The Hall was his life. Why couldn't Freddie understand that? Why did it have to come down to a choice between the building and her?

'She should know how much this place means to me,' he said, without looking round. 'I don't want to leave here. Especially now I have the farm.'

Dione snorted. 'No, Harry, I don't believe you. You're using the Hall as an excuse. You could easily take a weekend off now and again, just as you could easily go down to London to see her. But no, you have walled yourself in here, because here you feel safe.' Dione stood up, pulling on her gloves. 'I knew that Avery never really liked women – but I never suspected that of you.'

152

Harry said nothing, only watched as his aunt got into the humming taxi and waited until it pulled away from the silent house.

The clay and dirt of the building site stuck to Freddie's boots as she stood looking upwards with one hand shielding her eyes. She could only just make out the blurred shapes of men climbing the scaffolding above, and was startled when the lift landed beside the half completed building, a group of men getting out and ducking as a stiff breeze made the tarpaulin flap over their heads.

Having reluctantly relinquished her hold on Bart, Bea was determined to escalate matters between him and Freddie. She had suffered from Bart's indecision for years and she didn't want the same fate to befall Freddie – she loved her too much for that. Knowing that the relationship with Harry was at an impasse, Bea wondered for days how she could force Bart into declaring his feelings. A dozen scenarios were considered, then rejected, but finally she decided on her plan of action and confided in no one – not even in Jao.

Betraying nothing in her voice, Bea asked Freddie to deliver a note to Bart at work, giving her copious instructions on how to get to the building site where the offices were being erected.

'Fine,' Freddie said, agreeing easily, 'I'll go after I leave Penn's tonight.'

Bea smiled. No one would have suspected a thing. Freddie certainly didn't. She arrived at the site around five, but before she had gone more than a couple of feet she was stopped by the foreman who walked out of a Portakabin and faced her.

'What can I do for you?'

'I'm looking for Mr Wallace.'

'Sorry, but he's not here,' the man replied, raising his voice as a drill started up. 'Who are you?'

'I have a message for him,' Freddie shouted.

The man frowned. 'Are you his secretary?'

'No, it's a message from a friend of his.' She went on, 'I was passing this way and said I would drop it off. Do you know if Mr Wallace will come back this afternoon?'

The foreman shrugged. 'He never tells us when he'll call by,' he replied, glancing over Freddie's shoulder and screwing up his eyes. 'You might be lucky – I think that's him over there.'

Freddie turned slowly, her eyes focusing on Bart's figure as he got out of his car and glanced upwards. He had not seen her, that was obvious, and before the foreman had time to point her out to him, Freddie moved away. On the uneven building site she found her progress difficult, her glance often returning to the ground as she picked an erratic pathway between cement mixers and steel girders. Completely absorbed in his own thoughts, Bart did not notice her and only the sound of an appreciative wolf whistle made him glance over.

Freddie stopped, knowing that he had seen her. Suddenly embarrassed, she smoothed back the hair which had blown across her face and pushed her hands deep into her pockets, keeping her eyes averted. From where Bart stood, Freddie seemed woefully vulnerable, and as a fierce snap of wind caught the tarpaulin and a shout came from one of the men above, Bart responded automatically and called out to her, 'Get over here, for God's sake, you've no hat on!'

She ran towards him gratefully, his hand grasping hers as he pulled her towards the side of the car.

'What the hell are you playing at?' he said, reaching to the back seat and ramming a hard hat onto her head. 'You *never* come on site without a hat.'

Freddie said nothing and because the hat was too big it nearly covered her eyes, giving her a peculiarly vulnerable look, like a child dressed up in adult clothes.

'Freddie … ' Bart said.

She stared up at him, the hard hat nearly falling off her head. Bart reached over to catch hold of it. Stretching across her, his mouth was only inches from hers – and he kissed her.

Cambuscan was slumbering under a comforter of leaves. The spring trees were heavy with colour, the lake mottled with the thick wedges of reeds. Summoned home for the weekend, Freddie walked up the drive of Cambuscan, her thoughts alternating between Bart and Harry who was only a couple of fields away at the Hall. She walked deep in concentration, and jumped when Mike called to her from the stable yard.

'You startled me!' she said, smiling and giving him a quick hug.

He studied her carefully. 'You've lost weight.'

'I needed to.'

'Never!' he said, pulling a wry face. Together they fell into step.

'How's Meg?'

'At her mother's. She said she'll see you tonight.' Mike paused suddenly, stopping in his tracks. 'There's trouble.'

Freddie also stopped. 'What kind of trouble?'

'Your father's home.'

A cold shudder passed up Freddie's spine. It rattled against her heart and made her swallow. 'Has something happened?'

Mike had been dreading having to tell her and had rehearsed a hundred different ways to break the news, but in the end he blurted it out. 'He's heard that you and Harry aren't together – he knows it's off.'

Freddie blinked, realising how badly he would take the news. Greville Clements's dream of his daughter marrying a lord was over. All his ambitions, all his hopes were wiped out. In his eyes, Freddie had ruined her chances, and more importantly, she had ruined his.

Her voice was thin with panic. 'How does he know? Who told him?'

Mike shrugged. 'God knows, he just came back this morning in a hell of a rage and started shouting at your mother.'

Freddie glanced towards the house. For a fleeting instant she wanted to run, and keep running. 'Where is he now?'

'Waiting for you.'

She turned away, but he caught her arm as she stammered. 'I c … can't go in, I c … can't, Mike!'

Mike thought of the child Freddie had been, and the way

155

her white hand had patted the earth under Mrs Gilly's cross.

'Go on in and face him, love,' he said kindly. 'The wife and I will be waiting for you in the kitchen.'

Freddie hesitated, her face white. All the old fears came back in an instant and she couldn't move.

'Mike, I can't … '

Firmly, he steered her towards the front door. 'You can. And you will,' he said, his own stomach constricting with anger. 'But just remember this. You don't have to marry anyone you don't want, or do anything you don't want. It's your life, Freddie, *yours*.'

Freddie nodded, allowing Mike to lead her, but as she reached the front door she stiffened suddenly. Gently, she took Mike's hands away from her arms and straightened up; then with her head held high she walked into the hall of Cambuscan.

Sarah was fiddling with a flower arrangement, her plump hands nervously toying with the resistant blooms.

'Oh darling,' she said, turning round and hugging Freddie. 'I've been watching for you all day. I was looking for you out of the window … ' she continued rapidly, her voice pitched high with excitement, ' … and when you didn't come, I thought I'd just do this.' Sarah's gaze moved towards the flowers. Her skin was white with only a little make-up, her hair flat to her head. She acted like someone in deep shock. 'It's so nice to see you … I'm on my own so much now. The weekdays are so hard to bear.' She stopped and blinked as her eyes flicked to the door.

Greville walked in, smiling. His smile was charming, but as he came closer, Freddie could see that it was forced. The glorious face was still handsome, but there was a difference in his skin tone which was unhealthy and a jerkiness in his gestures which had never been present before.

Greville felt baffled and enraged by the young woman in front of him, knowing that she could have married Harry and had chosen a middle-aged American instead. She was a fool and a whore, that much was obvious. He had known enough fools and whores to recognise one. Slowly he shook his head,

156

like a kindly teacher admonishing a naughty child. Then suddenly, and without warning, he struck Freddie across the face with the back of his hand.

'You fucking bitch!' he said, breathing heavily. 'You fucking stupid bitch.'

Sarah gasped softly and then watched disbelievingly as her daughter slumped heavily to the floor. She made a movement to help Freddie, but after Greville gave her a warning look, she turned blindly back to the flower arrangement. Like an automaton she busied herself with it, her hands shaking, her eyes filling with bewildered tears. Behind her, she could hear their voices, but dared not turn.

'Get up!' Greville said, his voice dark with anger.

The sound of shuffling feet echoed grimly in Sarah's ears as her daughter rose awkwardly to her feet.

'Have you lost your senses?'

'N ... no.' Freddie heard herself stammer and paused. Her head rang from the blow and her skin burned, but her eyes remained fixed on her father defiantly.

'You could have been Lady Avery.' Greville laughed suddenly and Freddie flinched.

By the flowers, Sarah let out a muffled sob of panic.

'You could have been a *Lady*,' Greville repeated, his eyes flicking away as his attention wandered. What *had* he just been saying, he thought, what *had* he been saying?

Freddie watched her father warily, waiting for the next move. Was he pretending to be ill, she wondered. Or was he really losing his senses?

Greville pushed her away suddenly. 'Get out of my sight!' He shouted, rubbing his forehead as Freddie rushed passed him and made for the staircase.

Sarah hesitated for a moment and then hurried after her daughter, a piece of fern still clasped in her hand. She took the stairs two at a time, out of breath, her face flushed as she called after Freddie.

But Freddie kept on running, and only stopped when she reached the darkened playroom where she slumped heavily by the window, the doll's house on the ledge beside her.

157

'Sweetheart?' Sarah said plaintively at the entrance to the gloomy room.

Freddie said nothing. She just folded her arms around her body and rocked slightly.

'Sweetheart ... ' Sarah repeated, her voice as high as a child's. 'Please talk to me.' Sarah reached the window and sat down next to her daughter. The fern was still in her hand. 'You mustn't mind. You see, your father can be a difficult man ... ' She trailed off helplessly, without any hope of being believed.

'He hates me,' Freddie said, a simple statement of fact, nothing more.

Sarah faltered. 'No, no ... he's just not good at showing his feelings.'

Unless he happens to be in Eaton Mews North, Freddie nearly retorted, but stopped herself. There was no point striking out at her mother, she realised. There was no fight left in Sarah, only the dead acceptance of defeat.

'He's just disappointed, darling, that's all ... ' Sarah continued, as though Greville's anger was reasonable. 'He wanted you and Harry to be married.'

Freddie hung her head. Oh God, where was safety? Where in God's name could she find some peace? 'I've met someone,' she said.

Her mother's face was uncomprehending.

'I'm in love with someone.' Freddie was shaking and the words were hesitant. The blow had shattered everything; her confidence, and her belief that some day, one day, her mother would come to her rescue. It was never to be, she finally realised. Sarah was too afraid and too bound to her husband to ever side with her child.

'Who is he?' Sarah finally managed to ask.

'He's an architect,' Freddie said, bringing Bart into the wretched room, inviting him in. Protect me, she wished, without realising. Take me away, take me home.

'He's very successful. He's an American.'

Sarah's eyes were vacant. 'Is he nice?'

Freddie floundered. What an odd question. *Is he nice*? After all that had happened downstairs, what was *nice*?

'He's kind,' she replied, and both of them knew the weight of that virtue. 'He seems fond of me.'

Sarah toyed with the wilting fern in her hand. She felt bereft. Freddie would go away from Cambuscan. She would go away, far away. To America even …

'Freddie, how old is he, sweetheart?'

I could lie, Freddie thought, I could, but I won't.

'He's forty-five.'

'Forty-five!' Sarah repeated, her tone shocked, one hand going to her throat. 'He's nearly as old as your father.'

So he is, Freddie thought, so he is. Nearly as old and much wiser. And he would stand up to Greville Clements.

'Your father won't agree to it,' Sarah said suddenly. 'He won't agree. He'll put an end to it.'

'Oh no, Mother, I swear that he will never put an end to anything again,' Freddie said, her tone steady. 'He will *never* interfere in my life again.'

'Freddie, the man is too old for you … '

'I love Bart!' Freddie said firmly.

Sarah faltered. A middle-aged woman in a dress too young for her, too stupid to leave her husband, too craven to protect her child.

'Freddie, he's too old! You could have Harry … or any other young man.'

'I don't want a young man, I want Bart,' she said, putting her wishes into words. Take care of me, please, take me away.

'But, darling, is this man serious about you?'

The question stung Freddie because she didn't really know the answer. Bart was attracted to her and fascinated by her, that much she did know, but how much he loved her – or if he loved her at all – she had no idea. All she really knew was that she had to get away from Cambuscan. Out in the world there was a place and a person who would look after her. She wasn't certain if it was Bart, but she knew it wasn't Harry.

'Does he love you, Freddie?' Sarah asked again.

Freddie closed her eyes and took in her breath. She felt the pain of the blow to her face and at the same time all the myriad pains of her childhood. I will not be cowed, she swore to

159

herself, I *will* be happy, and I will make some man happy too.

'He loves me,' she said to her mother without hesitation, and in saying the words she bound Bart Wallace to herself inexorably. Then she turned, and facing Sarah, lied for the first time.

'Bart loves me and he wants to marry me.'

Chapter Twelve

The lie she had told her mother echoed in Freddie's ears as she paced the railway platform, glancing around repeatedly for any sight of her father, her hands clenching and unclenching with tension as several trains came and went. He could not really stop her, she knew that. Reason told her that she had come of age and no person alive could forbid her to do anything. But the old fears remained. Come on, come on, she urged the train, the station clock swinging overhead, I have to get back to London, I have to. The clock hands moved in slow motion, and Freddie's breathing was shallow as she waited and turned the years back in her mind until she was the lonely child again who had watched her father from the playroom window, and had been afraid of him.

Far in the distance the train finally came into sight. Freddie heaved a sigh of relief and bent down to pick up her cases – just as someone caught hold of her arm.

In the sitting room at Dorman Square, Jao was trying helplessly to comfort a distracted Trisha, her arms wrapped around her aunt as Bea poured her sister a brandy. The room was untidy, the unhooked telephone lying on the floor around Trisha's feet.

'Come on, drink this. It'll make you feel better.'

Trisha pushed her sister's hand away. 'I don't want a drink!' she snapped unexpectedly. 'That's your answer to everything, isn't it? You just throw back a few drinks, get pissed, and that makes it all better.'

Taking in a deep breath, Bea laid the brandy down on the coffee table. 'Trisha, relax. Please, just tell us what's going on.'

'Charlie has finished with me, that's what going on,' her sister shouted, pointing to the overturned phone. 'He says it's over.'

Bea blinked, trying to understand her sister's words. For over five years, ever since he had lodged with them, Trisha had been the lover of Charlie Harris, a freelance reporter who worked on overseas stories. A man of few words, and less humour, he had somehow captivated the giddy Trisha and she had grown to adore him. When he was abroad she wrote copious letters to him – few of which he received – and when he was back in Dorman Square she spent most of her time in the spartan flat below, her quick voice drifting up through the floorboards, the sounds of their love-making a heady accompaniment to the banging pipes.

'What's happened?' Bea asked bewildered. After her disappointment with Bart, this was too much. '*Why* is it over?'

'He met someone in Brighton.'

'*Brighton!*' Bea repeated stupidly. If Charlie had met someone in far off Brazil or Beirut it would have been somehow easier to bear. But Brighton?

'She's in a show there. An actress.'

'Oh dear,' Pam said quietly, with a faint note of censure in her voice.

They all ignored her.

'Listen, love, it'll just be flash in pan. It's bound to blow over.'

Trisha wailed hopelessly. 'He's going to marry her. He said so!' Her eyes looked at her sister beseechingly. 'Oh God, why did he do it?'

'Because he's a pig,' Jao said flatly.

Bea's eyes blazed at her daughter. 'You want to get that tongue of yours licensed,' she said coldly, turning back to her sister. 'Listen, Trisha … '

' … I should have made him happier,' Trisha sobbed, her luminously fair hair falling over her face. 'I should have made him marry me. Why didn't he want to marry *me*?'

Bea hugged her sister to her and stroked her hair. 'Perhaps if you talked to him.'

'No!' Trisha snapped. 'He says he doesn't want to see me again, that he's sorry, and that he'll be moving out.'

'Oh dear,' Pam said tactlessly. 'There goes the rent.'

Trisha looked at her sister fiercely. 'You're glad, aren't you? You've always wanted us to break up. You've been jealous ever since the day Charlie first came here and chose me, not you.'

Pam's mouth tightened. 'That's rubbish, Charlie Harris isn't even my kind of man.'

'Rubbish!' Trisha said violently. 'You'd have leapt in bed with him like a flash if he'd shown any interest.'

Bea looked at Pam in astonishment as an image of Charlie Harris came into her mind. She could see him at the old table in the kitchen, eating a pear in the summer-time, the juice running down his large hands as he passed a piece to Trisha. How could her sisters be rivals for this unremarkable man?

'Trisha, there'll be other men … ' Bea began.

Trisha shook her head, utterly dejected. 'Not like Charlie.'

'That's true,' Jao said drily.

'Oh, for God's sake!' Bea snapped. 'What the hell is the matter with you, Trisha?' she shouted. 'You're pretty, and you're still young – you'll find someone else.'

'I don't want someone else, I want Charlie!' Trisha howled in response, shaking off her sister's grip. 'I'll find some way of getting him back – you see if I don't.'

'It's not that simple,' Bea said more quietly. 'You can't make someone love you … '

'Well, maybe you can't, but I can.'

Bea reeled back as though she had been struck. 'I was only trying to help. I was only trying to make things easier for you.'

Trisha struggled to her feet. She was wearing a cotton nightdress and a pair of old bedroom slippers, her toes poking out of a hole in the left foot. 'You were only trying to make things *easier* for me!' she yelled furiously. 'Well, what the hell do you know about it?' She faced them all angrily. 'How dare you tell me what I should or shouldn't do! You've no man in your life, so what makes you an expert? You talk about love all the time, but you know nothing about it … '

Bea flinched, so shocked that she didn't notice how Jao glanced over to her anxiously. 'I've been married twice,' she said finally, her tone low with cold fury, 'which is a couple of times more than you have.'

Trisha stood up to her sister, her distress making her vicious. 'I could have been married … '

'You *could*, but unfortunately you *weren't*,' Bea replied cruelly, her vulnerability making her unexpectedly spiteful.

Trisha's expression was combative. 'I could have married Charlie, if I'd wanted!'

'Liar!' Bea howled.

Jao stepped back quickly. In her whole life she had only seen her mother really angry once and it had frightened her, just as Bea was frightening Trisha now.

'You talk about love,' Bea went on mercilessly. 'Hah! You hung around that man's neck and called it love. You washed and cleaned for him and made a martyr of yourself and called it love.' She pointed at her sister. 'Take a good look at yourself, and see yourself for what you are, and then you'll see why Charlie never asked you to marry him.'

Trisha's eyes were sharp with fury. 'You cow! How could you be so cruel? How *could* you say such horrible things, especially at a time like this!'

'You wanted that man at any price, didn't you?' Bea continued relentlessly. 'For years you've belittled yourself, and we've all sided with you and supported you. Well, it seems that all your efforts have got you nowhere – nowhere at all – because Charlie's found someone else and he doesn't want you any more.' Bea breathed in deeply. 'Now, tell me, how does that make you feel?'

Trisha's belligerence faltered and she swayed and then sat down heavily, her nightdress falling back to show the wide white curve of her calves. 'I love him… ' she said, defeated, tears pouring down her cheeks, ' … and I can't let him go! I can't!' She clutched her sister's hand. 'Tell me what to do, Bea. Tell me what to do.'

Gently, Bea touched Trisha's head, the large ring on her finger throwing an amethyst shadow onto the blonde hair. All her anger was spent, and she spoke from her heart when she said, 'We'll get him back for you, Trisha, I swear. I promise you, we'll bring the old war horse home.'

An hour later Trisha was in bed deeply asleep after taking two of Bea's Mogadon, Bea waiting by her bedside until she was certain that her sister was asleep. Then she had crept out, motioning to Jao to follow her into the kitchen where Pam sat with her eyes fixed on the table, her hands clenched. Slowly, savouring its effect, Bea drank her third vodka of the night.

'It's not true,' Pam said suddenly, 'I never wanted Charlie Harris.'

'Forget it,' Bea said, exhausted, 'Trisha was upset – she was striking out at everyone.'

Pam wasn't about to be consoled. 'But it's not true – whatever she says, upset or not. Poor Trisha.' She went on, her voice changing to hold an unexpected note of triumph, 'Whatever will she do now? I don't suppose she'll meet anyone like Charlie again ... not that we didn't warn her often enough about those trips he went on. You never know what kind of temptation ... '

'He's a journalist,' Bea replied impatiently. 'He has to go to cover the stories.'

Pam sniffed. 'All the same, it's a shame for Trisha. A tragedy. And when you think how happy she was ... '

'Pam,' Jao said quietly, 'If you don't get out of here now, I'm going to put my foot in your mouth.'

Quivering with rage, Pam made her way to her room and slammed the door.

Jao turned back to her mother. 'So, what happened?'

'You were there, you know.'

'Not with Trisha, Bea. With you.'

Her mother stiffened, then let out a long sigh. 'Bart is in love with Freddie.'

'Oh.'

'He told me.'

'Oh.'

'I can't blame him,' Bea said, draining her glass. 'He hardly knows what hit him.'

'And Freddie?'

Bea shook her head. 'I don't think she understands yet. She's still reeling from the disappointment with Harry.' Bea's throat ached with the effort of trying not to cry. 'I told Trisha you can't make someone love you and that's true. I had my chance with Bart, but there was always something missing.'

'But he found that something in Freddie?'

'Don't be bitter, Jao. If anyone has that right, it's me,' Bea said sharply. 'Bart and I knew each other for fifteen years, if anything was going to happen it would have done so a long time ago.'

Jao raised her eyebrows. 'I never knew you cared about him. I thought he was just a friend.'

'A good friend,' Bea said, her thoughts drifting, her tone embarrassed. 'You know, I used to imagine myself married to him.' Jao's heart ached suddenly. 'I used to see myself as Mrs Bart Wallace of New York and London. No more singing in hotel lounges, no more scratching and scraping to keep this sodding house going.'

Jao touched her mother's hand. 'Remember what you said to Trisha – you'll find someone else.'

'That,' Bea said swiftly, 'is the kind of remark we all make to comfort people, without ever believing it ourselves. I didn't bring you up to talk crap like that.'

Jao smiled wryly. 'No, you brought me up better than any one could ever have done. You're a bloody inspiration, Bea.'

Her mother shrugged, too moved to answer.

'Hadn't you better get ready for work?' Jao asked finally.

'I can't face it.'

'Oh, come on, you can. You don't want to disappoint your public, do you?' Jao squeezed Bea's hand. 'Come on,' she said, 'make the effort.'

Cajoled, Bea rose to her feet and padded into the bedroom. In silence she dressed in evening clothes and repaired her make-up, snapping on a selection of bracelets and then

166

pausing as she stood by the front door. A sharp wind blew in from the empty street as Jao winked at her mother.

'Knock 'em dead, Bea,' she said. 'And get a taxi home when you finish. Promise me?'

Leaning forwards, Bea pinched her daughter's thin cheek gently. 'You worry too much. Who'd run off with an old bag like me?'

Any man in his right mind, Jao thought to herself, looking into the unwelcoming night as her mother, Pimlico glamorous, walked off singing under her breath.

Freddie's return journey to London turned out to be an anticlimax after her fright at the station. Just as she had been about to board the train a hand had caught hold of her arm and she had swung round expecting to see her father standing there. Instead it was merely the porter, passing her the evening paper she had dropped at the barrier. With profound relief she had taken it from the man, but her hand had shaken violently and for minutes afterwards, until they pulled clear of the station, she had been trembling.

The journey was slow. The train dawdled along, stopping at every tiny station to pick up extra passengers and call at all their interminable stops. Staring out of the window, Freddie thought of her mother and of the lie she had told her, shocked at her duplicity, and at the desire which had motivated it. Did she love Bart Wallace, she wondered, hardly believing that she had said the words. Her eyes closed as she tried to clear her thoughts. It was true that the relationship with Harry was finished, and even though she had tried to be discreet, it was obvious that the news was common gossip. Yet there had been no argument with Harry when she went to see him the previous week, only a polite agreement that they should not see each other for a while. The politeness had been what hurt Freddie the most; surely anger would have been more reasonable? Anger or distress.

But it had been impossible to judge just what was going on in Harry's mind as he stood in the small bedroom where they had made love so often, his hands in his pockets, a look of resignation on his face. The Hall was blisteringly cold, even though the May blossom was out in the gardens and the first lilac buds hung around the drawing room windows. Freddie shivered. The building seemed to reflect Harry's mood, mirroring his strange detachment. And it was quiet, she thought suddenly, too quiet. No dogs barked, no music played. Nothing. Only stillness.

Carefully she had studied him – a silent young man in a house full of memories. She had wanted to touch him, to hear him recite the poem of Annabel Lee, or lift her hair to his lips with his scarred hands. But he did nothing, in fact it seemed as though the house had sucked the very warmth out of him, leaving him cold to the bone. Oh God, Freddie thought to herself, how Avery would have mourned the difference in his son.

Confused, Freddie had turned to go, embarrassed and humiliated by Harry's lack of response, and yet she had been unable to leave without making some gesture. Slowly she walked back to where Harry stood and laid her head on his shoulder. The smell of his skin and the memories of their love-making tore at her, and for an instant she could not move. Then she turned her head slightly and gently kissed the side of his cheek. Touched, Harry held onto her for an instant.

'I'll always love you,' Freddie said quietly, 'I'll always be there if you need me.'

'It's not you,' Harry said, trying to explain. 'I just can't ... '

She put her fingers over his lips. 'Don't explain.'

'Friends?' he asked hopefully.

'Better,' she said. 'Allies.'

Freddie opened her eyes, the memory of that meeting too painful to dwell on.

The lie she had told her mother dogged her down the railway line and whispered in her ear at every station, making her restless and uneasy. *Bart Wallace loves me* she had told her mother defiantly, predicting her own future and trying to make some place of safety for herself by grabbing at the one person who could provide it. But could he? And more to the point, would he?

Her flat was in darkness when she returned, only a few late cabs trailing the quiet streets of W1. Turning the key, she pushed open the door and walked in, taking off her coat; then she made herself some coffee and turned on the radio; the sounds of a French radio station filled the room. Freddie pulled back the silk cover on the bed, sipping her drink, her attention wandering until she remembered her father hitting her and quickly sat up, spilling some coffee on the sheet.

'Oh, hell!' she snapped, getting a cloth and scrubbing at the dark stain.

The doorbell rang unexpectedly. Freddie glanced at the clock in surprise. Frowning, she went to the intercom.

'Who is it?'

'Bart.'

The name jolted her and she paused before pushing the button to let him enter. His heavy footsteps sounded on the stairs and then paused outside her door. Freddie opened it and smiled in greeting.

'You keep late hours.'

He smiled easily. 'So do you. I've been waiting since nine-thirty.'

Freddie frowned. 'I'm sorry, were we supposed to meet?'

He passed her and sat down, glancing over briefly at the bed before looking away again. He seemed large in the room and exuded a warmth which seemed to fill the place.

'We hadn't made any arrangement to meet, no. I just wanted to see you, Freddie.' He gestured to her cup of coffee. 'Is there the chance that I could have a cup?'

'Of course,' Freddie said, moving away and busying herself in the kitchen. Even though she had been thinking of him all the way down from Yorkshire, suddenly to have Bart Wallace in her flat, in all his impressive reality, was somehow disconcerting. She also became aware of an unexpected feeling of attraction, and was uneasy, wondering how much the lie she had told her mother was affecting her judgement.

'Here,' she said, handing him a cup.

He accepted it and sipped the coffee, then took off his coat and leaned back into the chair. His expensive suit seemed oddly businesslike and strange on a Sunday night, and Freddie found herself wondering where he had been. Her curiosity made her stare, but when he looked up and caught her gaze, she flushed and glanced away, getting up to turn off the radio.

The flat held its breath, silent and shrouded, the drawn curtains holding back the world outside. The very air seemed heady, warm and comforting. The clock ticked like a heartbeat as they sat, unspeaking, the ornate masks watching them from the enclosed walls. In silence, Bart finished his coffee, and then passed the cup to Freddie, his fingers momentarily brushing hers.

Suddenly, letting out a deep breath, he caught hold of her and drew her towards him, the cup dropping to the floor as his hands gently stroked her face.

'Freddie, I ... ' he faltered, watching as her eyes closed, and then he began to kiss her. Gently, softly, his lips hardly touched her skin at first, whilst his hands moved over her face and neck, his fingers stroking her hair.

Moaning quietly, Freddie held onto him, pulling his body close to hers. His warmth seemed to scorch her as he pulled back and then lifted her hands to his mouth and kissed her palms, then her fingers, each touch so gentle that her skin trembled and she reached out to pull him to her.

His sheer size excited her, as did the feeling of his muscled body under his suit. When he took off his jacket and sat next to her on the side of the bed, Freddie could feel the hard flesh of his skin under the thin shirt and she shook as his mouth pressed over hers. Carefully his tongue moved over her lips, then slid into her mouth, working skillfully against her tongue, slowly and deliberately arousing her before he slid off her skirt.

Then he stopped and rocked back on his heels, kneeling in front of Freddie. His eyes were dark with excitement, his hands resting on her knees, the heat from his palms burning into her skin.

'Do you want this?' he asked, his voice hoarse.

Freddie paused for an instant then nodded. With a smile of relief and excitement, Bart moved position slightly and leaned

170

forwards, his lips brushing the skin of her thighs, his hands moving upwards and sliding her panties down her legs.

Totally preoccupied, Penn walked into the shop and tripped over the uneven floorboard, letting out a discreet exclamation as a sheaf of papers slid from his grip and spread across the floor. Sighing, he carefully bent his corseted bulk and gathered them up, laying them, out of order, on Freddie's desk.

'Being an ... '

' ... Emotional man,' she said, smiling broadly.

'You tease me, you really do!' Penn said, pushing up his glasses. 'I should be angry, but I'm not.' He paused importantly before delivering the next words. 'Being an emotional man, I can only say that I could cry with pleasure, for that,' he said indicating the pile, 'my dear Freddie, is the first chapter of my book!'

'Marvellous!' Freddie cried delightedly. 'I knew you could do it, Penn! I knew it.'

'It's good,' Penn said immodestly. 'Really – even if I do say it myself. You'll be surprised.'

Freddie raised her eyebrows. 'No I won't. I always knew you could do it, Penn.'

He stood next to her. 'So, when are you going to read it?'

'Would now be too soon?' she asked, grinning as he moved into the back room.

Unfortunately Freddie had only got to the foot of the first page when Jao walked in, smartly dressed in the hotel uniform, her feet slender in navy court shoes. Frowning, she glanced around.

'Christ, his taste gets worse,' she said. 'Does anyone buy this stuff?'

'Oh, you'd be amazed how many collectors come here.'

'What for? A good laugh?'

'Ho, ho,' Freddie said drily, one hand slapping down on the papers in front of her. 'This is Penn's first chapter.'

'Oh, boy,' Jao replied drily, reading the title. *Everything You Ever Wanted To Know About Italian Chests*. 'Well, the only ones

I'm interested in have hair on them.' She put her head on one side. 'Bags the sexy bits.'

'You're a mite skittish today,' Freddie replied, watching Jao carefully. 'What's happened?'

'Charlie's back in touch with Trisha and I was fired this morning,' she replied phlegmatically. 'Otherwise not much.'

'You were fired!'

Jao shrugged. 'I double-booked some bloody American and it turned out he was one of the directors.' She paused, changing tack. 'Talking of Americans, how's Bart?'

Freddie smiled and Jao's heart turned uncomfortably.

'He's well. More than well – he's terrific,' Freddie said, pulling out a chair and beckoning to Jao to sit down. 'I care for him, you know, I really care for him.'

'Good.'

'He's not like anyone else I ever met. After my father and Harry I was baffled, but he's gentle and kind and he's ... safe.'

'Good,' Jao said again.

Frowning, Freddie studied her. 'What is it?'

'Nothing.'

'Oh, shit, Jao!' Freddie said angrily. 'Don't horse about. What's the matter?'

'I promised myself that I was never going to say this ... '

'But you're going to.'

Jao nodded. 'Bea is in love with Bart.' Freddie took in her breath. 'She has been for years – ever since his wife died.'

'I didn't know.'

Jao scratched her leg thoughtfully. 'No, I know you didn't.'

A mixture of thoughts came into Freddie's head all at once. She loathed the idea that she had hurt Bea without realising it and yet she wondered why Jao had found it necessary to confide in her about Bart now. What was the point? Why hadn't she told her sooner, before they had fallen in love?

'Bea never said anything to me about Bart.'

'No,' Jao agreed. 'I didn't realise how hooked she was on him either – until she told me.'

Freddie pushed her hair back from her face. 'So why are you telling me, Jao? What do you want me to do?'

172

'You can't *do* anything,' she replied, glancing around her. 'I just wanted you to know, that's all. Just so you wouldn't … well … '

'What?'

'Rub Bea's face in it.'

Freddie stiffened. 'I wouldn't do that!'

'Oh, I know you wouldn't do it deliberately, but you might, without realising,' Jao said. 'You might talk about him and share all your little stories about him, and – I just don't want Bea to be hurt, that's all.'

'Tell me something, did Bart love Bea?' Freddie asked, suddenly aware that if he had, he should have told her, warned her. It would have been the honourable thing to do. *If* he had loved her.

'No,' Jao answered truthfully, not seeing the look of relief on Freddie's face. 'He thought of her as a friend, nothing else. Good chums. You know the kind of thing.'

Freddie hung her head, her happiness clouding. To hurt Bea, of all people. The woman who had always been kind to her and who had helped her through her teenage years. The woman who had been a better mother to her than her own.

'Oh God, I never meant to hurt her.'

'She knows that,' Jao said quickly, touching the back of Freddie's hand. 'And I didn't come here to damp down the fires of passion either. I came because I wanted you to know – and because I wanted to wish you well. You see, both Bea and I reckon you've had a shitty deal so far, Freddie, and we think you deserve some happiness. Bea wants you to make it work with Bart, then she won't mind so much. In a way, I even think she feels glad that she lost him to you, not someone else.' Jao smiled grimly. 'It was just weird the way Bea had to lose out in order to let you win.'

A shuffle of a premonition swept over Freddie and taking Jao's hand in hers she looked her squarely in the face.

'I promise you something,' she said calmly and with utter conviction, 'the time will come when I will do something for your mother. One day I will help Bea, and I swear I'll pay her back for her kindness.'

Jao left soon afterwards and Freddie sat with Penn's first chapter in front of her, untouched. She ran over what Jao had said and knew what it must have cost Bea to sacrifice Bart and watch him go to her. She knew and understood, because the very thought of losing him left her panicky. Jao was right, without knowing what she had done, Freddie had taken the man she loved from a woman she loved. I didn't know, Bea, she said to herself repeatedly, I didn't know.

She wants you to make it work with Bart. Wasn't that what Jao had said? To make it work. Well, Bea, Freddie thought, I want to make it work too. Her eyes flickered to the phone as she thought of Bart, now back in New York. For three months they had been together, both of them feeling bereft whenever Bart returned to the USA, although his trips grew shorter and shorter every time. He loved her, and she loved him. Unconditionally, totally, without question. He made her laugh, and their love-making was erotic but always tender. In Bart Wallace, Freddie had found kindness; she had come out of the long tunnel of a frightened childhood and had found in him safety at last.

And as she thought of him, she wanted him. The miles seemed suddenly too many, the distance too great. For one instant Freddie felt not security, but fear – if she lost Bart she lost herself. Before him there was no security, nothing fixed, or certain. There were no signposts, from arrival to end which could not be blown off course; there were no words which promised fidelity and loyalty which could not be altered or denied. For some women there was a safety, some metaphorical bridge over which they walked without having to struggle for their own footing. But not in Freddie's experience – her examples had been that of her mother and the Wilkie women, and she was suddenly afraid.

Carefully Freddie lifted the phone onto her lap and picked up the handset, then dialled very slowly, the numbers clicking into place audibly as the connection swung across the Atlantic.

Bart answered on the third ring. 'Hello?'

I love you, Freddie thought. *Come home.*

'Bart? It's Freddie.'

That he was glad to hear from her was obvious from his voice. 'How are you, darling?'

Come home. Please.

'I'm fine. Oh, Bart, listen to me ... ' she stopped, suddenly anxious. 'Are you on your own?'

Bart laughed, imagining the violet blue of her eyes and her strong eyebrows raised in enquiry. 'Sure, apart from the fact that the CIA are tapping this phone.'

'The CIA?'

'They tap all architects' phones, just to check that we aren't slipping ready-made bugs into our buildings when they should be doing it themselves.'

Freddie laughed hurriedly.

Oh Bart, for God's sake, don't make jokes now.

'Have you missed me?'

'I always miss you, darling.'

'*Really* missed me?' she pleaded. 'I've been so lost since you went back.'

He laughed again, but he was delighted. 'I only came back yesterday, Freddie,' he said, teasing her. 'And I'll be back in London on Friday.'

I can't wait until Friday,

'Bart, I wondered if ... '

'What?'

'Do you love me?'

He could suddenly smell the warm scent on her clothes and remembered when he had bought her a necklace so fragile that it lay in his hand like a golden wire. Laughing with sheer pleasure, Freddie had turned round and lifted up her hair so he could fasten the clasp, the fine down on her neck secret and erotic as he leaned forwards and ran his tongue over her skin.

'I love you, Freddie, you know that.'

Now, do it now. Go on, Freddie, now,

'Bart ... ' she faltered.

'What is it?' he prompted her, aware of some fierce desire in her voice, a passion which he could almost taste.

'Bart, I want to ask you something ... '

Get on with it, Freddie. Where are your guts?

175

Bart waited, wondering, knowing perhaps even then what the question was. The New York skyline loomed behind him, the other phones on his desk silent, the door closed. I am in a vacuum, he thought, strangely aroused, and here I shall stay until she releases me.

In London, Freddie closed her eyes, her hands shaking, although her voice was almost steady when she asked finally.

'Bart, will you marry me?'

PART THREE

Woman much missed, how you call to me, call to me,
Saying that now you are not as you were,
When you had changed from the one who was all to me,
But as at first, when our day was fair.

The Voice, Thomas Hardy

Chapter Thirteen

London,
Six years later.

Chris Ward walked into the bureau, unlocking the front entrance and pushing back the heavy glass doors marked The 107 Club. The carpet was thick under her feet, darkest green, the walls marbled in the foyer where the reception desk sat unmanned, the switchboard silent. Facing her across the large hall were four doors, all unmarked all covered in leather the same colour as the carpet. Only one door had a name written on it. The name, in gold lettering, was Frederica Wallace.

After making coffee in two porcelain cups, Chris knocked on the door and walked in. Freddie looked up from her desk and smiled, carrying on her phone conversation.

'Yes, I understand what you're telling me, but ... '

The caller interrupted and Freddie listened, sipping her coffee. Her hair fell to her shoulders in a thick bob, her carefully made-up face alert, a pair of emerald earrings and a wedding band her only jewellery.

'I think I know what I'm talking about, Mrs Wallace.'

'Daniel, I know you do,' Freddie answered, continuing at once, 'but Penny is a woman who has very specific needs ... '

She was interrupted again.

'I have specific needs, too! I just wonder if she understands that.'

'Penny's no fool,' Freddie responded gently, 'and you can't rush her in this relationship before she's prepared for such a commitment. You may be sure of what you want, Daniel, but she needs more time.'

The voice was plaintive over the line. 'I want to look after her.'

'I know, I know. But there's more to it than that. You know that Penny's been very ill, but she's recovered now and has a clean bill of health. I don't think she wants to be treated like an invalid any more. She wants to be a normal woman and lead a normal life.'

'But she's needs looking after.'

Freddie persisted. 'No, she doesn't. She needs to feel normal, that's all. And she wants to be with a man who is happy in her company, not someone who's constantly fussing over her. Penny is only thirty-four years old, and you're trying to make her into an old woman. Why, Daniel?'

There was a long pause before he spoke. 'I feel attracted to her because she's vulnerable.'

'Oh,' Freddie said simply, searching through his file for Malcolm Prentice's psychiatric report and pushing it across the desk to Chris. Covering the mouthpiece she said quickly, 'Read that,' and then continued her conversation with Daniel Haig. 'I don't think that wanting a woman to be reliant on you is really the right basis for a relationship.'

'She's not complaining.'

'Well ... '

'She's complaining to you?' he asked sharply.

Freddie's tone was careful. 'Listen, Daniel, she has to talk to me, just as you do. That's the whole point of coming here, so men and women can sort out their problems with the help of an intermediary.'

'Listen, I have to go. Someone's just come into the office,' Daniel Haig said suddenly. 'I'll phone back later.'

The line went dead in Freddie's hand and she shrugged. She looked at Chris. 'Oh dear,' she said, putting down the receiver. 'I hope you're reading that report, because I have a feeling that I'm going to need some help with Mr Haig.'

Chris smiled and sat down opposite Freddie, a 17th century French desk separating them. She had come to work at The 107 Club a year earlier, having heard of the bureau through friends. Like many people she had been curious about Freddie

Wallace and not a little envious. A young good-looking woman, with a happy marriage and an obvious flair for business could seem pretty awe-inspiring. But when she met Freddie, Chris had been taken aback by her informality and her intelligence.

Chris had come to Freddie looking for a job, and had expected to be intimidated, but Freddie was welcoming and charming, her questions never intrusive, only gently probing. In the course of the interview she explained that The 107 Club was a marriage bureau, exclusive and prestigious, but a marriage bureau nevertheless.

'We're here to fit people together, to get the right hand in the right glove,' she had said, smiling and crossing her legs. 'The people who come here are rich, successful and lonely – the last part is the most important. They've often achieved what they wanted in life materialistically, but emotionally ... ' She stopped talking suddenly and began to laugh. 'Oh God, listen to me, I sound like a salesman.' She got to her feet, extended her hand to Chris and said, 'Come on, let's go upstairs where we can really talk.'

Chatting all the way, Freddie took Chris to the first floor of the house at 107 Rutland Gate, pushing open the drawing room door and showing Chris into the most magnificent room she had ever seen. It was Christmas time, and a silver tree stood in the bay window, the branches hung with dozens of white lights which shimmered on the branches. In the marble grate a mock fire burned between caryatids. The mantelpiece was heavy with greetings cards and above it a portrait of Freddie hung in a gilt frame. Chris continued to look around her disbelievingly. She knew that Freddie Wallace was rich, just as everyone knew that The 107 Club was wildly successful, but this kind of opulence was even more than she had anticipated.

Unaware of the effect her home was having on her visitor, Freddie poured them both a gin and tonic and sat down. In the six years since she had married Bart, Freddie's world had changed irrevocably.

When they married her father had been too enraged to

181

attend and Sarah had cried off at the last minute as expected, leaving Mike Kershaw to give the bride away. At the church in London there were only a handful of guests as both Freddie and Bart had wanted to keep the ceremony quiet. Nevertheless Dione was there and all the Wilkie women attended, Meg Kershaw sitting proudly in the front row. The most surprising guest of all arrived as the couple took their vows, Harry slipping silently into the church, his scarred hands folded tightly on his lap.

When Freddie turned and caught sight of Harry, she saw again the boy who leaped gates in the sunshine, and smiled. He, for his part, saw a sensuality in Freddie which he had never seen before and, when he looked at Bart, felt little bitterness, knowing that he could never have brought about the transformation in her. In her white wedding suit, Freddie glowed like the good angel he had always loved; but she was no longer ethereal, and was now clearly earthbound and deeply in love.

For Bart there was only one moment of sadness in the whole wonderful day. After the service, at the reception at the Ritz, Bea came over to him and kissed him lightly on both cheeks like an old friend, but when she pulled away her eyes were filled with tears.

'I always cry at weddings,' she said, by way of an explanation.

'Bea,' Bart said softly, 'is there anything I can do?'

Bea thought of the buggy rides in Central Park and the apartment on Fifth Avenue, of all the things she had once expected to see and now never would. She had dreamed of standing in the place where Freddie now stood, and sending postcards home to England signed Mrs Wallace ... But it had been a dream, nothing more. Squeezing Bart's hand Bea smiled brilliantly and said 'Send me a postcard, will you?'

He nodded willingly. 'What do you want me to write?'

'Nothing,' Bea said, 'just leave it blank – I'll fill in my own words.'

An hour later Bart and Freddie left for their honeymoon. They went to the Paris Ritz, then onto the Cipriani in Venice, Freddie showing off her grasp of French and Italian, Bart

182

impressed and seeing old places with new eyes. They made love in hotel bedrooms well into the night, their bodies wrapped together, exploring and touching, each on a sexual adventure, Bart discovering in his young wife an eroticism he had never encountered before. Freddie moved him and she trusted him so much that she lost all inhibitions, making love in the bathroom, on the floor, or even on the hotel balcony one night when the city was silent and dark.

'Mrs Wallace you are insatiable,' he said, to tease her, and bent down to kiss her lips, his hair ruffled, his eyes already dark with excitement.

'Yeah, and aren't you the lucky one?' she answered, smiling as she reached for him.

Bart was so proud of Freddie that he lavished money on her, buying her clothes from Chanel in Paris and Armani in Venice. He also gave her jewellery, tucking pieces under her pillow, or in her pockets so she would find them unexpectedly. He was rich and for so long he had had no pleasure in his money. Now he could hardly resist buying each and every thing which caught his eye. The style Dione had uncovered in Freddie, Bart relished and encouraged, wanting perfection, wanting to enjoy her and be proud of her.

Dazzled by Bart's generosity, Freddie wanted only to please him and offered unfailing affection. It was easy to love him, he was warm and open, with no wrinkles to his personality, and on the third night of the honeymoon, Freddie talked about her father. She had told Bart some of the truth before they married, but had found that she could not confess everything – many secrets were too dark and had been hidden too long. But with Bart's gentle probing she began to talk, and the wounds he had long suspected began to emerge.

Bart listened and when she stopped talking he held her, and finally, when she told him about Mrs Gilly, he could imagine her as a child at Cambuscan, feeling what she had felt, her injuries his own. Loathing Greville, he made a silent vow that he would always stand between Freddie and her parents, giving her the constancy and security she had searched for for so long. Then later that night, as she slept, he

183

found himself lying awake, the memory of a child's terror riding the night with him.

When Freddie woke the following morning, on the pillow beside her was a toy rabbit, and a note pinned to the ribbon round its neck. On it, Bart had written:

Meet Mrs Gilly, mark II ...
She's not real so she can't be hurt.
She won't grow old, or die, or leave you.
Like me she's here to stay.
Your past, my love, is now mine. Let me
have the pain of it ... The future is ours.

Bart

After the honeymoon they returned to New York where Bart was eager to show off his wife. Always socially adept, Freddie was a willing hostess and a gracious guest, but being English and very much younger than the wives of Bart's colleagues, she was viewed with barely concealed suspicion, and longed to return home to England. Not that she voiced her opinion to her husband – instead she dutifully attended cocktail parties and helped to raise funds for a variety of charities. But she enjoyed most their evenings alone, when they listened to jazz at the Blue Note, or drove round town in Bart's Bentley convertible like a couple of teenagers. Anxious for her to like New York, Bart treated Freddie like a royal tourist, but soon he was aware that she was not comfortable in his home town.

'You're not happy here, are you?' Bart asked, only six weeks after their marriage.

She glanced up surprised. 'I'm happy anywhere with you.'

'But you'd be happier at home?'

'Yorkshire?' she asked frowning.

'No, I meant London.'

Her face lit up. The answer was obvious, Bart thought with only a little sense of disappointment.

'Oh, Bart, are we going home?'

Quickly he took her hand and pulled her down onto his lap. 'I've expanded the office in London. After all, there's more than enough work there to keep me fully occupied. I'll still need to come over here for a couple of months a year, but otherwise we could use London as our base.'

Smiling, Freddie laid her head on Bart's shoulder. 'Won't you miss New York? It's your home.'

Bart's hands tightened around her. New York was his home, or had been – with Gill. A year ago he would have said that he would live and die there, but since meeting Freddie, a new world had been revealed and offered up endless possibilities that he was anxious to explore. His beautiful wife was at home in Europe and England – places he had never really enjoyed before – and when he went with Freddie to Paris it was a different city to the one he remembered. It was as though these places he had known on business trips had been only half seen by him. With her twenty-year-old eyes, Freddie saw only the world's excitements, and with her, Bart began to regain some of the enthusiasm he had thought gone for ever.

'I've had enough of New York,' Bart said eagerly, his mind made up. 'Let's go back to London.'

After visiting many properties, the house they finally settled on was 107 Rutland Gate, Knightsbridge, a large white town house on four floors. Freddie fell in love with it at once, although Bart was reluctant to commit himself until the surveyor had assessed the property. When the results came back positive, he was still wary, taking a second look with Freddie one night in late September.

'What do we want with a house this size?' he asked, sweeping the room with his torchlight. His voice echoed in the empty rooms.

'We can have parties – and lots and lots of children,' Freddie said, winking at him.

He laughed. 'But it's huge … '

'It's not nearly as big as Cambuscan.'

'Point taken,' Bart replied, walking with her into the hall and looking around. Freddie's face was luminous with pleasure as he watched her and focused the torch's beam on her face. She smiled in the light, as though posing for a photograph, and then spun round on her toes, pointing out the reception rooms where they could have guests and hold cocktail parties for Bart's business clients.

'I could end up rivalling Dione,' Freddie said ingenuously, pulling open another pair of doors and walking into an empty lounge. Bart followed her, trailing the room with the torchlight. It was bare, apart from a couch and a rolled up carpet.

'Oh, we could be happy here, Bart, believe me. We could have a family here.'

Bart shook his head indulgently, already convinced as he walked over to her. The torchlight shone on Freddie's face, her eyes brilliant.

'I think I'll just turn off the light,' he said softly, flicking the torch off and guiding Freddie over to the couch. His lips brushed her neck gently and then he pulled back, looking into her shadowed face.

'What was that you said about children?'

'We could fill this place with them,' Freddie said happily.

'Then we'd better waste no time in starting, had we?'

Unwilling to infuriate Greville, Sarah tried not to mention their daughter, but finally, one evening at dinner, she laid down her knife and said, 'I think we should see Freddie.'

Greville glanced up. 'Why?'

'Because it's silly having a feud with your own daughter,' Sarah said, her voice high with a mixture of righteousness and quaking defiance. 'We should let bygones be bygones.'

'She let us down.'

'No, she didn't!' Sarah said quickly. 'She didn't marry Harry, that's all. She married Bart instead and he seems nice and he's very rich.'

Greville looked at his wife disbelievingly, the familiar sensation of detachment washing over him. His eyes shifted uncomfortably, feeling tight in his head. His throat constricted. Sarah would never understand, Greville thought, never. Freddie could have been a Lady, with a title. Lady Avery. With all the respect and social cachet such a title brings. But no, she married an American, a man with an accent like a film actor – she married Bart Wallace when she could have

186

had Lord Avery. Greville's head ached as it did so often these days. Why had Sarah lost that son? Why? He would have had an heir, someone to be proud of. But no, Sarah had lost the child. Silly, clumsy Sarah. And now she still expected him to make love to her, she pleaded with him, and repelled him.

'I think we should see her.'

Greville blinked, what *had* Sarah been saying? His thoughts turned to Madelaine in the mews house. All her little tricks weren't enough any more; all those little dressing up rituals and magazines couldn't arouse him any longer. He rubbed the back of his neck, wincing as his fingers caught a bruise under his collar. Bruises and blood …

'Well, Greville, what do you say? Please, darling, please.'

Greville blinked, suddenly seeing Madelaine's face superimposed over his wife's. *Please Greville, please* Madelaine had begged exposing her bare buttocks already reddened with weal marks.

Greville pushed back his chair violently and stood up. 'Do what you like, Sarah, I'm going back to London tomorrow anyway.'

Sarah arranged for Freddie and Bart to come up to Yorkshire, but somehow the visit never materialised. Once the ties were refastened however, Sarah soon reverted to her previous behaviour and phoned her daughter often, regaling her with stories of Greville's bewildering conduct. Yet however oddly Greville acted, Sarah remained besotted by him and resented any criticism from her daughter. Not that Freddie referred to her father often, too cautious of reopening the old wounds as, tentatively, the two women re-established their relationship. Freddie knew that she would always come second to her father in her mother's eyes, but in the security of her own marriage she found herself finally able to make allowances for her mother – if only from a distance.

The first year of the Wallace marriage passed in a hectic rush of activity. The house was decorated, the business settled in London, and many invitations extended. The first person to visit was Jao, whistling with approval as she saw the new house, and it was not long before the other Wilkie women followed Jao's lead. Dione had kept up a regular correspondence with Freddie and visited often when she was in London, her clear upper-class tones crackling through the rooms as she told indiscreet stories and hooted with unrepentant laughter. Continuing the education she had so adeptly begun, Dione introduced Freddie to many of her friends, setting up a network of acquaintances which stretched from Knightsbridge to Rome, and from Rome to Paris. Proud and confident of Freddie's social skills, she brought the painter Buccione to meet her, and when Freddie threw a cocktail party for Bart's colleagues, Dione arrived late with Prince van Thessiery on one arm, and a silent Caesar on the other.

It was inevitable that such goings-on were reported, copied and envied, and before their first wedding anniversary Freddie had crept elegantly onto the very first rung of her career as a society hostess. She was fortunate in her staff, too. With Bart's help, she had hired competent people in George and Jean Allen, a middle-aged couple who had previously worked for a baronet. Other help was brought in when they had parties, which they frequently did.

Freddie was delighted with her new home, and Bart was delighted with his new wife. Their love was so intense and so all-embracing that, although Freddie had stopped taking precautions, neither of them was too concerned when she didn't get pregnant. Yet after the second and third years of their marriage passed, Freddie began to worry and confided in Jao.

'I don't understand it,' Freddie said. 'I thought I'd be pregnant by now.'

Jao shrugged. 'Speaking as one who spends at least one week of every month praying to the calendar, I'm not the best person to advise you about child-bearing.'

'But doesn't it seem strange?' Freddie asked. 'D'you think I should see a doctor?'

'I think you should stop brooding on it,' Jao replied evenly. 'Give yourself something else to think about. Buy something to amuse yourself – I hear the Moscow zoo is up for grabs.'

'Sarcasm was always your strength,' Freddie said coolly, crossing her legs. 'I've been busy with Penn's book ... '

'That book will *never* get written!' Jao said emphatically. 'I have as much chance of filling a D-cup bra as he has of getting that into print.'

Freddie ignored her and went on, musing about the work she had been involved with lately. 'I did some research for the Leningrad museum recently, and I translated that catalogue for the Monet collection.'

'All of which Dione arranged for you,' Jao said, helping herself to another glass of wine. She was as thin as she had always been, her legs looking even longer than usual in dark tights. 'Why don't you do something off your own bat?'

Freddie frowned, surprised. For the last few weeks she had been thinking along the same lines. Not that she wasn't grateful for all Dione's contacts, but although the work was interesting, she had a nagging sense that people thought she was merely dabbling – she knew that Bart did.

'Don't wear yourself out, darling,' he said, coming home and finding Freddie working. She had made herself a small office next to their bedroom and kept some of her research books there, although the bulk of them remained in the library below.

'I'm not, I just want to do a good job, that's all,' Freddie replied, glancing over her shoulder and smiling at him. 'It's important to me.'

'Why? You don't have to work.'

Laying down her pen, Freddie slid round on her seat to face him. 'We have a marvellous home and a great deal of money. We are very lucky, Bart, and because of that I feel guilty sometimes.' She raised her hands to stop him interrupting. 'Even Dione only humours me with the research she puts my way. Who else would be working for these kinds of people without having a degree or studying for years?'

'You're good.'

She nodded. 'Yes, but so are others who will never have my chances. Money and contacts secure things for me – not my talent.' Freddie paused, suddenly ill at ease. 'I didn't do any of this on merit ... '

Bart sat down beside her. 'You work for charity too, Freddie, don't forget that.'

'Oh, I know, but somehow I feel I could – should – be doing more. I don't want people to think I'm just a spoilt, rich woman.'

'Correction. A *beautiful*, spoilt, rich woman,' Bart said, teasing her. 'Listen, Freddie, I love you and I think you've earned your good fortune.'

She pulled a face and then leaned forward, her forehead against his. 'OK, point taken.'

So for another three years Freddie was the ideal wife. Sexually adventurous, a loving, witty, charming hostess with a superb house and an enviable group of friends. For the Wallaces there was always a table available at Harry's Bar or the Ritz; at Christmas hampers came from Fortnum & Mason, and in the autumn they visited New York. Whilst Freddie continued to be based in London, she also frequently travelled abroad with Bart, and took on increasing amounts of research work, easily filling her time and her thoughts.

To outsiders, her life was blessed. But no children came. Never. No pregnancies, no miscarriages, no false starts. As the time passed, Freddie thought back to her mother and the anxious waiting for an heir, and repeatedly she blamed herself for not conceiving. Bart never did – anxious at first because Freddie was distressed, he attended several specialists and clinics and was given a clean bill of health, as she was. But Freddie still didn't conceive, and when Bart was approaching his fifty-first year, he felt a sudden longing for children – and he wanted them *now*. He had no desire to be too old to see them grow up and was painfully aware of the passing years, never articulating his fears to Freddie, but intermittently brooding.

Bart didn't have to tell Freddie that he was concerned; they were too close to need words to express their feelings. Freddie knew that Bart wanted a child – not in the way her father had wanted an heir – but as a way of distributing some of his vast resources of affection. In the past they had always been enough for each other, but now there was a desire for more – and they both felt it.

190

Taking the matter into her own hands, Freddie decided that she had to find an outlet to stop her worrying incessantly about not being pregnant. After all, she had heard the many stories about people adopting and then conceiving suddenly – simply because they were relaxed and not preoccupied. What she needed, Freddie thought, was a job, a proper job. Her mind made up, she then wondered exactly what that job should be. Well-read, bilingual, and glamorous, her options were numerous, especially as she had a powerful lobby of contacts to call upon. But that wasn't what she wanted, Freddie realised. No, she wanted something of her own, something to occupy her thoughts fully; a job which would help others and consume her. Then, and only then, was she certain that she would get pregnant.

'A marriage bureau!' Jao said, rolling her eyes at her mother, 'she has *got* to be deranged.'

Bea shrugged. 'Oh, I don't know. It's not a bad idea really.'

'Freddie Wallace? Hot off the society pages of *Harper's* and daughter of ... '

' "The Handsomest Man in England!" ' they chorused together.

' ... running a marriage bureau? It's bloody crazy.'

Amused, Bea folded her arms and leaned back in the kitchen at Dorman Square regarding her daughter thoughtfully. Since Jao had been so ignominiously fired from her receptionist's job, she had pursued a variety of careers, having about as much success as her aunts. Alternatives had included hairdressing, working as a personal assistant to a record company executive, and then as an airline hostess, but none of the jobs lasted for longer than a few months. The reason was obvious to Bea. Smart mouthed as her daughter might seem to outsiders, Jao was the most easily hurt of any of the Wilkie women, and the one who most believed in romantic love. Jao would have been disembowelled rather than admit it, but her life was held poised for the moment she met the right man, and then ... '

'It's so humiliating,' Jao went on.

191

Bea raised her eyebrows. 'Why? Freddie's going to run the bureau, not join it.'

'She doesn't need to,' Jao said softly. 'She and Bart are still besotted with each other.' She winced at her own lack of tact. 'Oh, God, sorry.'

Bea's hand snaked across the table and clutched her child's. 'It's OK. And stop worrying, you'll meet someone, I promise. Look, it was even in your cards the other night.'

'Sure,' Jao said drily, although her spirits lifted with automatic optimism. 'So if you're such a good clairvoyant, what happened to that car I was supposed to be getting last November?'

Rising to her own defence, Bea said stiffly. 'I'm not always right on time.'

Jao's thoughts drifted back to Freddie. She had seen her the previous afternoon when they had met in the Royal Academy restaurant. Freddie had walked in briskly, her face alert with triumph as she sat down.

'I've got it!'

'Keep your voice down or they'll all want some,' Jao responded drily.

Undoing her coat Freddie leaned across the table conspiratorially. 'Last week I met one of Dione's old friends, a man called Theo Gunther. He told me all about this club he used to run in Rome, a kind of salon – '

'As in hairdressing?'

'As in Marie Antoinette,' Freddie replied evenly. 'Do listen, Jao! Well, this place became a sort of meeting point for the fashionable people and after a while he noticed that lots of his guests got involved … '

'The Hammersmith Palais has the same kind of reputation.'

Freddie's eyes were steely. 'You can be as snide as you like, but you're not going to stop me talking about it.'

'Would that I could.'

'Theo gave me an idea … '

'Oh God.'

'I'm going to open a marriage bureau!' Freddie said triumphantly. 'I'm going to make it very up-market to attract all the

192

right people and then I'm going to introduce them to each other – making sure they have similar backgrounds and interests, of course.'

'Of course.'

'There are so many people who haven't found the right person …'

'Yeah.'

'It could work, Jao. I have the money to set it up and I could run the bureau from home. We've got the room, after all.' Freddie paused. All the unused rooms at Rutland Gate had become an uncomfortable reminder of the reason why they had bought the house. The space needed filling, and Freddie had finally decided how to do it.

'There is just one tiny point, which I'm surprised that you've missed,' Jao said calmly. 'All these upper crust people have their own network of contacts. They mix together and marry together …'

Freddie leaned further over the table. 'No, I'm not talking about the upper classes. I'm talking about people who've struggled in their careers and have become successful materially but then turn round at thirty or forty or fifty and realise they've no one to share their lives with.' Freddie paused, 'There are so many professional people who have no family and few friends, who can't meet people because they work all the time and get out of touch. I know men who can only go out and meet a girl in a bar – but what good's that? They have a great time, but they don't meet the kind of women they want to marry.' She fiddled with her earring thoughtfully. 'When I was New York with Bart last month I went to some singles clubs …' Jao's eyebrows rose. 'All in the interests of research, you understand.'

'Oh, naturally,' Jao agreed wryly.

'There is a whole dating subculture –'

Jao cut her off impatiently. 'Freddie with the greatest respect, you didn't have to fly first class by Concorde to find that out. Go down to any club one Friday night and you'll see the same kind of people all looking for "the right person." ' Jao was suddenly angry. 'What the hell would you

193

know about loneliness anyway? You've got a good marriage.'

'I was lonely once, Jao,' Freddie said quietly. 'And I've seen what a lousy marriage looks like from very close quarters. My parents lead a bloody odd life. My mother, I now realise, is sexually fascinated by my father, and as for him – well, I'm not sure I want to know what his preferences are.' Freddie paused, 'I grew up with the example of my parents marriage set against the genuine affection of the Kershaws, and when I became involved with Harry, well … that was a kind of loving too, even if it didn't work out.'

'You've hardly been round the track though, have you?' Jao said evenly. 'I mean, there are some who would say that your experience is somewhat limited. One happy marriage doesn't make you an expert on everyone else's love life.'

Freddie frowned. 'I know that, Jao, but I've got Theo to help me. He's going to manage the business whilst I learn the ropes and I'm going to hire people who have worked in marriage bureaux before.' Freddie stopped talking, and glanced at a couple who had sat down on the table next to theirs. 'What do you give for their chances, Jao? Will their affair work out, or not? I don't know, but I recognise something in myself. I'm lucky, and I want to spread that luck around a bit. Besides, I have a knack for feeling things – an intuition sometimes – and people interest me. If I use the money I've got to set up the bureau, I could do something valuable, I could achieve something.' She leaned back, the speech over. 'So what do you think?'

'It's not up to me, is it?' Jao responded. 'It's more a question of what Bart thinks.'

Bart was enraged by the idea, slamming the door of their bedroom, his hands loosening his tie as he threw his brief-case on the bed. They had argued before, but not this violently, he thought, sitting down and resting his head against the back of the chair. Who would have expected Freddie to come up with such a bizarre scheme? He had never been bothered about her wanting to do research – as he had said to Dione, it kept her occupied – but a *marriage bureau*! Had she gone crazy? And to think of setting it up in their house! She had to be mad.

'You need something to occupy your mind,' he had snapped when she told him.

Surprised by his anger, Freddie remained calm. 'That's the whole point, Bart. I want to do this in order to "occupy my mind." There's no purpose simply sitting around wondering why I don't get pregnant … '

'That has nothing to do with it!'

Freddie spun round to face him. 'It has everything to do with it and you know it!' Her eyes were brilliant with fury. 'You want a child, well so do I – but mooning around thinking about it all day and all night won't make it happen any faster. I need to be occupied. You have your work, so what's the difference?'

'The difference,' Bart said with deadly reason, 'is that I have to work, you don't. I don't want my wife to work. We have enough money to live very well, we don't need more money.'

'I'm not doing it for the money!'

He shook his head in disbelief. In the four years they had been married, Bart had kept up his regular exercise and was still meticulous about his appearance. But his hair was greying more around the temples, and his large eyes were heavily lined at the corners. He looked prosperous, but he also looked middle-aged.

'Listen, I've been thinking – why don't I retire?'

Freddie blinked. 'What!'

'If I retired, we could travel and do what we wanted … '

'We *do* travel and we *do* do what we want,' Freddie said sternly. 'You would die without your work, Bart. You know you would.'

Bart shook his head. 'Have it your own way,' he said, still angry. 'But you can forget the bureau idea.'

Freddie was not about to be dictated to and stood her ground. 'Bart, I have enough money of my own to set up this bureau,' she said, calmly defying him. 'If I want to do it, I will set it up. It doesn't have to be run from here, you know.'

They ate in separate rooms, Jean Allen taking a tray into the library for Bart, and another upstairs to Freddie's office. In their own domains each of them picked at their food,

Freddie finally throwing down her napkin in disgust. She did not want to give in and yet was reluctant to argue any further with Bart. They both expected the other to give in; Bart because Freddie was still very young and therefore pliable, and Freddie because Bart had never denied her anything before. But neither of them gave an inch, and instead Freddie spent an hour on the phone to Theo Gunther in Rome, asking him about his club and making voluminous notes. At two in the morning, Bart finally came upstairs, undressed, and climbed into bed beside Freddie. Immediately she shifted away from him, slapping his hand away when he rested it on her thigh.

'Go to hell, Bart!' she snapped.

He swore and then laughed softly. 'Is this blackmail? No sex until I give in?'

Freddie said nothing as his hand roamed over her thigh and then moved up to her breasts, fondling them gently. Against her better judgment, Freddie turned round to him and then, just as he was about to kiss her, he moved away and snapped off the light.

'Oh no, Freddie,' he said laughing. 'You shan't take advantage of my body until you drop the idea of the bureau.'

Infuriated, Freddie struck his shoulder with her fist.

'And it's no good trying to get round me,' he said, still laughing. 'I'm no push-over.'

Bart's evident amusement infuriated Freddie more than anything else, and in the morning she was still smarting when she woke to find him already dressed and ready to leave.

'You know, I was thinking, darling,' he said drily. 'There's no way you could work office hours … ' He snapped the locks together on his case. ' … You'd never be up in time.'

'Bart, listen to me a minute,' Freddie said, pushing back her hair and wrapping her arms around her bunched up knees. She looked small in the bed and for an instant all he wanted to do was to climb back in with her. Her voice was soft, honeyed, as she looked at him. 'Are you annoyed because it's a marriage bureau? I mean, if I had wanted to run a interior design business from here, would you have felt the same?'

196

Bart sat down on the bed and stroked her cheek. 'Well, it would have been less of a shock.'

Jumping to her feet, Freddie howled at him. 'Then you're nothing but a bloody hypocrite, Bart Wallace!' she shouted, throwing a pillow at his receding back.

Freddie had implicit faith in her idea and continued to talk to Theo and to discuss the matter with several women he knew who had worked in marriage bureaux. She had no wish to antagonise Bart, but she was firmly convinced that the bureau would not only be successful, but acceptable. When there were so many lonely people, she reasoned, why was matchmaking looked upon with such pity? You paid a plumber to fix your taps, so why not pay someone to find your partner? After all, you had a partner longer than a bath tub. At least you were supposed to ...

It was obvious, even to Freddie, that the main drawback to the scheme was her lack of experience. Having hunches was not enough. What Freddie really needed was a person who had seen it all, done it all, and survived it all. Which was where Bea came in. Within days of Freddie telling Jao what she wanted to do, Bea had been approached, and after laughing uproariously at the suggestion, was reluctantly tempted by the idea of the bureau.

'Have you any idea how these places are run, Freddie?'

Freddie nodded and pulled out a sheaf of notes onto the floor at Dorman Square. 'We have to investigate our clients. We'll need a full background, professional c.v., a birth certificate – to make sure they don't lie about their age – a medical examination, a handwriting test, and a psychiatric report.'

'Is that all?' Bea said drily. 'Oh, come on! No one on earth is going to give you all that information, Freddie.'

Freddie nodded her head. 'They will – if we don't make them feel uncomfortable about it.'

'Then what?'

'Then we talk to them.'

'Talk?'

'Yeah, you know, with the lips.'

Bea smiled grimly. 'And you think that's it? Just ask them

what they want, write down their particulars, and then match them up with a partner. Hey presto!'

Freddie faltered momentarily. 'Well ... that's the basic idea.'

'Freddie,' Bea said kindly, 'you are such an innocent. Have you any conception of how difficult is for a man and a woman to meet, fall in love, and marry? And the older they get – especially if they're divorced or set in their ways – the harder the dating gets.'

'You see!' Freddie said delightedly. 'You know all about their problems. You could sympathise with them.'

'I'm not married!' Bea said in exasperation. 'What kind of example am I?'

'You've been married twice, what better example could anyone have?' Freddie replied smoothly, giving Bea a sly look. 'Besides, who knows, when we've set the bureau up, you might meet someone.'

But if Bea could be persuaded to help out temporarily, Bart was immovable. Cajole him as she might, he was not going to give in, and after two weeks, Freddie capitulated.

'All right,' she said quietly at dinner one night, 'I'll forget the idea.' Her tongue ran over her lips, her hand reaching for her glass. Slowly she sipped her wine. In the subdued light she was exquisite. Dressed in a plain cream shift with her hair piled up on her head, she had all the refinement and elegance of a woman perfectly at ease with herself and her world. She looked glamorous, the kind of woman any man would want to possess – and she looked like the last kind of woman to want to open a marriage bureau. Bart frowned, suddenly seeing Freddie with different eyes. She wanted to help, did she? Wanted to put something back, in gratitude for all she had. It was a fine notion, and he felt suddenly ashamed for having opposed her. Any other woman would have been happy to be lazy and indulged; any other happily married woman would never have given a second's thought to all her unhappy, unmarried sisters. But then, any other woman wouldn't have been Freddie ...

'What are you going to do with all the money you make?'

he said simply, wanting her and wanting to give her anything to make her stay with him. For tonight and for ever.

Freddie laid down her glass. 'What did you say?'

'I said, what about the money?'

Freddie's heart lifted, her voice shaking as she answered, 'You know how interested I am in the art world, Bart, well, I want to invest half the money I earn and donate the rest. The National and the City Art Gallery need funds and I'd like to help keep some works in this country before they snap them all up and ship them to California. They nearly lost that Reynolds portrait the other day, and if it hadn't been for someone donating the money at the last minute, the painting would have left England for God knows where.' She rose to her feet and walked towards Bart slowly. 'So many paintings and antiques get sold to private collectors.' She reached his chair and took his hand, kneeling beside him. 'It would be nice to think that my money could help the galleries to hold onto some of them for a little longer.'

Bart lifted Freddie up and hugged her. 'Such fine ambitions, Freddie, such noble ideals,' he teased her. 'Don't you ever get worried that they might never come true?'

'No,' she said simply. 'I don't dare.'

That was now two years ago. It had taken over a year for the bureau to become established, its reputation growing unobtrusively, but steadily. The office was set up in Rutland Gate, the ground floor given over to The 107 Club, whilst the living quarters remained above. Many people, amused by the idea of a marriage bureau, pitied Bart and teased him about his tolerance, whilst he felt only a pride in his wife and a rich satisfaction when the bureau began to prosper. Besides, what the hell did he care what people thought? They had talked enough when he married Freddie – the middle-aged man and the young girl – so what difference did it make if they kept talking? As long as he had her, the rest could go hang.

As she had promised, Bea had come to help out temporarily, but she missed the down at heel glamour of the hotel lounge and after two months, left. By that time however, Freddie had hired Tina Shore, Liz Ford and Dot Cummings –

all women who had worked in the dating business before, and all of whom possessed understanding, intelligence and experience.

Having married a man much older than herself, Freddie had adapted her style accordingly, and although she dressed in high fashion, she had a sophistication which made her look older than her twenty-six years – a fact which was a decided advantage when it came to her dealings with women more mature than herself. Dignified and intelligent, Freddie impressed her employees, but was friendly enough to be approachable. After all, as she said to Bart, they might own the bureau, but the employees could make it or break it. She was wise enough to listen too, making notes and taking advice, well aware that her success or failure would be public knowledge, and that any humiliation she might suffer would rebound on her husband as well.

Driven by newly found ambition, Freddie soon found herself absorbed by the bureau. In the first few months she fussed over the decor, anxious to make it welcoming but expensive, and knowing that it had to appeal to women as much as men. But when the decorations were completed and the headed notepaper arrived, the long wait began. As Theo had warned her, the build-up of business would be slow unless she advertised, and yet that had its own drawbacks.

'It looks down-market to tout for business,' Theo explained over the phone from Greece where he was setting up a new night-club. 'It's difficult, Freddie, because you don't want to make yourself like every other bureau in town and yet you want people to come to you. You've got to make it clear that your bureau is – '

'Unique,' Freddie finished for him.

'Yes. That's the word.'

'But how do people hear about us if we're not in the papers?'

Theo laughed, a hoarse bark down the phone. 'Freddie, you're not unknown. Use your head and get the press on your side. It's a good story and they'll love it. I can just see it: "Lady Bountiful Wants To Save All Her Cinderella Sisters." '

Freddie winced. 'I'm not sure about the headline, but I get the idea,' she said evenly.

'I'll have a friend on *The Times* get in touch with you. It might not come to anything, but it's worth a shot,' Theo said, his voice fading on the phone line. 'Good luck.'

The article came out in *The Sunday Times* lifestyle section three weeks later, together with a photograph of Freddie in a black Chanel suit. Even though the journalist had tried to make her into some kind of socialite do-gooder, Freddie was amusing in the piece and although she could have come over as just another smug, rich bitch, Freddie's common sense and obvious enthusiasm won out. The only sour note was the smaller photograph at the bottom of the page, together with the revised caption, 'Greville Clements – Still The Handsomest Man in England?'

When Bart read the piece in bed that Sunday morning he couldn't help laughing and when the phone rang beside him he wasn't in the least surprised to hear Greville's voice.

'What the hell are you letting my daughter get up to?' he bellowed, impressively loud. 'I've just read the morning paper ... '

Bart was in lazy, good humour. 'Good photo of you ... '

'Don't fuck me about!' Greville said heatedly. 'Are you both crazy? What in God's name is she doing opening a marriage bureau? I didn't know anything about it.'

'That's not surprising,' Bart replied coldly, his temper rising. 'You haven't been in touch with your daughter for years.'

'That is a matter between us ... '

'Like hell!' Bart replied heatedly, sitting up on the side of the bed, his hand gripping the phone. 'Freddie is my wife now. If you've got anything to say, you can say it to me. I'm not letting you upset her any more.'

Alerted by Bart's raised voice, Freddie came to the bathroom door and frowned at her husband.

'I want to speak to her,' Greville said sharply.

'She's not here,' Bart replied. 'But I'll tell her you called.' He put down the phone without another word.

'Dear God, who was that?'

'Your father,' Bart replied. 'The son of a bitch.'

A familiar sense of dread washed over Freddie. Her voice dropped. 'What did he want?'

'To tell you that he wasn't amused by the morning press. Apparently he disapproves of your bureau,' Bart said fiercely, still stinging from the telephone conversation. 'That shit doesn't bother with you for years and now he wants to tell you what to do.' Getting to his feet, Bart stormed into the bathroom. 'Arrogant bastard!'

Freddie followed him. 'Did he say where he was ringing from?'

Pulling off his pyjamas, Bart turned to face her. 'No, why?'

'I was just wondering whether he was phoning from Eaton Mews North or Yorkshire.'

Bart frowned. 'Would it make a difference?'

'Yes,' Freddie said softly. 'It would.'

All through that endless Sunday Freddie expected her father to arrive. Her nerves tingled when she heard a car door slam, her hands shook over the phone each time it rang. She told herself that she was behaving idiotically, that she was a grown woman with a husband to protect her, but the marks of her childhood were too deep to ignore and Freddie only relaxed when the day ended and she and Bart went up to bed that night, a copy of the magazine lying open on the coverlet.

Whilst Freddie showered, Bart picked up the paper and stared at Greville's face, then carefully he began to doodle on the photograph. With his pen he scribbled an ink moustache and glasses over the glamorous features, added lines and blacked out teeth, and then, with a smile of triumph, he planted a large wart on Greville's chin, complete with hairs.

'You know,' he said innocently when Freddie walked back in, 'he might be a shit, but your father's ageing well.' Winking, he passed her the magazine and watched with relief as she looked at it and then began to laugh, the tyrant of her childhood reduced to a comic strip figure.

The bureau provided Freddie with the fulfilment she needed, and much of the time and attention she would have given to a child, she gave to her clients. At first she was sympathetic but hesitant, but after watching the three advisors she had hired, she soon learned what to say, and how to say it. Not that the three women didn't have their own different methods. Tina Shore was young and vivaciously optimistic. Her catch-phrase 'This is the one' echoed down the phone repeatedly, her quick fingers rifling through the files, discarding or approving, her endless stream of conversation never flagging as she encouraged her clients. At only twenty-eight she was the youngest of the three. Liz Ford was a cool thirty-five. Autocratic, well-bred and glacial she was the favourite of the moneyed clients, especially the men, and was the ideal advisor for the kind of person who wanted a detached assessment without sympathy or gushing enthusiasm. Tall and well dressed, she was married to a stockbroker and had one child. She was as committed to the clients in her own way as Tina was in hers. Of the three, Dot Cummings was the most down-to-earth. At forty-seven, she was happily married to her second husband after her first had left her with three children under ten. Lancashire grit and hard work had resulted in Dot raising her offspring with the minimum of trauma and the maximum of common sense, and she used these qualities to good effect at the bureau.

'I shoot from the hip,' she told Freddie when she came for her interview. 'I've never lied to my clients, never deluded them and never wasted anyone's time by trying to make a couple fit when the magic's missing.'

'How do you know when the magic's there?' Freddie had asked.

Dot leaned forwards, a stocky woman in a navy suit, her eyes steady behind gold-rimmed glasses. 'I just know – like you do.'

Dissimilar as the three women might be, they were the perfect mixture for The 107 Club, as every client could find the type of advisor with whom they felt the most comfortable. So, for the eighteen months, the three women, together with Freddie, coped with the flow of clients, although as time went on the bureau became busier and the work load heavier.

Although Bart was delighted with his wife's success, at the

same time he began to feel a little resentful. At first he had been very much involved with the business, but as the momentum built up and the club began to earn a name for itself, he found he could take a back seat. He did not mind that, but he did resent the hours Freddie worked, for they reduced the time he and she spent together – even though his own business was making him work longer hours and take more frequent trips abroad. When he finally brought up the matter Freddie was apologetic, but surprised.

'Oh, darling, have I been neglecting you?' she said one night when he came home to find her still in the bureau at eight o'clock. Everyone else had gone home, leaving Freddie to pour over a file alone. She looked rapt, her whole concentration on the task in front of her and Bart found himself unexpectedly jealous as he watched her.

'It's just that I want to see more of you, Freddie,' Bart explained, kissing the top of her head. 'Let's go out for dinner.'

Freddie stroked Bart's cheek, but frowned and indicated the file with her hand. 'I'll just finish this first,' she said, glancing back to Daniel Haig's file. 'This man's a television producer. 'He's very successful and very rich but his attitude to women is bizarre. I can't make any sense of it.' She turned back to a report on the file. 'Bart, will you just look at the psychiatric assessment where it says he's inclined to be jealous?'

Resigned, Bart sat down and read the extract out loud. ' "Mr Haig would appear to be very jealous when it comes to his relationships with women. This is probably understandable in the light of his circumstances. Having married a woman he loved deeply, he was distressed to find her in bed with her previous lover only six days after the wedding." ' Bart's eyebrows shot up. 'Where in bed?'

Freddie frowned. 'In bed, in bed. What d'you mean?'

'Were they in bed in the marital home?'

Freddie nodded.

'So the wife obviously wanted Mr Haig to find out, otherwise they would have gone to a hotel.'

'Maybe,' Freddie mused, 'but that's all in the past. What

I'm trying to sort out is Daniel's emotional state at the present time.'

Undoing his coat, Bart turned back to the file and continued to read. ' "Mr Haig has a high profile lifestyle and would like to think he is gregarious by nature, but in reality, he forces himself into behaving like an extrovert when his natural inclination is to be introverted." ' Bart laid down the file and frowned. 'That psychiatrist of yours is a nut.'

Freddie smiled indulgently. 'Thank you for that considered opinion.'

'And do you want to know why?' Bart continued, interrupting her. 'Because it is perfectly obvious to anyone with half a brain that most people on earth would stay at home in comfort rather than be forced to attend tedious cocktail parties. It doesn't take a degree in psychiatry to work that one out.'

Freddie leaned back in her chair. 'Have you finished?'

'No,' Bart said evenly. 'That Malcolm Prentice is a fake. If he was practising on a island somewhere in the back of beyond, the natives would have had him in a pot long since.'

'You are so open-minded,' Freddie said, teasing him. She knew that Bart loathed Malcolm Prentice, and had done ever since she had hired him to interview potential clients. 'You were always against the clients having to see a psychiatrist.'

Bart shook his head. 'Not true. They can see as many as they like. It's probably good company for them. What I object to is the fact we believe what they say.'

'The psychiatrists, or the clients?'

'Both.'

Freddie smiled wryly. 'Why would they lie to us?'

'Dear God, Freddie, you should know more about human nature by now. The clients lie because they have something to hide, and the psychiatrists lie because they want to make it look as though the clients have more to hide, and thereby appear to earn their ridiculous fees. I can remember how accurate Malcolm Prentice was about that Boulton man. After interviewing him for nearly two hours he summed him up as having "difficulties with women." ' Bart raised his eyebrows.

205

'Oh, he had difficulties all right. Mainly because he liked to tie them up with garden hoses and spray them with insecticide ... '

'Boulton was an oddity,' Freddie said, trying not to laugh. 'He ended up working at a garden centre, didn't he?'

'Ho, ho!' Freddie said drily.

'And if my memory serves me correctly, one of your first clients, Hortense Duval, was another one who took Mr Prentice in,' Bart continued, determined to make his point. 'His psychiatric report described her as,' he paused to savour the quote,' "uncomplicated and conservative" – even though she turned out to have a record in France for insurance fraud. I mean, how uncomplicated can you get for Christ's sake?'

Freddie's was serene. 'OK, smart arse, so you've made your point. But neither Boulton nor Duval ever got on the bureau's books – '

'But they would have done, if we had relied solely on what Malcolm Prentice said.'

'You know something, Bart?' Freddie said sweetly, 'I'm glad you're not here to help me out all the time, because to put it bluntly, you really get up – '

'Coming back to Daniel Haig,' Bart said, grinning, 'what do you intend to do about him? From what I've now read,' he tapped the file and assumed a pompous tone, 'it seems to me that he has allowed himself to fall in love with a woman who could not fit into his lifestyle. This is probably due to the fact that either he doesn't really want to get involved with her, or that he is somewhat peculiar and can only love a woman who is totally dependent on him.' Bart grimaced. 'But if she was totally dependent that wouldn't be satisfactory either because she couldn't join in his lifestyle and he would soon resent that.'

Freddie raised her eyebrows, enjoying Bart's performance. 'So what do you suggest?'

'It is my opinion that you should keep Mr Daniel Haig on a short leash. Don't let him get too involved with anyone just yet.'

'But he's only interested in Penny ... '

'And how does she feel about all of this?'

Freddie thought for a moment, her judgement factual, as it always was in business. 'She feels pressurised, and she's not sure that she could cope with his way of life.'

'Then there isn't a problem,' Bart said, slamming the file shut. 'She's not really committed.'

'Just because she can't fit into his social life?'

'A man's lifestyle matters to him. It's important, Freddie.'

Freddie glanced up as he said the words and looked into his eyes. The statement did not refer to Daniel Haig, but to Bart himself. In the words Bart was sending out a warning to his wife. His expression was as loving as it always was, but the implication of what he said was not lost on Freddie, and with a little jolt of anxiety she got to her feet.

'So?' she said, leaning against the desk and running her high-heeled foot up Bart's leg. 'Where are you taking me?'

'Dinner?'

'Sounds good,' Freddie said, smiling seductively as her foot wandered higher.

Bart caught hold of her calf and returned the smile. 'But then again, if you're not hungry ... '

That night Freddie dreamed of Cambuscan. Even though it was early May, the blackthorn winter was reluctant to leave and had gathered all its forces to chill the country for a final few bitter days. The pavilion looked lost under the frost, its little pillars melting into the white background, its steps smothered with ice, the bay tree sinister and black against the steel sky. Slowly, without effort, she wandered beside the lake and glanced down into the frozen water, but nothing stirred. A quick sensation of being watched made Freddie turn back to the house. Yet no one looked out from any of the windows and after a long moment she moved on under the forbidding sky.

Dreaming still, Freddie remembered that according to legend this was the time when the Ice Saints walked, coming over the moors and tapping on the windows to call for the damned. Suddenly she could hear her father's voice retelling the old story and imagine the white fingers pressed at the glass panes, every noise whistling down from the fierce moors and every creak in the night living proof to the frightened child of the dead feet walking, walking, coming for her …

In her dream in Cambuscan's icy garden, Freddie trembled, noticing how the light was failing and how malevolent shadows were crouching amongst the black bushes, the shadow of the bay tree uncomprehendingly turning into the shape of a figure. Terrified, Freddie hurried towards the house, but fell suddenly and struggled desperately to get up as she heard the sounds of many running feet behind her …

In that instant Freddie woke, crying out as a dark sense of fear swallowed her whole.

Yet the morning after, the dream was almost forgotten as Freddie interviewed Chris Ward in the drawing room above the bureau. Having already talked to her over the phone, Freddie suspected that Chris would be an ideal advisor. But when Chris came to see her, Freddie was puzzled by the woman's obvious nervousness. Easy conversation did not relax her, and neither did the drink Freddie gave her, and after a little while Freddie began to wonder if Chris Ward was suitable for the job after all.

'You've had some marvellous experience,' Freddie said admiringly. 'Eleven years working as an advisor – you must have had some triumphs.'

'Some,' she agreed, her knees together, her hands on her lap. She was middle-aged, with dark, permed hair, her make-up restricted to powder and lipstick. Under level eyebrows, her eyes were clear but wary, and when she moved all her actions had the slow steadiness of someone bone tired.

Instinctively, Freddie began to question her about her personal life, sure that she was professionally adept, and that the key to her nervousness might be due to some emotional problem.

'Your details said that you worked in Bath before,' Freddie smiled easily. 'How long have you been in London?'

'Six weeks.'

'It's a hard town to settle into, isn't it?' Freddie said calmly. 'So many of our clients find that loneliness is their greatest problem.'

Chris blinked quickly.

'They see people all rushing around looking like they've got somewhere to go to, or someone to meet … ' Freddie paused, Chris's eyes on her, ' … it makes them feel useless, and very alone.'

'My husband died at the beginning of the year.'

Freddie sighed, then refilled Chris's glass. 'You must miss him very much.'

Chris nodded. 'I was married to him for over thirty years – I dare say that's longer than you've been alive. We did everything together. The house, the garden, holidays, everything.' She sipped her drink anxiously. 'When he was at work, I went to my work in the bureau and we'd meet up afterwards – sometimes go for a bite to eat or a drink – and then talk about what we'd done all day. I can't seem to function without him. I'm not very capable alone.' Chris stopped, suddenly alarmed. 'I shouldn't have said any of this, should I?'

Freddie frowned. 'Why not?'

'You'll think that I can't do the job, that I'll be too caught up with my own problems to worry about other people – but you'd be wrong. I was a good counsellor, and I helped a lot of people before – and I can again, if you give me a chance. Honestly, I can.'

Freddie drained her glass and leaned forward in her chair. 'I have over a thousand people on the books now … '

'So many?'

Freddie nodded. 'Yes, so many. You see, although the registration fee is high, people come to us because they trust us. They know that we'll check the clients out and that everything is confidential and that they're safe. That matters to everyone – but especially if you happen to be on the board of a leading bank.' Freddie paused. 'People can't afford to be lonely, but most of all they can't afford to be seen to be lonely. It's a stigma in this society.' She returned to the question of her clients. 'In amongst those thousand clients, I probably have about two hundred widows or widowers. They are the people who have two burdens – they are lonely and they are grieving. Chris, the other three advisors are all first class, but

209

none of them have your experience. I would very much like you to work here.'

'You would?'

'I would!' Freddie said happily, watching as Chris smiled and relaxed.

'I was so afraid ... '

'That I wouldn't take you because you've been bereaved?' Freddie raised her eyes. 'God, Chris, to lose your husband was tragic – I can't imagine how that must feel – but just think how you can help all the others. I never know what to say to them, but you do. You can understand them, and that's all that anyone can really hope for, isn't it?'

Chris remembered the conversation as she watched Freddie that morning. In the year which followed she became her right-hand woman, Freddie's closest ally in the bureau. As she was much quieter than the other advisors, Chris attracted the people who were either shy or badly hurt, and before long she had built up an impressive list of clients. Careful, thorough and reliable, she was the best listener of all of them, and kept long hours at the bureau, taking calls at seven o'clock at night, or eight in the morning. Knowing that she could trust Chris implicitly, Freddie never minded her late nights or early morning arrivals, and often peered through the window from upstairs at seven-thirty to see Chris unlock the front door and make her way into The 107 Club.

All the same, Freddie did not relinquish any of her own responsibilities or clients, and week by week the bureau became busier, reaching its most frenetic around Christmas when so many people were afraid of spending another festive season alone.

'I hate bloody Christmas,' Jao had said the previous night, 'and I hate bloody men.'

Freddie raised her eyes at Trisha and leaned back in her chair. The kitchen of Dorman Square hadn't altered one jot, and as her hand reached into the ginger jar which always held liquorice, she heard Bea's voice singing low from the bedroom at the end of the hall.

'I just can't seem to meet anyone worth knowing ... '

'So come over to the club one night and we'll go through the books,' Freddie said evenly. 'I've asked you a million times.'

'I don't want a misfit.'

'How the hell can you judge without looking first?' Freddie said, her tone exasperated. 'You might find someone to spend Christmas with.'

Trisha nodded at her niece. 'It's a good idea … '

'And you can shut up!' Jao snapped. 'Just because Charlie's all over you again.'

Incensed, Trisha got up and walked out. Freddie glanced back to Jao. 'How do you know that it's back on?'

'She's shaving her legs every night,' Jao replied phlegmatically. 'That always means that they're having sex.'

'Oh God, whatever happened to feminine intuition?' Freddie asked, laughing.

Half slumped over the kitchen table, Jao laid her head down heavily on one slender arm. Her blonde hair pooled under the overhead light and her voice was quiet when she spoke. 'I got fired again.'

'You get fired more often than a gun,' Freddie said drily. 'So what are you going to do now?'

Jao shrugged, 'I've got an interview with a vet tomorrow.'

'For a job, or for treatment?'

Laughing, Jao sat up, her good humour restored. 'All right, you've had your joke. It might be OK.'

'Except for the fact that you don't like animals.'

'I like small animals.'

'So what happens if he has to look after a cow?'

Jao rolled her eyes. 'He's a London vet – how many cows do you know in Hammersmith?'

'Four footed, or two?'

Laughing Jao got to her feet and made them both a coffee and a sandwich, then she sat down again and after eating half her sandwich greedily, looked over to Freddie.

'So, how's Bart?'

'Well,' Freddie replied evenly. 'He's away at the moment.'

'He's travelling a lot now, isn't he?'

Freddie shrugged. 'The business needs him, and he needs the business.'

They continued to eat in silence, Freddie thoughtful. She knew how much the architectural practice meant to her husband. As her business had expanded, so had his, and he took advantage of his success by taking on new partners and travelling more. The considerable money he made was welcome, but not as precious as the work itself. It had filled his life and given him satisfaction when his life was empty after Gill's death, and when Freddie's business had taken off he had found himself turning back to his profession for company again.

Although still very much in love with Freddie, Bart was deeply disappointed that they had not had children and now seemed unlikely to have any. As a release he poured his unfulfilled feelings into his work – just as Freddie had done. Both of them were happy and secure with each other, but by the time eight years of marriage had passed, each was compensating for the lack of a child by focusing hard on their work.

'Bart will be home soon though?' Jao asked, cutting into Freddie's thoughts.

'Of course he will,' Freddie replied, feeling a quick knock of anxiety as she changed the subject.

At that precise moment Bart was in Chicago and had just ordered some coffee and sandwiches to be sent up to his room before sitting down on the bed to check over a sheaf of reports. The work was well done, the drawings his firm had made were accurate and they gave him a sense of pleasure as he scrutinised them. For nearly two hours he worked and when he finally looked at his watch he swore, remembering how he had promised to ring Freddie. His hand moved towards the phone hurriedly.

'Freddie?'

'Bart, hi! I was wondering why you hadn't called.'

A twinge of guilt nagged at him. 'I was working, sweetheart, sorry.'

'No matter,' Freddie replied, pushing away a client's file

which was lying on top of the bed. 'I was working too.' She paused. 'So when is my favourite hod-carrier coming back home?'

'At the weekend. I'll be in around ten, Saturday.'

Freddie smiled, relaxing with relief. 'I'm looking forward to seeing you.'

'Me too,' Bart said warmly. 'Oh by the way, I heard something interesting today on the grape-vine. An old friend of mine, Warren Roberts, has just opened a restaurant in London – d'you remember him?'

Freddie frowned. 'No, I never met him, did I?'

'Oh, maybe not, perhaps I just told you about him,' Bart replied. 'Anyway, I've got the telephone number so I thought we should get in touch.'

'Fine,' Freddie replied, holding onto the receiver tightly. 'I love you.'

Bart smiled and closed his eyes, savouring the words. 'I love you too, darling.'

'We'll have a good time, won't we?'

'The best.'

'Bart … ' Freddie said softly, over the transatlantic line, 'hurry home.'

Chapter Fourteen

The restaurant was in Maiden Lane. With its low ceiling and its mullioned windows, it had the kind of dark glamour which invites confidences and love affairs. As Freddie and Bart walked in, they noticed one of London's brightest literary agents, an impressive art collector, and an actress over from Los Angeles, all seated at strategic tables, the surrounding crowd talking loudly as a pianist played the blues in an alcove behind.

Carefully avoiding a large Christmas tree, and threading their way between the tables, Freddie spotted Theo Gunther and rushed over to have a word with him, returning to her table a few moments later to find Bart deep in conversation with a fair-haired man.

'Freddie,' Bart said, sliding his arm around her bare shoulders, 'this is my old friend, Warren. Warren Roberts.'

Freddie smiled, extending her hand. 'Well, it's lovely to meet you at last. Bart told me you were friends in New York.'

'For a while,' Warren agreed, his tone composed, but reserved.

'Your restaurant's wonderful,' Freddie continued, surprised by the stiffness of his manner. 'And you've got some pretty impressive guests.'

Warren glanced around, as though to see for himself, and Freddie stole a look at him as he did so. He was about six feet tall, slimly built, his eyes deep set under heavy brows. Although he was fair, he did not have the delicacy of Harry's pale, fine features, and his skin was darkly tanned, his mouth set. To Freddie, he gave the impression of someone trying

214

hard to control himself and she found him oddly disturbing.

'Well if the food lives up to the guests, you should be onto a winner, Warren,' Bart said. 'I feel quite upset that you don't need our friendly support.'

'Some friend,' he replied smiling evenly. 'I wasn't even invited to your wedding.'

'Oh, you mustn't mind,' Freddie replied. 'It was a very quiet affair.'

'Besides, you weren't even back in London then,' Bart said, picking up the menu. 'So don't try to work a guilt trip on me.'

Smiling in response, Warren glanced over to Freddie. 'I hope you enjoy your meal,' he said and moved off.

'Brrr!' Freddie said, watching him go.

Bart glanced at her. 'Huh?'

'C – O – L – D,' Freddie spelt out. 'That friend of yours is a mite on the uptight side, wouldn't you say?'

'Warren?' Bart replied, surprised. 'No, he's just a little shy, that's all.' His gaze drifted across the restaurant to where Warren was standing, talking to a new arrival. He seemed perfectly at ease, and when he moved away, he exchanged a few words with another diner. 'He's OK. He's enjoying himself. Look at him.'

'I'd rather look at the menu,' Freddie replied, reading down the courses and then glancing back to Bart. 'How long have you known Warren?'

'I met him in New York about – what, it must be ten years ago now. He'd opened up a restaurant there and was a huge success at the age of only twenty-nine.' Bart smiled at the memory. 'He was always quiet though, but charming – a man it took a long time to know.'

'Was it worth it?'

'Was *what* worth it?'

'Was getting to know him worth the effort?'

Bart was surprised by her tone. It was unusual for Freddie to dislike anyone on sight. 'Yes, it was. He comes from a tough background and I admired the way he got to the top against the odds.' Bart paused, expecting Freddie to probe him further, but when she remained silent he went on. 'Warren was

215

one of the few Englishmen who made it big in New York. But when he did, he sold out and just dropped out of sight for a while.' He looked at Freddie. 'There was a rumour that he got married but I'm not sure – though now he's back I'll find out.'

Whatever Freddie thought of Warren Roberts, the food his restaurant served was superb. Course after course appeared exquisitely presented, delicate sauces accompanying the succulent meats, the vegetables fresh and the wines either warmed to the right temperature or chilled to perfection. After each course, the dishes were cleared quickly, the next course following smoothly, the meal culminating in a delectable dessert.

As Bart was finishing his cheese, Warren came over to the table again.

'Sit down, Warren, and join us,' Bart said. Warren joined them, smiling distantly at Freddie.

'That was a great meal,' Bart enthused.

'Thank you,' Warren said, genuinely pleased by the compliment as he turned to Freddie. 'Did you enjoy it, Mrs Wallace?'

'Call me Freddie – and yes, the dinner was delicious, Mr Roberts.'

'Warren.'

'Warren,' she repeated, surprised by how uncomfortable she felt. She was never ill at ease with people, and yet this man was making her feel gauche. 'Bart told me that you had an amazing restaurant in New York. He said it was very select.'

Warren smiled. 'Oh, I am very select.'

'She's intrigued by your past, Warren,' Bart said smiling and signalling to the waiter for more coffee. 'Freddie can't help grilling people. She does it for a living.'

'Yes, I heard you owned some marriage bureau.'

'The 107 Club,' Freddie said, rising to her own defence and suspecting that he was laughing at her.

Warren's expression was calm. 'Is there much of a call for a matchmaker?'

'Too much,' Freddie replied bluntly, adding, 'are you married?'

216

'I was.'

'But not now … Well, perhaps you should come and see me, I could introduce you to some very nice women.'

Warren flinched, but Bart looked up and grinned. 'She never offered me the same service,' he said lightly. 'You ought to take her up on it.'

Freddie glanced over to her husband, surprised that he hadn't noticed the animosity between her and Warren. Tactfully she changed the subject. 'It must be hard work running a place like this.'

'I've known harder. You see, all this,' he indicated the restaurant with one sweep of his hand, 'came about through hard work. I was born in Glasgow and brought up in Stepney, had little education and less opportunity, but I learned fast – at the Savoy, in fact – and then went to New York with private backing to open my own place ten years ago. It made a name for itself and it became a very "select" watering hole.'

Freddie bristled. 'I meant it as a compliment. I didn't mean to offend you.'

'You didn't,' Warren said, adjusting his jacket and turning to Bart. 'I've got to circulate, I'm afraid. Come in again soon, I'd like to catch up on old times.' He stood up. 'And tonight you and your wife must be my guests.'

Politely Freddie thanked him. Bart pressed him to stay.

'No, honestly, I can't,' Warren said, pausing suddenly and glancing back to Freddie. His face was expressionless. 'It was a pleasure to meet you.'

'And you,' Freddie said, reverting to her usual charm as she smiled. 'You are a very interesting gentleman.'

'Oh no,' Warren said quietly, 'I'm not interesting and I'm no gentleman – and no matter how rich or successful I get, I remain a waiter at heart.'

Bart was delighted with the evening and told Freddie so repeatedly, his pleasure enhanced by his reunion with Warren Roberts. 'I can't believe it, you know he's hardly changed since I last saw him – and that must be five years ago now.' He tugged off his socks as he sat on the edge of the bed. 'He

217

looked well, didn't he?' Bart paused, thinking. 'But he's a quiet one. You know something, Freddie? He's a loner; he doesn't really fit in and he never has, although sometimes I wonder if he wants to keep himself apart. Other times I think he's just shy. He's a weird guy.'

'You can say that again.'

Bart turned round to look at Freddie. 'You don't like him, do you?'

Momentarily wrong-footed, Freddie glided into the bathroom and called out to him through the door. 'He just seems so ... uneasy. Like someone who holds themself in all the time and never relaxes.' She leaned towards the mirror and looked at her face critically. 'I felt uncomfortable with him, Bart, and to be honest he's not the kind of man I'd like to spend time with.' She took off her clothes and walked out of the bathroom with only a towel wrapped around her. 'You're more my type.'

Smiling, Bart stood up and opened his arms to her. Freddie undid the towel and stood naked in front of him before slowly letting the towel drop to the floor. Then she moved towards him, her breasts and thighs pushing against his body as she unfastened the belt on his trousers and glided her hands across his stomach and back. The muscles on his buttocks felt tight under her fingers, his excitement obvious as she continued to undress him.

'You forgot your dessert,' she said, smiling and pushing him back onto the bed, her mouth moving over his.

Hungrily Bart's arms fastened around her as he pulled her over and rolled on top of her, his lips moving over her neck and breasts. Then the phone rang ...

'Jesus Christ!'

Freddie continued to kiss him. 'Let it ring.'

'I can't, darling, it might be business,' Bart replied, as he answered the call. For several minutes he made notes on the pad by the bed and then put down the phone and turned back to her. 'Sorry, Freddie, but I have to go out. There's been an emergency on site.'

'You're an architect, not a doctor, Bart!' Freddie exclaimed, infuriated, as she pulled the sheets around her and turned away from him.

Bart made no reply and dressed hurriedly, finally laying a hand on her shoulder as he was about to leave. 'I'll be back soon, I promise.'

'Huh!' was all she said.

Chapter Fifteen

The patch of kirsch was sticky and resistant to the cloth as Warren Roberts bent down and began to rub at the stain on the dance floor. At eight in the morning none of the staff had arrived yet, but Warren was always there early to check the takings from the previous night and to approve the menus for the following evening. It was his policy not to open at lunchtimes, and the restaurant offered only dinners and a small dance floor for the select few. The whole place was no larger than the drawing room at Cambuscan, the limited space deliberately forcing intimacy and sometimes indiscreet conversation.

At first, Warren had been uncertain what kind of style the restaurant should adopt. He knew that he had a first class financial brain and had hired probably the best chef in London, but he was still a novice in the art of creating atmospheres and found that part of his business difficult. Having trained as a waiter, he had learned the hard way that customers wanted first class food, first class service and comfort. But he knew there was something else, something indefinable which made a good restaurant great, and he had been determined to find it in London, just as he had in New York.

Weeks of research had followed. Always the perfectionist, Warren investigated all forms of decor, beginning with the interior designers, then seeking inspiration at the British Museum, the Wallace Collection and finally in the clubs, both homosexual and straight. At first, little seemed to fire his imagination and the uncompleted restaurant in Maiden Lane waited uneasily for its identity, like a baby waiting for a name at its christening.

The story of his life, as he had summarised it to Freddie, was correct but abridged, a version fit for public consumption. The truth was different. His parents had been poor, unglamorously, blood-spitting poor Polish immigrants. Their home had been a rented flat in a Glasgow neighbourhood hounded by violence, poverty and vast flanks of condemned tenements. They had moved to Stepney when Warren was nine and things had improved slightly. His father secured a good job with a furrier who made coats for Harrods, although his working conditions remained miserable. A skylight provided good illumination but no other comfort; in the summer he sweated and in the winter he was stung by the freezing cold and glare of snow overhead.

As a child, when Warren Roberts was still Dani Rabinski, Warren visited his father frequently, watching as he took down the tied notches of hides and began to work on them, scraping, stretching and cutting, his tools precious to him and washed and polished each night before he left. It never occurred to his father to question his trade or wonder why he was making luxury goods for a pittance of a wage when they would be sold on for exorbitant amounts. It never occurred to *him*, but his son considered this a weakness on his father's part, especially as his mother repeatedly bemoaned the injustice of the situation.

'You kill yourself, and for what?' she would say, doling out their dinner, her spoon banging on the sides of the tin pan. 'When is old man Levin going to give you a rise? When?' she pestered, knowing the answer as well as he did. 'You should go ask for yourself,' she continued. 'You don't ask; you don't get.'

But old man Rabinski never asked, too afraid that he would lose the job and the only means of providing for his wife and children.

Warren's childhood was, of necessity, brief. His schooling was basic and he was encouraged to get out and make a living

221

fast. The choices open to him were limited, but he already knew with certainty what he wanted.

'A waiter ... ' his mother said happily when he came home to give her the news. He had always been the dark horse, the quiet one who liked reading and who had caused little trouble, apart from the occasional outburst of inexplicable rage. But he had also been smarter than her other sons and expected to do better.

'You could get on,' his mother encouraged him. 'Why should you waste your life mopping up other people's spills?' Her voice was quick with ambition for her son. 'You could even get your own restaurant one day.'

So Dani Rabinski began his apprenticeship in a hotel in West Kensington where his keen intelligence was soon observed. Amongst the sloppy and uninterested boys, he stood out. He was cleaner than most and asked pertinent questions, though his solitary nature made him few friends. His employers rewarded his quiet diligence with a rise, the chef and maître d'hotel looking upon him as reliable and therefore valuable. Dani never turned up for work late or untidy; he was never rude to the customers; and if he did not attract many friends over the first few years, he did attract many regular customers who liked his composure and listened to his advice when they ordered.

All seemed to be going well for Dani until, on his nineteenth birthday, he arrived home covered in blood.

'My God, it's a wonder you weren't killed!' his mother moaned, dabbing the blood off his face with a flannel. 'Get hold of the police,' she called to her husband frantically.

Dani gripped her hand firmly. 'Leave it alone.'

'Leave it?' she repeated, incredulously. 'No!'

Her son tugged at her arm. 'Please, leave it. For me.'

His mother pulled away. 'No! This is serious, you have to take a stand. The people who do this kind of thing are little more than thugs.'

'*Leave me alone!*' Dani shouted.

Mrs Rabinski blinked and stood back as he walked out.

Her husband was standing by the door.

'What happened?' he asked, dumbfounded.

'He just went crazy … '

And he went away – all the way to New York. Stunned by his own loss of control, Dani left London and arrived in Manhattan with little money and a massive parcel of guilt. The fight in which he had been injured was the result of two fellow waiters taunting him. At first Dani had not responded, but finally, when they had called him a coward, he had reacted and struck out. With the first blow, all his pent up violence erupted and when the first man slumped to the ground unconscious, Dani continued to beat the second. Blow after blow he pummelled into the man, blindly enraged, and was only stopped by the intervention of the other waiters.

When Dani realised what he had done, he felt sickened and afraid, knowing that he had been out of control. The only solution was to get away. In New York he found menial work at the Plaza and drilled every emotion out of his life, learning to control every thought and action. Endless runs around Central Park burned off energy and aggression, constant exercise in gyms left him exhausted, and silent. He said little to anyone, unless he was at work and then he became another person, shyly charming and at ease with the customers. Driven constantly in an attempt to escape his own personality, Dani learned his trade thoroughly and impressed his employers over a period of years, so much so that when they found out that he was undertaking a course in business studies at night, they paid his fees in order to secure his future services.

Voraciously ambitious, Dani pushed himself to the limit mentally and physically. He was rewarded with passes in his studies although he was not satisfied with such nondescript achievements and resat the examinations, earning distinctions a year later. The change in his circumstances was obvious as he reached his mid-twenties. Fanatically careful with his finances, he had managed to save enough money to run a discreet car and keep himself soberly, but well dressed. Only his social life refused to flourish – until he met Louise Fowler who came to work as a receptionist at the hotel. With her, Dani found he could express himself, and relaxed more, loving her and beginning finally to enjoy life.

It was Dani and Louise's shared ambition which led him to change course and apply for several jobs in hotel administration. Although he failed his first few interviews, he was finally accepted to become the under-manager of an exclusive hotel in Manhattan with an international clientele. At the Plaza, his employers were incensed with his disloyalty after having paid for his management studies. But they were unable to deny the truth when Dani pointed out that there were no suitable jobs available for him in the forseeable future – and he was in a hurry. The hurry was due to the fact that he finally knew exactly what he wanted – to marry Louise and run his own restaurant in New York.

But before Dani could fulfill his ambitions, he needed to bury the person he had been and he changed his identity. In a final gesture, Dani Rabinski wrote his Polish name on a piece of paper and then leaned out and dropped the scrap into the grey water of the East River, watching as it floated waywardly down towards the open sea. Without any apparent emotion or pain, Warren Roberts was born. He had no mother and no father and gave birth to himself, not in blood but in silence.

'How could you!' Freddie screamed, throwing an ashtray across the room as Bart ducked, the glass smashing against the wall behind him.

Astonished by the uncharacteristic outburst, Bart started towards her with his hands raised. 'Cut it out! I have to go, you know that.'

Freddie backed away and Jean Allen, the housekeeper, beat a hasty retreat into the kitchen.

'I hate you for this!' Freddie shouted, her voice raised with frustration.

'I have to go,' Bart repeated, trying to reason with her.

'Why?' his wife asked, facing him, the barrier of a couch between them. 'You know that the party's arranged for Saturday, just as you know that Dione's made a special trip over to see us. Does nothing matter any more, except your work?'

'That's not fair!'

'*Not fair!*' she bellowed. 'What's "not fair?" You go away so much of the time now, Bart. Why?' Her voice dropped, sudden anxiety filling her. 'Don't you still love me?'

'Of course I love you,' he said, smiling weakly. 'Frankly, darling, I don't know why you're making such a fuss.' He pushed his hands deep into his trouser pockets, offering her no contact. 'It's always been part of my job to travel. I have to go, but I'll be home soon, darling. I promise.'

'Well, you just take care of yourself, OK?' Freddie said, feeling drained, and knowing that whatever she said, Bart would still go.

In Dorman Square, Bea Wilkie was baking a cake for the pianist at the Bayswater hotel, who was celebrating his thirty-ninth birthday just before Christmas. She had been hard at work all day, struggling with a complicated recipe and the intricate icing instructions, her fingers covered in white sugar when Jao came home. Without a word of greeting, she walked into the kitchen, glanced at Pam who was reading, and then made herself a sandwich. The wall clock ticked over their heads, the lights across the square visible from the kitchen window as dusk fell.

'Well, hello to you too,' Bea said drily, watching her daughter.

'Who's that for?' Jao responded sulkily, pointing to the cake.

'Jack. It's his birthday tonight, and I thought I'd make a surprise for him.'

'It certainly will be when he sees it,' Jao said sarcastically. 'It's not right. The icing should be more set by now.'

Steadily Bea wiped her hands on her apron and glanced across the kitchen table. 'OK, so who rattled your cage?'

'No one,' Jao replied. 'I'm just tired, that's all.'

'I can't see what you're so tired about,' Pam chimed in, looking up from her book. 'You're hardly rushed off your feet at that shop.'

Jao was immediately on the defensive. 'It's a surgery – and what the hell do you know about it anyway?'

225

'Not as much as I should! But then I never had your opportunities, did I?' Pam continued plaintively. 'I never had the chance to make something out of my life.'

Bea sighed and raised her eyes heavenwards, her attention returning to the cake.

'All right, so if you'd had the chance, what would you have done? Gone to university?' Jao queried, her tone combative.

Pam hesitated momentarily, but recovered. 'I could have done a lot of things. I was bright at school.' She glanced at Bea. 'You ask your mother and she'll tell you. I was the smartest there by a long chalk ... ' She trailed off, her cheeks colouring as she said defiantly, 'I could have been a doctor, if I'd wanted to.'

'Oh, do me a favour!' Jao responded sharply. 'You haven't the brains ... '

'Jao!' Bea snapped, as Pam's face paled. 'That's not fair, take it back!'

'Why?' her daughter countered nastily. 'Pam isn't clever, so why should I lie about it just to make her feel good? We're always so bloody careful of her feelings and she's just a bad tempered old maid.'

Taking in a deep breath, Pam glanced away, her eyes filling with tears. It was an old ploy.

'You've never liked me, not like you like Trisha. I was always the odd one out.'

'I want you to apologise to Pam now,' Bea said sternly, her eyes fixed on her daughter.

'Why?'

Bea leaned across the table, her voice threatening. 'Because you have no right to speak to anyone the way you've just spoken to her.'

Jao's face was sullen. 'But she's – '

'Firstly your elder, secondly your flesh and blood, and thirdly because she is a human being and you can't go around striking out at people just because you happen to feel bloody-minded.' Bea's tone was dark. 'I'm ashamed of you, Jao. I've never known you to be so spiteful.'

Jao glanced round at her aunt, her voice strangled. 'OK ... I'm sorry.'

226

'And so you should be.'

'That's enough!' Bea said impatiently. 'Just let the matter drop, please.'

As Jao and Pam glared hotly at each other, Bea leaned across for the birthday candles and began to arrange them on the cake. 'I think Jack will be really thrilled,' she said to no one in particular. 'I can't wait to see his face.'

Pam wasn't listening, instead she was brooding on Jao's words. 'You've been spoilt, that's your trouble,' she said.

Irritated, Bea looked up as Jao turned on her aunt again. 'Spoilt! Hah! That's a laugh, especially since Bea's been carrying you for years.'

'Stop it!' her mother said angrily, walking round the table to face her sister and her daughter. 'What the hell is the matter with you both?'

'I'm fed up!' Jao shouted,

'I have more reason to be fed up than you. You've got your life ahead of you,' Pam wailed brokenly. 'What is there for me?'

'Oh, shut up and get out of my way!' Jao replied, pushing her aunt to one side in temper.

Pam stepped back, caught off balance, and immediately bumped into her sister who was standing right behind her. As if in slow motion, Bea fell backwards, losing her own footing and extending her hand towards the table to break her fall. Suddenly aware of what she had done, Jao turned, watching the dangerously slow movement of her mother's arm as it arced over the table and thudded, deadly, into the birthday cake.

All three women looked at the ruined mess, Bea's eyes huge with disbelief, as the phone rang.

Jao walked over to it with stiff legs. 'Hello?'

'Hi, Jao, it's Freddie. Is Bea there?'

Jao glanced over to her mother and said sheepishly. 'It's Freddie. She wants a word.'

'I can think of several at this moment, and not one of them has more than four letters,' Bea replied, snatching the phone from her daughter's hand. 'If you've got troubles, Freddie, go to hell, but if you want to go out on the town, you're welcome.'

227

'Would an invitation to a party on Saturday be any good to you?' Freddie asked, smiling down the line.

The house was blazing with lights, the porch welcoming with its boxed bay trees strung with ribbons and Christmas decorations. As Jean Allen let in the guests, the sounds of laughter and conversation poured out into the street, huge arrangements of flowers flanking an impressive buffet in the dining room. The chill of the December evening dampened no one's spirits as Dione held court in the drawing room surrounded by admirers whilst her husband read alone in the library. Freddie, dressed in ivy green, stood by the fireplace in the hall, welcoming everyone as they walked in.

'Hello, Penn,' she said, kissing his bearded cheek. 'How's the new book coming on?'

Pennsylvania gasped with delight. 'Oh, Freddie,' he said, his voice breaking. 'How lovely, how lovely to see you. Are you well?'

'Blooming,' she answered. 'Go on in, Dione's here. I told her you were coming.'

'Dione!' he sighed. 'Oh, I know I'm emotional, but it will be so lovely to see her again.' Penn sighed dreamily. 'I still miss you in the shop, Freddie.'

'I miss you too,' Freddie replied, smiling at the memory of Penn's corsetted figure, the Egyptian urns which flanked the window, and the smell of old papers coming from the drawer where he kept the naval maps.

'Have you brought someone with you, Penn?'

He shook his head. 'I have no luck in love. But never mind me, you're happy aren't you?'

'Blissfully,' Freddie replied, turning her attention to the new arrivals.

Bea was dressed in black velvet, her hair flicked around her face, her lips deep vermilion to show off her immaculate teeth. Behind her, Jao and Trisha were deep in conversation, Trisha wearing a pale shift, Jao sparce in a lace dress and a pair of long evening boots. Waving, Freddie called out to them and hugged each of them in turn.

'Where's Pam?'

'Crying self-pityingly into her sherry,' Jao said, glancing round. 'So where are all the eligible men?'

'Not here, you chump!' Freddie replied. 'We'll go through the books next week and find you someone.'

Jao nodded half-heartedly. 'Not that I expect anything.'

'Freddie!' a voice said, interrupting her.

Both women turned to see Dione walking towards them, a glass in one hand and an obscure Count on the other.

Jao's eyes brightened as she turned to Freddie. 'Who's he?'

'Count Leopold ... '

'Count me in!' Jao said, smoothing her dress and weaving towards the man with a determined air. A moment later she was engaging him in deep conversation. Freddie smiled at Bea.

'You know,' she said wryly, 'if only we could get her to be less shy with men.'

Bea laughed and then, spotting someone she knew, moved off. Freddie turned to Dione. Her hair was pulled into an immaculate French pleat, her make-up a flawless patina on her fair skin. By then at least fifty-five she still looked no more than forty, thanks to the continued magic of Signora Guardi in Florence.

'Wonderful party, my dear,' Dione said, genuinely impressed. 'You have to come over to Milan again soon. I really can't bear all these excuses you keep giving me. I thought Harry was bad enough, but really ... '

'They're not excuses, Dione,' Freddie answered. 'I have a business to run.'

'Which I have heard all about, but never seen.' Dione linked arms with Freddie and raised her eyebrows. 'So, do I get a tour of the famous 107 Club, or not?'

They walked downstairs to the bureau together, using the back staircase, Freddie flicking on the lights and pushing open the heavy glass doors silently. The full elegance of the reception area made Dione smile, and when Freddie showed her into her exquisite office, she glanced round and nodded with satisfaction.

229

'Very chic,' she said, sitting down and crossing her legs. 'But where do you keep all the notes?'

Like a magician, Freddie pressed a concealed button under her desk and the false front of one wall opened to reveal row upon row of files, alphabetically arranged.

'Goodness, so many!' Dione exclaimed, her eyes raking down the stacks. 'How *do* you find partners for all of them?'

'I don't,' Freddie replied, sitting down. 'I just pair up the lucky ones. I sometimes think that I'm not in the matchmaking business, more like the gambling world.'

'So love comes down to luck, does it?' Dione asked, feigning innocence.

Since she had arrived that evening, Dione had been aware of a change in her beloved Freddie. Nothing obvious, just a subtle difference in her which was worrying. At first Dione put it down to her imagination, but after watching Freddie with her guests she had realised that Freddie's gaiety was a little too frantic, and her hospitality just a little too intense. Lovely as she was, and Freddie *was* in splendid shape, she seemed to Dione to have lost some of her serenity, and that, more than anything else, made Dione anxious.

'Is love all down to luck, Freddie?' she repeated.

Two clear blue eyes met hers. 'I'm worried about Bart.'

'Oh?'

Freddie pushed her hair away from her forehead. 'He's travelling a lot. I suppose you've already noticed that he's not here tonight ... '

'Not really, my dear. But then I have a husband who prides himself on being socially invisible, so I'm not the best person to judge.'

'I started this bureau,' Freddie said softly, 'to keep myself occupied when I didn't get pregnant. I wanted it to be a success and I really believed that when I stopped thinking about having a baby day and night I would conceive.' She paused. 'But I didn't, and although Bart and I are still happy, he misses a child as much as I do. So, what's happened?' She raised her eyebrows. 'We did what everyone else does – what all my clients do, in fact – we concentrated on our work to take

230

our minds off things. The trouble is that we both concentrated so hard that we've started to grow apart.' Her eyes filled with tears and Dione leapt to her feet, wrapping her arm around Freddie's shoulder.

'Oh dear,' she said simply. 'Trouble in paradise.'

'I love him so much,' Freddie went on, helplessly. 'And I know he loves me, it's just that we've drifted and we can't get the closeness back.'

'Poor Freddie,' Dione said, handing her an embroidered handkerchief and leaning against the desk with a questioning look on her face. 'Whatever are you going to do?'

Freddie shrugged. 'I don't know. I feel such a charlatan running a marriage bureau whilst my own relationship is on the rocks.'

'It's not that bad, is it?'

'I don't know how bad it is!' Freddie replied, shortly. 'And that's part of the trouble.' Her eyes were huge with anxiety. 'If only I could get pregnant, Dione. Then everything would be all right.' Her hands banged down on the desk in front of her. 'If I could just get pregnant, everything would be all right.'

The party was a complete and extended success. To the general approval of all present, Penn did a remarkable series of charades which culminated in his pretending to be a Greek urn; and Bea's impromptu rendering of 'My Man' drew such applause that the clapping could be heard half way down Rutland Gate. Having composed herself, Freddie was again the elegant hostess and at four-thirty in the morning, waved the last of her guests home. Finally alone, she slipped out of her dress and bathed slowly, drying herself before curling up in bed, her hair damp on the pillow.

She dozed fitfully but did not sleep. When seven o'clock came round she heard the newspapers arrive, then half an hour later the familiar sound of Chris's key in the side door as she let herself in, using a quiet Sunday morning to catch up on paperwork. Willing herself to rise, Freddie for once slid back into bed and lay unmoving, her eyes open, until eight when the phone rang.

'Freddie? It's Mummy.'

It took only a small flight of imagination to see the hall at Cambuscan and the fire burning in the morning room where Sarah would be making the call. Outside, Mike would be starting up the Land Rover and the frost would be shimmering on the iron weather vane.

Sarah's high voice tinkled over the phone. 'I was just thinking of you. Are you all right?'

'Fine. I'm really well, thanks,' Freddie added for emphasis. 'How are things at home?'

'Lonely, darling. You don't know how lucky you are to have such a lovely husband,' Sarah said, conveniently forgetting her initial distrust of Bart. 'I hardly see your father, he's seems so busy all the time. I know he always was, but well, lately, it's been even worse.' She rushed on. 'I'm worried about him, darling. But still, that's something I have to sort out and it's no good burdening you with my problems when you're so happy. I don't want you to worry about me. I can cope, I always do. I'm a lot stronger than I look … It's just that I miss you so much when you're so far away, and I don't see you any more … '

'I'm always phoning,' Freddie said defensively.

'I know, darling, and I appreciate it, honestly I do. But it's not like having my baby at home with me, is it?' Sarah's voice assumed a wistful quality as Freddie closed her eyes tightly. God, why can't you listen to *me*, for once, she thought. Why can't you help *me*.

'I used to think that things would be so different for us, that you would marry a nice young man from around here, and have lots of babies and I could have had lots of grandchildren to fill my days.' Sarah laughed gaily, as a child might. 'Silly of me, wasn't it? But I do so dread getting old, sweetheart, especially as your father doesn't seem to care about me … ' Sarah stopped suddenly, changing the subject, her woes now expurged. 'My pleasure now is knowing that you're happy and even though you're so far away, I can bear it when I know your marriage is a success. Unlike mine … You enjoy your life, Freddie darling, and don't worry about me. Just be happy.'

When Freddie replaced the receiver her hand was shaking. The memories of her childhood leap-frogged over one another in her head. Her fear of her father, her mother's dependence on her, and her own jealousy about the baby who was born dead. Without thinking, Freddie's hand went down to her stomach and slid under her night-dress as she imagined herself pregnant, picturing a swell of belly becoming the child she wanted, the child Bart longed for. If only I could have a baby, she thought, if only …

Chapter Sixteen

Warren Roberts woke early and turned over in bed, his sleep interrupted by the sound of a police siren howling in Maiden Lane below. Stretching, he got to his feet and went into the kitchen of his flat above the restaurant, flicking through his mail and yawning as the coffee percolated on the stove. It was a biting morning, a brush of late snow on the window ledges and a gesture of grey slush banked up against the pavements. Sipping his coffee, Warren glanced at the morning paper and then padded into his study.

The room had little character because he had wanted it that way. It was in keeping with the rest of the flat, designed in the minimalistic vein with no fuss and little detail. The television, compact disc recorder and video tape machine all disappeared behind disguised cupboards, the furniture kept to the bare essentials. Anyone coming into Warren's apartment would have had no clues to the type of man who lived there – and that was exactly the effect he wished to create.

Yet if he chose such spartan surroundings for himself, Warren was astute enough to realise that it would be an uncomfortable environment for most people so he adapted his style for the restaurant downstairs. His careful research had stood him in good stead and the restaurant had an atmosphere which was unique. Many gifted artists had been hired to create the impression of an old English coffee house, like the famous establishment about which Ben Jonson wrote. Using *trompe-l'œil* effects, they had managed to create an interior which looked aged. The walls had been hung with mock pamphlets from the 17th century and with a host of faded engravings. The only contemporary note was in the alcove where a pianist played nightly from seven to midnight. Unknown London composers were invited to contribute all manner of new music. This was the secret side of Warren Roberts, the man who was always ready to give the underdog a chance.

Warren's restaurant, in the centre of London, with all the frenetic hustling going on outside, was dedicated to a memory of a past which was nostalgic and intriguing and soon fascinated London, and as such, society. Almost as soon as the place opened, Warren realised its impact and enjoyed its success, although his celebrations were limited as he had no one really close with whom he could relish his triumph. At first he had been tempted to get in touch with his parents, but had hesitated, still ashamed, and too well aware that Warren Roberts had banished all trace of Dani Rabinski ... just as all trace of Louise had long since disappeared.

Whilst Warren sipped his coffee and read through his papers that morning, he was toying with the idea of opening another restaurant abroad. Toying, but not deciding, because he had sense enough to know that the magic may not work every time and that there was only one thing that people liked more than success – and that was failure. Yawning, he leaned back and flicked on the television news, watching the pictures flash on screen, his thoughts wandering. A newscaster appeared on screen, followed by a series of pictures of Beirut and finally one of New York. A memory tugged at him and he frowned momentarily, snapping off the set and going into the bathroom to shower.

The water did everything but expunge the memory of Louise ... She had stayed with Warren in New York and finally married him, giving birth to a daughter whom they called Alia, a Polish name deliberately passed down to remind the child of her forefathers. Alia became Warren's chief reason for his success – his spur and his succour. Coming home Warren dreamed his dreams with Louise and whispered them to his child, passing on his ambitions and his hopes. As the child grew, any violence and aggression in her father faded. Alia was his bolt-hole and occupied the core of his heart.

Then one day in early spring, Alia and her mother were knocked down and killed in a hit and run incident and Warren's grief was so immense that he vomited when he received the news. In the morgue he identified his wife, his voice low, the words difficult to articulate, but when he saw his child he said nothing. Alia's eyes were closed, her face unmarked, and for an instant he touched her hair, fully expecting her to move as if she would wake. But under his touch Alia remained unmoving and cold. This time no words came, only a shutting down of the heart which left Warren silent. Without voice. Nothing. In his daughter's death was the end of all goodness and the closure of his soul.

It took very little time for Warren to revert to his previous reserve, the violence and frustration held in check, but only a little way below the surface – such a very little way. He visited the graves often, but finally left New York, turning homewards to escape. In London, he told himself, the pain will cease. In London, I will find some rest. But although he had kept himself busy since he returned, the emptiness inside him remained. Only the recent phone call from Bart, and his visit to the restaurant with his wife, had given Warren a genuine sense of pleasure.

'So, Warren, you're going to work your magic in London, hey?' Bart had asked, full of his usual boisterous good humour. 'I'm glad,' he continued genuinely, 'really glad that you're over here. It'll be good to see you again.'

Warren nodded, for an instant afraid to trust his voice as he felt a wave of emotion. He liked Bart and counted him as a true friend, although they had never really been that close. As an intensely private man, Warren had disclosed little of his personal life, but Bart and he had shared many conversations, and Warren relished Bart's easy enjoyment of life and his openness. By contrast, Bart felt drawn to Warren for his complexity – where he was uncomplicated, Warren was intense; where he was unlikely to probe the meaning of life, religion, or morals, Warren would provoke him into discussions, forcing him to think. As opposites, they valued each other, and it was with real pleasure that Warren, still grieving two years after the death of his family, reopened the friendship.

'I was going to get in touch ... '

'Bullshit!' Bart said affably. 'You were going to see if the restaurant was a success first.'

Warren smiled slowly. 'On the button, as usual.'

'I got married.'

'I heard.'

'And you?' Bart said easily, hoping that his friend was similarly blessed.

'I'll tell you all about it when I see you,' was all Warren said.

Yet when Bart took Freddie to the restaurant, Warren was too busy to confide and although he phoned Bart the following day, Bart was on site and unable to take the call. The foreman took a message and stuck it on the notice-board instead, but the day passed without Bart returning to the Portakabin and he went home without knowing of the phone call. A week passed without any communication between the two, so Warren, surprised that Bart hadn't been in touch, decided to call at Rutland Gate.

Rapt in thought, Warren rang the bell several times and was about to walk away when Mrs Allen opened the door.

'Good morning.'

'Morning,' Warren said. 'Is Mr Wallace home?'

She paused. 'No, I'm afraid he's already left,' she said, adding swiftly. 'Mrs Wallace is at home though.'

Warren hesitated. He had no real desire to see Freddie and was just about to make an excuse when Freddie walked into the hallway behind Jean Allen. Outlined against the light she stood erect, wearing a red suit, her hair lose on her shoulders, her eyes made-up carefully although her mouth bore only a trace of lip gloss. Smiling warily, she approached her visitor.

'Good morning.'

'Morning. I'm sorry to come unannounced, I just thought

237

I'd call and see Bart. I was acting on a whim.' Warren hesitated, as though he already regretted his actions. 'But apparently he's away.' Warren passed Freddie a book. 'I hardly had a chance to talk to him the other night, so I thought ... ' He trailed off, pointing to the volume she had taken from him. 'It's Turgenev – he might like it.'

Freddie's eyebrows rose. 'That's kind of you. Thank you.'

'Well ... I just hope he enjoys it, that's all,' Warren replied lamely.

Turning away, Freddie glanced over to Mrs Allen. 'We'll have some coffee, Jean. Oh, and take Mr Roberts coat, will you?'

'I can't stay.'

Freddie's poise faltered. Warren noticed the change and felt guilty. 'Well, perhaps just a couple of minutes.'

Smiling distantly, Freddie walked into the drawing room with Warren following her. Without being obvious, he glanced around, instantly realising the great wealth which had made such comfort possible.

'So how are things?'

'At the restaurant?' he queried.

'Yes, at the restaurant,' Freddie agreed, surprised that she found him so difficult to talk to.

'I was thinking of opening another one,' Warren said, immediately regretting the words. Not having confided in anyone since Louise died, he was severely discomforted to find himself exposing his thoughts to a virtual stranger.

Freddie's blue eyes watched him with interest. 'Well, if it's anything like the new one, it should be a great success.'

'Maybe ... ' Warren said simply, embarrassed.

By now believing what Bart had said about Warren's inherent shyness, Freddie was relieved as Mrs Allen came in and laid down their coffee. Warren took a cup from her, refusing milk and sugar.

'I heard about your bureau,' Warren said. 'It must be quite a success.'

Freddie stirred the spoon in her cup. The milk streaked the dark liquid and muddied it. 'It is, thank God. There are a lot of people who need partners, people who are lonely … '

'Who isn't?' Warren answered, sipping his coffee and looking over the cup at her.

Freddie bristled, thinking he was being flip. 'People need someone to talk to.'

'And are you easy to talk to?'

'Usually, yes,' Freddie said, aware that she had shown some flicker of animosity. Ashamed of her bad manners, she changed the subject. 'More coffee?' she asked suddenly, turning her attention to his empty cup.

Warren shook his head, 'No. No, thanks. I have to go anyway.'

Intensely relieved, Freddie rose to her feet. 'I'll tell Bart that you called, Warren. He'll be delighted with the book, I'm sure.' Together they walked to the door. 'I would invite you over for dinner one night, but I'm not sure that would be much of a change for you.' Her tone lightened, now that he was leaving. 'But if you want to take a chance, we would be delighted to have you.' She paused by the front door, smiling warmly. 'I'm sure Bart will be in touch soon,' she said and watched as Warren turned up the collar of his coat and walked off.

Mystified, Freddie closed the door and leaned against it, thinking. She was adept with people, even the most difficult. A privileged upbringing and Dione's social ministrations meant that Freddie could mix with any class or type of person and her own interest and tact made her a good conversationalist, her warmth inviting confidences. All such qualities made her ideal for the job she did, and she had never once found herself at a loss for what to say – until she met Warren. Shaking her head, Freddie thought back to his visit. Was he shy? Reserved? Or was there something else? She thought back over what she knew about his past, unable to contain her usual curiosity. Warren had been a poor boy who had struggled to achieve – OK, Freddie reasoned, so how did that normally affect people? Was he full of resentment? She dismissed the idea, no, that wasn't it. So was it anger? The thought struck a chord and she pursued it – was Warren

Roberts an angry man? And if so, why?

Freddie's thoughts occupied her on the way downstairs to the office. She had told Chris that she would spend the morning shopping, but she had changed her mind. Her brain was humming. Perhaps she should just follow up that woman who had come in yesterday. Pushing open the door of The 107 Club, she walked in, smiling at an anxious looking Chris.

'Hi.'

'Hello,' Chris replied, walking towards Freddie and pushing a file into her hands gratefully. 'I'm glad you decided to come in – the temporary's not … ' she jiggled her hand as though to find the word, ' … working out. She seemed to be doing fine yesterday, but this morning she's been in the office and hasn't made any calls – and when I knocked on the front door she just waved me away.'

Freddie glanced over to the closed door. Liz Ford was on holiday and her short term replacement had been recommended by a friend of hers. At first Mala Levinska had seemed ideal. She had worked in a New York marriage bureau and was very experienced, but the latest development worried Freddie. Silently, she walked to the office and opened the door, without Mala knowing she was there. Seated in front of the video recorder, Mala Levinska's kohl-rimmed eyes were fixed on the screen, her tongue constantly explored her teeth as she watched. The heat in the office hung in the high eighties, boosted by the frenzied ministrations of a fan heater.

Abruptly, Mala Levinska pushed a new video tape into the machine. A man came up on screen, his voice over-confident from nerves. Immediately Mala screwed up her eyes and stared at him, her attention riveted. 'What a shit ball,' she murmured. 'How the hell am I supposed to find some woman crazy enough to want him? How many blind morons are there?' Mala turned up the volume as the man began to talk on screen. *'I'd like a fun person … '*

'Don't they all!'

' … who's at home in the city and the country.'

Mala Levinska watched greedily, punctuating the man's conversation with her own running commentary. 'Hah!'

240

'She would have to be attractive …'

'Even if you look like shit.'

' … and loving.'

'Jesus! No woman is going to want to go to bed with you – unless you're paying good money.'

'I've been alone a long time …'

'What a surprise!'

' … and I need a companion now and children.'

'So adopt,' Mala Levinska snapped, flicking off the video. She heard Freddie behind her and turned suddenly. About to say something, she stopped, intimidated by the sheer fury in Freddie's eyes.

Worried about Bart and unsettled by the forced conversation with Warren, Freddie was in no mood to listen to reason or excuses – not that there could be any. How dare Mala behave that way. To humiliate her clients! To laugh at them, make fun of them, belittle them! Freddie's hands clenched in rage and for an instant she felt tempted to knock Mala Levinska off her seat. This was her life, her work – The 107 Club – prestigious, genuine, the place where clients came to get away from the savagery of the world. And this woman, this cow, Freddie thought, was trying to spoil it.

'Get out!' she said, her voice deadly.

'What?'

'You heard me. Get out. Now!' Freddie snatched up Mala's coat and threw it at her.

'What the hell … ' Mala said, ducking. 'Oh, come on, I was just having a little joke.'

'Get out!' Freddie said hoarsely.

Mala's tongue ran over her teeth quickly. 'You don't impress me, Mrs Wallace,' she said bitingly. 'Don't tell me you're not in this for the money. Hah! You don't con me. I know you really don't give a damn for Little Mr and Miss Lonelyheart, spending Christmas alone and getting no cards on Valentine's Day … '

Freddie's anger was terrifying as she leaned forward and grabbed Mala by the arm. In silence she hustled her to the door and then violently pushed her out onto the street.

241

'Now, get away from my business,' she said, her voice fearsome. 'And don't ever – *ever* – come near me again.'

Blazing with indignation, Mala faced Freddie with a bitter smile. 'I'll get my own back, Mrs Wallace,' she said.

Snorting with derision, Freddie turned, but in the moment she took to close the door, Mala's voice hissed through to her. 'You'll regret this, bitch! You just see if you don't.'

Back in reception Chris was waiting for Freddie with a cup of coffee in her hand, but when her employer returned she was too angry to even see Chris. Walking past rapidly, Freddie made her way back to the office and counted the video tapes, making sure that Mala hadn't taken any with her, then she turned off the fan heater, the low hum dying to nothing. Her head banged with fury, her eyes blazing as she tidied the desk, removing any remnant of Mala Levinska, When she had finished, she walked into her own room and returned with a vial of perfume, spraying the room as thought Mala had left a foul odour behind.

Chris watched in amazement, as did Tina and Dot who had come out of their offices when they heard the commotion. None of the women had even seen Freddie angry before, and all of them agreed later that they had no desire to see her angry again. Such was her fury that her clothes seemed to crackle as she passed, and when she had finally re-organised the office she folded her arms and faced them.

'I'll take on Liz's clients whilst she's away,' she said, encouraging no arguments. 'And if I ever catch any of you laughing at our clients, by God, you'll regret it.'

Then she turned and walked into her own office, sitting down heavily at her desk, her hand hovering over the phone.

Timidly, Chris walked in with the coffee. 'Would this help?'

Freddie glared at her and then, as though she suddenly recognised her, relaxed, smiled ruefully, and took the cup. 'Sorry, Chris, it's just that woman made something snap inside me.' She sipped the drink. 'I couldn't bear to see her sneering like that.'

'It's OK. She's gone now.'

'Yes,' Freddie agreed, her thoughts wandering. She had

over-reacted, she knew it, and was surprised at herself. At the same time, she knew that her anger had been partially due to the tension between her and Bart. The only thing she had believed secure and inviolate was the bureau, and Mala Levinska had momentarily threatened it. Freddie shook her head. This was no way to go on, she reasoned. She had to be calm and work her marriage out – after all, she spent all her days working out other people's love lives. It would be laughable if she failed with her own.

'Get me the file on Daniel Haig, will you?' she asked Chris, her tone back to normal, her mind settling as the familiar file flopped on her desk. Carefully she turned the pages, looking at Daniel's photograph and reading his details again, her eyes flicking over his graphology report and his medical assessment. Within minutes, she was musing on the idea of introducing him to a new client – all worry about Bart postponed, her composure restored.

When Freddie left the bureau at seven that night there was a message waiting for her on her private answering machine upstairs.

'Don't bother to wait up for me, sweetheart,' Bart said, his voice aggravatingly kind. 'I'll be very late tonight. We can talk in the morning.'

Freddie re-ran the message twice, her disappointment rising and falling like a spring tide. The words were kind enough, but there was no real regret, just a simple statement of fact.

Fighting a seductive impulse to wallow in self-pity, Freddie went into the bedroom and sat down heavily on the side of the bed, slowly taking off her jacket and slipping off her shoes. Unutterably weary, she leaned back against the pillows and curled up in a foetal position, thinking of Cambuscan and of the iron-coloured water of the winter lake. Then she spotted the book by the side of the bed and slowly she reached out for it, reading the title, *On the Eve*, and the name Turgenev. With little enthusiasm, she began to read, and was startled when the phone rang a little while later.

'Bart?'

'Hi, darling,' he said, easily. 'I just wanted to say good-night.'

Freddie smiled with relief. 'Good-night, my love,' she said softly. 'I miss you.'

Their affection met across the phone line and for an instant both of them regretted their recent distance. 'Do something for me, darling, will you?' Bart asked.

'Of course, what?'

'Phone Warren and ask him over for dinner on Saturday – a sort of pre-Christmas celebration,' he said. 'The number's in my book by the bed. I meant to ring him today but I didn't get time.'

'That's funny. He came over to see you this morning,' Freddie said, looking down at the book in her hand. 'He left you a novel.'

'Jesus! He never gives up,' Bart said laughing. 'Warren was always trying to get me to read more. But although I had the education, he had the instinct.' The memory made him smile. 'Don't tell me, it's by a Russian.'

'Yes,' Freddie agreed. 'Turgenev.'

'Even the name makes my head ache!' Bart replied, then changed the subject. 'If I can, I'll get away soon.'

'Please.'

'If I can, darling. If I can,' he said, ringing off.

Freddie replaced the receiver and then, after looking at Bart's telephone book, picked up the phone and dialled. It rang several times before Warren answered.

'Warren?'

He was on his guard. 'Yes. Who is it?'

'Freddie. Freddie Wallace,' she said, pausing. But he said nothing. 'Bart's just asked me to invite you to dinner on Saturday – after everything I said this morning! Can you come?'

There was a short pause. Freddie imagined him either considering the idea or looking at his diary. Finally, he responded. 'Fine.'

'Around seven-thirty then,' Freddie said lightly.

'Listen, I'm sorry, but I have to go. It's getting busy down-stairs in the restaurant.'

244

'Oh, I didn't mean to keep you … ' She trailed off, embarrassed. 'Sorry.'

'No problem,' Warren said quickly. 'I'll look forward to it.'

On the other end of the line, Warren replaced the phone carefully, his hand resting on it for an instant as Freddie's voice murmured in his head, her tone clear and unhurried; an elegant voice belonging to an elegant woman, who had, with perfect civility, just invited him to dinner. He should have been more polite, he thought guiltily, but he was out of practice socially. In the restaurant it was different. He was the boss, able to converse with his customers and remember all the little details about them, so that they felt welcomed – 'How's your wife?' 'Did your son get into Cambridge?' 'I saw your film the other day, it was excellent' – All these details came naturally to Warren, because he had an excellent memory and wanted to please his clientele and encourage them to return.

But privately he was ill at ease. The huge vacuum Louise and Alia had left had never been breached by anyone – in fact, he didn't really want it to be. Superstitious and wary, his grief made him believe that anyone else who even tried to take his wife and child's place would be taken too – how, he didn't know, whether killed, stolen, or maimed – but they *would* go. The extent of his punishing grief was so intense that he lived warily and kept reality away. Unsettled by the telephone call, Warren fastened his dinner jacket and sighed, thinking of Freddie, not with desire, with something much worse. With curiosity.

They had only met twice, once in the restaurant and again that morning at Rutland Gate, and yet he had found it impossible to prevent his thoughts from turning to her. The things she had said, he forgot, but he could see her wide bottom lip, free of lipstick, the touch of her fingers on the palm of his hand … Warren shook his head and fastened his watch to his wrist. His few indulgent love affairs after Louise's death seemed suddenly a weakness instead of a relief, and he was angry that the first woman who had really interested him was Freddie – the wife of his friend, Bart Wallace.

245

As Warren walked down to the restaurant, he knew that he had to control his thoughts and dismiss Freddie Wallace from his mind. He knew himself too well to pretend that there was any other way. He was too intense a personality to be relaxed about anything. If he worked, he worked obsessively; if he trained, he trained obsessively; and when he loved, he had loved blindly, wildly, completely, and obsessively. The violence in his nature, he had subdued by fanatical control, and now he would have to rein in his feelings with the same discipline.

At the bottom of the stairs Warren paused and then pushed open the door to the restaurant kitchen. Immediately five pairs of eyes turned towards him, each apprehensive as he walked around examining the preparations, leaning over pans on the cookers and silently running his glance over the stainless steel worktops.

'What's wrong with this fan?' he asked finally, pointing to one of a bank of fans over the cooker range.

The chef's eyes followed his gaze. 'I don't know, Mr Roberts. It was working a little while ago.'

'Get it fixed,' Warren said. 'It'll be as hot as hell in here later, and no one can work well under those conditions.' He moved on, each man watching him. 'Mike,' he said suddenly, turning round, his eyes searching out the waiter in question. 'You were rude to a customer yesterday.'

'I wasn't,' the man replied. Thin and freckled, his face was mottled with embarrassment. 'The woman was – '

'A customer,' Warren said, silencing him, 'and as such she deserves the best service.' He paused. Beside him the pots bubbled and hummed under the pan lids. 'This is a warning. If I have one more complaint, you're out.'

The waiter nodded. Anywhere else, he would have argued, or thought his treatment unjust, but he was so keen to stay at Warren Roberts' restaurant that he took the warning without murmur, shuffling guiltily under his employer's gaze.

When he had finished his inspection, Warren moved out into the restaurant. As he pushed open the kitchen doors, the animated rustle of voices drummed on his ears. The occupants of the nearest table glanced up and smiled, a woman raising her hand in greeting. Slowly, Warren moved towards her, the sound of the music layered with the noise of conversation, quick laughter, and the chink of knives and forks. Under the subdued lighting the guests became like figures from a Caravaggio painting, the women flattered into beauty, the men sentient in the shadowy light. Hands looked bolder, eye sockets deeper, cheek-bones *sfumato* smudged; and as he passed his guests, Warren wondered how many romances would begin and end in this place.

Arriving at the woman's side, Warren took her extended hand and noticed her tongue running over the teeth as she appraised him. Mala Levinska had visited his New York restaurant with a variety of escorts, and had made no secret of her attraction to him.

'Lovely place,' she said keenly. 'As nice as the one in New York.'

Warren smiled without any real sincerity. He had never liked Mala, either in New York or London.

'Thanks,' he said evenly.

'You still friendly with Bart Wallace?' Mala asked, her kohl-rimmed eyes alert.

Warren resented her curiosity, but was far too adept to show any emotion and nodded instead towards the empty plate in front of her. 'Did you enjoy your steak?'

Mala's eyes held his gaze for a long moment. 'I could make a meal out of you, darling.'

Smiling wryly, Warren moved away.

As was his custom, he spent the whole evening in the restaurant, accepting some customers' invitations to have a drink with them and politely rejecting others from people who were either new to him or ones whose custom he did not want to encourage. Experience had taught him that some people believed that a glass of wine could secure them a table for evermore, their name remembered and ranked amongst the customers who received preferential treatment. It was the usual way of business, but it was not Warren's way. He was very careful about the people who came to the restaurant.

247

Knowing that its reputation and prices guaranteed a certain section of society, Warren welcomed the showbiz crowd and the European nobility who descended on London, whilst keeping a careful eye on the rowdier, younger set.

Yet as Warren paced around his territory that night his attention wandered and he found that when greeting someone his thoughts moved back to a house in Rutland Gate and to a polite woman whose eyes were alert with intelligence. Certain that the temporary infatuation would pass, he was alarmed to find that as the evening continued he was re-running their phone conversation repeatedly and experiencing unwelcome guilt for his rudeness.

In the kitchen word went out that the boss was in a foul mood and looking for trouble. As a result, every dish was checked and re-checked, all the fans now humming again, the steam gobbled up as it left the pans, the chef's vivid face assuming an anxious expression as he spotted a plate about to be carried into the restaurant.

'Hold on a minute!' he shouted to the waiter, moving over and wiping away a minute trace of sauce that had smeared the edge of the plate. 'Watch out for that, he hates to see mess.'

The waiter nodded, his nerves already jangling. 'Sorry,'

'You will be if he catches you,' the chef replied, turning back to the cooker.

By eleven the temperature was in the high eighties, and Warren glanced into the kitchen repeatedly, his manner unusually restless. Looks were exchanged between the chef and the waiters, but no one dared to comment as the hectic activity continued. Orders were barked out, food turned, flipped, steamed and scalded in pans; desserts were teased and frothed into opulent tempters; the bins were filled with fish bones and vegetable skins, then emptied and refilled with fruit peelings and cartons and innumerable disposable cloths. Through the kitchen door came the dull hum of conversation as the restaurant filled to the maximum, the waiters weaving adeptly between the tables, whilst the pianist played an old blues number in the alcove by the door.

In an attempt to turn his thoughts away from Freddie,

248

Warren tried to absorb himself in the restaurant, but found to his astonishment that he was preoccupied, his conversation forced. Although they had noticed nothing amiss, Warren thought that the guests watched him as critically as he watched them; that the staff were as unsettled as he was; and that the whole glorious magic of the restaurant was only sham, as empty as his life was. Struggling to control his feelings, Warren felt his collar growing tighter as a nearly-forgotten anger rose up in him.

His hands balled into fists, the violence held down under the surface, but beginning to show through, like a needle under a layer of skin. An old memory of the fight on his nineteenth birthday came back, quickly followed by the sensation of guilt which had led him to destroy Dani Rabinski and give birth to Warren Roberts. Other memories jumped onto his back; Louise and all her sweetness, Alia, the day she was born, and the last time he saw her, dead and cold under his touch.

For the first time in years, Warren was losing control. Recognising all the symptoms, he suddenly rushed through the kitchens and ran, panting, into the alleyway outside. Greedily, he breathed in the night air and then loosened his collar, unbuttoning the cuffs of his evening shirt and hailing the first taxi which came into sight.

Mrs Allen had done a good job and the table in the dining room of Rutland Gate was perfectly organised, a bowl of specially ordered flowers standing in the centre of the table set for three. Humming under her breath, she fiercely polished the last knife and laid it beside Bart's plate, standing back to observe the finished result. Cheerfully the china and cutlery beamed up at her, arrayed like smiling children on a playground, innocent and unstained. Satisfied with the effect, she turned to find Freddie behind her.

'Lovely,' Freddie said with pleasure. 'You've done a good job.'

'And the meal should be even better, Mrs Wallace,' the woman replied eagerly. 'I think you'll be pleased.'

'I know I will,' Freddie replied, walking out of the dining room towards the drawing room where she paused by the mirror, glancing at her reflection. The dark velvet of her dress threw her white shoulders into relief, her eyes smokey under make-up, her heart beating powerfully. She and Bart had begun to make love that afternoon, Bart gentle and Freddie willing, but when he had received a call from the site hurriedly he had left. Freddie had remained calm, fighting her momentary irritation.

' ... Just for an hour or so, darling.'

'Well, make sure it is, Bart,' she had responded. 'You remember we've got your friend over for dinner tonight.'

'Warren should be your friend too,' he had replied, dressing and glancing over his shoulder towards her. 'I'll be back around seven-thirty – in plenty of time, I promise.'

Freddie glanced at the clock again. Seven-twenty. Oh, come on, Bart, she willed him, come on. But by seven-thirty he was nowhere to be seen and at a quarter to eight the doorbell rang.

'Oh hell!' Freddie snapped, rising to her feet and composing herself as Warren walked in.

He was as ill at ease as she was, glancing round, obviously looking for Bart.

'My husband's been delayed, I'm afraid, so we'll have to amuse each other until he gets here,' Freddie said, her tone even. 'He's had a lot of problems with a site over at Croydon,' she went on, pouring them both a drink. 'You can't imagine how much time these offices have taken up.'

Warren took the glass from her and smiled as Freddie sat down on the chair next to his. Dressed in a lounge suit, Warren looked impressively well-dressed and fit, and when he leaned towards the table to reach for his drink, Freddie caught sight of his expensive and rare German watch.

'So what have you been doing today?' she asked, crossing her legs.

'I went to an auction at Bonhams,' Warren said, pleased to see her interest kindle. 'I got some good pieces.'

'What do you collect?'

'Cigarette cards.'

250

Freddie laughed, then realised with horror that he hadn't been joking. 'Cigarette cards?' she repeated stiffly. 'I don't know much about those.'

'I've got a huge collection,' he went on impassively. 'English and European – the older ones, of course – ones such as the 52 Kimball 'Beauties' are not only rare, but quite valuable.'

Freddie smiled, willing Bart to walk in, well aware that every time she and Warren spoke the conversation was doomed.

'I collect masks myself,' she said, indicating several on the wall behind him. Warren turned to look, his blond hair thick against his collar, one hand lying along the back of the settee. 'I've been buying them since before I was married,' Freddie went on then froze when she heard the phone ring. It rang twice, then stopped and Mrs Allen walked in. Apologising to Warren, Freddie slowly rose to her feet and left the room, her hand shaking as she lifted the receiver in the library.

'Darling, I'm so sorry … '

'Like hell!' she snapped.

'There's been trouble with the drawings.'

'I don't want to hear it, Bart. I want you home instead, which is where you should be on a Saturday night.' Freddie dropped her voice. 'Warren's here and I'm struggling to entertain him. He is not my friend, Bart, he's *yours* and frankly, I don't like him.'

'Listen … '

'No, you listen!' she said, furious. 'You have horsed me around once too often, Bart. I thought that after this afternoon we had some kind of understanding – but obviously it was all on my part, not yours.'

'I have to work … '

'No, you don't!' she said, cutting him off. 'You work for the same reason I do, to forget your problems. We can't go on like this, Bart,' she said softly. 'I love you and I want us to be happy, but this … this is impossible.'

'I'll make it up to you, Freddie,' he said, hurriedly, feeling a sudden real sense of guilt. She was right, he had been overworking, just as she had. Both of them had been refusing

251

to admit that the burning issue of children was forcing them apart. 'Tell Warren I'll be delayed, but that I'll be along later.'

'Tell him yourself!' Freddie said hotly, walking into the drawing room and putting Bart's call through to Warren. With her arms folded she watched as they talked, and was amazed to see Warren relax and even laugh a couple of times before he put the phone down and turned to her.

'Maybe it would be better if I left. If I remember the Bart of old, he was always forgetting the time when he was busy. He could be home soon – or not so soon.'

Letting her arms drop to her sides, Freddie smiled half-heartedly. 'I've been a terrible hostess, Warren,' she admitted, 'and I think we got off on the wrong foot from day one. I can only apologise and ask you for a favour – I would be very pleased if you would stay and dine with me.'

Elegant and apologetic, Freddie waited for his response. Warren felt a terrible and profound rush of admiration for her. He wanted to leave and avoid further contact, but he couldn't. He was too fascinated by this young woman in a glamorous evening dress whose eyes were dark with disappointment. For several seconds he watched her and then as though his mind was made up, he nodded.

'There is nowhere in London I would rather be.'

Freddie frowned, surprised by his words, then added lightly. 'Don't be too sure, you haven't eaten the dinner yet.'

Chapter Seventeen

With only four days left to Christmas, the Wilkie women were panicking. Most of the three storey houses around Dorman Square were already hung with a smattering of reckless festive lights, but the most haphazardly spectacular were being hastily hung up in the Wilkie house, Bea hovered in the hallway downstairs with a formidable Christmas tree propped up against the wall beside her. Having bought the largest she could find, she had had it delivered home and then found to her astonishment that delivery did not include walking up two flights of stairs with an unwieldy Norwegian spruce.

After pressing a reluctant Pam for help, Bea was just jabbing Charlie's bell without success, when Jao walked in. Her eyes rested for a long moment on the spruce. 'What is that?'

'A portable helicopter,' Bea replied acidly. 'What the hell do you think it is? It's our Christmas tree.'

'We didn't need such a big one,' Pam muttered, her body almost obliterated by the vegetation. 'I know that no one ever listens to me, but I think – '

'There's no reply from Charlie's,' Bea interrupted, one hand fixed firmly around the trunk of the tree.

'Well there wouldn't be. He and Trisha have gone out for the day,' Jao replied, regarding the spruce thoughtfully. 'I don't know if it will go up the stairs.'

Bea sighed and tightened her grip on the trunk, her face half hidden behind an impressively full branch. 'All that

253

flaming money they charged me, *including* delivery.' She pushed away the branch with her hand. 'But apparently delivery is to the door only, my dear, not the family hearth.'

'You can't put it by the fire, or the whole place will go up in flames,' Pam chimed in, walking over to the bottom stair, her plimsolled feet silent on the linoleum. 'Everyone knows that.'

'Perhaps you'd like it in your bedroom then?' Bea responded drily, turning back to Jao. 'Listen, we have to get this damn thing upstairs so grab hold and when I count to three, lift.' Her daughter nodded enthusiastically. 'We'll pause on the landing and then turn it before we heave it upstairs.'

'You'll never – '

'Oh, dry up, Pam! Just go and open the front door for us. Oh, and move the flowers off the sideboard in the corridor.' Summoning up all her strength, Bea turned back to Jao. 'Right. One, two, three!'

With their combined effort the tree seemed suddenly rocket launched and crashed resoundingly into the ceiling before lurching forwards and wiping all the mail off the hall table. Rapidly disappearing under a mass of green foliage, Jao let rip with a stream of impressive curses as her mother grasped the trunk again and began to progress towards the stairs, the spruce held before her like a gigantic, animated spear.

'Stand back!' she screeched, lunging up the first five stairs, the branches scraping against the banisters and flicking backwards like a cat-o'-nine-tails to catch her legs. Jao provided extra leverage by pushing her mother from behind. 'Open the door, Pam, I'm coming!' Bea shouted triumphantly, flushed with success as she arrived on the landing and paused to take a breath, momentarily losing her grasp on the tree.

It was a fatal error. Free of her grip, the Norwegian spruce fell forwards drunkenly and jammed against the corner of the landing, its branches haphazardly jutting from its trunk as it took on a malevolent resistance. Much as Bea shoved, the tree would not budge, its tip squashed into the corner, its sturdy lower quarters as defiantly stubborn as a mule. Blowing out her cheeks, Jao joined her mother, but as much as they pushed, jiggled and levered, the tree remained jammed, and after another few moments, Bea sat down on the stairs, defeated.

'It's stuck.'

'You don't say,' Jao replied, looking balefully at the monumental tree.

'You'll have to move it, it's blocking the stairs,' Pam called down over the banisters.

'Actually I was thinking that we should decorate it here and then put in a lift,' Bea replied cuttingly. Her sister sniffed and disappeared again.

Jao glanced over to her mother. 'What about a rope?'

'Suicide's no answer,' Bea replied.

Jao burst out laughing and then frowned as the doorbell rang. 'Who's that?'

'God knows,' Bea replied, 'but let's hope it's a six foot Norwegian.'

It wasn't, but it was someone strong enough to help.

'What in God's name happened?' Bart asked, walking in and glancing up at the beached tree on the landing with an amused look on his face.

'It's the new loo brush,' Bea replied lightly, putting her head on one side. 'It gets into all those awkward little corners … Give us a hand, will you?'

Bart ran up the stairs immediately and began issuing orders, calling to Pam to open the door and telling Jao to hold his jacket. After several minutes of concerted effort, he succeeding in raising the tree upwards again. Then with the help of Bea and Jao, he managed to turn it round the corner of the landing and place it triumphantly in the sitting room.

'There.'

A burst of spontaneous applause sprung from Bea and Jao, Pam watching gloomily from the doorway.

The tree was dressed an hour later with a selection of lights which refused to work until Charlie returned and fixed them. For the rest of the evening they flickered erratically (despite Charlie's protestations that they were working perfectly) and gave the room the air of a third rate discothèque.

'We'll keep out of the way,' Bea said to Bart, closing the

255

kitchen door. 'Charlie's got a look on his face which means business.' She poured them both a drink and added deftly. 'Speaking of which – how's your business? We all missed you at the party last week.'

Bart stared at the whisky and soda in his hand. 'I'm busy, too busy. Oh God, Bea, I'm worried about ... things.'

'Ah,' Bea said enigmatically. 'Could you be a little more specific?'

'You know how much I love Freddie?' Bea nodded, the passing years had made that fact less agonising for her to bear. 'And she loves me,' Bart continued. 'We want a child, Bea, that's the trouble. It didn't matter when we were first married, but it's got so much more important in the last years. I'm getting no younger.'

A loud bellow of rage came from above followed by the sound of Charlie's feet clattering down the stairs.

'Oh dear – war.' Bea turned back to Bart. 'You were saying?'

'We've lost the closeness we had.'

'You've been married for nearly nine years, Bart, no one keeps the first flush of wedded bliss going for ever.'

'It's more than that,' he said firmly.

'So why don't you talk to Freddie, Bart? She'll listen, she's always ready to listen.'

'I should be home now,' he said in astonishment, almost as though his own actions surprised him. 'I've got a friend over for dinner and yet I still stayed on at work. The work had to be done,' he said, defending his actions and glancing across to Bea for reassurance. 'But I should be home now.'

'So go home!' Bea said flatly.

'I will. I just wanted to talk to someone for a while,' he said, running his hands through his hair. 'Just to see if I could work it all out in my head.' He frowned, hesitating and wondering if he was betraying his wife. But he had to ask someone for help, and Bea had always been his closest confidante. 'I love her,' he said aloud, thinking of Freddie suddenly, and wanting to cling onto her, to grab his last chance of sexual and domestic euphoria. 'I have to save this marriage ... '

256

Before Bea could respond, the kitchen door opened with a dull thud as Jao came in.

'Charlie's got a fit of the sulks,' she said, peering into Bart's face, 'and you look awful. What happened?'

'I'm just tired, that's all,' Bart lied, glancing around irritably as Pam walked in. She was trying to mend the ear-piece of her reading glasses and muttered to herself as Trisha followed her, reading the paper avidly.

Bea raised her eyes to Heaven. 'We were having a private chat in here ... '

'Have you read about the kidnapping, Bart?' Trisha asked innocently, ignoring her sister. 'Apparently this married couple broke up and the court couldn't decide who would get custody of the goldfish, so the husband kidnapped it.'

She paused, supposedly reading the article in front of her. 'He then sent a letter to his estranged wife saying that unless she paid the ransom, he'd send a fin in the post.' Her voice cracked suddenly as she burst out laughing and dropped the paper.

Jao glanced at Bart. 'I can see why you keep coming here, it's the quality of the conversation, isn't it?'

He smiled bleakly in response.

'Charlie's back,' Pam murmured, her eyes fixed on the broken glasses as she heard the sound of heavy feet running upstairs. 'I suppose we can get the tree finished now that he's recovered his temper,' she said, adding innocently, 'Incidentally, how's Freddie, Bart?'

Jao fixed her eyes on her aunt, but Pam was too cunning to look up and continued to scrutinise her glasses.

'I'm bored,' Trisha said suddenly, preventing any response from Bart. 'Charlie and I are going over to some friends of his who've just got a new bath installed.' She paused, thinking. 'One of those new things. You know, an Emile Zola.'

Jao raised her eyebrows. 'An Emile Zola? What the hell are you talking about now?'

Trisha's smile was impish. 'You know what I mean – a *J'accuse*. Jacuzzi!'

Bart burst out laughing, but Trisha's attention had already

257

returned to the paper as she hummed softly and left the room with Pam following her reluctantly. Jao however remained, sipping her coffee as she scrutinised Bart and her mother. Having had their private conversation interrupted, Bea was busily arranging some holly and mistletoe, her mouth scarlet with lipstick, her eyes made-up, the brows darkly confident. Chatting easily, she was animated, her deep voice luxurious in the warm kitchen, her hand now and then banging lustily on the kitchen pipes to quieten them. Jao watched her and treasured her mother's familiar actions as though each was an individual photograph in an album; page after page of beloved instances, an extended arm, a glance over the shoulder, a quick tug at her jumper which had ridden high over her hips.

Bart watched Bea too, and wanted to explain to Jao that he was only a friend, no more. Knowing that she was protective of Bea, he wanted to assure her that he did not want anything other than advice. But no words came to him, and he stayed locked in confusion. Nevertheless, he did notice a quick exchange between the two women when Bea leaned across the table for some more holly. Glancing over to Jao, she instinctively read the expression in her daughter's eyes, and seeing the concern there, smiled reassuringly then turned away, her hand lying beside the soft fruit of the mistletoe.

At the same time that Bart was sitting in the Wilkie kitchen, Warren was telling Freddie about his time in New York. He found, after his initial unease, that having begun to confide, he could not stop himself. As though he had taken a drug which battered down all his inhibitions, he spoke quickly and eagerly, the burning intensity of his feelings taking Freddie vividly back with him to his past. She listened, as she always did, and made few comments, somehow realising that many of the secrets were painful and of long standing.

'So why did you change your name?'

Warren hesitated. There were some things too shameful to admit. Like the fight. 'I wanted to escape,' he said stiffly, pulling back.

Freddie saw the change in his attitude and moved onto

another subject. 'Do you really think you'll open up another restaurant?'

'Maybe,' Warren said, leaning back in his chair, his reserve restored. 'I like to work.'

'I do too – if it's work that interests me.'

'And a marriage bureau does?'

Freddie nodded. 'Yes, it suits me,' she said truthfully. 'But sometimes I get too involved with the clients. I never learned to keep my distance.'

Warren smiled politely. 'Do you really match many of them up?'

Freddie nodded, laying down her napkin and ringing for coffee and brandy. 'We match up quite a lot, but it's more than that – I listen to what they say, and often no one else ever has. Sometimes,' she went on, 'they've been to other bureaux and been horribly disappointed. People had just signed them up without taking the trouble to understand them. I'll give you an example,' she said quickly. 'There's a woman who desperately wanted to get married to have children. That's the whole reason why she went to a bureau in the first place. So one of the consultants rings her up and tells her all about this wonderful man and gets her all excited – and then asks her if she minds that he's had a vasectomy.'

Warren laughed shortly.

'It's not funny!' Freddie snapped. 'She was really hurt, and not surprisingly. It's like asking a hydrophobic if they'd like to work as a coastguard.'

He laughed again. 'I'm sorry, it's not funny.'

'No, it isn't,' she agreed. For a moment they were silent. Freddie dismissed Mrs Allen for the evening and then showed Warren into the drawing room. Their rapport, which had been so fragile, had snapped, and Freddie found herself longing for the sound of Bart's key in the lock.

Sitting down, Freddie crossed her legs and turned back to Warren. 'You said you'd been married,' she began, then noticed the flicker of alarm in Warren's eyes. 'I'm sorry, I didn't mean to pry.'

'I was married … ' he hesitated, not knowing if he should

259

pull back, or go on. The room was very warm, an exquisite Christmas tree twinkling expensively against the silk-lined walls. ' … to a woman called Louise. We had a child … '

His thoughts slid backwards. He couldn't have stopped them even if he had tried. His mind skidded down the years like a runaway car and finally came to rest on a spring morning in New York.

' … She was called Alia.' He closed his eyes, a low moan escaping his lips. 'She was only six when she was killed.' Freddie felt the colour drain from her face. 'It was a hit and run accident.' Warren's voice rose, threatened loss of control humming under the words. 'Oh God, she was so little … she was everything to me. All my heart. Even Louise wasn't as precious as her.' His hands shook violently, the memory so savage that he pressed his palms to his forehead in anguish. The years dissolved suddenly – he was back in the morgue identifying his child with all the same pain, the low ache of a stomach emptied by vomiting, the dry scratch of disbelief breaking into a howl of rage. His mind scattered into fragments, his control gone, the only thing remaining was a sense of loss so powerful that it tore at him.

'Oh, God!' he said desperately. 'I can't live with it any more.'

Immediately Freddie moved over to him and sat beside him on the settee. Her eyes filled with pity as she laid her hand on his shoulder.

Warren shuddered as he felt her touch and then turned to her, both of them reaching for each other at the same moment. In silence, Freddie held onto Warren as he clung to her, compassion making her comfort him.

'I'm sorry, so sorry … '

Then slowly he lifted his head and looked into her eyes. His expression was one of incredible anguish, and yet as he gazed at her his expression altered and a low murmur of desire crept over him.

'Freddie,' he murmured.

His breath seemed to burn her as his lips touched her cheeks and moved downwards, pulling aside the collar of her

260

dress as they traced the hidden warmth of her shoulder. Freddie closed her eyes and tried to push him away, but he clung to her fiercely and she finally felt herself respond. Their mouths met greedily, then moved away, their lips moving hotly against each other's cheeks and necks.

'I want you,' he said simply. 'Where can we go?'

Freddie shook her head, trying to form an excuse. But Warren persisted, touching her face with his hands and tracing the line of her shoulders, as he asked her again. 'Where?'

Recklessly, and without considering what they did, he followed her upstairs. Driven by pity and need, they wanted each other with an urgency unknown to either of them before and when Freddie led Warren to a guest room, they fell blindly together onto the bed.

'Freddie,' he repeated, undressing her and then himself.

The bedclothes accentuated the shape of Freddie's body and for an instant he did not want to touch her, knowing that when he did so, as when he finally entered her, not one aspect of her would be the same. Carefully he drew back the sheet and then moaned, moving on top of her, all foreplay dismissed in excitement. Freddie moved under him, the first stirrings of guilt murmuring in her ear as she kissed his neck and his cheeks, her lips moving over his chest, whilst his hands explored her body and his skin lay burning against hers. In her marital home Freddie made love to Warren Roberts, calling out in pain and excitement – then falling silent.

After he had come to a climax Warren looked down at Freddie and then sat up on the side of the bed, staring disbelievingly in front of him. Neither of them said a word. Warren clenched his fists and hung his head, his longing for her as violent as the shame he felt in betraying Bart.

On her side of the bed, Freddie pulled the sheet around her breasts, her heart pounding in complete bewilderment. Warren could not see her, but he heard her breathing as he sat motionless in the darkened bedroom. Many minutes passed, until he could hear nothing other than the sound of her breathing. In, out, in, out, a rhythm of its own. Slowly he began to breathe with her, taking in her life, her soul, part of her very being. In, out, in, out.

Finally his hand reached behind him and touched her back, then traced his fingers down her skin.

'Freddie, I'm so sorry,' he said. 'I should never … '

'It was my fault too,' she replied softly, her voice faint with anguish.

Listlessly their fingers laced together, until Warren turned suddenly and pulled Freddie backwards so that she fell against the sheets, her dark hair spread out against the whiteness. Then his lips moved over hers again, but this time Freddie shook her head and tried to turn away. Warren frowned and then caught hold of her arm, making her cry out, her mouth opening to his as he leaned over her. Driven by frantic desire, he made love to her again, and finally Freddie responded, wanting frantically to block out the remorse, clinging to him and touching him as she had never touched Bart, their passion achieving a form of eroticism through guilt. In desperate silence they lost each other and themselves, but when Warren held Freddie's face between his hands to look at her she glanced away and tried to get up.

'Don't go,' he said simply. 'Please. I care for you, Freddie.'

She sighed, suddenly regaining her senses, knowing what she was doing and knowing also that she had betrayed Bart. Struggling to rise, she tried to push off Warren's arms, but he held onto her, desperate to keep her.

'Warren, let me go!' she said, suddenly afraid.

'Freddie.'

'Let me go … ' she snapped, her voice cut off as he struck her across the face.

Rigid with shock, Freddie lay still, memories of her father flooding back to her.

'I'm sorry,' Warren said blindly, his voice panicky as he touched her face and pulled the sheets around her. Freddie shivered uncontrollably. As he looked at her face, Warren felt a drowning sensation. His memory returned to the fight on his nineteenth birthday, and he caught hold of Freddie's hands, rubbing some warmth into them.

'Freddie, I'm sorry. Oh God, I don't know what came over me. I'm so sorry.'

She remained silent.

'I love you,' he went on, in the darkened room. 'I want you,' Warren said, the words boiling inside him. Come with me, save me. 'I love you.' She shook in his arms, dark head bent down, faceless in the dim light.

He was frantic with grief. 'Oh God, I never meant to hurt you.'

'I'm all right,' Freddie said finally. 'I'm not hurt.'

'I never meant to hurt you … ' he repeated.

Freddie's voice was distant and contained as she rose and dressed carefully. 'It's all right,' she said, over and over again. 'It's all right.'

Warren also dressed, knowing that their love-making, begun so recklessly, had distanced them, not joined them.

'I want to love you, ' he said, pulling on his jacket. 'I never meant … '

Slowly Freddie turned and looked at him. She saw all his confusion and guilt and felt so weary that there was no room left for anger. With both hands, she cupped Warren's face and looked into his eyes. She saw in them two forces working together – destruction and tenderness.

'Warren, we must forget this ever happened.'

'No!'

Freddie nodded emphatically. Please, she prayed, don't argue, just go. 'Forget it, Warren.'

'I need you,' he said, his voice crying out to her, and she realised the truth of his words. She knew that he was tortured and afraid, and yet she also knew that he was capable of violence and obsession. She felt drawn to him, and afraid of him.

'Warren, please go. There's nothing for us. It was a stupid mistake, but it's over.'

His gaze matched hers steadily as he shook his head. 'No, Freddie, it's only just begun.'

Chapter Eighteen

Bart returned an hour later to find Freddie in the shower. Tapping on the glass, he grinned to see her jump and when she put her head around the partition he kissed her wet hair, wrapping a towel around her as she stepped out. She was crying softly and clung to him.

'Hey, hey now,' he said, holding her at arm's length. 'What's the matter?'

'I missed you, Bart,' she said honestly. 'I want us to spend Christmas together. I want us to be as we were.'

He was touched by the words as they reflected his own feelings so exactly. Finding no solution at Bea's, he had walked for hours, then finally come home, dreading having to face Freddie. But she was already waiting for him, and she wanted what he wanted – to save their marriage.

'God, Freddie, I never stopped loving you. I just got worried and kept working to prevent myself thinking about things.'

'I did the same, I did the same!' she said rapidly, clinging onto him and realising how much she loved him. 'But it doesn't matter, we can make it all right again, can't we?'

Bart nuzzled her hair. 'Of course, Freddie, of course we can. Everything will be all right, believe me.'

But her heart kept beating quickly. Of all the people to deceive – Bart, who had never lied to her and who had never betrayed her. Guilt stabbed Freddie like a splinter of glass in her heart.

Determined to repair their marriage, she made plans the next day, and booked a last-minute Christmas holiday in Paris. The tickets were duly delivered, the packing rushed, and Chris was told of Freddie's plans the moment she arrived that morning.

'Good, you should get away for a break,' she said, 'I'll look after everything at this end.'

In a hurry to escape her thoughts, Freddie made all the arrangements assiduously, blocking out the memory of Warren and concentrating all her energy on her future with Bart. She even dared hope that in time to come, her adultery might prove to have been the shock she had needed to force her to take steps to save her marriage. She hoped so, but knew too that the appalling guilt would never fade entirely, and would always be there to remind her of what she had done.

She was angry with herself, especially at her naïvity in allowing herself to be seduced merely because she had felt pity for someone. Yet she knew Warren's grief for his family had been real and could only hope he would dismiss their love-making as a single act of recklessness and keep his distance. He was the wrong person to become involved with, she thought frantically, remembering the frightening intensity of their sexual attraction.

Having made arrangements to meet Bart at the airport, Freddie finished packing and then stopped suddenly, remembering something. Hurriedly she went into the drawing room and flicked on the answering machine, but just as she was turning away, the phone rang. Freddie tensed, waiting to see who the caller was.

'It's me, Warren.'

Freddie stood by the phone, listening, unutterably relieved that she had allowed the machine to answer for her.

'I don't know where you are but I'll call later.' His voice was controlled. 'I miss you. I miss you every moment.' He stopped short. 'I love you.'

The phone went down, severing the connection. Gone, Freddie thought with relief, turning away again. Then she stopped, her mind racing. Dear God, she had to wipe the tape or Bart would find the message! Clumsily her hands fumbled with the dials. He wouldn't believe it at first, she knew that. No, he would have to listen to it again and again, and then what?

The tape rushed back to the start, the message obliterated. Freddie leaned back against the table, her legs unsteady. If only she could wipe the past as easily, she thought. If only.

Frozen under a thick sheet of ice, the lake at Cambuscan looked black and unfathomable, the little white pavilion banked with snow, a few ebony crows cawing as they flew homewards.

Freddie got out of the taxi and stood before the house, her eyes turning towards the weather vane over the stables, the iron cockerel stationary under snow. The afternoon light was heavy, the sky pressing down over the silent garden, the clouds the colour of smoke.

As Freddie walked in, Meg Kershaw rushed over to her smiling.

'Well, what a sight for sore eyes!' she said, hugging Freddie. 'We didn't know you were coming.'

'I came on an impulse,' Freddie answered simply, moving towards the drawing room. 'Is my father home?' she asked, already knowing the answer.

'No, he isn't,' Meg said sharply. 'He's away at the moment.' She changed the subject as she took Freddie's coat. 'Didn't you go away for Christmas?'

Freddie smiled. 'Paris,' she replied. 'It seems a long time ago now.' But it was only six weeks, she thought, six weeks which had changed her life.

Slowly Freddie pushed back the double doors of the drawing room, watching, the familiar scene of her childhood widening before her eyes. The room was the same. The wallpaper, the paintings, the furniture, the footstool by the fireplace, the silk fringe around the rug, and the raised piano lid silhouetted against the window – nothing had changed.

Transfixed, Freddie moved inside, then turned as she heard footsteps behind her.

266

'Freddie, my dearest, dearest girl.'

Her mother's voice was shrill with excitement, her hands outstretched as Freddie hugged her. 'Oh, Freddie, how lovely to see you. How lovely.'

'I wanted to come home, Mummy,' she said simply, drawing back. 'I wanted to spend a few days with you.'

Frowning slightly, Sarah looked over her daughter's shoulder. 'Where's Bart?'

Freddie paused. 'Oh, he's not coming.'

'Not coming?' Sarah repeated innocently. 'Why ever not?'

'He's tied up with business. '

'Business? Again?' her mother persisted. 'Oh, all these men are the same,' she said, moving towards the fire, where she sat down and tugged at her skirt as it rode up over her plump knees. She stole a curious glance at Freddie, wondering just what had triggered this sudden visit – then decided that whatever it was, she didn't really want to know. Instead she made up her mind not to ask any questions at all, and rang for afternoon tea.

Bart Wallace had always been too old for her daughter, Sarah thought; it was sad if things hadn't worked out, but maybe it was for the best. After all, she was on her own most of the time too ... Perhaps Freddie would move back and live with her.

The thought cheered Sarah immensely and she served tea with a light heart, chattering on as her daughter listened patiently to a stream of inconsequential anecdotes about people she did not know. The afternoon darkened, the lamps going on around four, the fire banked high against the Yorkshire cold, the curtains drawn. Relentlessly, Sarah continued to chatter, showing Freddie a recent photograph of her father, her pride in Greville still apparent.

'Well, what do you think? I took it in the summer, in the garden.' Sarah put her head on one side and scrutinised it. 'He wouldn't smile. He never does,' she sighed.

Freddie's eyes fixed on the picture, studying it so hard that for an instant it was almost as though her father was actually looking back at her. She blinked and then noticed that his dark eyes were slightly more sunken, a faint suggestion of ill health unavoidable on the print.

'I'll put it back on the piano,' Sarah said happily, placing the picture beside Freddie's wedding photograph from which Bart smiled out warmly. My God, Freddie thought, how I love that smile and how I love that man.

'He said he might be home for the weekend.'

Freddie was alert. 'Who?'

'Your father, sweetheart,' Sarah explained patiently. 'Who else?'

At eight o'clock that night the restaurant was still quiet as Bart made his way down the stone steps and looked around for Warren. A few early diners sat chatting and did not glance up, and only the head waiter moved over as he noticed the man standing in the doorway. As he approached he recognised Bart and smiled a welcome.

'Mr Wallace, how nice to see you again. Have you booked for dinner?'

Bart glanced round. 'No, I came into see Mr Roberts. Is he here?'

The waiter pointed to the bar tucked away at the side of the restaurant and, nodding, Bart moved over. Warren was sitting with his back to him, nursing a glass of mineral water as he usually did. He never drank spirits early in the evening. Totally unaware of Bart's entrance, he was thinking of Freddie and wondering why she hadn't returned his many calls, his irritation rising daily when she didn't contact him, either by phone or letter. He couldn't believe that she didn't want to see him, and throughout the six weeks since they had made love his obsession with her had grown steadily. She was his first thought in the morning and stayed with him throughout the day, the memory of her sliding over him like a second skin. His fingers touched her, his mouth moved over hers, his voice spoke to her; all his actions were for her and consumed by her. Yet she didn't ring.

Arriving by his side, Bart tapped Warren on the shoulder. He spun round, his face grim, his mind working overtime.

268

'Bart,' he said simply in greeting, a slap of guilt making him brusque. 'I didn't know you were coming for dinner.'

Sliding onto the bar stool beside Warren, Bart ordered a whisky and took several swallows before he answered. 'I just thought I'd drop in.'

Warren's throat tightened. Had Freddie told him? 'How's business?' he asked inanely.

Bart shrugged. 'Fine, but Freddie's gone.'

Warren winced. 'What?' he asked sharply.

Immersed in his own thoughts, Bart turned back to him with a look of resignation. 'It's her blasted mother – she's gone up to Yorkshire for a visit. I spoke to her this morning over the phone, but it's not the same as having her at home. I feel out of touch with her. D'you know what I mean?'

Warren glanced away. *Out of touch with her.* Yes, he knew what Bart meant. Yes, he wanted to say, in my head I touch her constantly. I made love to your wife. *Your* wife, and I'm ashamed that of all men, I betrayed you.

'I'm asking you for advice, as a friend,' Bart went on, the words so ironic that Warren scrutinised his friend's face carefully. Are you baiting me? he wondered. 'I've neglected her so much lately,' Bart continued, holding the glass in his hands tightly. 'I want to make it up to her.'

'You couldn't help being away. You've been busy.'

Bart looked at his friend with affection. 'Don't make excuses for me,' he said simply. 'I was wrong.'

In silence they sat side by side, Bart remembering how he had first met Warren Roberts, the quiet outcast, the one man at the smart party who was not trying to seduce a woman or engage in small talk. Glad of his companionship, Bart glanced over to Warren and saw him as a man of few words, and less treachery.

'How long has Freddie gone away for?' Warren asked at last.

'She says until the weekend, but you know how soft-hearted she is. If her mother starts begging her to stay on, then she will,' Bart replied. 'They live in Yorkshire, the family's got a house there.'

It's called Cambuscan, Warren remembered, almost hearing Freddie's voice as she had told him of her childhood, her descriptions so vivid that he had felt the quick scrape of the water rushes on his hand. As a child, he had been used to cramped rooms and a shared toilet and could hardly imagine a house with so much space for a family with one child.

'I've been a blind fool,' Bart said suddenly, making Warren flinch.

'Why?'

'I have a wife any man would want, and I've neglected her.'

He knows, Warren thought suddenly, he knows and he's playing with me.

'But I'm not going to neglect her any longer. I want her and I'm going to keep her.'

Warren turned back to his drink, seeing a challenge in Bart's words and fighting an impulse to tell him the whole bloody truth.

'So I was thinking, when Freddie gets back to London ... I want you to do something for me.'

Warren took in a deep breath. 'What?'

Bart's eyes were fixed on him so avidly that Warren turned away, ashamed.

'I want you to organise a surprise party for her. Here.' Bart said triumphantly. 'A big surprise.'

'Fine,' Warren said, sickened with his own betrayal.

'You're a good friend,' Bart said finally, glancing up in surprise as Warren got to his feet. 'Do you have to go now?'

'I'm sorry, but I have see how they're getting on in the kitchens,' Warren replied, smiling quickly before turning away and motioning to the barman. 'Another drink over here for Mr Wallace. It's on the house.'

At Cambuscan, Freddie was walking over the field towards the Hall, her eyes fixed on the ground in front of her. So finally it had happened, she thought. Finally she was pregnant. The truth winded her momentarily and she stopped, leaning against a tree and gazing out across the winter fields.

I'm pregnant, Freddie repeated to herself. I am going to

have a child. But not Bart's child, Warren's. She took in her breath and glanced upwards as though some solution lay etched on the clouds. What do I do, she thought for the hundredth time. What do I do?

'Freddie?'

She turned slowly, her hand shielding her eyes from the weak sun. 'Harry!' She smiled, and hurried over to the gate. 'Oh, Harry, I'm so glad to see you.'

He smiled broadly and unlocked the barrier.

'Time was when you would have jumped that,' Freddie said, walking through. 'How are you?'

They stood, embarrassed and uncertain what to do. For an instant they might have embraced, but the moment passed and they fell into step instead, walking down the field towards the Hall.

'You look good,' Harry said.

'You look better,' Freddie replied easily. 'How are things?'

'The Hall's finished – except for the wing which was burned years ago. I've left that alone for the time being.' He smiled, the lines around his eyes creasing the fine skin. 'I've been following your success in the papers, Freddie. You're doing well.'

'The bureau's thriving,' she agreed, glancing over to him. 'Do you remember when we went to Paris all those years ago, with Avery and Dione?' He nodded. 'We wondered then what would happen to us – if we'd look back and think ourselves failures or successes.'

'Oh, Freddie!' Harry said, laughing softly. 'You're only thirty now, and I'm only thirty-three – I think we've got a little way to go before we judge our lives.'

Freddie smiled to herself, her boots leaving impressions on the damp earth as she walked. Almost before she realised it, they had reached the grounds of the Hall, Harry opening the side gate and standing back for her to pass through. The old orangery had been renovated, the high windows replaced, a couple of peacocks cawing out into the cold air.

'You fixed the orangery!' Freddie said with delight, running over and looking in at the windows. 'I never thought you'd manage it.'

271

'It's my life's work,' Harry said, glancing through the window as he stood next to her. 'It's what I wanted to do.'

Freddie smiled and continued down to the house, staring admiringly at the beautiful building which welcomed its visitor. The Hall, my sometime rival, now my friend, Freddie thought wistfully.

'Harry, you've done so well,' she said, linking arms with him and standing in front of the Hall as she had done so often before. 'It's magnificent.'

High and wide, the walls stretched outwards and upwards, the stone pillars replaced, the old rotten doors renovated and standing open to the Yorkshire air. No trace of the fire remained, and none of Avery and his bizarre schemes – no marble chippings, or hoards of film company personnel to churn up the gardens and over-heat the old stone with their lights. Nothing, except the perfection of harmony in a Yorkshire landscape, and the sense of a building which had risen, triumphant, to an applauding world.

'I can't believe it's the old place,' Freddie said, looking at Harry in disbelief. Then she ran towards the front doors and into the Hall.

Harry followed, delighted by her approval. 'I've wanted you to see it for years – but I didn't know how to approach you.'

'You should have phoned, Harry,' she said.

'I didn't know if I'd be welcome.'

Freddie stopped and frowned. 'I said once that I would always been there for you and I meant it,' she said firmly. 'Whenever and wherever.'

He smiled faintly, and for an instant looked like the young boy she had first met, with all the world before him.

'I heard you got engaged,' Freddie said, sitting down on a window seat in the hall.

'And *dis*engaged,' Harry said, shrugging his shoulders. 'I put the house first, Freddie, and she didn't like it any more than you did. I'll never learn.'

'Maybe you're not supposed to, Harry,' Freddie said wisely. 'Only a dedication like yours could have brought this house back from the dead.' She paused. 'You're not lonely, are you?'

'With the calibre of guests he has?' A familiar voice said behind her.

Spinning round, Freddie saw the elegant figure of Dione walk down the central stairs and approach her with her arms outstretched.

'Dione!' Freddie shouted, running to her gratefully, thinking that some God had sent his guardian angel to help her. 'Oh, Dione, you don't know how pleased I am to see you.'

Over her head, Dione glanced at her watching nephew and winked.

They walked and talked for nearly half an hour. Dione told Freddie all her news and made her laugh telling her about the count who had attended Freddie's Christmas party. Apparently he was discovered to be gay, but his outraged father had sent out a denial to all the daughters of the European aristocracy in the hope that his son might still secure a wife. Dione laughed when she told the story and then confided that she had spent thousands at the last Dior sale, her extravagance supported by a lucky buy at auction.

' ... a Viennese chair, my dear, which just happened to be exactly what one of the Rothschilds wanted.' She smiled warmly at the memory. 'My God, it's good to be lucky sometimes.'

'I've missed you,' Freddie said, stealing a quick glance at Dione's face.

'And I you,' she replied. 'But you've been so very successful and so very busy.' Her thoughts shifted back to their conversation on the night of the party at Rutland Gate. 'So, how is your life?'

Freddie took in a deep breath. 'I'm pregnant.'

'That's wonderful!'

'No, it's not. You see, it's not Bart's child. We hadn't made love for a while, Dione. I don't really know why. We just seemed to drift apart.' She glanced away. 'Oh God, Dione, what have I done?'

'Don't you love Bart any more?' Dione asked, stopping in her tracks and glancing around. Harry was nowhere to be seen.

'Of course I do!' Freddie snapped. 'I know what you're thinking, but you're wrong. I don't love anyone else. It was just a mistake, Dione, a terrible mistake. You can't imagine how guilty I feel ... '

'So who *is* the father?'

'I can't tell you.'

'Oh, Freddie, whatever possessed you?'

Freddie hung her head, childishly guilty. 'I don't know. It just happened, that's all.' Her voice rose, 'I can't explain it and I won't make excuses. I just don't know what to do.'

'Well,' Dione said practically. 'You have two choices – to tell or not to tell.'

'I can't let Bart think the baby's his.'

'All right, so tell him. If you do, of course you realise that you will have destroyed him. To hear that his young wife has committed adultery and is carrying another man's baby is hardly likely to make him run cheering into the streets.'

'But if I don't tell him, I'll be lying to him.'

'Yes, and if you do, your marriage will be over. Is it so far gone? Is it over?'

Freddie frowned. 'No! After ... after I acted so stupidly, we went to Paris for Christmas and things were marvellous between us – just like they used to be.'

'So to all intents and purposes, this child could have been conceived on that trip?'

Freddie nodded, then shook her head briskly. 'I *have* to tell Bart the truth – anything else would be dishonourable.'

'My dear Freddie, the dishonour has already been done. The question now is how to avoid hurting others.'

Stung by her words, Freddie breathed in deeply. 'I thought you would advise me to tell Bart the truth ... '

'Why? So that you can absolve your stupidity and guilt by passing it over to him?' Dione caught hold of Freddie's arm. 'The whole truth, my dear, is an instrument which can only be played by an expert.'

'Meaning?'

'Meaning keep your secret. That way Bart will have the child he wants and you will save your marriage.' She paused suddenly. 'You're not in love with this other man, are you?'

'No,' Freddie said firmly.

'Then that's one problem we don't have to face.'

'I don't know if I can carry this off, Dione,' Freddie said honestly.

'You have to,' she replied, her tone imperious and unbending.

Freddie stood silently beside Dione. She knew that if she had confided in Bea, Bea would have been shocked and would have demanded a confession. Bea would also have despised her betrayal of Bart. But who else could Freddie have turned to in London? To Jao? No, she would be bound to take her mother's part, and there was no one else to ask for advice – certainly not Sarah.

If she remained silent, she could give Bart the child he wanted. If she remained silent, she could bring him happiness in his middle-age and secure her marriage. If … If …

'If I have this child, Dione,' Freddie said, 'every time I look at it, I will know who its father really is; and every time I look at Bart, I will know I have deceived him.'

'And the other choice?' Dione replied. 'Abort an innocent – to rid yourself of an embarrassing result of a reckless act of sex?' Dione's voice was precise. 'We all have our secrets and our sins, Freddie – count yourself lucky that you can bring happiness through yours.' Her hand touched the back of Freddie's wrist gently. 'It will be difficult, but you *will* do it. You're young and you're strong. This accident could turn out to be your salvation.'

Returning to Cambuscan Freddie met Mike Kershaw and was deep in conversation with him when she heard a car draw up, and turning, saw her father.

'Oh, my God,' she said, 'I thought he wasn't coming up this weekend.'

Mike followed her gaze, his protective instinct to the fore. 'D'you want to come in the back way? He'll not know you're around if you do.'

Freddie touched his arm gently. 'No, thanks. I might as well get it over with,' she said, walking off towards the house.

275

Pushing open the drawing room doors, she stood facing her father and for an instant was too surprised by the change in him to speak. 'The Handsomest Man in England' was getting old and the angel's head was losing its shuddering beauty. His hair was thinning, his skin, once so perfect, had begun to wrinkle and his eyes were dark rimmed.

'It's good to see you again, Frederica,' he said without enthusiasm. 'Mind you, it's a pity that your husband can't be here.'

'Yes, Father,' she replied coolly.

'Still, I suppose he's busy.'

'Yes, Father,' she replied again. 'He's always busy. In fact, he's doing some work for the Historic Building Society now.'

'You never said,' Sarah muttered, smiling uneasily.

'He only told me last night,' Freddie continued evenly, her defiance obvious to her father. Her eyes were blue and steady. Not violet, as they had been when she was a child, before time had altered them and made them less special. Now they were only blue.

'Excellent,' Greville said uninterestedly.

'Yes,' Freddie said, weighing her words carefully. 'It was nice to have some good news from him – although I have some even better news to tell him tonight.'

Greville's eyes flickered with a mixture of suspicion and curiosity. 'Oh?'

'I'm pregnant,' she said simply.

Sarah leapt to her feet, hugging her daughter, whilst Greville merely smiled and raised his glass to her. 'At last,' he said, 'I was wondering when it would happen.'

'In its own good time, Father,' she said chillingly. 'In its own good time.'

When Freddie finally went up to her room she was hardly aware of the phone ringing downstairs, and was surprised when the high voice of her mother called her. Already tired, she moved listlessly out into the corridor and looked down the stairwell.

'There's a call for you, sweetheart,' Sarah said, nodding her head towards the library. 'Take it in there.'

'I want to see you,' a voice said, as Freddie picked up the receiver. 'I can't live without you.'

'Oh God,' Freddie replied, sitting down heavily. 'Warren, don't ... please don't phone me here.'

'Where then?'

'Nowhere!' she snapped. 'I don't want to talk to you, or see you again,' Freddie said more quietly. 'What we did was wrong.'

'Shit!' Warren said violently. 'Bart neglected you ... '

'I also neglected him ... '

'Oh, grow up!' Warren said harshly, despair making him irrational. 'Come back, or I'll come for you, Freddie. I can't think of anything but you,' he said, uttering the agonising truth. Daily and relentlessly, his obsession with Freddie had grown.

'It's over, Warren. There was nothing to it. We just made a mistake, that's all.'

The bad news tingled towards him.

Warren was too stunned to respond and instead glanced towards the bedroom in his flat. In the wardrobe he had hung a selection of clothes, ready for her when she returned, expensive clothes with elegant labels, bought with care.

'No,' he said simply. 'It can't be. I won't let you go. You're *mine*.'

'I'm married to Bart,' Freddie replied, her voice steady, no emotion showing. The child had first priority now, not her, not Warren, not even Bart. The child was her first concern. Her child and Warren's – only Warren would never know it was his. 'Bart and I have talked. We're going to give our marriage another try.'

'No, Freddie! I love you. It would work out for us. I promise.'

'It wouldn't!' she said flatly, her mind closed to his. Every feeling of pity suppressed. 'I'm sorry, but it's useless, Warren. We're not close, we were just stupid, that's all. To pretend otherwise would be wrong. I'm sorry, really I am. Thank you for ... ' She trailed off, tears close to the surface. 'Take care of yourself.'

Severing the connection, Freddie closed her eyes and pressed her fingers to her lips, remembering Dione's words. Then carefully she dialled the number at Rutland Gate. Bart picked up the phone immediately.

His voice was thick with lack of sleep. 'Who is it?'

'Your wife,' she said with intense relief. 'I want to come home.'

Warren stumbled down the stairs from the apartment and hurried through the restaurant, pushing aside a waiter as he flung back the door and moved out into the street. Dressed only in his dinner suit, he hurried through the freezing streets. His shoes repeatedly lost their grip on the icy pavement as he rounded Maiden Lane, his eyes fixed ahead of him. Seeing him coming, several pedestrians stood back to let him past, the vicious cold whitening his face as his hair flopped heavily over his forehead.

He was oblivious to the temperature, aware only of Freddie and her words, each syllable shadowing him down the darkening streets, each phrase lit up on the hoardings. His jacket flapped open, his shirt was damp with perspiration, his fists balled up tight as he ran across Piccadilly. One car screeched to a halt, another swerved as he dodged the traffic, his eyes wild as he turned, illuminated by the headlights.

At last, exhausted, he hailed a taxi and after giving his instructions to the driver, slumped into the back seat. In the minutes which followed streets passed, neons blazing garishly, theatre lights drawing in people in evening dress. But Warren heard nothing and saw less, and when the cab finally stopped he glanced round, startled, before realising where he was. Staggering out, he pushed a selection of notes into the driver's hands.

'Listen, mate, are you drunk?' the cabbie asked. 'Cos this ain't no place to be out late if you are.'

Without replying, Warren dismissed the man with a wave of his hand and began to make his way towards the dockside. In the floodlight the ships were huge, the warehouses empty and forbidding. Night sounds scuttered around him, rats scurrying and chains clanking in the biting wind as Warren climbed over rubble, skirting the illuminated bank of the Thames where a brazier was burning and two night-watchmen stood talking and stamping their feet.

Breathless, Warren stopped to force air into his lungs, the cold chilling him and making him shiver as he leaned back against a warehouse door. When he had regulated his breathing, he pushed himself upright and moved into the warehouse, feeling his way in the dark. Finding the stairs, he began to climb upwards, floor after floor. Beneath him a door creaked but he never turned. He reached for the night sky, the vast dark wilderness which he could see through the broken roof, and he climbed on silently, the pain which filled him too immense to find a voice. Up and up he went, his hands gripping the steel rails, his expensive leather shoes scuffed by the iron steps.

Warren had come to this place as a child, on his own, knowing that at night it was deserted and therefore quiet. In this place he had talked aloud – to no one but himself. Here he had dreamed his dreams and here he had come that day before he left England ... The memory stung him as he pushed himself upwards faster and faster, finally reaching the roof and hauling himself up. Steadily he looked out over the night sky and at the water lapping coldly against the dockside below.

Then he moved towards the edge of the roof and hesitated, looking around. Frowning, he turned and peered into the semi-dark, finally catching sight of the hole in the roof and moving towards it. Just as he reached it, he slipped and landed heavily on his knees, his hands thrown out before him, landing either side of the jagged gap. The drop to the warehouse was over fifty feet, but Warren wasn't going to jump. Instead, in a gesture of blind agony, he leaned down into the hole and screamed out his pain.

Over and over he cried out, the sound tearing at him, his body crouched over the dark hole, the noise of his anguish filling the empty building and souring the night tide.

Chapter Nineteen

Stunned by the news of his wife's pregnancy, Bart was at first too shocked to accept it, and then too delighted to think of anything other than the coming child. There had been a moment when Freddie had been tempted to confess, but Bart's euphoria had been such that Dione's words came back to warn her. 'The whole truth is an instrument which can only be played by an expert,' she had said, and Freddie, knowing how right she was, kept silent.

Bart was not alarmed by the prospect of becoming a parent for the first time in his fifties, for he had long wanted to commit himself totally and irredeemably to a child of his own. Not a day passed without plans being made for its future and not a night passed without Bart's hand stealing over Freddie's skin and lying protectively over her swelling stomach.

And what of Freddie? She was again Bart's wife in all ways. Having clawed back her marriage, she was grateful to the child she carried, and protective of her husband. Nothing would harm Bart, she swore, *nothing*. She would have this child for him, and although she would never forget that Warren was the father, Bart must never know. To the world outside, she and Bart were going to have their first child – the perfect couple crowning their happiness with a family. Overdue it might be, but a baby was finally on its way, and with its coming it would secure a future and a marriage.

When Freddie did think of Warren she felt two emotions – guilt and pity. The phone calls still came intermittently, but only to her private business line. Every time she heard his voice she explained carefully that they had nothing to discuss. After a few months had passed, she stopped saying anything and merely replaced the receiver, locking him out of her life. She knew how such behaviour would hurt him. As a child she had been injured repeatedly by rejection. But there was no choice. She had to keep Warren away from her, and from her family. Sleeping with him had been an error of judgement – one occasion of weakness which could have cost her every-thing – but instead it was to be the saving of her marriage. And *nothing* was going to threaten that now.

Freddie was sensitive enough to see Warren's side of the story. Having shared his deepest griefs and shown his weaknesses he had tried to force a relationship between them, desperate to cling onto the woman he had confided in. Warren had found sympathy and tenderness in Freddie and had thought mistakenly that he could make her love him. But he never realised that she was afraid of him – and afraid of the overwhelming sexual desire she felt for him. For months after they had slept together, Freddie would dream of his body and long for him, waking filmed with sweat, aroused and guilty.

But all Warren knew was that the woman he wanted, did not want him. Freddie had walked back into the arms of her failing marriage and had chosen Bart instead of him. Unaware of the depth of his obsession, she did not know how Warren's disappointment swelled under the weight of her recovered good fortune.

Having decided on her course of action, Freddie meticu-lously prepared the groundwork, visiting her gynaecologist, Teddy Reynolds, and telling him the true parentage of her child. A thin, freckled American with a Deep South accent, he listened without expressing any surprise, his quizzical eyes watching the woman in front of him.

'So you intend to let your husband think the child is his?' he asked.

Freddie nodded. 'It's better for everyone.'

Teddy Reynolds leaned back in his seat. 'Are you sure?' he drawled easily. 'If you made a clean breast of things … '

'I've thought it all out,' Freddie said calmly, 'and I've decided what to do. I'm not in love with the real father and I know he wouldn't make a good parent.' Freddie lifted one hand to her face in embarrassment. 'Bart wants this child. He's longed for a family for years – and he'll make a marvellous father.'

'And you love him?'

She never hesitated. 'Yes, Yes, I do. We went through a bad period, but he's a good man and he's changed so much since he knew about the baby. He's kind, considerate – ' her voice was adamant ' – and he wants this child. He really wants this child.'

Teddy Reynolds glanced down at his notepaper and began to doodle large loopy swirls on the white paper. 'So, according to your dates,' he wrote some figures in a row, underlining the last one, 'Your child is due on September 18th.'

The summer slumped in, hot and sultry, the London air steaming. By June, Freddie was getting heavy, her pregnancy obvious. She began her work at the bureau later in the mornings and finished earlier at night. The clients were generally delighted by her pregnancy – a married woman expecting a child was exactly the right person to advise them – but a few were patently jealous, and made their thoughts apparent.

'I don't suppose you'll have time for us now,' one said to Freddie.

'I always have time for you, you know that,' Freddie replied evenly.

'With a child?' the woman responded. 'I doubt it. You've got it made now, haven't you? Rich husband, kid on the way – no problems.'

No problems, Freddie thought wryly, watching as the client left the room and Bart walked in.

'Hi, sweetheart, I've just seen Warren,' he said, kissing the top of Freddie's head and slumping into the seat opposite her. 'He looks God awful.'

The blood pumped loudly in Freddie's ears, but she said nothing.

'I asked him what the matter was, but you know Warren,

he never tells anyone anything. You know something? I think he was offended that we never held that party at the restaurant. After all, I had talked to him about it – he must have felt slighted when I didn't go back to fix it up.' Bart looked at his wife and frowned suddenly. 'What's the matter?'

Freddie swallowed painfully and leaned back against the seat.

'God, Freddie, are you OK?'

The room spun around her, images of her love-making with Warren flaring up before her eyes.

'Freddie?' Bart repeated, getting up and putting his arm around her with infinite tenderness.

'I just felt … faint,' she managed to say.

'It's too hot in here, that's why!' Bart snapped, getting to his feet and returning a moment later with a cold flannel. Chris followed behind him with a glass of water. 'We should get some better air-conditioning put in.' He fussed around. Freddie's pregnancy had made him wildly protective. 'Come upstairs and put your feet up, darling.'

Freddie smiled at Bart indulgently, as his face creased into a worried frown. Bart was so delighted by the prospect of becoming a father that he idolised Freddie simply because she was carrying his child. All his old worries now seemed foolish. His life was rich and his marriage secured. Their mutual relief held them together fiercely.

'You have to take care of yourself,' he went on. 'I don't want anything to happen to you, Freddie. I neglected you once, it won't happen again. Besides, we have our baby to think of now.'

The deception was completely successful in all areas, although Freddie had found the news of her pregnancy hard to break to Bea. She decided to telephone Dorman Square, rather than visit in person, and as congratulations swung over the telephone line she imagined Bea singing later that night at the Bayswater hotel, and knew that the memories would come back, Freddie's words mingling with the lyrics of an old love song. Would she guess, Freddie wondered, would Bea guess? Intuitive, honourable Bea – did Freddie really imagine that she could deceive her? For a moment Freddie had the ludicrous desire to confess, to tell Bea the truth. Then, almost as she surrendered to the temptation, she stopped herself – Bea would never condone her action, and she could not expect her to. The secret would have to be kept, and carried, by Freddie alone.

Then one early morning in late summer when she was just coming out of the Burlington Arcade, Freddie noticed a figure on the other side of the street and stopped dead in her tracks. Directly across the street, standing immovable on Piccadilly, Warren Roberts watched her. His eyes were unreadable, his expression blank, and although he had not seen her for months he wanted her as much as ever; even though her pregnancy was obvious under the white cotton dress; he wanted her.

Transfixed, Freddie stared back, her dark eyebrows drawn together in a frown, one hand lifted to shield her eyes from the sun. She had not expected to see Warren again, and when she did, a rush of unexpected longing shook to life inside her. Every pore of her body seemed suddenly exposed and sensitised, every hair tensed, every thought absorbed by the man who now watched her and beckoned her to go to him. Her mouth dried, the sunlight punching her, each sun mote leaden with guilt.

Then suddenly the sound of a passing ambulance siren broke the high summer spell, and Freddie walked away quickly, one hand resting protectively on her stomach. Her eyes were fixed ahead and only when she had gone several yards did she turn … but Warren had gone. Taking in a deep breath, Freddie calmed herself. Warren's restaurant was nearby – how could she expect to live in the same city and not see him? She had to get used to the idea that their paths might cross – and she had to be prepared.

Others were getting prepared too; Sarah, Dione, the Wilkie women, and Pennsylvania Parry.

'Dearest, loveliest Freddie,' Penn gushed, rolling into Rutland Gate, his red face swaddled with its ginger beard and wet with tears. 'I'm sorry. I always get so emotional.'

'So what else is new?' Freddie asked, smiling and kissing him on the cheek.

He blew his nose loudly and grasped her hand. 'You look wonderful and I'm so pleased to see you're having a baby. It's right for you. Perfectly. I don't even mind that you're not doing any research for me any more – even though I never found anyone else as good.' His thoughts wandered, then returned to his original theme. 'When you left, I grieved, Freddie, *grieved* for you.' He swallowed, 'But now, to see you happy and having a baby … You look just like a Madonna,' he said, sobbing again.

Freddie smiled and linked arms with him, leading Penn into the drawing room and sitting him down to let him compose himself.

'Oh, Penn, don't get upset,' she said kindly. 'I want to ask you something.'

His corsetted bulk moved stiffly as he leaned towards her. 'What is it, dearest Freddie?'

'I want you to be the baby's godfather.'

His response was immediate, a flood of violent tears, followed by some concerted nose blowing and several determined nods of the head. 'Love to, love to,' he blurted out finally. 'What an honour, especially for an emotional man like me. An honour.'

Dorman Square was restful. Heavy-leafed summer trees swayed thick with moisture from a sudden light shower and the smell of cut grass drifted over from the communal garden. From the many open windows came the sounds of radios, children laughing, and someone practising piano scales. Encouraged by the idyllic atmosphere, Freddie rang the bell and shifted the flowers in her hands, her smile already formed before the door was opened by Trisha.

'Freddie!' she said delightedly, ushering her guest in, relieving her of the bouquet, and chattering all the way up the stairs to the first floor. 'Everyone's out,' she said, nudging open the sitting room door with her bottom. 'You should have called first.'

'I thought I'd surprise you all instead,' Freddie said by way of an explanation. 'How's Charlie?'

'He's fine,' Trisha replied, blushing, her manner as naïvely beguiling as ever. 'He's not wandered off with any more actresses,' she said, touching the wooden sideboard for luck. 'And he doesn't go on those long trips any more ... and frankly, I'm glad.' She paused, laying the flowers down carefully. 'It's great about the baby. When's it due?'

Freddie faltered, surprised by Trisha's delight. 'In September, September 18th.'

Trisha's eyebrows rose. 'That's not long, is it? Have you got everything you need? You know, nappies, and things like that. I remember when Jao was little it was chaos here for months; things drying all over the place, and sour milk.' She wrinkled up her nose, her eyes resting on Freddie's stomach momentarily. 'Does it kick?'

'Of course. Do you want to feel it?'

Trisha nodded again and giggling, rested her hand on Freddie's stomach just as the door opened and Bea walked in. At once Freddie felt a rush of affection on seeing the woman who had steered her through a wretched adolescence, made pizzas for her at two in the morning, comforted her, and loved her unconditionally.

'Bea,' she said and then stopped, her pleasure at seeing her friend suddenly obliterated by a sharp flicker of guilt. *What if she knew about the baby; what if she guessed?*

But Bea never hesitated and stepped forward with her arms extended. 'Ah, sweetheart, the baby – at last,' she said, hugging Freddie, the swell of Freddie's stomach between them. 'This is such good news.'

Trisha watched them for a moment and then pointed to the flowers. 'What about these?'

'Oh, I nearly forgot!' Freddie said, reaching over to the sideboard and giving Bea the bouquet. 'I wanted to ask you something ... ' She hesitated, wondering about the wisdom of what she was about to do. 'It was just an idea.'

'So, get on with it!' Bea said, exasperated.

'I want you to be the baby's godmother,' Freddie said finally.

286

Bea's eyes fixed on the flowers. Godmother to Bart's child. Godmother to the child of the man she had once loved.

'Well?' Trisha said ingenuously. 'Aren't you going to answer?'

Carefully, Bea glanced at Freddie. 'You're like a second daughter to me,' she said, 'so ... I'd love to be godmother to your child.'

When Freddie returned to Rutland Gate, Jean Allen was in the hall, sifting through the second post. She glanced up with a brisk smile.

'There's a letter for you, Mrs Wallace,' she said, passing it to Freddie. 'Lunch will be ready in about an hour.'

Freddie looked at the handwriting with unease, a nudge of premonition making her wary.

Jean Allen turned to go and then thought of something. 'Incidentally, Mrs Wallace, there's an ant's nest by the kitchen door.' She straightened her narrow shoulders confidently. 'But I'll have it destroyed in no time.'

'Oh, good,' Freddie said absent-mindedly, walking upstairs with the letter and lying down on the bed. Around her, the hot summer air swung heavily, and the smell of boiling tar on the road outside crept in through the open window. Suddenly nauseated, Freddie turned over onto her side and ripped the letter open.

> Freddie,
> can't sleep, can't think, can't live, but I'm going to try
> to put my feelings into words.

Freddie glanced at the signature, recognising Warren's handwriting and knowing already what it would say. The note was written in a heavy hand, not well formed and hinting at an inadequate education.

> When I saw you a few weeks ago you were pregnant.
> It was a shock, although it shouldn't have been.
> You're married after all, and Bart ... I was going to say
> that he'd make a good father, but I don't want to

admit it. I want you back, Freddie, I don't care that you're having his child, I just want you back. I thought I wouldn't give a damn after so long. I thought I'd hate you, but I couldn't. I thought I'd get used to losing you. I even used to kid myself that I'd got your memory … But it's the other way round, Freddie – your memory's got me. I'll love you and the child. I'll take you both on. You don't love Bart. He neglected you and left you alone. He didn't appreciate you. You know how he hurt you. I don't want to injure him, but God, I want you. What are you doing to us?

Warren.

The letter left Freddie feeling like an animal recaptured after a spell of freedom. Slowly she crumbled the paper in her hand and rolled onto her back, nausea welling up in her violently as she did so.

Chapter Twenty

The baby was born on September 20th in a private clinic off Harley Street, Teddy Reynolds in attendance. He arrived a little after midnight, Freddie refusing an epidural, the pain endured not avoided. Crying only once, the child made his way into the world, dark haired, like his mother and Bart, his eyes shuttered. Bart had chosen to be in at the birth, but found himself helpless in the face of Freddie's pain and amazed that after the birth she recovered enough to smile at him and reach out for her son. Together the new parents watched as the baby lay silently against her breast, Freddie scrutinising each of his sleeping features, looking for signs of his father in him, whilst Bart found himself hopelessly emotional, his speech fast, his eyes filled with tears.

'He's wonderful,' Bart said repeatedly, the miracle of the child rendering him childlike himself. 'Wonderful.'

Freddie smiled and rested her head against her husband's shoulder, but after he left she found herself leaning over the cot and watching her son avidly. Finally he woke, his eyes opening briefly without focusing. Freddie stiffened.

The nurse peered over her shoulder. 'What lovely blue eyes he's got.'

'All babies have blue eyes,' Freddie said, her heart banging as she pulled the blanket around her son. 'They'll change when he gets older.'

'That's true, dear,' the nurse said obligingly. 'Babies' eyes do change colour.'

'They'll be brown like his father's,' Freddie interrupted, glancing back at the child. 'They'll be brown, won't they? Just like your father's.'

But they remained blue. High summer blue. Clear, light sharp blue. Warren Roberts' blue. A blue with intelligence and clarity in it – a blue she remembered well. Not that anyone gave the matter a second's thought, and when Sarah came down to visit her daughter in the hospital she was ecstatic.

'He's so handsome,' she trilled lightly. 'Just like you were at his age.' Her hands picked at the bedspread restlessly. 'You look a little tired, Freddie, you must rest now, d'you hear me? And if you can't rest at home, you can both come to us. I know Bart won't mind.' She glanced over to her husband who had just walked in. 'Freddie can come to us, can't she, Greville?'

'Frederica can if she wants,' he replied, walking over to the baby and looking down. Freddie's heart beat faster, certain that he, of all people, would spot something, some little give-away. But he didn't seem to, and merely straightened up, a faint scent of lemon cologne wafting over to his daughter.

'He seems fine.'

'He's splendid,' Sarah said defensively.

'Oh?' her husband replied coolly. 'I didn't realise you were such an expert on babies.'

When they left the nurse came back, pink with excitement. 'Is that your father?' Freddie nodded. 'Oh, he's very handsome, isn't he?'

' "The Handsomest Man in England", ' Freddie murmured, smiling to herself and thinking of the first time she had heard the words – on that day when Harry jumped over the gate. It had been so long ago, when everyone had expected her to stay in Yorkshire, marry, and have a handful of children. But instead of marrying Harry, she had aligned her fortunes with Bart, and now she had a child. A son, born into a secret and carrying a hidden inheritance every bit as priceless as the Avery line.

'I expect you're hoping that the baby will inherit your father's looks,' the nurse went on.

Freddie touched the sleeping child's face and smiled. 'Handsome is as handsome does,' she said softly.

Pennsylvania had no idea what a baby was supposed to look like, he just knew that Freddie's son was more handsome and more talented than any other child who had ever breathed. He visited her on the second day after the birth, bearing a large panda from Hamleys and a bunch of carnations. His stout form rested uncomfortably on the edge of the hospital bed.

'Oh, what a lovely, lovely baby. ' Out came the handkerchief. 'It makes me want to have one myself.'

'That would be a novelty, Penn,' Freddie said drily.

'Oh, I mean that I'd like to be a father.' He extended one monumental finger towards the sleeping child and stroked its cheek. 'There, there ... Oh, babies make one so sentimental,' he cooed into the crib. 'My godson. What a marvellous, wonderful boy.'

Jao was the next to visit, her fair hair tucked under an oversized cap, her thin legs in cord trousers and a man's tweed jacket completing the outfit. When she walked in, Freddie blinked.

'What happened to you? You fall off a float?'

'Ha, ha!' Jao responded, leaning over the crib. 'Oh, he's great – it almost makes me broody. Almost, but not quite.' She passed a bunch of violets to Freddie. 'So, how are the stitches?'

'Let's put it this way – the pattern would never sell.'

Jao grinned. 'And the happy father?'

'Ecstatic,' Freddie replied calmly. 'He's thrilled with the baby.'

'I'm not surprised, at his age,' Jao said, glancing back to the child. 'So what's its name?'

'Conrad.'

'Conrad,' Jao repeated approvingly. 'Nice and English. I had a horrible vision of Bart calling it Chuck or something.'

'We did consider Alvin,' Freddie said wryly, 'but we didn't want to give him a name he couldn't live up to.'

Jao nodded sagely. 'And I suppose the proud grandparents have been down to see the heir?'

'Yesterday,' Freddie agreed. 'As usual, my father had his effect on the female staff and for the rest of the day I had some nurse drooling over the bed-clothes.'

'Nasty.'

'Very,' Freddie agreed.

Jao changed the subject deftly, her tone suddenly serious. 'I'm glad it worked out, Freddie, and I'm glad you're happy. That said – I have to go. I've got another job interview.' She slipped off her seat and taking one last look at Conrad said 'You know, he reminds me of someone.' Freddie's breath caught in her throat. 'I can't remember who, but it'll come back to me,' Jao said, waving and walking out.

Startled by Jao's words, Freddie stared at her child. But as the days passed she found nothing in Conrad's appearance to alarm her. In fact a number of people remarked on the resemblance he bore to his father and to herself. Bit by bit she relaxed, her optimism coming to the fore again, her thoughts bright for the future … until she returned home with her son.

Away from the cloistered world of the hospital, Freddie refused all offers of help, having decided to look after Conrad herself. But her initial curiosity about her son's appearance soon developed into something more worrying and before long she was spending hours scrutinising Conrad's face for any sign of Warren. The constant anxiety soon tired her. Exhausted by the birth and by guilt, she paced the nursery at night and slept little during the day, developing an irrational fear that when she was absent, Bart would come into see the child and somehow *know*. The thought terrorised her and the strength she had before the birth soon evaporated, leaving her frantic and isolated.

Freddie's condition deteriorated so much that an anxious Bart rang Teddy Reynolds for advice. He was only temporarily reassured by the doctor's assurance that Freddie would settle down in time.

' … But she's exhausting herself. She's not sleeping, and she's not rational any more.'

The doctor tried to soothe him, knowing Freddie's history and suspecting the real reason for her erratic behaviour. 'If you're really worried, perhaps I should come and visit her.'

Yet when Bart suggested it to Freddie, she over-reacted and refused point blank to see the doctor. What could he do? She asked herself repeatedly. What could he say or do? Nothing. She was the only one who knew what to do and she knew that her place was at home, with her child.

Ten days passed. Ten sleepless days and nights. Conrad was a quiet baby but Freddie remained a distracted mother. Nothing could prise her away from her child. Nothing. She didn't work or show any interest in the bureau. All phone calls were taken on the portable phone, all visitors greeted in the nursery and at night Conrad slept in his cot by his parent's bed, his mother's hand clenched tightly onto the rails of the crib. Over-tired and overwrought, Freddie became with-drawn. Bart was frantic with worry about her.

Meanwhile, at Cambuscan, Sarah was blissfully ignorant of her daughter's condition and phoned every day, taking Freddie's blithe assurances on face value.

'When are you going to visit us at home?' Sarah asked repeatedly.

Freddie thought of her father and a hunted look came into her eyes. 'Soon, Mum, soon. When Conrad's a little bigger.'

'I could come down to you ... '

'Not just yet, Mummy. But soon. Soon.'

Of all the fears which circled Freddie's brain, the most terrifying was that Bart should find out that Conrad was not his child. The fear was not primarily for herself, but for her husband. She had watched Bart since Conrad's birth and seen the difference in him, the besotted affection given so gener-ously, the tenderness making his goodness apparent. No child could have been blessed with a better father, and Freddie realised that if Bart ever found out that Conrad was not his son, the truth would destroy him.

Such fears bedevilled Freddie and made sleep impossible. Something had to give way, and she knew it, for she was lucid enough to realise that she could not spend her whole life defending her son from prying eyes. Someone, some day, would know the truth and the truth would ruin her. Maybe, she thought with a rush of despair, Bart would find out and brand her an unfit mother; maybe he would steal Conrad in the night and take him away from her ...

Freddie's guilt made her so irrational that in the end she could only see a future without husband, child, or security. All the things she prized and had fought for so fiercely, she would lose because of her own deceit. Freddie peered into Conrad's cot, her heavy hair falling over her face, her panic transmitting itself to her son who cried out suddenly and continued crying, his screams bringing someone running up the stairs.

Freddie heard the footsteps and panicked. It was Bart! He *knew* and was coming to take her child away. With shaking hands, Freddie gathered her son up in her arms and backed up against the far wall of the nursery, hugging the baby to her breast protectively as the door was thrown open and Dione rushed in. In total disbelief, she glanced at Freddie, noticing at once that her face was bloodless, her eyes huge, her arms gripped around her screaming son.

'Freddie,' she said cautiously, 'are you all right?'

Freddie said nothing in reply, but some kind of reality permeated through the horror and she recognised Dione and blinked. 'Don't let Bart take him away from me, will you?'

Dione frowned. 'No one's going to take the baby, Freddie,' she said gently, shocked by the deterioration in her. 'Conrad is your baby.'

Freddie nodded frantically, but backed further away. 'Yes, he is my baby. He is my baby.'

'Then why would Bart take him away from you?' Dione asked, well aware that Freddie was close to collapse.

Freddie stared into Dione's eyes without replying, her lips pale and swollen, her eyes heavy-lidded. 'You know why, Dione,' she said helplessly, sounding like a child.

'Freddie, listen to me! Bart has no reason to take Conrad away from you. He loves you and he loves his son.'

Freddie shook her head stiffly. 'No,' she said, her eyes filling. 'He's not his father.'

'I know,' Dione said firmly. 'You told me, Freddie.'

'He'll guess, you see, Bart has brown eyes and the baby has blue eyes,'

'*All* babies have blue eyes.'

'Not when they grow up!' Freddie said helplessly.

Dione sighed. 'Listen, everyone in your family has blue eyes. Bart's natural child wouldn't necessarily have brown eyes like his ... '

Freddie was impervious to reason. 'No, no, he'll know and he'll take him away. I know it. He'll take him away.'

'Yes, he probably will!' Dione said, her eyes fixed on Freddie mercilessly. She could see what guilt had done, how the secret of Conrad had unbalanced Freddie, but she wasn't about to let her give in. 'He will take your child, Freddie, and do you know why? Because you're not fit to be a mother.'

Her words slapped Freddie into reason and she blinked, her mind clearing. 'How dare you say that – '

Dione saw the change and pushed on. 'I dare say it, because it's true. You aren't fit to look after this child. You're letting your guilt ruin everything. Look at you!' she sneered. 'You were a beauty and now you're a hag. You don't wash, don't brush your hair and can't hold a reasonable conversation – Conrad *should* be taken away from you.'

Freddie drew herself up to her full height, her voice firm, her eyes blazing. 'How dare you talk to me like that!'

'I dare, because I remember when you were a girl – with all the promise in the world,' Dione hissed. 'You've disappointed me, Freddie. Not by your adultery – that was a stupid mistake – but by this. This is indulgence, not guilt. Indulgence.' Dione's voice was frightening. 'Get yourself together, girl, and take your place in the world. You have a good husband, a healthy child and a fine future – if you can just let go of the past. Forget it, and grow up!'

Swiftly she walked over to Freddie and took Conrad from her arms, settling him down in his cot.

About to protest, Freddie said. 'But I – '

'Be quiet!' Dione snapped, cutting Freddie off and steering her towards the bathroom where she turned on the cold tap in the shower. Then still fully clothed, she shoved Freddie under the water.

'Welcome back to civilisation!' she shouted triumphantly, Freddie gasping and crying out as Dione folded her arms and leaned against the glass doors.

Chapter Twenty-One

'He didn't like me,' Claire Rivers said simply, her humiliation apparent. 'I could tell.'

Freddie laid down her pen and watched the woman in front of her. 'How do you know that?'

'He said he'd ring – and he didn't.'

Sighing, Freddie made a note on her file. 'I'm afraid men do that a lot,' she said sympathetically. 'Actually I have a belief that they think the phone takes a little of their soul away every time they use it.'

Claire smiled wryly. 'So it happens to your other clients too?'

Freddie nodded. 'Most of them. I can't understand it. The women say they'll ring – and they do. The men say they'll phone – and they either don't, or they phone three days later, or they hesitate so long that they talk themselves out of ever wanting to phone at all!'

'I'm glad,' Claire said softly. 'I thought it was just me. You know ... it's embarrassing.'

Freddie had heard the same words so often, and yet she replied evenly, 'Just stick with it, Claire. We'll find you someone, I promise.' She got to her feet and showed the woman out, adding 'And I'll make sure he knows how to use the telephone too.'

A year and a half had passed. Conrad was thriving and Bart was hugely relieved that his wife had recovered from her temporary instability. Freddie enjoyed her family and put her worries in a mental glory-hole – where they stayed. Freddie found that after going through the crisis from which Dione had saved her, she was now stronger, and less likely to panic. When Bart had mentioned Warren, Freddie had suggested that he keep friends with him, but confessed that she had never liked him. The explanation was feasible to Bart, after all, he had seen the animosity between the two, and as time passed, his friendship with Warren faded and any conflict of loyalty between friend and wife ceased.

With fierce discipline, Freddie calmed herself. Her anxiety, although never completely absent, was controlled, and her guilt faded gradually as the months passed and she heard nothing again from Warren. For her, Warren ceased to live, and his memory did not linger. Instead Freddie concentrated every thought on her son and her husband. Having been dangerously aroused once, and having seen the result of that eroticism, Freddie was grateful for the comfortable sex she enjoyed with Bart which was full more of tenderness than of passion. A considerate lover, Bart was careful with his wife, and she was constantly pliable. If Freddie did think about sex with Warren, the thought was immediately banished, the shame welling up in her, her hands spreading protectively across Bart's back whilst he lay on top of her, her wedding ring an ever present reminder of her betrayal. Constantly kind, Bart relished his home, and found himself working shorter hours, his business finally relegated to second place as he settled with his family.

Bart adored Conrad. He did not love him, or enjoy him, he *idolised* his son. Every morning he rose early to play with the child, every weekend was spent with his son, and every thought was prefaced with 'When Conrad's older ... ' or 'do you think Conrad would like to ... ?'

Intensely grateful, Freddie encouraged such devotion, watching as Conrad developed from a tiny infant into a strong toddler. His body was stocky, his legs sturdy and the few words he spoke were greeted with ecstatic joy by his doting parents. But his eyes remained blue and there was a certain intensity in his character that was not typical of either of his parents.

297

'Look at that!' Bart said, pointing to his son with indulgent astonishment. 'He was determined to get that toy.' He watched as Conrad lifted the stuffed animal and held onto it grimly. 'He knows what he wants! Yes, sir, he knows what he wants in life.' Bart glanced over to Freddie and smiled. 'You know, I've never seen a child so damn feisty. It makes you wonder where he gets it from.'

The only disadvantage of Bart's great love for his son was that he constantly tried to monopolise the child. Outsiders were allowed only so much time with him; Bea's audiences were limited; and Conrad's grandparents saw very little of the heir to Cambuscan. Not that Greville was interested in his grandson, but Sarah was, and constantly pleaded with Freddie over the phone.

'I could come down to see you both, darling. I don't mind,' she said. 'I've hardly seen the little soul.'

'Listen, Mummy,' Freddie said patiently, understanding how her mother felt and trying to make some recompense. 'Bart's going off to New York next week and I was going to come up and surprise you.'

'Oh, sweet Freddie, how lovely, how really lovely!' her mother trilled over the line. 'I can't wait. When will it be?'

'I think Tuesday,' Freddie said. 'I'll ring and confirm everything at the weekend.'

Bart's trip to New York had been postponed twice until it became imperative for him to go. It should have made it easier that he still had retained a small flat in New York, but the apartment was no longer frequently used as Freddie stayed in London, Rutland Gate being more suited to a child's needs. Besides, Bart found little to call him back to America as his family were all dead and he no longer had roots there. Since his marriage to an English wife and the birth of his child abroad, he felt a deeper bond with London than with New York and was more than a little reluctant to go away.

For her part, Freddie was grateful for Bart's absence as she could finally visit Yorkshire again, taking her son with her. Since Conrad's birth, she had not gone home. Instead Sarah had made frequent trips down to London, Greville accompanying her only twice and never staying at Rutland Gate. He showed little interest in his grandson and Freddie bitterly resented the fact that he spent so little time with her family whilst he willingly spent days with his mistress only a handful of streets away. Her resentment was an old one, endurable because she had grown used to her father's treatment; but his lack of interest in her son was new, and it scorched her.

It hurt her so much that subconsciously she developed a real need for her father to accept Conrad, knowing that if he could be persuaded to love the child, her son's inheritance was secure. And that mattered to her. It was not so long ago that Sarah had lost the son she wanted so desperately. The son and heir to Cambuscan. Freddie frowned, wondering if perhaps that was the reason for her father's attitude to Conrad. Perhaps he resented the fact that his son would not inherit, and that instead his grandson would one day take over the Clough fortune.

Ruefully Freddie shook her head. If Greville knew the real truth what would he do, she wondered. If he knew that his grandson was really the son of a restaurant owner and not the wealthy and respectable Bart Wallace, what would he think? The thought jangled on Freddie's nerves. Her father, who had cheated on her mother all their lives, was now rejecting a child who could so easily have been born to his mistress. He was rejecting the interloper without even knowing it. The thought unsettled her and when Bart walked back into the bedroom Freddie jumped.

'Hey, what's the matter?' he said, sitting down on the bed next to her.

'Sorry. You just startled me, that's all.'

He glanced round the room, the walls were hung high with blue damask, and the wide bed sported a carved French bedhead, a gold display cabinet full of *objets trouvés* facing them. Divided into dozens of tiny compartments, the Venetian cabinet contained many of the eccentric pieces Freddie had collected, such as a 17th-century Spanish purse and a diminutive gold salamander with garnet eyes.

'I love the way you've decorated this house,' Bart said, kissing her gently on the cheek and taking her hand tenderly. 'It's a show place.'

'It's a home,' Freddie corrected him, her arms going around him, her hair brushing against his chin.

'And we've got Conrad,' Bart added, 'to make it complete.'

Freddie nodded, raising her face. 'Yes, we've got him too.'

His mouth found hers and he kissed her softly, then drew back to look at her. 'I love you.'

'I love you too,' she replied.

'I don't want to go to New York,' he said abruptly, picking up a strand of her hair and weighing it in his hand. 'But I'll be back soon, and then I thought we'd all go away somewhere.'

Freddie closed her eyes, contented. Thank God, she thought. After all that had happened, thank God.

'Do you think we should sell the New York apartment?' Bart asked suddenly, watching as Freddie's eyes opened and she glanced at him in surprise.

'Sell it? Why?'

'I was thinking that I could concentrate on the practice in England ...'

'But you like to go back to New York at times, you know you do. Besides, you were brought up there. It's your home. How would you feel if you sold up entirely?'

Bart's eyes were gentle as he shook his head, his left hand tracing the line of his wife's cheek. 'It's not my home. My home is where you are, and where my son is. My home is with you.'

Parting was not easy. Having found contentment, neither Freddie nor Bart wanted to say goodbye and Conrad cried constantly the morning Bart left. Hurriedly, Freddie finished her packing and that same afternoon George Allen drove them up to Harrogate. The journey was comfortable but achingly slow, the miles punctuated by stops and delays; and yet, as usual, Conrad was quiet and slept often, waking and stirring in his mother's arms only when they stopped for petrol.

When they finally arrived, they drove slowly up the winding drive, the car's headlights illuminating the late summer evening and blazing over Cambuscan as they made their way up to the house. Automatically, without thinking, Freddie got out of the car and lifted her son into the air.

'Look, Conrad, it's Cambuscan. It's your home,' she whispered, smiling as he blinked in the cool summer night.

Sarah was waiting for her daughter and after kissing her quickly on both cheeks, opened her arms to take hold of her grandson, her head bent over him as she moved into the drawing room. Freddie followed and then hesitated. By the fire stood her father, a Havana cigar in one hand and a look of disinterest on his face as his wife approached him.

'Look, Greville, hasn't he grown?'

Conrad regarded his grandfather thoughtfully, his blue eyes meeting Greville's dark glance.

'He's a big boy,' Greville said dully. 'And you've put on weight too,' he concluded, turning back to Freddie.

'It's due to a happy marriage,' she replied, glancing up and down her father's thickening waistline. 'Not that that's your excuse.'

Her response startled Greville. Having intimidated Freddie all her life, he was surprised when she stood up to him and took an instant to compose himself, inhaling on his cigar moodily. Bart Wallace's money had cushioned her, he thought meanly, as he glanced over to the boy in Sarah's arms and winced. A strong child obviously, the child he should have had, the son he wanted. Angrily he flicked some ash into the fire and sniffed.

'I'm really glad to see you, Father,' Freddie said, trying to make the words sound genuine as she walked towards him, and for the first time in her life stretched up and kissed him on the cheek. He recoiled as though she had spat on him. Humiliated, Freddie drew back and then saw that his eyes were full of something she could not fully comprehend; a look of fear almost. Dear God, she thought with bewilderment, I frighten him.

'He's so good,' Sarah said, rocking Conrad, her absorption with the baby making her immune to the tension around her. 'I've never seen such a good boy. Although you were good,

Freddie. Oh, sweetheart, you were hardly a bit of trouble.' She glanced over to her husband. 'Isn't it nice to have your father here? I didn't know he was coming myself until he turned up out of the blue.' She tittered, like a giddy teenager. 'But I'm so glad he came. Now the whole family is together.'

Freddie smiled and kept her gaze averted from her father, knowing that he watched her and that he was waiting to say something. The atmosphere filled suddenly with his malice and his cigar smoke. It choked the room, gagged the windows and became so oppressive that Freddie found herself touching her neck nervously. Why had she come home, she asked herself. Why? She knew the relationship between her and her father would not improve, so why come here?

The answer came back immediately. Because you wanted to show Conrad Cambuscan, that's why. But Cambuscan was only lovely when her father was absent, she realised. When he was there, the rooms were full of reminders of her childhood – of Greville's silences, his criticisms, his thousand resentments. Each corner and cushion was imprinted with the unhappiness of Frederica Clements, the child of this house, the lonely daughter who looked out from the top window, the disappointing heir. Heir to what, she wondered. Not the joy of Cambuscan, but the threat of cold fingers on the window at night as the Ice Saints walked over the moors and called to her …

'What is it?' Sarah asked, alarmed when Freddie dropped her bag and struggled to her feet.

'Nothing. I was just so tired that I nearly dozed off,' she lied, picking up Conrad and saying good-night hurriedly.

Yet when she went to her room she did not sleep well and kept her son in her arms all night.

In the morning her fears seemed ludicrous and when Freddie came down to breakfast, her father was nowhere to be seen. Relieved by his absence, she fed Conrad in the kitchen and talked to Meg. Mike Kershaw was already out in the garden, mending a fence which had blown down overnight.

'Your son's very like you,' Meg said, glancing at Conrad. 'You were just like that when you were little. Same expression, everything.'

Freddie glanced at her son as he lay in her arms. A quiet baby, born to carry secrets.

'He does have a look of his father,' Meg went on, 'not that we see much of Mr Wallace up here.' She wiped her hands on her apron and glanced over to the door as Sarah walked in. She seemed preoccupied, her voice a little more strident than usual, her gestures irritating as she fussed around the housekeeper.

'Mr Clements wants beef tonight ... '

'I'm afraid that's not possible, Madam,' Meg replied vigorously. 'It'll have to be lamb. We did agree on lamb yesterday.'

'He doesn't want lamb!' Sarah snapped. Freddie looked up in surprise.

Meg pursed her lips. 'I'll have a word with the butcher.'

'Well, if you would,' Sarah said, fiddling with some vegetables, her hands nervously playing with the cabbage leaves. 'I would be grateful.' She smiled at her daughter. 'I have to spoil your father, otherwise he gets so ... well, you know.' She tugged off a leaf. 'He's probably tired. After all, he's been working so hard in London all week and it's our duty not to irritate him.'

Silently, Freddie and Meg exchanged looks.

The day which followed was uneventful, the morning dragging its feet into a long, warm afternoon. Conrad was playing on a blanket on the lawn as Freddie lay nearby watching the fading sun and the shadows of dusk nuzzling at the edges of the lawn. But for all the beauty of the evening a chill overtook her and she sat up suddenly, looking round.

There seemed no reason for her unease. Conrad was still gurgling happily by her side and when she glanced over towards the open doors of the conservatory, her mother waved to her. Cambuscan held its breath. Time continued elsewhere, but not in that garden. Not then. Inexplicably, there were no movements, no sounds, no life, only a quick certainty that inescapable disaster was imminent. Even Conrad seemed to sense something. Crying suddenly he screwed up his eyes and extended his arms towards his mother. Freddie hugged him, her voice soothing. I want to be away from here, she thought, I want to be home. Yet she knew there was no escape; that wherever she was, the evil would reach her.

Getting to her feet, Freddie held onto her son and, gathering the travelling rug over her arm, walked quickly towards the open doors of the conservatory. Her mother frowned and seemed surprised, but just as she opened her mouth to say something, they both heard the sound of a car winding up the drive and turned towards it. Together they moved inside the house, Freddie laying Conrad down in his cot upstairs and running back down to the drawing room to find her father standing in front of her mother, a look of satisfaction on his face.

'Freddie, your father's leaving me,' her mother said, turning round and looking at her daughter with an expression of total bewilderment.

'What?' Freddie asked, turning to her father for an explanation. 'What are you doing to her?'

'This has nothing to do with you!' Greville responded sharply, avoiding Freddie's eyes and cutting off the tip of his cigar. In silence, he sucked the end before lighting it. 'You have no say in this matter, so keep out of it.'

'I have no say in it?' Freddie repeated, incredulously. 'This is my mother, so I have plenty to say – '

Sarah shifted in her seat. 'Oh sweetheart, don't argue with your father … '

Freddie looked at her mother in astonishment. 'What are you talking about? He's leaving you!'

Sarah raised a finger to her lips, silencing her daughter as she used to do when Freddie was a child. 'Your father won't really leave me, he'll come back.'

'No, I won't,' Greville replied evenly. 'I've had enough of you, both of you, and I want a new life.' He paused. Both women watched him. 'There's someone else.'

Sarah screamed once. It was a childish gesture, almost pathetic, an involuntary expression of pain tugged out of her. 'No, no, Greville. You love me … '

'I never loved you,' he replied, unemotionally. 'I *endured* you. How could you expect a man like me to be proud of you? You're a nothing. A silly, fat, little toad.'

'Greville,' Sarah said simply, getting to her feet and then

dropping back into the seat, her face slack. 'Greville, don't … '

'I used to tolerate you because I had to, but now I can tell you just how much I loathe you … '

'That's enough!' Freddie said darkly, stepping between her father and her mother. 'You're not good enough for her, you upstart.' He winced at the word. 'You might think you've got the whip hand now, but you're wrong. You're nothing: a man no one likes, someone people only put up with. And why? Because you're rich.' The words pounded the air. 'And the money's not even yours! It's my mother's, just as this house is – '

'He can have the money and the house, if only he'll stay!' Sarah cried out desperately.

Stunned, Freddie swung round on her. 'But Cambuscan's yours!'

'But I want to keep your father!' Sarah wailed, her face red with emotion, her eyes filled with tears. 'I'd give everything for him.'

'But he's worthless,' Freddie said, her own anger changing to disbelief. 'He's always cheated on you.'

'He only did it because I disappointed him!' Sarah shouted, her voice rising with hysteria. 'It was my fault. I should have given him a son … '

Freddie breathed in deeply. 'You gave him a daughter.'

'It wasn't the same! You were always a disappointment to him,' Sarah shouted finally, seeing the look on her daughter's face and stopping, one hand covering her mouth.

Stricken by the words, Freddie said nothing and walked out. A moment later she heard the sound of her father's car leaving and watched until the vehicle was finally out of sight.

'Freddie?'

She turned listlessly, seeing her mother in the doorway, her figure slumped, her expression begging for forgiveness. 'I didn't mean to hurt you.'

'Yes, Mummy,' Freddie said wearily, getting to her feet. 'I know.'

'Your father's not well,' she went on, 'that's why he's been behaving like this.'

The thought had already occurred to Freddie. The colour

305

of Greville's skin and the unease of his movements hinted at more than a guilty conscience.

'Has he seen a doctor?'

'No,' her mother replied, moving away from her. 'He says he's never felt better ... He'll come back,' she said, fiddling with her hair in front of the window. 'He's just upset, that's all. I'm just going to lie down for a while,' Sarah went on. 'He'll be back, you'll see.'

Freddie did not believe her father would ever return. Like an automaton, she fed, bathed, and finally laid her son down to sleep, Greville's words banging in her head relentlessly, the small mews house as clear in her memory as it was the day she first saw it. How could you do this, Father, she thought bitterly, how could you?

Undressing herself, Freddie frowned suddenly. She realised that her premonition in the garden had been valid, yet her anxiety remained. Why? Why was there no sense of relief? Was something else going to happen ... ?

Missing Bart suddenly, Freddie picked up the phone by the bed and dialled the New York apartment. She knew that he would probably not be there at five in the afternoon, but she could at least leave a message on the answerphone to greet him when he got in.

The phone rang out several times as she waited, and then to her surprise it was answered.

'Bart?'

His voice was a lifetime away. 'Hello?'

'It's Freddie.'

'Freddie,' he repeated.

Alarmed by the unemotional response, fear swamped her. 'What is it?'

He seemed unable to talk properly, his words staccato. 'I saw Warren on the plane. Warren Roberts.' She was silent. 'He said a lot of weird things and he asked me for a loan to help him to get his new restaurant off the ground ... '

The connection faded, severing his words.

'Bart!' Freddie shouted, panic rising rapidly. 'I can't hear you, Bart. Please, speak up.'

His voice came back. Like a weary bird making for home.
'I explained that my money was tied up in investments and
that I had little ready cash, but he wouldn't believe me ... '

Again Bart's voice faded. Freddie breathed heavily as she
banged her hand against the phone.

'Bart, speak up, I'm losing you.'

I'm losing you.

'He seemed odd and he kept drinking, and after a while he
got really angry, saying that I wasn't a real friend and that I
despised him.' Bart paused, trying to make sense of what he
had experienced. 'He didn't believe me and thought I was just
making excuses not to give him the money.'

'What happened?' Freddie asked softly. Oh God, don't let
it be what I think. No, not now.

'He got more and more drunk and then started saying
things about you. About how you and I were so lucky to have
the perfect marriage.'

She listened, but there was no anger in his voice. Only
disbelief. Let him not be hurt. Please, not Bart.

'Then he got nasty and said that perhaps our marriage
wasn't quite as perfect as I thought ... '

Bart trailed off at the other end. Sitting on the edge of the
bed in the flat, he had spent the last hour running over
Warren's words, dissecting them, shifting them, trying to
make sense of them.

'Bart, what else did he say?' Freddie pleaded over the dying
ocean. 'Tell me.'

'Nothing else ... not really. He just gabbled, too drunk to
make any sense.' But there had been an awful sense to the
senselessness and a niggle of doubt had swelled inside Bart's
head. He remembered the animosity between Freddie and his
best friend, the way she had avoided him and the evening he
had visited Bea and left Freddie to entertain Warren alone. He
had neglected her, he knew that, but whilst he was away, had
she found someone else to pay her attention ... and had that
person been Warren?

'He said how easy you were to talk to – and how he had
confided in you about his wife and daughter ... '

Freddie swallowed, her mouth drying.

' ... but you never said anything about that to me, Freddie, you never mentioned it.'

'It wasn't important, Bart.'

'Wasn't it? It seemed very important to him. Far too important.' His voice rose suddenly, pain in every syllable. 'It's not true, is it? Oh Christ, Freddie, tell me it's not true.'

Freddie felt as though her heart was ripped out of her. 'Is what true?'

'You and Warren – you didn't make love, did you?' The words aged him. Suddenly he felt so old, so defeated. His wife, his lovely Freddie ...

'No,' she lied. 'It's not true, darling. It's not true.'

But the words sounded like lies and both of them knew it. Both of them knew it and couldn't pretend.

'Freddie, tell me the truth,' he said gently. 'Please, tell me the truth.' Oh, but I know, he thought, I know ...

The miles separated them. He couldn't see her face and she couldn't reach out to him.

'Bart,' she said fiercely. 'I love you.'

It was not enough.

'Freddie, did you sleep with Warren?'

'No! No, I didn't,' she said. Damn me to hell fire, God, if that's what you want. Damn me. But in the next life, not in this. Let me live this one out with Bart.

'Promise me you didn't, Freddie. Promise.'

'I promise,' she lied.

He heard the words and bent over the phone, his whole body aged. Not fifty-six any longer, long past that age. Not a man in his second marriage, given a new life. No, just a man who had begun his dying. From now onwards, Bart knew, there would be no escape from pain.

'Bart,' Freddie said gently over the phone line. 'Listen to me – I love you, no one else ... ' Her words trailed off and inspired no response. 'Bart, do you hear me?'

It was my fault, he thought. I had a magnificent wife and I neglected her, and so she turned to Warren. The person I trusted above all others.

308

Freddie continued blindly, wildly. 'Oh God, Bart, come home and we'll sort this all out.' She glanced about her and saw Conrad's little shoes and said, without thinking, 'Listen, Bart, listen. Think of Conrad. Think of *him*, darling, we can't let anything spoil our life and our son's life.'

Bart's head burned, her words suddenly galvanising him. 'My son ... *is* he mine, Freddie?'

Is he mine? The words hummed over the telephone line and in the instant Freddie paused, in the one instant she took to respond, he had his answer.

The phone line went dead. Panicking, Freddie redialled but this time no one answered. Crying out helplessly, she dialled again and again, until the tears ran down her face and her hands shook uncontrollably. Answer me, Bart, answer me, I love you, everything will be all right again, I promise. I never meant to hurt you, I never meant to betray you. Bart ... Bart ... In despair, she threw the phone to one side and got to her feet, pacing the floor, the events too huge for her to comprehend. Bart knew, he knew – the one thing she had dreaded had happened, and now what?

'Oh God, I love you,' she cried out hopelessly in the dimly lit room as she snatched up the phone and dialled the number again. 'I love you, Bart ... Talk to me! Please, talk to me!'

Chapter Twenty-Two

Bart never spoke to Freddie again. He never spoke to anyone again. The shock of knowing that Conrad was not his son forced Bart out of the apartment and down to the garage below street level. Ignoring the mechanic's greeting, he revved the engine up and then drove sharply out into the Manhattan traffic, weaving in and out of the lanes, oblivious to the car horns around him. He drove for miles, out of the city, towards the suburbs, towards the rows of residential houses with their residential families. Like his had been once.

Gradually his foot went down on the accelerator, a fraction of an inch, then further, then down, down, drowning in speed as he came out of the city onto silent roads. The noise of the engine roared in his ears, his eyes fixed ahead, the roads becoming one road, leading nowhere, except oblivion. If he could just drive it all out of his system, he would stop. He would drive away the anger in his heart, his stomach and his brain. I loved you, Freddie. Worse, I trusted you – just as I trusted Warren.

The car soared past houses, almost flying, soaring like a bird waiting for a trade wind to take it home. Summer's gone, snow bird, time to go home. Bart drove on, the car now driving itself, no longer an engine but a part of his anger. I thought I was happy, and I thought I was a father. The accelerator hit the floor of the Bentley, the car speeding, roaring on, nose diving into the vacuum beyond ... and beyond that, what? Sea? Silence? The dead end of all dead ends.

I loved that child, Bart thought, brushing his eyes with the back of his hand. I loved him as my flesh and blood, not as Warren Roberts' son. Played with him as mine, looked for my expressions in him and planned for his future. Bart cried out once in panic, and then took a turning quickly, his fear accumulating. But he didn't slow down.

I searched Conrad's face for my own face, Bart thought despairingly. I searched his eyes for my eyes, his soul for my soul and believed that when I died he would live on for me. He was my son. Another bend came up suddenly and Bart flinched, moving his foot over the brake and then hesitating as he remembered … *Conrad was not his son* …

The bend snatched at him, grabbed the car from under him – and then he responded, wanting to live, his foot jamming down on the brake, pumping it, treading water, gasping for air, going under and over and losing everything as he dived below the surface and drowned in his own anger, the car's gas tank exploding as it hit the wall.

PART FOUR

Where shall the lover rest
Whom the fates sever
From his true maiden's breast,
Parted for ever?

Where Shall The Lover Rest? Sir Walter Scott

Chapter Twenty-Three

Three years later,
London.

In the back of the car, Freddie read the papers lying on her lap, glancing briefly at the photograph and then scrutinising the details.

No: 2354876

Name: Thomas Fairchild FORREST
Occupation: Doctor
Employer: n/a
Date of Birth: 28.5.53
Astrological Sign: Gemini
Address: 17, Rowland Gardens, London SW7
Religion: Church of England
Political Affiliation: Lapsed Tory
Education: Harrow; London University
Place of Birth: Rochester
Appearance: 5' 11"; brown hair; brown eyes
Foreign Languages: None
Martial Status: Divorced
Children: Twins, aged seven
Hobbies: Visiting galleries, theatre and travel
Salary: £40,000
Personality: Outgoing and friendly, but can be a loner.
Request: To meet someone 25-35, independent and feminine, who likes children. Hopefully blonde and slim.

Carefully, Freddie read the medical and psychiatric reports, frowning at Malcolm Prentice's handwriting whilst the car sped on, Conrad sleeping in his car seat beside her, a safety-belt strapped across his chest. For some reason, Prentice's report bothered her and she had to admit that as time passed she was less certain of the psychiatrist's abilities. Direct, impersonal questioning was one thing, but she knew that people lied to defend themselves, and were more likely to lie when confronted with an authority figure. So in the end she decided that she would read Malcolm's reports, consider the information, and then speak to the client and make up her own mind.

'We're here, Mrs Wallace.'

Freddie glanced up, surprised. 'Already, George?' she said, turning to Conrad and waking the sleeping child. 'Come on, sweetheart, we're home.'

He woke slowly, stretching out his arms to his mother as Freddie lifted him and walked up the steps of 107 Rutland Gate. In the hall Jean Allen turned to greet her, a stack of sheets in her arms.

'Did you have a good trip, Madam?' she asked, nodding towards the study. 'Your post and messages are in there, on the desk.'

'I'll have a look in the morning, thanks,' Freddie replied softly, not wanting to wake the dozing Conrad as she headed towards the stairs.

She reached the first floor before she caught sight of Molly, her son's nanny, waiting for her. On the landing the girl stood smiling awkwardly, her plain face made-up in a crude copy of Freddie's maquillage, her greasy hair arranged hopelessly into a loose chignon at the nape of her neck.

Feeling a wave of pity, Freddie smiled and passed Conrad to her. 'He's still half-asleep,' she said, falling into step with Molly as they made their way to the nursery upstairs. 'You look different.'

The girl flushed with embarrassment and pride. 'Do you like it? I copied you ... ' She trailed off uncertainly, her admiration for Freddie making her even more gauche than usual.

'Molly, do you know something?' Freddie asked suddenly,

as she watched the girl undress Conrad and tuck him into bed.

'No, Mrs Wallace. What?'

'I could never have managed without you,' she said. 'You've been marvellous. You've been a godsend.'

Molly was clumsy with gratitude and shrugged. 'I just wanted to help. That's all.'

Freddie slid her arm around the girl's shoulder. 'And you do. Always.' She paused, looking at the make-up. 'But why did you put all that stuff on your face?'

Molly was stricken. 'I wanted to look like you.'

'Well, I don't think that's a good idea,' Freddie said, steering Molly out of the nursery and into her bedroom. 'I don't think you should copy anyone,' she went on, pulling out her make-up and scrutinising Molly's face in the mirror. 'Now wash all of that off, and I'll show you how to do it properly,' she said. She waited until a grateful Molly came out of the bathroom drying her face on a towel. 'Someone did this for me once,' Freddie explained, thinking of Dione and Signora Guardi in Florence. 'So the least I can do is to pass on what I know.'

Tired as she was, Freddie worked patiently on Molly's unremarkable face, her mind going back to the day the girl had first come to see her. Molly had run away from Yorkshire after her mother's death and arriving in the capital had turned to Freddie for help. Clutching her case, she had waited in the drawing room after Mrs Allen had admitted her, not daring to sit down and very much in awe of the house and the woman she had come to see.

Molly's father had worked as a foreman for Freddie's father, and in typical Yorkshire fashion had instilled in his family the legend of 'them and us'. The wealthy were not to be trusted, he insisted, his natural jealousy embittered by his uneasy association with Greville Clements. But Molly had not inherited that jealousy and her admiration for Frederica Wallace had increased over the years, especially when she married an American and divided her time between the USA and England, her life infinitely glamorous to a young girl who had never left the Yorkshire town where she was born.

So when Freddie entered the room that day and she was

317

finally confronted with her heroine, Molly faltered, smiling unsteadily, her fingers plucking at her skirt.

'I've just arrived in London. I thought that ... I wondered if I could work for you. Here.'

'I don't want to be cruel,' Freddie said, distantly, 'but London's not the place for you. You should go home.'

'I can't.'

'Yes, you can,' Freddie replied, the echo of Conrad's crying sounding from upstairs. 'You wouldn't be happy in London, believe me.'

'I would if I got a job,' Molly insisted, too anxious to even notice the child's cries above. 'I could do anything ... '

'It's not that simple,' Freddie responded, her voice high with tension as she walked to the door and called out to the housekeeper. 'Mrs Allen, go and see to Conrad, will you? I'll be up in a minute.'

A quick scurry of feet on the stairs followed as Freddie took in a breath and absent-mindedly touched her face with her hand. Molly stood in the centre of the room, shabby and nervous, her height making her stoop slightly.

'How ... how old are you?'

The girl faltered. 'I'm ... seventeen.'

'Seventeen,' Freddie repeated dully. A quick winter shower pattered against the windows, a few raindrops vaulting the open window and landing on the piano, one running insolently down a photograph frame. Hurriedly Freddie smoothed the water away with her fingers, her husband's picture looking out at her as she did so.

'Mrs Wallace?'

Freddie flinched. She had momentarily forgotten that there was anyone else in the room with her and it took her an instant to respond. 'What is it, Molly?' she said finally. 'What can I do for you?'

'You don't have do to anything for me,' Molly replied eagerly. 'I know I'm only seventeen but I could help you. Housework, cleaning ... ' Molly trailed off, just as Conrad began to cry again. His sobbing escalated, as it had done so often in the weeks after Bart's death.

Glancing towards the door, Molly said timidly. 'Perhaps I could look after the baby?'

'The baby,' Freddie repeated woodenly, turning to face Molly with eyes that saw nothing.

Alarmed, Molly stepped back suddenly and knocked off a small ornament which shattered on the panelled floor. 'Oh God, I'm so sorry!' she blustered, falling onto her knees and picking up the pieces. 'My father always says how clumsy I am,' Molly continued plaintively, her voice breaking with anguish, a piece of glass slicing into her thumb and making it bleed.

The sight of the blood brought Freddie back to reality. Quickly she knelt down and taking her own handkerchief, tied it around the girl's thumb, the crimson wetness soaking into the clear white cotton.

'You must go home, Molly,' Freddie said gently. 'This is not the place for you. I can't help you at the moment. It's not that I don't want to, I just can't.'

The rain stopped as suddenly as it started and a cool breeze shuddered uneasily amongst the trees as Conrad's crying persisted.

'You don't understand, I can't go home,' Molly continued. 'My mother's dead ... '

Freddie held the girl's hand and nodded. ' I'm sorry.'

' ... and my father wouldn't have me back.'

'Of course he would,' Freddie said eagerly. 'You're his only child, he must love you.'

Oh God, why did I say that? she asked herself, hardly believing her own words. She had been an only child, and that had made her no more precious to her father.

'Go back home, Molly. It's the best thing to do. Honestly.'

'I can't go back!' Molly replied with venom, her eyes fixed fiercely on Freddie. 'I can't go home, and you can't make me.' Her voice softened, pleaded. 'Please, let me stay. I'll stay for nothing. You don't have to pay me, just let me stay.' Her words fell heavily in the air between them, until, in exasperation, she tugged at her sleeve, pulling it back to reveal her forearm and upper arm dark with bruises, some recent, some fading.

Shocked, Freddie touched the marks with her fingers. 'Who

did this to you?' she asked, suddenly responsive to the girl's needs.

'My father. My father did it,' Molly replied flatly. Above them Conrad cried out again, his distress underlining Molly's. 'I could help you with the baby, really I could. I'm good with children.' She drew herself upright and looked into Freddie's eyes. 'You look so tired, I could help you and give you more free time to spend with your husband.'

The words closed over Freddie's head like a freak wave. 'My husband?' she repeated, looking into the girl's eyes and seeing her own distress reflected there. 'I have no husband, Molly. My husband is dead.'

Nearly three years had passed since then, Freddie thought, as she brushed Molly's hair and turned her towards her reflection in the mirror. You are no beauty, she thought, but you have a great heart.

'There,' she said finally. 'What do you think?'

Molly looked into the mirror at her smoothed face and then back to Freddie, her face luminous with admiration and gratitude.

'It's perfect,' she said, her voice hushed. 'Perfect.'

Molly adored her employer unquestioningly, although her relations with the Allens had initially been strained. In fact as soon as Molly moved in she was regarded with suspicion, her Yorkshire accent, her plainness, and her insecurity making her a perfect target for the housekeeper's distrust. Yet as time passed, even Jean Allen had to admit that the unprepossessing waif who had turned up on the doorstep was actually a considerable help.

Freddie, always fiercely protective of her son, was at first wary and unwilling to pass Conrad over to Molly, but as the weeks passed, she found that she relied on her more and more. Anxious to help, Molly did many of the tedious chores, the domestic tidying and shopping accomplished without murmur, with Molly returning home laden and as ungainly as ever.

Well aware of Freddie's grief, Molly was discreet, her presence apparent only when she was needed. Not that she

320

resented this state of affairs at all, instead, mesmerised by the distracted Freddie, she took the chance to study her and to try to fathom out the circumstances of her husband's demise, which had never been fully explained to her. All she knew was that Mr Bart Wallace was dead, and that his widow was in mourning.

For her part, Freddie offered Molly no explanations at all, and when the girl never questioned her directly, she began to relax. 'What are you doing?' Freddie asked one morning, walking into the drawing room to find Molly stooped over a small display cabinet.

She jumped up, startled. 'I was only looking. Honestly.'

'It's OK, I know that,' Freddie continued. 'Do you like china?'

'I … I … ' Molly stammered, looking into Freddie's eyes. She could not fathom the expression in their blueness, and was wondering helplessly if there *was* anything to fathom when Freddie smiled at her. Relieved, Molly smiled back, a violent flush of colour rushing from her neck up to her cheeks.

'I don't know much about it … china, that is,' Molly answered. 'But I like looking at your things. You've got such a lot of lovely bits and pieces.'

Molly glanced around the room as she said the words, her gaze taking in the polished Georgian furniture, the clever English paintings, the sombre Persian rugs, the silk covered suite, the sprinkle of cards on the mantelpiece and the invitations to private viewings on Cork Street. Dizzily, Molly continued to look, remembering the wardrobes upstairs into which she had peeped to see the long lines of clothes hanging on padded hangers and the flirtatious lace of a négligéé peeping out like a wayward child. When she looked, she could always catch the dark scent of Freddie, as memorably her as the occasional strand of hair nuzzling against the collar of a discarded gown.

Totally unaware of the girl's thoughts, Freddie also looked around, but her vision was different. She saw a window which stared out onto an empty street, a clock which had wound down, an invitation to a cocktail party which had come and gone, and a photograph of her husband.

'We … I … collected things over the years,' she said stiltedly, her attention wandering again, the girl's admiration suddenly embarrassing. 'Do you want to take Conrad for a walk?'

'But I thought … ' Molly faltered, confused. 'Well, you're the only one who usually takes him out.'

Freddie studied her for an instant carefully. 'Yes, I know, but I trust you, Molly,' she said. 'And I do so need someone to trust.'

The conversation came back to Freddie as she stood by her bedroom door watching Molly walk, heavy-footed, to her room. Years had passed since then; time in which the girl had developed a deep bond with her son. Thoughtfully, Freddie moved into her bedroom and flicked on the bedside lamps, kicking off her shoes and walking over to a small table by the bed. On it lay an antique silver tray, complete with a brandy decanter and one glass. It did not require a huge effort for Freddie to remember Jean Allen's initial response;

'I want a tray with brandy left by my bed in the evenings,' Freddie said only days after Bart died.

The woman's eyes were momentarily beady. 'In your bedroom, Madam?'

'Yes, in my bedroom,' Freddie repeated. 'Every night.'

For Freddie, sleep had become a stranger. From the second she had been told of her husband's death, the years of rest ended. She had always been a sound sleeper before, but now experienced the endless, silent hours which turned every night into a battleground as the insomnia stalked her. Yet gradually, as time passed, the nightly struggle had lessened. Now it was merely getting off to sleep she found difficult – not staying asleep – except occasionally, when there was another reason for unease, such as memories.

Sitting down on the side of the bed, Freddie leaned forwards and reached for the brandy, remembering that tonight was the anniversary of Bart's death. Carefully she pulled the stopper out of the neck of the decanter, lifted it over the tumbler and slowly poured an inch into the glass. Then, as though to increase her anticipation, she spun it voluptuously around the bowl several times, its familiar and comforting aroma making her close her eyes, her lips finally opening to receive the first, and most profound, sip. The brandy lingered against her mouth, rubbed its quick feet down her throat and danced in her stomach, an initial sensation of peace welling up in her.

She knew it would not last, that the sense of euphoria would fade, but she had become adept at judging the sensation and found that after one good draught of brandy she would slide off to sleep easily if she allowed herself to. Sighing, Freddie rested against the pillows, looking up and tracing the sounds of the feet going from nursery to bathroom overhead, then moving on into Molly's bed-sitting-room. Soon the low sounds of music sunk through to Freddie, as the brandy began to take effect and the night took its usual course, following the same pattern of remembrance and guilt.

When it came, the news of Bart's death had not been expected, but not unexpected either. It had not crept up on her unawares or struck her in the belly, making her retch with the pain of it. Instead, it had simply occured. A bulletin, a news flash, a headline. It could have happened to anyone, any of the myriad people who flash up at six o'clock, faces uniformly milked after disasters. But this night, it was her disaster. This night the news was all hers. A car had crashed. A vehicle, driven at speed, recklessly, had gone off the road and smashed against a wall ... A great shock, of course. Almost as great a shock as a witness saying it could have been deliberate.

Freddie blinked, fully awake. A kettle whistled from Molly's kitchen above as she put out her hand and took another long drink of brandy. She knew she should get undressed and climb under the covers, otherwise she would fall asleep where she lay and wake later, disorientated and chilled. But the journey down from her mother's home had been so tiring, and tomorrow there was so much to do. She drank again hurriedly, the mischievous warmth tingling in her hands and feet making her suddenly light-headed as her eyes closed.

Immediately the image of her husband's face was thrown

up against her shuttered eyelids. A man of standing, of honour, a father figure who had replaced a refractory parent, a man who had loved his wife and his child. A man who had died three years ago that night.

The street light outside the house on Dorman Square was fused, or missing, or vandalised. Whichever it was, it was giving out no illumination, and as Jao searched for her key in the darkness she cursed her mother, the council, and finally the Government, her muttered anarchy ceasing only when she managed to get the front door open and jab on the hall light. Several letters waited for her on the dresser and the new puppy, also named Miku, growled by her feet, standing protectively in front of the Hoover, just as his predecessor had done.

'Hi, Miku,' Jao said half-heartedly, leaning down and then withdrawing her hand as the dog lunged towards her. 'You bloody idiot!' she snapped as the animal returned to its loving vigil over the Hoover. 'It's a flaming Hoover,' she continued. 'Even you can't be that short-sighted.'

'Don't pick on the dog!' A voice called out to her from down the hall. 'You know how he loves that thing.'

'It's a machine,' Jao replied, walking into the kitchen, and facing her mother. 'Dogs don't fall in love with machines.'

'Mine does,' Bea replied phlegmatically, pouring out some wine for her daughter. 'You're late,' she said, her deep voice totally without reproach as she got to her feet and teetered to the cooker on high-heeled pumps. 'I've kept something warm for you.'

Jao slumped into a chair and glanced across to her aunt.

'We were playing a game ... ' Trisha said.

'Oh, goodie,' Jao replied drily, knowing that the sarcasm would be lost on her aunt.

'We were naming all the weather forecast stations.'

Jao frowned.

'You know, like Faroes, Dogger ... '

Jao's face was impassive.

' ... and I said that it was very bigotted of the BBC ... '

324

'Bigotted?'

'Yes,' Trisha repeated delightedly. 'Cos they say "Germans bite"!' Having delivered the punch-line, she began to laugh, the noise beginning in the back of her throat and then escalating down her nose, like the sound of a cat sneezing.

Jao watched her aunt in solid amazement.

'Well, do you get it?'

Smiling dimly, Jao nodded and then looked round the table at the best dishes and the guttering candles. 'Are you celebrating something special?'

'Nothing much,' Trisha replied, unsmiling as she leaned into the candle-light. 'We're just celebrating the news that Charlie's got an assignment in New York.'

Again Jao blinked at her aunt in astonishment, knowing how she always dreaded the call which took Charlie away on assignments abroad. Not that the cosseted Charlie would have guessed; all he knew was that before he left Trisha showed more interest in sex than usual, and hid love letters in his luggage which he found later. The latter trait he had found endearing until she had, in a rush of inspiration, hidden one breathless outpouring under his camera's shutter cover. She had expected him to find it when he arrived, imagining how his eyes would glisten with emotion and how he would tuck the tiny piece of paper against his heart until he returned. Unfortunately it dropped out in the middle of a hotel foyer in Cairo and was found by the cynical, sweating journalist who was accompanying Charlie. He had repeated the dreadful outpourings continually during the long assignment, burning every word of passion indelibly into Charlie's brain, and when he returned he could, with the dedication of a moonstruck Romeo, repeat Trisha's words by rote. And he did, every night for a week, thereby immortalising himself in her eyes and ensuring her enthusiastic participation in some pretty innovative sex – after he had first made her promise not to write any more love letters.

Fascinated by the enduring hold Charlie had over her aunt, Jao glanced at the bearded, balding journalist, the candle-light toying fitfully with the deep scar which ran across his forehead. It gave his face a roguish look, not at all in keeping with his temperament, and a kind of devil-may-care bravado which matched nicely with the combat fatigues he was wearing. Not that he had seen much combat in a townhouse in Pimlico, chewing listlessly at a piece of nut loaf.

Sexy old Charlie, Jao thought wickedly and smiled.

'What are you laughing at?' Bea asked suddenly, passing a stack of dirty plates towards her.

'I was just thinking about something that happened at work today.'

'You're lucky you've got work to go to,' Pam said, walking in.

We're off, Jao thought. I've only been in ten minutes and we're already arguing.

'Jesus, Pam, the way you grumble!' Jao snapped. 'You'll only be happy when I'm unemployed.'

'Be fair, Jao, she never said that ... '

Jao turned on her mother quickly. 'She didn't have to, it was what she meant. It's not my fault if she can't make a go of things. She could get more work if she was a bit more agreeable.'

'That's not true!' Pam replied shrilly, banging her hands on the table and making the candles splutter. 'You know how difficult things have been lately. I've worked hard with my training and I'm a good aromatherapist, everyone says so. People have always complimented me on my massage.'

Content with one of Charlie's ectomorphic arms wrapped around her shoulder, Trisha sniggered.

'I am!' Pam insisted blindly.

Bored, Charlie yawned and rubbed his eyes. 'Well, I'm for bed.'

'I'll just check your bag to see if you've got everything for the morning,' Trisha said coyly, getting to her feet and following him out of the kitchen.

'They've been sleeping together for years, so why the hell does she have to act so damn childish?' Jao asked her mother. 'It's not a flaming secret.'

'Maybe it should be,' Pam responded sharply.

'You're just jealous!' Jao hissed. 'Just because she's got a man and you haven't.'

326

A flash of triumph sparked in Pam's eyes. 'You can talk! You've hardly got a queue of men lining up outside your door.'

'Bitch.'

'That's enough!' Bea cried exasperated, snapping on the light and blowing out the candles. The kitchen was suddenly exposed. Every damp-riddled corner and faded inch of linoleum was illuminated, the pipes behind the sink striking up a violent drumroll until Bea leaned over and hit them with the breadboard.

'We need a plumber to fix that,' Pam moaned.

'Call one then,' Jao said dully, her eyes still fixed on her aunt's profile. 'I'll give you the cash. After all, I am earning money, which is more than some people.'

If Bea heard the remark, she made no comment and merely squeezed past Pam and walked down the hall to her bedroom, her daughter following her. The room was hot and the morning paper lay crushed under the sleeping peke, who had temporarily abandoned the Hoover. Silk wallpaper which had once been oyster coloured was now mottled with damp patches, and in a far corner a crack in the wall was eclipsed by a faded Rubens print.

Passing her bedside table, Bea picked up her Tarot cards and slipped them into her bag deftly.

Jao looked at her and frowned. 'You never give up, do you?'

Her mother was immune to criticism. 'It's money. Good money,' she said, sitting down on the bed and pulling off her shirt and trousers. 'It'll pay for the plumbing.'

'Crap! It's got nothing to do with the money, Bea, you just like doing it.'

Pulling on a long dress over her head, her mother muttered. 'Well, why shouldn't I? I've got regular customers who've been coming to me for years.' She smoothed down her skirt and winked at Jao. 'They pay well for reassurance, and I give them that.' She curled one arm around her daughter. 'D'you want me to read for you?'

'I don't believe in it, you know that.'

'I told you you were going to do well in business,' Bea said,

327

cajoling her. 'Didn't I? And you got the job at the gallery ... '

'I was made for that job!' Jao replied hotly. 'That wasn't a prediction, that was a certainty.'

Bea squeezed her daughter tightly, then slid the cards out of her bag and began to shuffle the pack, singing under her breath.

Shuffle, shuffle, shuffle the cards went, flashing primary colours as Bea's hands, ringed with two large garnets, worked deftly. Finally she slapped the pack down on the desk and looked at her daughter with her eyebrows raised quizzically. 'Well? Cut them, Jao, and let's see what's coming up for you.'

Hesitating, Jao's hand hung over the pack and then, lifting her eyes to heaven, she cut the cards.

'It's marvellous,' Bea said, picking up the two piles and laying out the cards on the desk top. 'Look, here's the new gallery, you could do well there – and a man. Oh look, Jao,' she said, her face breaking into a tremendous grin.'Someone's going to come into your life. I told you you'd find someone in the end.'

'Yeah, sure,' Jao said, trying to sound uninterested. 'And if this one doesn't work out, I could always poison the dog and run away with the Hoover.'

Bea slapped the back of her daughter's hand. 'Don't be ridiculous. Have you any idea what vacuum cleaners cost these days?'

Jao laughed loudly, her optimism restored. After all, even though she didn't believe in the cards, her mother had predicted many things which had come true over the years. And besides, what was the harm in it?

'You always say I'm going to meet someone. Always.'

'And so you are,' Bea replied with gusto. 'You just have to have a little hope.'

'Hope I have – a man is what I lack,' Jao said wryly.

'Well, you know what the Arabs say – "A man who has health has hope, and a man who has hope has everything."'

Jao grimaced. 'Some Arab.'

'Some hope!' Bea said, laughing.

Freddie was dreaming. The brandy had done its work and

even the memory of the anniversary had been obliterated as she had finally drifted off to sleep. Against the white pillow, her hair looked black, some falling across her face like a domino mask. She breathed deeply, rhythmically, the house quiet around her, the empty glass lying on the bedspread beside her hand. It seemed in her dream that there were bells peeling, but as Freddie rolled over she woke with sudden understanding and reached for the telephone. A familiar voice greeted her.

'You're there.'

Smiling, Freddie replied. 'You're right.'

'Are you OK?' Jao asked.

'Fine,' Freddie replied, suddenly chilled and pulling the bedspread around her. 'What time is it?'

'Twelve-fifteen. Were you asleep?' Jao asked, carrying on immediately. 'God, I'm sorry, I never thought ... '

'It's all right. I'm glad you called,' Freddie replied patiently, leaning back against the pillows and turning off the lamp. There was no moon, hardly any light at all coming through the curtains. 'It was ... it is ... three years ago tonight since Bart died.'

'I know, that's why I rang,' Jao replied anxiously. 'Do you want me to come round?'

'No, no, it's all right,' Freddie answered, touching the pillow beside her and imagining her husband lying there. His hair had been greying, but where? At the temples. Yes, of course, but where else? His face took shape on the pillow, but not flesh, more like a death mask pressed down over a living head. Freddie snatched her hand away and stared at the white pillow-case.

Guilt made her frantic. 'Oh God!'

'Freddie,' Jao shouted. 'Are you there? Are you OK?'

Startled, Freddie lifted the phone back to her ear. 'I'm fine. I was just thinking about Bart ... trying to remember what he looked like.' She paused, fighting back tears and opening a drawer in the bedside table. 'I've got his watch – they gave it to me after the accident.' Slowly she ran her forefinger over the cracked face, the white dial yellowed by the fire.

'Maybe I should come round,' Jao said.

'No,' Freddie said simply, glancing at Bart's photograph. 'He looks older now. Isn't that funny? I never thought he was old when I married him, although my mother never stopped mentioning it – "It might seem all right now, Freddie, but you don't want to be looking after an old man whilst you're still a young woman." ' She paused. 'I never got the chance, did I? He died instead – I bet that confounded her.'

Jao recognised the tone in her friend's voice and winced. 'Bart was … special,' she said uncertainly, not knowing quite what to say.

'He was,' Freddie replied, pushing the photograph away and reaching for the brandy decanter. 'And he was good, and everyone knows what happens to the good.' She poured a stiff drink and gulped it quickly. 'The good die young. Or not so young, as in Bart's case.'

'Oh don't, Freddie! Don't get upset.'

'I was supposed to marry a nice young man, wasn't I? And have nice babies. A nice young man like Harry. I should never have married Bart,' she said helplessly, then checked herself. Be careful, she thought, remember Bea loved him, and Jao is her mother's child. Remember not to hurt them. 'I did love him, Jao.' The brandy made her thoughts soggy, incoherent. 'Always be certain of that – I did love him.'

'I know, Freddie, I know,' Jao said, and after another second Freddie rang off.

The bedroom was chilly, far too cold to be comfortable. Freddie pulled on a jacket and walked into the bathroom and turned on the tap. When the water was icily cold she filled a glass, drank the liquid quickly and then dabbed her mouth dry afterwards. The second brandy had had no effect and when she walked out of the room her head was clear, her thoughts concentrated on the bureau below.

Freddie made her way downstairs through the stubbornly silent house. No sounds came from the nursery or the basement as as she paused in the hall and pulled the office keys out of her pocket. Eagerly she unlocked the door and flicked on the light switch, the elegant reception area inviting her in

330

as she made her way towards her office. Once inside, Freddie sat down, her hand resting for a moment on a *pietra dura* container which Harry had sent her when he heard of Bart's death. A piece from the Avery collection, a gesture of a grief shared, for Harry, more than anyone, knew what it was like to lose a loved one.

Freddie sighed, her breath juddering in her chest. After Bart's death she had found the grief to be all-consuming, the questions unanswerable, the guilt grinding into every action and every thought. Her mother had phoned regularly from Yorkshire, insisting that the house in Knightsbridge should be sold and that Freddie should return home to live with her 'after all that had happened'.

Freddie never knew exactly what she meant. Was she referring to her own impending divorce? Or Bart's death? Or something else? What else was there, she thought helplessly, knowing full well – Yet whatever Sarah knew or suspected, she still pleaded with her daughter to return, even though Freddie was equally adamant that she was going to stay in London with her son, in the house where they had lived with Bart Wallace. Things would continue as before. Only now she was a widow.

Bart had left Freddie well provided for in her widowhood, so much so that with her own considerable funds, Freddie Wallace was extremely wealthy. Some people resented it. Jean Allen was one, although she voiced her opinions only to her long-suffering husband when the door to their quarters was securely locked. Others were less discreet, Bart's colleagues mulling over the rumours which circulated around London, the suggestions of infidelity, and the unending innuendoes about Bart's death. Because Freddie had had so much, people envied her and now found their satisfaction in striking her when she was down. Their jealousy was expressed in a thousand vague suspicions, their gossip spreading across a hundred drawing rooms as Freddie's reputation took a severe nosedive. The prestigious circles which had welcomed her as Bart's wife now rejected her as Bart's widow. People murmured about her, and she retreated as the invitations

331

ceased, women afraid that the stunning Frederica Wallace might seem just too tantalising a morsel for their weak-willed husbands, men too frightened of her reputation to risk involvement.

Freddie leaned her head back against her chair and thought back, wondering how the rumours had started. Who had known about her affair with Warren? Her affair, she repeated, what affair? One incident, that was all. One sex act, one stupid, reckless event which had cost her everything. One moment of pity which had turned into attraction – for she *had* wanted Warren, she admitted that much to herself. But who had known about it? Freddie thought suddenly of Warren's obsession, of his determination to made a relationship out of a fleeting attraction. His telephone calls, his letters, his frightening absorption with her. But who else had known about it? Who?

Only Dione, and she was too clever and discreet to betray Freddie – so the question was never answered. For months Freddie's life rocked, and then gradually day by day, it settled. The Wilkies rallied around her, as did Harry, Dione and Penn but others kept their distance. Soon Freddie was restricted to the role of businesswoman and mother, nothing more. All emotion disappeared, interred with Bart Wallace. For a long time Freddie wore black, then adopted dark purple, her face and neck violently white in contrast, a figure out of time and place, carrying her own time with her.

The humiliations had been many. Freddie sighed, remembering how she had attended a party with Dione a year after Bart's death.

'I hope you didn't mind my bringing someone along,' Dione had said, drawing a reluctant Freddie into the Chelsea drawing room.

The hostess's eyes flicked to Freddie as did every other pair of eyes in the room. One couple turned away immediately, another glanced down, reluctant smiles winched into place, shuffled greetings exchanged furtively like betting slips as the hostess attempted to make conversation.

'We were just talking about Mary's new interest,' she said

lamely, aware that all attention was on her and mortified that she had been put in such a position. Hurriedly she changed tack. 'What do you do?'

'I still run The 107 Club,' Freddie said quietly.

'Oh yes … the marriage bureau,' the woman replied. 'It must be difficult … in your situation … I mean, since your … ' She floundered hopelessly.

Freddie was beyond caution. 'You mean, since my husband died?' she asked. Dione watched her carefully. 'No, it's not difficult. It's not difficult at all.'

Having heard the exchange, Dione slid beside Freddie and guided her away. The evening drummed along, animosity tinkling amongst the wine glasses. Each morsel was devoured without sense or feeling as the atmosphere tightened. And yet, even though she was nauseous with embarrassment, Freddie was still sensitive enough to realise that by bringing her, Dione was jeopardising her own social standing. Not that she seemed to care, and pretended to be unaware of the commotion their presence was causing as the hostess sank like a failed souffle into her taffeta gown.

'You're doing well, Freddie,' Dione whispered into her ear encouragingly. 'Never let them think they've fazed you.'

'They have,' Freddie said quietly.

Dione shot her a quick look. 'Nonsense. You've got the money and the beauty to live down anything, Freddie, including a reputation.' She glanced round at the assembled company. 'Brazen it out – before long they'll forget. They always do.'

Chapter Twenty-Four

So Freddie did fight back and Dione wasn't the only person to be surprised and heartened by her revival. Bea also rejoiced, remembering all too well the grim days after Bart's death. Mercifully, she did not know the truth, and neither did she hear the rumours as she moved in different social circles. She never knew about the whispers concerning Freddie's adultery, and the query over Bart's death. All she knew was that Freddie's husband, the man she herself had once loved, was dead. That was enough for her to know – and to bear. So whilst the gossip had tinkled in expensive drawing rooms, at Dorman Square Bea had mourned simply and without complication.

But now it seemed that Freddie had recovered – and about time, Bea thought. Three years was long enough to hibernate, even as a widow. Not that Freddie's parents had done much to help her recover. Sarah was as giddily inept as she had always been, and Greville was distant, too involved with his mistress to spare attention for his daughter.

Nothing had changed up in Yorkshire, Bea thought, looking around her kitchen; and nothing had changed here either, she realised, not since Freddie had visited as a teenager and had helped clear up the bathroom. Bea knew that in a minute the pipes would start banging again and that later the floor boards would creak, making crafty footsteps in the dark. As it had done so many times before, the kettle hummed next to her; a well worn oven glove hung suspended from a hook, the scrubbed pine table marked with scratches and the imprints of hot dishes. Almost before she looked up, she could see the copper pans on the shelf which ran along the side wall, and the ginger jar which used to hold liquorice.

Bea sighed and got to her feet, rinsing a beaker under the tap and moving onto the bathroom where she washed out some tights, hanging them to dry over the bath. When she had finished, she glanced round and saw the blunt razors left in the soap dish, and the make-up smeared on the towels – all items typical of the Wilkie household and of the women who lived there. A feminine place, a house without men – as Freddie's was now.

What was it all about? Bea wondered suddenly. All the men and the marriages, all the anguish concerning Bart, all the disappointment when he married Freddie – what the hell did it all amount to in the end? Nothing, she realised suddenly with a sense of unexpected comfort. It amounted to nothing because the taps still banged as they had always done and the pigeons still strutted on the fire escape …

Bea frowned and leaned against the wash-basin. The only thing I can't understand, she thought suddenly, is that I never saw what was to come. Why couldn't I see your future in the cards, Freddie? Why?

In the small hours sleep scuttered around the room and made lunges towards the pillow, but it didn't settle, and at four Warren opened his eyes. His lids felt heavy from forced rest, his mouth dry, his limbs stiff with tension. As his mind focused, his first thought was of Freddie and the plans he had made in the swinging moments between wakefulness and sleep.

Plans which seemed ridiculous now. She did not want him, that much was plain. Their love-making had been a single event, with no chance of a repeat. All his letters had been returned or, he suspected, destroyed, his phone calls ignored. And he had resented it. At first he had believed he could convince her to continue the relationship, and after Bart's death he felt sure she would reconsider. But Freddie never did and although every atom of his intelligent brain told him the situation was useless, he longed for her.

And he kept longing for her – his infatuation, already dangerous, turning into an obsession when Bart died. He could not remember the conversation he had had with Bart on the plane that last time – he only knew that he had resisted the temptation to tell him the truth; but that was the limit of his nobility. What he had said had been enough – he knew that. So when he heard of Bart's death, although he fervently wished otherwise, he immediately suspected suicide. The word crushed into him like the steering-wheel of a car on impact. *I am responsible for his death*, he told himself continually, *I have indirectly killed my friend*.

From then onwards, Warren was haunted by guilt. His betrayal of Bart had ended in his friend's death, whether accidental or deliberate, and he realised that he had to live with that knowledge. Yet at the same time, Warren knew that Freddie must be suffering a similar guilt and he felt a kind of grotesque relief – at last they had something to share, some secret to protect, and they could do it together.

He never thought that she would loathe him, seeing no comfort in him, only a reflection of what she had done. Daily, dangerously, his passion for Freddie and his determination to make amends, grew. His obsession consumed him. It was in everything he touched and everything he felt. Freddie. Freddie. Other women came into his life, and left; work continued, exercises were done, conversations held, daily chores undertaken, but at the back of his skull a hammer pounded relentlessly ... *Make amends, make amends, make amends*.

Warren thought of the fight he had had when he was nineteen; he thought of Louise and Alia, killed; and he thought of the violence under his skin and the effort he took to control it. And then he thought of Freddie and remembered her kindness and saw in her the gentleness of the world. She was his absolution, and he had injured her. The one person who could offer him relief, he had almost destroyed. The only solution was to convince her to turn to him. When she did, he would love her and make her forget. He would make recompense for old injuries. When she came back, he would live again. They would live again. When ... When ...

A thick summer sky, heavy with insects, hummed round the stable block as Harry whistled for his dogs. They came out hurriedly, bounding into the warm air and barking in greeting as he held open the back seat of the Land Rover. Climbing in, Harry turned on the ignition and then paused with the engine running, his eyes fixed on the letter from Freddie lying on the passenger seat.

He had read it twice since Mrs Gibbons had brought it to him, and he had almost phoned her, but resisted, no longer certain of what to say. Later he would write back, but for now he could only think of Freddie as the girl in the summer hayfield, laughing over the gate, the young woman he had wanted to impress so much the morning he had fought Mike Kershaw. He remembered her courage when she had run into the fire and how she had brought him back to life with her body, pulling his soul home to the earth when his eyes burned with the memory of his dead father.

Harry's hand went out to the letter and he remembered all the other letters they had ever written. Missives from London to Eton, then Cambridge; the silly, idiotically romantic letters left lying in wait for her on the bed upstairs. Harry sighed, looking down at his hands, the palms still scarred. Why did I not marry you, Freddie, he wondered. Why?

His head went back suddenly, his eyes fixing on the Hall in front of him. Was it too late now? Was it past, that tenderness? He sighed. Freddie was known now, a woman who had made her place in the world. What could he offer her, except a home in a county she had left long ago? She was a widow, she was now free – but there was no comfort in the news, he thought, only grief for the woman left behind.

I could phone her or go and see her, he thought, suddenly galvanised. We were friends, it would be a perfectly reasonable thing to do. But as soon as he thought the words, he dismissed the idea. The Freddie he knew was gone; she had gone with the boy who jumped over the gate. They were still

337

out there somewhere, unaged and unchanged, still walking about the cornfields and exchanging secrets in low voices ... but not here, not now.

With a quick gesture, Harry released the brake and drove off down the drive, the dogs barking in the back seat behind him, his eyes seeing only a young girl turning to wave in an open field.

Freddie opened a new bureau that year in Rome, and the following year, around the time of the fourth anniversary of Bart's death, she opened another in New York. Her business acumen and the experienced, friendly personnel she hired in both places made them instant successes. With her increased wealth she made some clever investments in the art world, rescuing one Van Dyck at the last moment from its intended destination in Palm Springs.

The rumours about her and Bart had largely fizzled out after four years, just as Dione had said they would. Besides which, Freddie no longer mixed with her old circle of acquaintances, instead she kept faith with her few true friends, and occasionally wondered who had originated the rumours. She wondered, but she never found out. It remained as much a secret as Conrad's lineage and she didn't pursue the matter, trying to distance herself from her past.

She adored her son as much as Bart had done, and he became a loving, if rather thoughtful, child. Many times Freddie crept into his room and watched him as he slept on his stomach, his breath damp against her cheek as she leaned over him, her lips nuzzling his neck. Sometimes he stirred, mewled in his sleep and then fell silent again, his eyes under moist eyelids, flickering as he dreamed.

But this morning he awakened and stretched out his arms to her. 'Mummy.'

She smiled. 'Hi, sweetheart. Did you sleep well?'

He nodded, his soft, brown hair ruffled. 'I dreamed of a cat with one eye.'

'Oh! Like this?' Freddie said, covering her right eye with her hand and grimacing.

338

He giggled with delight. 'Yes, do it again! Do it again, Mummy, please!'

She obeyed, then sat on the side of the bed and looked at her son thoughtfully. 'Would you like to go to Milan with me, Conrad?'

He opened his eyes wide. 'Why?'

'To visit Aunty Dione,' she replied. 'You'll have fun there, she has lots of cats.'

'OK,' he said easily, slipping out of bed and calling for Molly.

Molly emerged yawning, her glasses askew and her hair messy. ' 'Lo Conrad,' she said, glancing over to Freddie and smiling.

'We're going to Mil ... '

'Milan,' Freddie said, helping him with the word and then turning to Molly. 'Do you want to come too, we could make it a holiday?'

As Freddie had anticipated, Molly was delighted by the idea and shooed Conrad into the bathroom, her voice high with excitement. Smiling, Freddie went into her own room to dress and then applied her makeup quickly, rubbing a smudge of lipstick off her front tooth and fixing a leather belt around her waist.

'Not bad,' she said, her hands lying flat on her stomach as she looked in the mirror. Slowly she turned, putting her head on one side and screwing up her eyes. She was in good shape, too disciplined to let her appearance slip, her sleek bloom carefully attended. Like Dione, she visited Signora Guardi twice yearly, and kept to an exercise regime religiously, her appearance cultivated to perfection.

Yet Freddie never asked herself why she attached such importance to her looks. The question was too painful to consider. Beautiful and clever, she should have married again, but could never even consider the idea seriously. Bart had died because she had been unfaithful – to love someone else would be the final act of betrayal. So Freddie never looked into the future, but just lived for the day, and concentrated on her life with her child, and her business. Incredibly she didn't miss sex either. The desire she had felt for Warren had been frightening and unmanageable, and although she still dreamed of his body and the rough grasp of his hands on her skin, she felt too guilty to start a relationship. Too guilty and too afraid.

Shrugging off the memory of Warren, Freddie walked downstairs, hearing the dull sounds of activity from the basement as she walked into the kitchen and began to make herself some coffee, nearly dropping her cup when the housekeeper rushed in.

'Good morning, Mrs Wallace,' she said evenly. 'We've got ants.'

Freddie raised her eyebrows. 'Oh really? Where?'

'All over our sitting room,' Jean Allen replied. 'I can't think where they come from. After all, it's not that I don't put stuff down.'

'It's April, the weather's getting warmer,' Freddie replied patiently, sipping her coffee.

'We'll be overrun by summer if we don't do something now.'

Freddie sipped her coffee. 'I can't understand it myself. Why don't you get some of that spray stuff?'

Jean Allen glanced over her shoulder. 'I'm onto it, Madam, they won't beat me. What d'you want for breakfast?'

Freddie's appetite had already flagged. 'I've had all I want, thank you.'

'As you like,' Jean Allen replied evenly, her thoughts elsewhere. 'I think I'll try that new American insecticide. You just smear it on and the ants get their feet stuck in it and starve to death.'

Smiling indulgently, Freddie made her way to the bureau. Chris looked up as she pushed open the glass doors.

'Morning,' she said, passing a photograph of a new client over to her. 'What do you think about that?'

Freddie scrutinised the picture, then pointed to the man's tie. 'What on earth is that?'

'A bow tie,' Chris said, laughing. 'You must have seen one before.'

'Not in snakeskin.'

'He told me he got it in Malaysia. It's quite extraordinary, isn't it?'

'It looks like he's got a bug under his chin,' Freddie replied, grinning. 'For God's sake, don't let Mrs Allen catch him wearing it or she'll spray it with something.'

'He won't tell me his real age either,' Chris went on. 'All he would say was, "I'm as old as my tongue and not quite as old as my teeth!" '

'Oh, great. I love the cocky ones.' She said, walking back into her room and pushing one of her heavily embroidered cushions behind her back as she sat down.

Her office had changed little since Bart's death although a few personal touches had been added. Two china bowls stood on her desk filled with flowers and one of Conrad's baby bootees had been bronzed and was now used as a paper-weight. Over the door, Bart's first letter to her was displayed in a gilded frame, his wedding ring hanging just below it on a piece of silk. The room spoke of comfort and of memories and it had a peculiarly relaxing effect on most of her clients.

'I had an interesting phone call first thing,' Tina Shore said, walking in, full of energy. 'This guy asked what we did here. So I said,' she paused for effect as Freddie watched her, ' "We guarantee a meeting of intelligent people with interesting professions, money, and good contacts ... " '

'And I said that makes us sound like the Masons,' Dot Cummings interrupted, standing in at the doorway, her Northern accent heavy with disapproval. 'Anyway, it was probably just another of those blasted journalists, trying to find out about the bureau.'

Freddie frowned and leaned back in her seat. 'Are they up to their old tricks again?'

Dot nodded. 'Ever since they heard you were thinking of expanding again.'

'I don't like it,' Freddie said emphatically. 'I don't like people prying into my business.'

'He also wanted to know why he needed to see a psychia-trist, a doctor, a graphologist and an astrologer.'

'Those are the rules, and have been ever since I opened the

341

bureau.' Freddie frowned, suddenly uneasy.

'You'll never guess who else I saw,' Tina went on eagerly. 'That horrible woman who came here years ago to help out. Oh, you know, the one with the black around her eyes ... '

Dot snapped her fingers as she remembered. 'Mala Levinska!'

'Yeah, that's the one,' Tina agreed. 'She looks so smug, and said she was going to start a business.'

Freddie's eyes narrowed. 'What kind of business?'

'A marriage bureau,' Tina said, wincing. 'She also said she was going to call in and have a word with you later on today.'

'Like hell!' Freddie snapped angrily. 'I won't have that woman on my premises.'

'Well ... ' Tina hesitated.

Dot took over immediately. 'She said that you'd better not refuse to see her, as she had something very private to discuss.'

The room shuddered around Freddie, a dark nudge of premonition flooding her. She didn't want to see the woman, loathing her and mistrusting her, and yet ... and yet ...

'All right, I suppose I'll have to see her,' Freddie said, turning to Dot. 'But only for ten minutes, d'you hear? Ten minutes only.'

Mala Levinska waited until six-thirty before making her entrance. Everyone had gone home apart from Chris, who had stayed protectively and she jumped, startled, when the bell rang. Getting to her feet, she shot Freddie a rapid glance as she released the glass doors and stood back to let Mala Levinska enter. Her appearance was unchanged, the kohl-rimmed eyes as unemotional as ever, as her tongue flicked over her teeth.

'So,' she said, sitting down and facing Freddie in her office. 'We meet again.'

'D'you want me to stay?' Chris asked anxiously, but Freddie shook her head.

'No, you go home now, Chris. Thank you.'

They both waited for the doors to close again before Mala continued. Glancing round she said. 'Well, the place looks profitable, and you've opened up new premises all over the world, I hear.'

'Let's cut the small talk, shall we?' Freddie said sharply. 'What do you want?'

'I'm opening a business,' Mala said smoothly. 'A marriage bureau.'

'So what? You're no competition to me.'

'I intend to make it a success,' Mala went on. 'And to break you.'

Freddie blinked. 'I beg your pardon?'

'I'll let you carry on as you are, Mrs Wallace,' Mala said with mock magnanimity. 'But you're not opening any more bureaux and before long, everyone in London will be coming to mine.'

'Really?' Freddie said, with biting sarcasm. 'And how do you think you're going to manage that? Arson? Or are you going to have me killed perhaps?'

'Your son isn't Bart Wallace's child.'

Freddie's chest tightened, her hand going to her throat. 'What ... what are you talking about?' she stammered finally.

'What I said – your son isn't Bart's child,' Mala repeated, smiling with relish. 'Can you imagine what would happen if this was made public? All your clients would be so shocked. Bearing another man's child whilst you were married to someone else – that's hardly the kind of thing people expect from a matchmaker, now is it? Besides, Bart Wallace was such a nice man to cheat on – and he died so tragically. An accident, wasn't it? Or was it?' She paused, to let the words sink in and do their damage. 'And of course, there's always your son to consider, isn't there? It would be hard on him.'

'Get out!' Freddie shouted, springing to her feet. She's bluffing, she has no proof, she thought. She's guessing, she must be. How does she know? How? 'Get out of my office!'

Mala was impassive. 'Before you start thinking you can bluff your way out of this mess, I have proof.' She waved a copy of some medical notes in front of Freddie's eyes. 'It's astonishing what a little bit of luck and a little bit more money can buy,' she went on. 'A nurse got me this. She owed me a

343

favour actually. She just photocopied your notes.' She pushed the paper over to Freddie. 'You can keep that, it's only a photocopy. Only one little mystery remains – who is the real father?' She paused to deliver the final blow. 'I wondered about that, but, as luck would have it – and I do seem to have been lucky with this – I remember seeing a certain Warren Roberts come out of your house very late one Saturday evening. A few days after you fired me actually.' Her voice was thick with malice. 'He bumped into me and looked very shaken. Very shaken indeed.'

Mala paused, watching how Freddie faltered. Oh yes, this will pay you back for your high-handedness, you cow, she thought. Over six years I've waited and now finally I've got my own business – and as I go up, you're going down. She thought of Warren suddenly and of how she wanted him. Her jealousy nearly choked her. That had been the final blow. To discover that Freddie Wallace was having an affair with the man *she* wanted – it was too much to bear. And it must all be true, Mala thought, otherwise Freddie would have denied it. From now on, I'll be the first matchmaker in the world – not Freddie Wallace.

'Don't be too upset, Mrs Wallace,' she said, getting to her feet and walking to the door. 'Everyone's luck runs out in the end.'

Chapter Twenty-Five

Shaking, Freddie's hand reached out and turned on the desk lamp. The light came on, subdued, soft, intimate. The kind of light which made people talk and encouraged confidences, a mother earth light. Freddie sighed, the bitter memory of Mala's visit still in her mouth as her eyes moved to the wall opposite, her gaze resting there for an instant before she walked over and felt for a concealed button. As she pushed it, the false front opened to reveal over six years of files stacked up in alphabetical order, each file representing a person looking for a partner.

Slowly Freddie's gaze moved along the shelves, O running to P, Q running to R. Her glance stopped suddenly at the initial R. She blinked. R as in Roberts. Warren Roberts. The name rang around her head like a siren. Warren Roberts. She inhaled deeply, her legs shaking. Fear dragged at her, as did the old memory, her insecurity roaring back into life.

I love you, someone said. But the voice wasn't Bart's and she automatically closed her eyes.

The word teased her. Love. She knew she had been wanted, desired and loved – just as she knew that Bart's love should have been enough for anyone. Freddie closed her eyes against the memory of another love. Hurried, furtive, guilty – the illogical agony of lust made love. Freddie shook her head and glanced over to Bart's photograph. Anything else was a lie; love was Bart. Love was a man asleep next to you in a shared bed. Love was the man who married you, who protected you, who instinctively caught your arm as you crossed the road. Love was a man who felt a responsibility to his woman, because in his protection was her strength and in her strength was his need. Bart Wallace, Freddie thought, I loved you. You, the father figure, the giver of the heart.

Her eyes closed, and the guilt swelled – as did the unexpected longing for Warren. Hearing Mala say his name had brought him back, a spiteful incantation calling him from the past. And with his name had returned the memories – his face and the shape of his hands, the smell of him and the scent of his hair on the pillow. There were other things that Freddie could not forget about that late night in December ... He had confided in her and touched her and she had listened, trying to commiserate, to console. He was only slightly older than her and his body was so much younger than Bart's, as was his voice, and when he first caught hold of her hand, the caress was so gentle that it was almost as though there was no passion in it. Almost as though it was innocent ...

Freddie swallowed, the memory too painful to comprehend fully and tears welled up in her eyes, not for herself, but for her betrayal of Bart. Then the memory returned again, twice as strong, making her suck in her breath to steady herself. No, she said to herself, I have to forget the past. I've done well now, for myself and for my son. I've made people happy. She leaned her head against the wall, suddenly panicky as she remembered Mala's words. Just let her try and take this away from me, Freddie thought fiercely, just let her try.

Sudden images of all her old fears spun around in her head, mixing with the image of Mala Levinska ... and of Warren Roberts. Intense, fierce, lost, a man whose personality could be described as compulsive, a man who, had he come to her as a client, would have been considered unsuitable. Freddie could imagine Malcolm Prentice's report. 'This man is dangerously possessive ... This man does not know how to lose ... '

Freddie's grip tightened on the files, her knuckles whitening under the skin, her nails gorging the cardboard covers.

'Go away!' she screamed aloud. 'You're gone. It's in the past.'

Frantically her eyes flicked towards Bart's photograph on

346

the desk. 'I'm sorry for what I did, and for what I am about to do,' she said, her voice calming down and losing the edge of hysteria. 'I don't want to hurt Conrad, but I won't be terrorised any longer.' Her mind winged back to Cambuscan and the dark days of her childhood, seeing herself reflected in the image of the bay tree, a solitary figure, set apart. Oh God, she thought, what if it were discovered that Conrad wasn't the legitimate heir, that he was an interloper? How much could she risk? How much? And if Warren discovered that Conrad was his son, how would he react? After losing his daughter so tragically, how would he behave knowing that his son had been withheld from him? Obsessive and driven, how would he react?

Freddie's hand stretched out towards the phone, then hesitated, trembling over the instrument. She had been about to call Dione to ask for her advice, turning to her mentor as she had so many times in the past. But slowly Freddie's hand dropped to her side. No, not this time. This time she was going to stand on her own. The time for asking advice had come and gone, the decision was now in her own hands.

A sudden strength galvanised Freddie. She knew she had a battle to face, just as she knew that Mala's visit would change her life – but she was no longer afraid. Slowly, Freddie sat down, her breathing returning to normal, then she reached for a piece of headed notepaper and began to write.

Darling Conrad,

As I write this you are upstairs playing,
totally unaware of what has happened. Dear
child, I can't say this to your face because you are too
young to understand, but I did
want to explain on paper.
Someone came to see me tonight and what they said
may well change our lives. I don't want you to
be hurt, Conrad, but I cannot go through my life
being afraid – not all the time. It has taken
me until now, in my thirty-fifth year, to find

347

the courage to say 'enough'.
Of all the things I tried to give you in your
short life, I believe that peace was the most
precious. Rest easy, little one, there might
be problems to come but remember I love you
and I will do everything in my power to protect you.
Play on, my darling child, the world is yours.

Your loving mother.

Freddie folded the paper, slid it into an envelope and hid it behind Bart's photograph in the picture frame. She knew she would never give it to her son, just as she knew that in reality she had not been talking to Conrad, but to herself.

'Why Paris?' Chris asked, her eyes troubled behind glasses as she studied Freddie sitting impassively at her desk at 107 Rutland Gate.

'Why not?' Freddie replied, rising to her feet. She pressed the button on the wall, lifted out a file, and began studying it. Her hair was drawn back from her face and held at the base of her neck in a snood. It was a fashion she had borrowed from the 1940s and had made her own, just as she had adopted a curiously stark way of dressing, relieved only by the sumptuous materials she favoured. Severe jackets and skirts were made sensual by fabrics such as velvet or brocade, her opulently feminine figure highlighted, not disguised, by the tailored lines. The individual fashion suited her and she had the style and elegance to carry it off superbly.

'Why do you need another bureau?' Chris persisted. 'The one in New York is making a fortune and so is the place in Rome. Why bother with Paris?'

Freddie glanced over her shoulder. The look was patient, deliberately so. 'I want to expand, that's why.' She sat down again. 'Paris is a city that has happy memories for me.' She paused, thinking back. 'And besides, that appalling woman, Mala Levinska, is opening a bureau there.' They exchanged a glance of understanding.

'I loathe that woman,' Chris said, not daring to ask about her visit the previous week. 'I can't believe that she's opening a marriage bureau, and I can't think why anyone would go to her for advice.'

'Because she's a good actress,' Freddie said evenly. 'She has a lot of experience in the business and people don't know what she's really like until it's too late and they've signed on the dotted line.'

'She should be stopped,' Chris said firmly.

Freddie's blue eyes blinked coldly. 'Oh, she will be. I think the time has come for Ms Levinska to be given a run for her money.'

Chris smiled delightedly. 'So you're going into competition with her?'

'That's just about the measure of it. The days of Mala Levinska and her kind are numbered. "No pay, no lay," ' Freddie murmured, remembering.

Chris frowned. 'What?'

'Apparently it was Mala's little motto, and it sums up her attitude neatly.' Freddie glanced at Chris, her head on one side. 'But she won't last much longer. I'm going to teach that bitch a lesson, Chris. Are you game?'

Laughing with mischievous delight, Chris nodded as Freddie answered the phone. Yet privately she wondered why Freddie wanted to compete with Mala Levinska. For financial gain? Hardly – most of the money made in the bureaux was either invested or donated to charity. Freddie Wallace's name was synonymous with fund-raising in the art world just as in society everyone associated her with The 107 Club. Over the years Freddie had carved out a special niche for herself, earning herself a seat on the board of the Louis XIV Gallery in Paris and the Georgian Institute in London. So why was she taking Levinska on, Chris wondered. To prove herself in some way?

Freddie's intelligence, once sparked, had proved formidable, and her reputation as a highly regarded business woman was more than secure. So what was the real reason for her rivalry with Mala? Chris coloured suddenly, staring down at her hands, surprised that she had been so stupid. Of course, the answer must lie in Freddie's past, in that hazy, shaded past which had clouded the time after Bart Wallace's death, in the rumours of suicide, and the casual inquiries of people as to why a man like that would kill himself. It *had* to be something from her past, Chris realised, feeling violently protective of her employer. Whatever it was, she thought, she would be on her side. Freddie Wallace had done more good for people than she had ever done harm. Whatever was going to happen, Chris would stand by her.

It didn't matter to Chris that she did not know the full story of Bart's death, or the circumstances surrounding it. All that mattered was that Freddie Wallace had saved her after her own husband's death, giving her a job and a place in the world. For that, she owed her employer unquestioning gratitude and loyalty.

'Is there anything else?' she asked Freddie when she came off the phone.

'No, not at the moment, thanks,' she replied, turning back to the file in front of her.

Frowning with concentration, Freddie flipped over the top page of the file and read the psychiatric notes from Malcolm Prentice, sighing when she saw the word 'vulnerable'. Then she turned over the next sheet of paper and read Craig Benson's medical report. The client was an academic, a fit man in his forties who had some nervous trouble with his stomach, but otherwise was in good health. Freddie pushed aside the medical report as her eyes fixed on the graphology analysis. The words 'creative' and 'original' jumped up from the page. Yet the photograph showed a spare little man, prematurely aged, a full-lipped mouth disguised by a beard, eyes shielded behind spectacles.

Freddie was mulling over the information when Tina Shore walked in, full of her usual optimism. 'This one's going to be lucky. I can feel it!' she said eagerly. 'Are you ready to see Dr Reiner now?'

'Is he here already?' Freddie asked, glancing at her watch. 'All right, send him in.'

A moment later Dr Harvey Reiner walked into the office,

took a seat and smiled nervously. His appearance was undistinguished, almost comic, his clever academic brain disguised by an unprepossessing face and a badly fitting suit.

'I'm early,' he said, his voice bearing marks of a Dutch accent. 'I hope that's not inconvenient for you, Mrs Wallace. I so hate being late that I have a tendency to arrive everywhere far too early. At the university they always say ...' He trailed off, embarrassed to have talked so much.

'What did they say at the university, Dr Reiner?' Freddie prompted him.

He relaxed visibly. 'That such actions betray anxiety ...' He paused again. Perhaps he had said too much, perhaps this woman would think he was emotionally immature and refuse to take him on. Nervously he shifted in his chair. He could barely afford the large fee to join the bureau on the wage the university paid him as professor of semantics – but on the other hand he had no choice but to pay, and pray that this woman could find him someone. After all, his own efforts over the last few years had been pitiful, his attentions met with surprise or ridicule, his unattractive appearance isolating him.

Harvey glanced at the open file lying on the desk in front of Freddie and forced himself to smile. He had found the selection process humiliating, an admission of his own failure and loneliness. Acknowledged as a fine scholar, it was humbling to find himself in a marriage bureau – no matter how exclusive.

'I read your file,' Freddie said easily. 'You've had a very distinguished career. You must be very proud of what you've achieved.'

Harvey coughed with embarrassment. 'I was well educated and lucky,' he said without any false modesty. 'And I always wanted to study.' He cleared his throat. 'Was everything in order? I mean, well, am I suitable? I know I don't have a great deal of money and that some of your clients are rich ...' His diffidence made him awkward and when he reached out for his cup, he slopped some coffee into the saucer. 'I don't have much to offer really, but I'm affectionate ...' He paused, and thinking that the words implied sexual intimacy, his mortification was complete.

351

Intuitively aware of what he was feeling, Freddie reassured him. 'Affection is something of a rarity these days, Dr Reiner. I think you should feel proud of the quality.'

His eyes searched hers for any sign that she was mocking him, but there was none.

'I read your details and your history,' Freddie continued slowly. 'I'm sorry about your wife.'

Harvey nodded, unable to talk. His unhappiness had taken many forms since his wife had left him unexpectedly. Whilst other men would have turned to religion, or women, his work was his saviour, his time spent with literature and theories. Shock was his Host, the continual litany 'why me?' his psalm. But time still continued and after three years the loneliness had become unbearable, his confidence broken by rejection.

'When she left it was a great shock,' he said finally, breathing in and calling on his courage. 'But now I want to find someone.' He glanced up, looking for approval. 'Do you think it's wrong of me?'

'She's gone, Dr Reiner,' Freddie said softly. 'And I think that it's time you met someone new. I'm also glad you came here.'

Harvey's voice faltered. 'You'll take me on then?'

'Of course. Why ever not?' Freddie replied, turning away and passing a form to him, her mouth widening into a smile. 'Just sign this and we're on our way.'

Obediently he signed and passed it back to her. 'Do you think I have a chance?' he asked wistfully. 'Do you really think I have a chance of meeting someone?'

It was a question Freddie had heard repeatedly. *Do I have a chance of meeting someone?* Sometimes it was asked genuinely, a plea for reassurance, but at other times it was asked arrogantly by people who believed they had every chance, individuals who took love without giving any. Most of these people Freddie turned away, her instinct warning her against them, her own history making her a sure judge of character. Others she accepted, knowing that the bravado covered massive insecurity.

Most of the time she was right and as she grew to know the client their arrogance peeled off, their vulnerability exposed gradually over the weeks and months. Sometimes their

352

confidence returned when they met someone, at other times their egos took a beating as they were constantly rejected. And sometimes they made her laugh, especially Beth Holland. A tall, angular woman with a PR job in fashion, she had come from a large family in Middlesborough. Her brothers and sisters had all followed the same route and married early, whilst she had pursued a career and avoided wedded bliss. The choice had been the right one, until she woke up one morning and realised …

' … that my life stank.'

Freddie smiled easily, encouraging her to continue.

'I'd run my whole existence to the five Ps,' Beth explained. 'You know what I mean, Preparation Prevents Piss Poor Performance.' Freddie smiled as Beth continued. 'Only, when it came to a lasting relationship, I hadn't done my *preparation* and I'd missed out on the *performance*.' Her accent was suddenly pure Middlesborough, her eyebrows raised. 'So that's why I joined your bureau.' Her voice dropped and she stood up, taking two long legged steps towards the door and closing it. 'That advisor of yours – Liz Ford? She's a great girl, of course, Mrs Wallace … '

'Freddie.'

'Freddie,' Beth agreed. 'But she's a bit of a snob. All that "too pure to pee" accent, it's not me. In fact, I can't understand half of what she says.' She smoothed down the jacket of her expensive Lacroix suit. 'That's why I asked for you to take me on instead. I've been on the books for nearly six months and I haven't met anyone suitable yet.'

Freddie looked down at her file and ran her finger along the list of men from the agency Beth had dated. There were fifteen. 'And not one of these was any good?' she asked, pausing as she came across one name. 'What about Tony Shaw? Most of the women think he's pretty attractive.'

'No one's opinion could live up to his own. That bloke doesn't hold a conversation with you, he gives you the benefit of an appearance.' Beth leaned towards Freddie. 'And do you know, at the end of the evening he had his hand up my skirt so fast I found skid marks on my tights.'

353

Freddie laughed and then continued to read the list of names. 'Frederick Meades?'

'Too old.'

'Paul Howard?'

'He had halitosis, and he told me that he dreamed he walked on water.' She laughed uproariously. 'I told him to be careful, the last bloke who did that came to an untimely end – and I didn't mean Donald Campbell.'

'OK, OK,' Freddie said grinning and putting up her hands in mock surrender. 'What about Michael Netherlandt?'

'Dutch.'

Freddie's mouth twitched. 'What's wrong with the Dutch?'

'Nothing, if you happen to be called Gerta.'

'I see,' Freddie said. 'Well what about Gregory Thines?'

'We went out for dinner,' Beth explained, 'and at the end of a dull evening, he had the nerve to tell me that he has a list of women who wanted to meet him so he felt he couldn't commit himself to another date until he'd seen "what else was on offer." '

Freddie made a mental note of Mr Thines' comment, and then raised her eyebrows. 'But I thought you were seeing quite a lot of Daniel Haig and things were pretty serious there?' she said, thinking of the man she had had on her books since she first opened the bureau.

Beth glanced down at her hands. 'He's a nice man and we have a good time, but he's possessive.'

'Well, he had a lousy time with his wife,' Freddie said, getting to her feet and drawing out his file. 'Has he told you about it?'

'That he found her in bed with her not-so-ex-lover only days after the wedding?' Freddie nodded. 'Yes, he told me, and I'm sorry, but I don't feel … comfortable with him.'

'Well that's all right, I understand,' Freddie said sympathetically. 'But in some ways you two do seem compatible. He has a good sense of humour and he wants to settle down … '

'And he's rich,' Beth said wickedly. 'Believe me, I know he's got a lot going for him. Flashy media job, good car, all the things I want, but … '

354

'But?'

'He makes me uneasy, and he wants to rush things too much.'

Freddie glanced at Daniel Haig's photograph and remembered the many conversations she had had with him. He was fond of Beth but wondered if she could mix with his friends, or whether her background would clash uneasily with his own. Yet gradually, as the weeks passed, he had made allowances and when they had last talked, he had told Freddie that he was serious about Beth and was even thinking about marriage.

'He's very fond of you.'

Beth shrugged. 'I'm fond of Persian cats but I wouldn't marry one.'

Yet if Beth Holland could take the bureau and the dating in her stride, Cleo Taylor could not. She came to see Freddie one afternoon, hanging back at the door for minutes before she plucked up courage to go in, and when she did she said little and confided less.

As her footsteps faded on the steps Freddie pointed to the door and said to Chris. 'That was the one that got away.'

Chris shrugged, not entirely convinced by Freddie's judgement. 'You never know. She might just be thinking things over.'

She was, and returned three further times before agreeing to undergo the selection process. When everything was finally completed, the results were sent through to Freddie. According to Dr Benson, her medical report was sound, but the psychiatric assessment from Malcolm Prentice was decidedly strange. He even took the trouble to deliver the report in person, his clear Welsh voice declaiming dramatically. 'Crazy as a fox, I think.'

'Listen, Malcolm,' Freddie said drily. 'You're the psychiatrist. You're paid to tell me, not guess.'

He regarded her critically over the edges of his bifocals. 'Have you ever thought of undergoing therapy yourself?'

She nodded. 'I have it every week at the hairdressers. After I see the results, I resort to something called primal screaming.'

Malcolm Prentice sighed and turned back to his notes. 'With regard to Cleo Taylor, her background could have a lot

355

to do with her character development, although she doesn't go into much detail about her family. I think she's either immature, or psychotic.'

Freddie laced her fingers together and smiled half-heartedly. 'So she's somewhere between Lizzie Borden and Postman Pat? Couldn't you be a little more exact? I would appreciate it.'

Malcolm Prentice bridled. 'Psychiatry is not an exact science.'

'Neither is matchmaking,' Freddie replied coolly, 'but as my clients are paying a large fee, I feel I owe it to them not to fix them up with any potential assassins.'

In the end Freddie asked Cleo to come and see her so she could judge for herself. The following afternoon, Cleo duly arrived and she and Freddie talked for several hours, continuing long after Chris came in at six to say she was going home and Molly phoned down from the nursery to tell Freddie that Conrad was having his supper. But Freddie made no effort to terminate the appointment and neither did she rush Cleo. Instead she waited. For what, she didn't know. She knew only that Cleo Taylor wanted to talk and Freddie was prepared to listen.

Round about the subject of Cleo's childhood they went, skating past each other on thin ice, Cleo occasionally scratching the surface and then moving off again. Catch me if you can ... if you can. Patiently Freddie followed her leads whilst scrutinising the pretty woman who sat in front of her. She had tiny hands with chewed nails, hair worn with a long fringe, eyes constantly alert. Cleo was then twenty-four years old and worked as a commercial designer, her mother remarried and living with her stepfather in Israel, whilst she lived alone in Blackheath. The family was wealthy, that much was obvious from the conversation, but Cleo's education had been cut short suddenly when she was removed from school and sent away to the Sorbonne in Paris.

'Did you miss home?' Freddie asked, pouring them some more coffee.

Cleo picked up the cup and held it with both hands as a child would. 'I suppose so.'

356

'You know something? I don't think you did,' Freddie said gently. 'I think you were glad to be away from home.' Her voice was soft. 'I think you were afraid of something, Cleo. Am I right?'

The girl stiffened in her seat and stared, her eyes full of terror. 'I wanted to … '

'What? What did you want?' Freddie coaxed her. 'You can tell me. So many people have told me secrets and not one of them ever left this room. Trust me.'

'No, you wouldn't take me on if you knew.'

'Knew what?'

Cleo blinked. 'I want to join the bureau. I want to be married. I want to be safe.' Her eyes closed, tears trickling out from the corners. 'I can't tell, can't tell.'

Freddie rose to her feet and went over to the girl. Carefully she prised the cup from her hands and then kneeled down in front of her chair. 'Did they hurt you?'

Cleo's eyes snapped open. 'I never said, I never told you!'

'No, I guessed, didn't I?' Freddie said firmly. 'You never told me. I guessed. Was it your father?' Cleo shook her head. 'Your mother?' Again, Cleo shook her head. 'Your stepfather then?'

Cleo's eyes widened, her hands gripping Freddie's as she leaned towards her. 'I never told you! I never did. I promised I wouldn't.'

'What did he do, Cleo? What did he do to you?'

'He raped me!' she said finally, her hands releasing Freddie's and then brushing her thighs repeatedly as though she was trying to clean herself. 'And then he … '

'What?'

'Then he … he urinated over me.'

Whatever the clients looked like, whatever age, religion or whatever background they came from, they all had one thing in common – fear. Freddie understood such fear well, as nothing would have induced her to expose herself. In fact nothing would have persuaded her to fall in love, or trust any man ever again.

Chapter Twenty-Six

Distressed and confused, Warren returned to Maiden Lane and brooded. In the years since it had opened, the restaurant had made him a great deal of money. So much money that he had found himself wondering what to do with it, periodically tempted to effect a reconciliation with his family, but always resisting the impulse – until now. That morning he had at last revisited the old workshop, climbing the stairs and imagining the look on his father's face as he walked in. But the notice on the door had been final. The furrier no longer traded there, it said, workshop being closed due to his death. Warren rocked with the news.

For years Warren had imagined his return. He dreamed of a joyous family reunion, of revisiting his old childhood haunts, of his money making amends. His family would be proud of him, forgiving, all past differences absolved because their son had made good ... But now it was too late, he thought bitterly. He had left it too late.

As he hurried into his private entrance to the restaurant at Maiden Lane, Warren tried to collect his thoughts. He had been stupid to go back. What he needed was not in the past, it was in the future. What he needed was a family of his own. His thoughts turned to Freddie Wallace and he shook his head incredulously as he made his way up to his flat, locking the door behind him. The emptiness of the place angered him unreasonably and he moved into the bathroom, splashing his face with cold water, the blank tiled walls pressing in on him.

He had to have her, there had to be a way.

Leaning forwards, Warren pulled open the bathroom cabinet, his hand tightening around a bottle of scent. It was the type Freddie always wore, the perfume she had on her skin the night they made love, the smell which had clung on his own skin for hours afterwards. Slowly he opened the bottle and breathed in the scent; the perfume came full-bodied, the memory potent. Shaking, he poured a few drops into his right hand and then rubbed his palms together, cupping his hands around his face and closing his eyes as he breathed in the scent of the woman who consumed him.

Mala was jubilant as she walked into her bureau and spun round on her high heels. Her kohl-rimmed eyes took in every detail as she reached greedily for the newly filled files, the names neatly typed out, the fees quickly banked. In the three weeks since she had opened, she had had the satisfaction of seeing a healthy procession of clients coming to her. Some had come from the previous bureau where she had worked; some were dissatisfied, difficult clients who had been poached from Freddie and others were old friends of Mala's who had their own reasons for wanting to ruin Freddie Wallace. Men like Tony Shaw. He had been an old lover of Mala's and after he had been rejected by Freddie when he made a half-hearted pass at her, his malice had festered. So Mala encouraged him to be disruptive; she laughed when he told her about the women clients he seduced; and she provoked his antagonism by clever reminders of Freddie's rejection of him – knowing how such taunting fuelled his anger.

At the same time Mala brooded on her own jealousy, thinking of Warren Roberts and burning with envy. She did not know for certain that Freddie and Warren had been lovers. She had simply guessed, and Freddie's reaction when she visited her at the bureau had all but confirmed it. Mala narrowed her eyes, thinking of the nurse who had been so obliging. It paid to have people owing you favours, she thought wryly. But the medical information had been limited. All the woman could confirm was that Freddie's child was not Bart's son. Nothing more. The information she had read and passed on so assiduously to Mala was limited, lacking the most vital fact – the name of the real father.

But Mala had guessed. She knew deep inside her that it was Warren Roberts, and smouldered with bitterness and spite. Her head swam. She would destroy Freddie Wallace and get her revenge on the man who had rejected her. Day by day she would build up her own business and pick her rival clean. There would be no mercy, no weakness. Freddie Wallace had had her day, now it was Mala's chance to shine.

Jao was lying on her back on the bed, watching Bea put on her make-up for the evening show at the Bayswater hotel. Beside Jao, Miku snored happily, his chest rising and falling, his nose running slightly and leaving a damp patch on the counterpane. For the past few days Jao had not been able to get Freddie out of her mind and had rung her, only to be told by Chris that she was in Paris and not expected back for a while.

Yawning, Jao closed her eyes and thought of Rutland Gate, and of Freddie's son. He looked very like his mother, and although she had never been able to see anything of Bart in him, his expression betrayed a surprising resemblance to Greville. She scratched her nose thoughtfully, her mind wandering. It was odd how things turned out; she had tried dozens of careers, all of them failing miserably until Freddie had stepped in and introduced her to some of her friends in the art world. Jao had known a fair amount about paintings and applied herself to learning more, liking the artistic social life and anxious not to run up any further professional blind alleys. When people realised she was serious, Jao attracted the attention of some of the smaller dealers and began working as a runner. Jao grinned at the term 'runner' – a freelance art consultant who couldn't afford to own a gallery, someone who was forced to move around constantly visiting clients. A runner. It suited her temperament perfectly.

'Are you doing exercises, or just trying to scare the dog?'

Jao opened one eye and glanced at her mother. 'What?'

'You should have seen your face then. What a sketch!'

'I was thinking – '

'Then give it up before you pull something.'

Jao hauled herself upright and leaned on her elbow. 'Have I disappointed you?'

'Only when you wouldn't marry Prince Charles,' Bea said drily. 'Otherwise, no.' She frowned. 'What brought this on?'

'Oh, I was just wondering,' Jao said idly. 'I've not met anyone yet, have I?'

'You've not met anyone *suitable*,' Bea corrected her. 'Why? Is it worrying you?'

'Well, I was thinking about Freddie, and thinking that she's already been married … '

'And widowed,' Bea said, throwing her lipstick into her bag. Jao stared at the back of her mother's head.

'I heard the oddest thing yesterday,' she said cautiously. 'At a private view. Someone said that Bart's death wasn't an accident, but that he committed suicide.'

Bea's back stiffened. 'Rubbish! People have vicious tongues,' she said emphatically. 'Why would Bart kill himself when he had everything to live for? A loving wife, and the child he always wanted. It's rubbish. You shouldn't spread such malicious talk, not if you're a friend of hers.'

'OK, OK!' Jao said, pulling a face. 'I just thought you'd be interested to hear about it, that's all. I never said I believed it, did I?'

Yet as Bea walked out and hailed a taxi at the corner of Dorman Square, she felt profoundly unsettled. The idea of Bart killing himself was ludicrous. Yet she had heard something along the same lines herself years before. But why would Bart Wallace kill himself? He had what he wanted. The marriage had been shakey for a while, she knew, but things had improved and Freddie and he were happy again, especially when Conrad was born. Bea shook her head, and glanced out of the taxi window.

Oh God, she thought, don't let it be true, don't let there be any truth to it. I couldn't bear to know that Bart had been so unhappy. All I wanted was his happiness, it was the only thing which made losing him bearable. Her thoughts turned to

361

Freddie and her grief. Had she been too distraught for too long, Bea wondered. Had her agony been just for her husband's death, or for something else? ... But there were no answers to her questions and as her mind raced on she clutched her hand-bag, her eyes staring blankly at the road ahead.

Greville, too, was thinking of Freddie as he stretched out his arm and turned off the alarm by the bed. Madelaine slept on, her face, free of make-up, a mere blur, without character; her breath acid. Greville touched her shoulder, but when she stirred he moved quickly, his libido flagging as he changed his mind and got up.

The kitchen in the mews house was untidy, a greasy dish cloth swimming in a pan full of cold water, a selection of dirty cutlery thrown haphazardly into the sink. With a bad tempered grunt, Greville turned on the kettle and scratched the stubble of his beard. He had been foolish to leave Sarah so suddenly, but Madelaine had duped him, telling him that she was to inherit a sizeable nest-egg if she had a child. His greed had then forced his hand ... The kettle hummed listlessly, the gas light sputtering underneath. Of course she'd lost the kid, he thought, amazed that he had fallen for the oldest trick in the book.

Luckily Sarah had not started divorce proceedings, so he still had free access to all their joint accounts and the income from the business. But he would have to be more careful from now on. For years he had gradually been getting a grip on more and more of the Clough funds. Money had been secreted by a clever accountant, and doubled by an even cleverer stockbroker. Yet more funds had found a home in Switzerland. But if Freddie were ever to find out, there could be problems, and she was more likely to show an interest now that he wanted to leave her mother and she had a son of her own ... Greville turned off the kettle as it began to boil and poured the water onto a tea bag, stirring it thoughtfully. Madelaine had obviously not heard him moving around, he realised gratefully. With any luck he could get out of the house and to his club before she woke.

How soon would she take to get pregnant again? he wondered, burning his lip on the scalding tea. It wasn't as though they didn't try hard enough, not that that seemed to make any difference. Greville slumped into a chair in the sitting room, his eyebrows drawn together. Damn his bloody luck! Two bloody women and neither of them had managed to give him a son. Bloody Sarah! Bloody Madelaine! He cursed, his temper rising as he extended his hand and poured an inch of scotch into his morning tea, his thoughts clouding suddenly as he did so.

At Rutland Gate, Molly took off her glasses to polish them, then peered out of the study window. Freddie was sitting in the small enclosed back garden, listening to Conrad, her dark head bent down as he haltingly read a book to her, Conrad laughing suddenly as his mother made a face. Molly smiled, but didn't feel tempted to join them, even though Freddie encouraged her to use the garden, inviting her to eat outside with them and suggesting that she sunbathe on the patio in summer.

Molly never sunbathed; Molly never went out to parties; Molly never had a boyfriend, or visitors. Molly simply existed for Freddie and Conrad. That was all, and that was enough. Her only excursions of any distance had been to Yorkshire at Easter and Christmas, but nowadays, since her father had remarried, she had the perfect excuse to stay in London in December and enjoyed the festivities there.

Rutland Gate was now, to all intents and purposes, Molly's home. She idolised Freddie, and above all adored Conrad. He was her real joy, her child as much as he was Freddie's – not that she would ever say such a thing, she wouldn't dare risk being banished, sent back to Yorkshire. No, it was her secret. Not that people didn't guess. Her expression gave her away, her plain face reddening when Mrs Allen poked fun, or when Freddie praised her.

'I don't know what I'd do without you. I'd never have managed with Conrad on my own.' Freddie had said the other day. Molly beamed at the memory. Yes, she had done well and made herself indispensable. She frowned, struggling with the word.

It had been Freddie's idea that Molly attend adult education classes now that Conrad was at school. Naturally, Molly had agreed to it, almost speechless with gratitude when her employer paid her fees. She had chosen to study English Literature, coming back to Rutland Gate with a bag full of Dickens and Austen and talking to Freddie at length about the plots and characters, faithfully reiterating everything her teachers had taught her.

But if Molly found it easy to talk to Freddie, it was impossible for her to communicate with the likes of Dione Salari or Pennsylvania Parry. Molly frowned, remembering the latter's corseted gait and the way he cried at the smallest thing. She liked Jao Wilkie though, even when she swore violently and made jokes which Molly didn't understand. She liked Sarah Clements too, because, being little and childlike, she bought out Molly's protective instinct as she fussed around her and Conrad when Freddie was away. Not that Molly minded the extra work that Sarah's visits always caused; it made her feel more useful, knowing that she was relied upon so completely, even if Mr Allen did check the locks at night and made sure that everything was in order before going to bed. Molly could have done it herself easily, but Freddie had explained that Mr Allen needed to feel useful too. It was logical really, Molly thought, trying out the word and liking the sound of it. It was logical – but not quite true.

The truth was another thing, she knew. She waved quickly as Conrad glanced up at the study window. The truth was that she, Molly Garrett, was responsible for Conrad *because Freddie trusted her*. Her, and no one else. Oh, she might let her mother look after him sometimes, but when it came right down to it, Molly was the reliable one. After all, hadn't she been there for years? Since just after Mr Wallace's death? And hadn't she nursed Conrad and helped Freddie out when she was grieving? That counted for something surely, she thought. Yes, that counted for a lot. She smiled again, the light glinting momentarily on her glasses and blinding her so that she could see no further than the window and the small garden beyond.

*

364

'I think I might have someone for you, Cleo,' Freddie said, turning back to the file in front of her. 'But first I want to have a chat.'

'Have I done something wrong?' she asked immediately.

Freddie smiled patiently, recognising the insecurity in the words. 'Of course you haven't done anything wrong, Cleo. I just wanted to talk.' Freddie smiled warmly. 'I have someone I want you to meet, he's called Harvey Reiner, Doctor Harvey Reiner, and he's a very kind man.'

What does he do?' Cleo asked warily.

'He's a professor at London University. In semantics.'

'What are semantics?'

Freddie smiled. 'Ask him. Any explanation I could give would be only superficial.'

Cleo smiled uneasily. 'He sounds too clever for me.'

'That's the point. He is smart, but he doesn't want someone who's always trying to score points.' Freddie paused. 'Anyway, don't do yourself down, Cleo, you're very intelligent.'

'Not if I don't know what semantics means,' she said sullenly.

'He's not a good looking man,' Freddie continued ignoring Cleo's bad mood, 'but he's kind and very giving.'

Cleo fiddled with her hair, her fringe shading her eyes. 'Can I see the photograph?'

Freddie nodded and pushed it across the desk.

'Ugh!' Cleo said simply, throwing it back at her, 'he's horrible.'

For one moment Freddie was too stunned to react. 'How can you say that?' she said, her voice steely. 'He is a good man and worth meeting. I didn't say I expected you to marry him, I just thought that you could have a friendship ... '

'I don't want anyone like that!' Cleo screeched. 'He looks like a dirty old man.'

Stiffly, Freddie got to her feet and looked down at the girl. 'I suggest that we talk again in a few days time, when both of us have calmed down.'

'I'll still say the same thing!' Cleo said defiantly, walking to the door and slamming it closed behind her.

Wearily Freddie sat down and clenched her fists tightly. She didn't need arguments or tantrums, she had enough on her plate. Mala's threat was depleting her, and she knew it. Although she had tried to force Mala's hand, she had not carried out her threat of exposure. Why? Freddie wondered for the hundredth time. Because she only suspected the truth? After all, she couldn't know about Warren, no one did. So why was she hesitating? A timid bubble of optimism flared up in Freddie – perhaps she had never meant to carry out her threat. And yet she wasn't sure, and as every day passed and Mala's business thrived, Freddie found herself living on a knife-edge.

But Freddie refused to be cowed and deliberately provoked Mala, opening the Paris bureau to a fanfare of articles and a couple of television interviews. She knew that some of her clients had defected to her rival and had vague suspicions about Tony Shaw, but there was nothing concrete and she decided to brazen it out, hoping that Mala would take her revenge professionally, not personally. A month passed by, Freddie never more courted by the press and never more visible – yet she heard nothing, and in the days which followed she waited anxiously for Mala to strike.

But there was not a word.

Freddie frowned, rubbing her forehead with her hands. Of course, Mala may have been bluffing – but Freddie doubted it. She knew too much of Mala Levinska's temperament and history to be lulled into a false feeling of security. Perhaps she should give herself a break from the bureau, Freddie thought. She could put off her next trip to Paris and go up to Yorkshire with Conrad instead. Freddie smiled, thinking of Cambuscan. Yes, they ought to go up and have some time there. But what about Conrad taking time off school? What about that? The door of her office opened silently, Chris watching her for an instant before coughing discreetly.

Freddie glanced up. 'Sorry. What is it?'

'There's a man to see you outside. In reception.'

Frowning, Freddie glanced at her appointment book. 'I didn't think I arranged to see anyone.'

Chris shrugged. 'Well, he seems most eager to see you ... '

She was interrupted in full flow when Greville passed her and walked into his daughter's office.

'Hello, Frederica,' he said simply.

She was too surprised to answer him and merely watched as he picked up the *pietra dura* box on her desk.

'Nice, very nice.'

'It was a token from Harry when Bart died,' she said, taking the box out of his hands. 'What do you want, Father?'

'To see you,' he replied, as though it was the most natural thing in the world.

Freddie hesitated. 'Sit down then' she said finally, 'I'll get us something to drink.'

She ordered two coffees and then waited in reception with her arms folded, leaning back against the desk and wondering why her father had come to visit her. Her father, the man who had soured her childhood; the man who had left her mother for his mistress ...

'Here you are,' she said coolly, returning to the office and passing him a cup of coffee.

Greville smiled, his exquisite face showing depressing signs of age. The skin was unhealthy, the whites of his eyes faintly yellowed, but his mouth and teeth were as memorably perfect as they had always been.

Unaware of what his daughter was thinking, Greville glanced round the room, noting everything and itemising each object. His brain worked like a calculator – chair £300, books £250, paintings £14,000 ... He took in a breath to speak, finding words difficult and fighting the old belief that his daughter knew his thoughts and all his secrets.

'I came to ... '

'Yes, father?'

' ... see you,' he finished lamely.

So you've seen me, Freddie thought, now get back to your mistress. Her temper burned slowly, her eyes locking with her father's gaze. I refuse to be afraid of you any longer, she thought.

'How's Conrad?'

'He's at school,' Freddie replied. 'But he'll be home soon,' she added, cursing herself as the words left her lips. Why did

367

she say that? she thought. She didn't want her father to see her son. He'd never shown any interest before, so why pander to him now? Because he's your father, she thought with resignation, and because you still want him to be proud of you.

'I'd like to see my grandson,' Greville said lightly, sipping his coffee and grimacing as the skin came away on his lip. For a moment Freddie almost laughed and then controlled herself. Don't ruin it, she thought, maybe your father is here to make amends. You waited a long time for this, don't spoil it.

'You've done very well for yourself, Frederica,' Greville said, smiling again. 'I'm impressed.'

Freddie could feel her face redden, the long years of her father's cruelty melting under the few kind words. Maybe it's because he's getting older, she thought, or ill – maybe that's why he's softening.

'I chose something that people need. Marriage bureaux always do well,' Freddie said, trailing off, her confidence failing her.

'Do you have many clients?' Greville asked.

Freddie hesitated and then rose to her feet, smiling proudly at her father as she pressed the button on the wall. Immediately the false bookcase front swung forwards, revealing the rows of files exposed in all their systematic glory. Almost as though she soothed a child, Freddie reached out her hand and stroked the spines of the files, her heart banging. Look at what I've done, Father, tell me you're pleased with me. Tell me ...

'It's quite an achievement,' Greville said, his hand going up to his face, revealing the feeling of discomfort they both shared. 'I've been harsh with you in the past ... '

She said nothing, just remembered falling from the orchard wall, and the little white cross marked 'Mrs Gilly'.

' ... and I'm glad to see that you've done well. I worked hard too, you know, to build a career for myself.'

It would have been ungenerous for her to contradict and insist that his 'career' was due to a lucky marriage and the Clough money, so Freddie said nothing and remained standing beside the wall, the rows of files stacked behind her.

'I'd like to see Conrad,' Greville repeated, glancing at his watch, 'but I have to go now. Perhaps I could come and see you again?'

Freddie nodded, not trusting her voice, and for an instant she nearly moved towards him, but stopped herself. He saw her hesitation and walked over to his daughter, leaning down and kissing her briefly on the cheek. For hours afterwards, Freddie could hear every word that her father had said and smell the faint and familiar scent of lemon cologne on her skin.

Mala Levinska arrived at her bureau early the following morning, raging as she threw the sheaf of newspapers and magazines in her hand violently at the wall. Freddie's face looked up from the open page triumphantly.

'Bitch!'

The receptionist rushed out when she heard her. 'Miss Levinska, is there anything I can do?'

'Get out of my frigging way!' Mala howled, pushing the girl aside and slamming the door of her office shut. With trembling hands she lit a cigarette and inhaled deeply, her foot tapping angrily on the polished floor. I never thought she would call my bluff, Mala murmured under her breath. Well, we'll see who gets the last laugh. She must have thought I was joking. She thinks that her position is so secure that she's safe. Her temper bubbled unhealthily. Oh no, Freddie Wallace was too confident by half.

Her hand snatched up the telephone receiver and she dialled quickly. A man answered on the third ring. The conversation was brief and to the point as she outlined to the journalist the news about Freddie Wallace, the famous matchmaker. She knew the man would be interested in the story and although she couldn't tell him the name of Conrad's real father, the story was too sensational for him to resist.

'Do you have proof?'

'A copy of a medical document that proves the child wasn't Bart Wallace's. Besides, he committed suicide, didn't he?'

The journalist laughed shortly. 'You don't change, Mala. I suppose this is personal?'

Mala bristled. 'Freddie Wallace should be exposed!'

'So that her business is ruined and you can profit from the fall-out?'

Mala thought of Warren and swallowed. It wouldn't do for anyone to know that rejection was the prime reason which motivated her.

'Freddie Wallace isn't fit to run a marriage bureau.'

'How humanitarian you've become!'

His sarcasm made her wince.

'Listen, do you want the story, or not?'

'Sure, I'm always ready to right wrongs, Mala,' the man said drily. 'You know that.'

Chapter Twenty-Seven

The news spread quicker than ink on blotting paper. By the time Mala had done her work, Freddie Wallace had been exposed as a woman who had had an adulterous affair and borne another man's child. That would have been enough to ruin anyone, but the additional suggestion that Bart Wallace had committed suicide when he discovered that Conrad was not his son – that was the final and most damning blow. Reeling from the shock and uncertain where to turn for help, Freddie's first instinct was to take out an injunction to prevent further damage, but then she decided that by doing so she might just fuel further gossip, so she stayed her hand. She thought that there would only be a limited interest and that she might escape extensive exposure, but she was wrong. Freddie Wallace had enough of a reputation to attract the attention of a couple of the tabloids and their articles followed on quickly:

Matchmaker's Secret Affair Finally Revealed.
Frederica Wallace bears another man's son.
Her husband commits suicide when he finds out.

The papers went on in grim detail, but did not mention who the father was, as it was the one thing Mala only suspected but could not conclusively prove. Otherwise, Freddie was crucified. That a matchmaker could commit adultery! The woman to whom people paid a high fee for advice ...

When Freddie saw the articles she reeled, avoiding Jean

Allen's eyes when she came down for breakfast. Molly glanced up from her paper, her face red.

'I don't care what they say – it's not true, is it?'

Freddie nodded. 'Yes, Molly, it's true.'

The girl faltered, regarding the fallen idol, and then she got slowly to her feet and called for Conrad to take him to school. Just as they were about to leave, Freddie stood in front of the door, barring their exit. 'No, I think Conrad should stay home today.'

'But – '

She cut Molly off.

'He stays home,' she said emphatically and then leaned against the door for support as Molly took her son back into the kitchen.

She had gambled and apparently lost, but now she had to prove that she was tough enough to take all the recriminations coming her way. In deciding not to be blackmailed, she had risked all – now the only question that remained was how much could she salvage from the situation. Lifting her head high, Freddie pushed open the glass doors of the bureau. Tina Shore, Liz Ford and Dot Cummings all glanced up at her from the reception desk where they had been in a huddle, reading the morning press. Embarrassed, they shifted their feet, and only the arrival of Chris broke the silence.

'Morning, Mrs Wallace,' she said breezily. Freddie frowned. Hadn't she heard the news? 'We've got a busy day ahead. Three new clients.'

Liz exchanged a cool, questioning glance with Tina.

'If they still come,' she said, her voice thin with reproach.

Freddie swung round and challenged her directly. 'Liz, if you have anything to say to me, say it directly, will you?' She turned to the others. 'And the same goes for all of you. I've always played fair with you, I ask you to do the same for me.'

'But it's in the papers … ' Tina said, rushing on, ' … all about your son and your husband and you … Oh, I'm sure it'll all blow over.'

'I'm not,' Liz said coldly. 'I think it will damage the bureau very badly indeed.'

'What will?' Chris said, baffled. In silence, Liz handed her the paper and waited until she read it. Slowly, Chris let out her breath and then her eyes met Freddie's. 'I still say we have a busy day ahead,' she repeated. 'I don't care if the story is true, or not. You stood by me when I needed help, Mrs Wallace, so you can count on me now.'

Freddie's eyes filled and she glanced away, but even as she did so, Liz's voice cut through as sharp as a knife blade. 'I don't think I can stay on, Mrs Wallace,' she said. 'I wouldn't feel comfortable here now.'

Nodding, Freddie said quietly. 'I'm sorry, but if that's the way you feel, you must go. In fact, you can go now, Liz, if you want – I'll send on your papers and your salary.'

As she walked out, the remaining women looked at each other; Dot, tight-lipped, Tina, nervously smiling, and Chris, solidly dependable.

'Well?' Freddie asked them. 'What do you want to do?'

'I'm staying,' Chris said, smiling brilliantly when Freddie squeezed her hand in gratitude.

'I say – bugger the press!' Dot replied, her Northern voice filled with defiance.

'Well … I suppose it'll all be all right in the end,' Tina said, picking up the phone as it rang by her elbow.

Warren read the headlines and found himself shaking, his eyes flicking from the newspaper to the window and back again. For nearly an hour he paced the floor in his flat, his mind grinding over and over again, his thoughts fixed on the one thing he now knew for certain. *Conrad was his son.* Freddie had given birth to his child. He knew it by instinct, and now wondered only how he could find the proof.

Dangerously, he brooded, and by eleven o'clock had found a solution. He knew the name of Freddie's doctor – Bart had mentioned the man several times – and he phoned for an appointment, saying it was a matter of grave urgency.

Warren walked in calmly and sat down, passing the newspaper to the man, who had obviously already seen it.

'I have to tell you, Doctor, that Mrs Wallace is very shocked by all of this,' Warren said, his tone even, preparing himself

373

for the next words. 'But we have to talk. I think that you know the truth – you know that I'm the father, don't you?'

The doctor nodded, almost relieved.

Warren's heart was beating frantically.

'Mrs Wallace told me, of course, but I didn't write it in the notes, thank God.' He shook his head, eager to try and excuse the leak from his office. 'I can't believe that a nurse would do such a thing – would break a patient's trust like that. She left a little while ago and I can't even trace her. I think she went abroad to work. I can't tell you how badly I feel about all of this, Mr Roberts. It's never happened to me before in all my years of practice.'

Warren was all quiet understanding.

'I understand, believe me. But this *must* remain a secret between us.'

'Of course, Mr Roberts. No one will find out that you are Conrad Wallace's father. You can take my word for it. I assure you of that.' He paused, filled with real sympathy for the man in front of him. 'I'm so glad Mrs Wallace has your support. That will be a real comfort to her, I'm sure.'

When Freddie finished talking to her staff she walked back into her office and closed the door. Thank God Warren was back in New York, she thought. At least he wouldn't hear the news there. She sighed, not realising that at that moment Warren was in London tricking her doctor into his damning admission. He wouldn't find out, she thought. He couldn't so far away ... But others would hear the news, she realised, her hand reaching for the telephone. Slowly she dialled the number, her heart banging in her chest, her mind filled with the sounds of the past. The banging taps and the soft muffle of an old blues melody coming from under the bathroom door ...

'Hello?'

'Bea, I wanted to tell you ... '

'I've already heard.'

Freddie's stomach turned over, her legs shaking as she sat down. The words failed to come because she knew it was impossible to explain what she had done. In betraying her husband, she had indirectly betrayed Bea, the woman she had loved for years, the woman who had sacrificed her dreams for her.

'It's true,' she said finally, honestly. 'But it's not the way they're saying.' Bea made no response as she continued. 'I did have an affair. No, that's wrong. I slept with a man once, and that was all ... '

'All?' Bea asked incredulously.

'I mean that it was just one occasion,' Freddie swallowed, the words seemed almost to hurt her. 'But Conrad was the result. It was when Bart and I were going through that bad patch, and he was away so much. Well, when I knew I was pregnant, I didn't tell Bart. I was going to, I wanted to, but he was so thrilled by the thought of a baby ... ' Freddie paused, not realising that tears were running down her face. 'Bea, I know you can't understand or forgive what I did, but he wanted that child so much. He'd always wanted a family. If I had told him, what would I have done? Ruined our marriage and taken away the one thing he wanted most of all. It would have killed him.'

'It did,' Bea said coldly.

'Oh God, don't!' Freddie replied, clinging onto the phone. 'I've lived with this for years. Have you any idea what that's been like?'

'Did Bart commit suicide, Freddie?' Bea asked. 'That's all I want to know.'

'I can't tell you,' she replied, her voice faint. 'That's some-thing no one will ever know.' Freddie paused, willing Bea to speak, but she said nothing and the only sound which came over the line was the click when she put down the phone.

The day ground on interminably, hour after expanding hour, the office door opening and closing as clients came in and out. Some hadn't heard, some didn't care, others were maliciously pleased, and others outraged. Freddie held onto her courage and took it all, Chris watching over her carefully, forcing her to eat, sandwiches and cups of coffee materialising beside her at regular intervals. By four o'clock the strain was beginning to show. Telephone queries were met with quick rebuffs from Dot, and even the persistently cheerful Tina found her voice rising with nerves.

Then the phone rang suddenly by Freddie's elbow, making her jump.

'Mrs Wallace, this is the *Beacon*. We wondered if you would like to talk to one of our reporters ... '

'No,' she said simply, putting down the phone.

A moment later it rang again. 'We're going to run the story anyway, so it might be better ... '

'I said no!' Freddie snapped, severing the connection again.

Once more the phone rang. 'I said I wasn't interested!'

A chill blast of disapproval rushed over the line. 'What in God's name are you doing? Have you seen the papers?' Greville asked angrily. 'You're dragging our name through the mud. You're making us a laughing stock. I can't believe you did these things. Sleeping around! Passing off some bastard kid!'

'Don't you ever say that!' Freddie roared. 'Don't you ever call my child that name again, do you hear? He is innocent.'

'Which is more than can be said for you,' her father replied furiously. 'Do you realise what you've done?'

'And how is it so much worse than what you've done, Father?' Freddie replied. 'For years you've treated your family like dirt, and now you're threatening to divorce my mother to marry some tart – '

'Now, listen to me – '

'No! You listen!' she shouted, beyond reason. 'I've done some stupid things, but at least I've owned up to them. All my secrets are out in the open, Father, which is more than yours ever were.'

Greville flinched at the end of the line.

'I'm your father. You should show me respect.'

'And I am your daughter, you should show me love,' Freddie replied brokenly, putting down the phone.

For nearly an hour she sat motionless, exhausted and drained, and when the doorbell rang suddenly in reception Freddie froze in her seat, for an instant too weary to move and too wary to face anyone. Finally she got to her feet and straight-backed, walked to the glass doors, surprised to see the thin little figure on the other side of the glass.

Tapping her foot impatiently, Jao stood with her hands on her hips, an expression of belligerence on her face.

'Hi,' Freddie said timidly as she opened the door.

'That is a terrible photograph of you,' Jao snorted, flinging a copy of that morning's tabloid onto a chair. 'You should sue the bloody paper for that alone.'

Then she held out her arms to Freddie.

Chapter Twenty-Eight

He said nothing, merely kissed her, his mouth pressed over hers before moving down her neck, pulling her blouse aside as his lips ran over her breasts. Without speaking, he glanced into her eyes and then hurriedly tore at her clothes, his hands jerking them away until she was naked. Then he carried her into the bathroom. Quickly he filled the bath and lifted her into it, his arms wrapped around her, his head rested against hers. The water pounded against the marble tub, the noise surging in their ears as he folded Freddie's silk scarf and then carefully tied it over her eyes. She murmured but did not resist – all sight obliterated, every other sense heightened – and when he lowered her into the warm water she took in her breath but did not struggle against him.

Wordlessly he washed her, each fraction of her skin made slippery with soap, each pore explored and touched, and then when he had finished, he rinsed her, the water pouring deep and hard over her body, her back arching as she felt his breath against her cheek. But he did not kiss her, merely lifted her out of the water and dried her, slowly and intimately, her eyes still closed behind the blindfold. He did not hurry, and when she was dry he seemed to spend a moment looking at her and then moved away. Vulnerable and exposed, she waited for him, jumping when she felt his hands on her body again. A familiar scent drifted into her nostrils as she realised what he was doing. Gently, he stroked the talcum powder over her skin, his hands tracing the line of her legs and resting momentarily against the round of her stomach.

Then suddenly he left her again, his footsteps retreating into the flat as she stood naked on the bathroom floor. Freddie waited in silence, her ears straining for a sound, her eyelids flickering under the blindfold, and then she raised her hands and lifted the material away, blinking under the bright light. There was no sound coming from anywhere, just a total silence filled with excitement and a vague nudging of fear.

She did not call his name, but walked into the dark bedroom, her bare feet soundless on the floor, the blindfold still in her hand. He stood by the window, as naked as she was. He did not move towards her as she approached but remained looking out, only turning as she reached his side. His eyes fixed on hers and he frowned, but he did not move, and instead she touched his bare chest timidly, waiting for his response. Still without speaking, he regarded her, his eyes tracing the movements of her hands on his skin. A low sigh escaping his lips as she traced the line of his belly, his mouth opening and his tongue finding hers. Freddie moaned and clung to him, her body moving against his as he caught hold of her hair and jerked her head back.

The pain made her flinch and when he did not release her she began to struggle. In response he pulled her hair harder. Suddenly afraid, Freddie gripped his hands, her nails scratching at his arms as he dragged her down onto the floor and pressed her face against the carpet. His weight restricted her movements as he leaned over the bent arch of her back with his mouth next to her ear.

'Welcome home, Freddie,' he said finally. 'I've been waiting.'

Freddie awoke quickly and snapped on the light. Not remembering where she was, it took several seconds for her to realise that she was in her bedroom in Rutland Gate and that she had been dreaming. Breathing in deeply, she took a sip of water from the glass by her bed and then moved into the bathroom, the details of her dream coming back with glaring clarity. She was about to wash her face and then changed her mind and cleaned her teeth instead, scrubbing away with the toothbrush so vigorously that she made her gums bleed, the toothpaste foam was mottled with blood when she spat out.

He knows, she thought suddenly with total conviction, the toothbrush slipping from her fingers as she rinsed her mouth out with cold water. She might have thought that he would never find out, she might have hoped, but she knew she was deluding herself. Wherever he had been, in his New York restaurant, in Maiden Lane, anywhere – he would know. The old demons were already back, with the old longings and the memories. Freddie wiped her mouth with the hand towel and turned off the bathroom light without glancing into the mirror. I don't want to see myself, she thought, because I will hate myself for still wanting Warren Roberts, admitting in a dream what I would never admit in life. I shouldn't have dreamed of him, she thought bitterly, I should have dreamed of Bart.

Walking quickly out of Maiden Lane, Warren hailed a taxi and gave hurried directions, his eyes burning through lack of sleep. The sleeping city flashed past, the traffic lights lazily changing colours in the dawn light. Rubbing his chin, Warren was surprised to feel the stubble and wondered if he should return to the flat to freshen up, then decided that he would keep to his original plan. Rutland Gate was his destination. Rutland Gate where Freddie lived with his son.

His son, he repeated to himself incredulously. How could Freddie had deceived him to that extent? How could she have kept his son away from him? Their son, his child. When she knew what had happened to Alia, how could she deny him his child? *How*, he wondered furiously, how could she do that? He had struggled to control himself, to resist the temptation to confront her. Then, almost without realising it, when dawn broke he had hailed the taxi and was now standing, cold and silent, outside 107 Rutland Gate.

A dishevelled Mrs Allen opened the door to his knocking. Warren said nothing and merely pushed past her as he took the stairs two at a time and kicked open the door of Freddie's room. She woke, pale with fright, hardly understanding what was happening, then stumbled to her feet and ran after him as he moved back into the corridor and hurried towards the nursery. When he finally found the right door, he flung it open. Molly jumped back, holding tightly onto Conrad's hand.

'That is my son,' Warren said. 'Give him to me.'

Breathless, Freddie ran up behind Warren and glanced over to Molly. 'Take Conrad back to bed, will you?' she said, trying to keep her voice calm.

'How *dare* you!' Warren said, turning to her.

Freddie stood her ground, staring at the terrified Molly. 'Take him back to bed, please,' she repeated, watching with relief as Molly moved off with her son.

Warren turned to her, his eyes blank with fury. 'You seem a little nervous, Freddie. Why is that?' he asked. 'Could it be because you've been lying to me all these years?' He was shaking, trying to control his anger. 'That is my *son* – my son. Dear God, I lost one child, how could you keep my son away from me?'

His voice faltered and Freddie moved towards him.

'I'm sorry if I hurt you ... believe me.'

He said nothing in reply, but his hand stroked her hair back from her forehead absent-mindedly. 'I'd forgotten the colour of your skin,' he said.

The touch was so tender that Freddie felt herself drawn to him by the same desire which had first joined them. As his hand traced the line of her cheek she leaned towards him, his other hand pressing into the small of her back, his head bent down towards her.

'I love you. I've never loved anyone else the way I love you.'

Transfixed, Freddie closed her eyes and then suddenly realised what she was doing and stepped back. 'No, Warren,' she said calmly. 'It's not possible. I should have told you about Conrad, but I couldn't, surely you can see that? Please, tell me you understand.'

He blinked and then pushed her right shoulder roughly with the palm of his hand. All tenderness suspended.

'Understand?' he repeated mockingly. 'Understand? How Freddie? How the shit can I?' He pushed her again, forcing

381

his words home. 'I can't. I can't understand anything any more. I want to be as I was before I met you.' His hand jabbed at her shoulder, each blow harder than the previous one. '*I want to stop the wanting*. But I can't and I hate myself for it.' He paused, sighing, and laid his hand flat against her cheek, his fingers resting against her hair. 'I could hit you.' Freddie's heart pounded as she felt the pressure of his hand increase. 'Perhaps if I broke every bone in your body, I would be rid of you … ' He smiled helplessly. 'But it's not like that, is it? I could kill you, but you'd have more power dead than you do alive.' He stopped, seeing that he had frightened her, his anger lifting. 'That child is my son, *our* son.'

Pity moved Freddie to lay her hand on his arm. He closed his eyes at the touch as he had done all those years before in the drawing room, one week before Christmas, in the minutes before they made love.

'Love me,' he said piteously. 'Please, for God's sake, love me.'

Freddie shook her head slowly, her eyes filling. 'I can't … I don't love you, Warren,' she said, her voice softening as she realised that she had to calm him. Vindictive, he could make an implacable enemy. 'Please stop, before you destroy both of us,' she said, her voice gentle, pleading. 'You said you love me, Warren, well, if you do, let's try and work something out.'

He was moved by her words, but interpreted them wrongly, thinking that she still had some feeling for him. His voice was urgent as he pressed his advantage. 'Will you come back to me? With our son?'

Freddie hesitated, frowning. 'I can't.'

He couldn't understand her words, couldn't accept that she was rejecting him again. Stubbornly, he stood in front of her, his eyes fixed on hers. 'I'll ask you one more time, Freddie. Will you come back?'

'No, Warren. But I … '

She had no time to finish as he turned and began to run down the passageway towards the stairs. Running after him, Freddie shouted to him, but he only turned when he reached the front door.

'I'll fight you for that child,' he said, pointing at her, his face contorted with rage. 'He is my flesh and blood. He's my son.'

The Paris bureau was the first to suffer. The news that Freddie Wallace was disgraced was soon common knowledge and surprised everyone. People thought her reckless, and worse, stupid. A woman in her position should have a blameless past; no one would take advice from a woman like that, it was said, as the gossip floated maliciously over the phone lines from London to Paris, then to Rome, and onto New York. How could Freddie Wallace have been so indiscreet? And how could she have bourne another man's child? Soon the scandal was heard everywhere, the old rumours floating up to the surface like a bloated corpse. Bart Wallace had died in a car accident. Suicide, wasn't it, they asked each other. Well, if his wife was sleeping around at the time, what could you expect? They relished the details, dragging the opulent Freddie into disrepute, staining her success with their indignation.

It was time for her rivals to settle old scores. For years they had watched Freddie grow more prosperous and resented her success. Now all the New York wives who had felt intimidated by her, and the London society clique to which she had so reluctantly belonged, felt vindicated. Freddie Wallace had always thought she was so special, well, now she was an outcast whether she liked it or not.

Mala Levinska was the one who enjoyed the murmurings most. She relished the situation, watching in delight as her own business expanded and Freddie's faltered. Tony Shaw was doing his work well, she thought. People were muttering about the standard of Freddie's clients, hinting that she was not vetting them as carefully as she used to. Oh yes, everything was going perfectly to plan, Mala thought with sour glee. Soon Freddie Wallace would be nothing but a memory, and a dim one at that.

But Freddie hung on, gritting her teeth and continuing as the weeks passed and the business began to suffer, convinced that she could outlast the gossips and regain her previous esteem. Yet she knew the wooing had lost its magic. The suitor was no longer amenable to advances, the clients too vulnerable to gossip to be pliable.

Anna Price was one of the first to complain. Having worked hard to raise the fee to enter the bureau, she had expected an immediate return on her money, and when she did not form a relationship with anyone, had decided that it was Freddie's fault. Her animosity increased rapidly and when she heard some of the rumours, she could no longer disguise her enmity. She was not open to logic, her bitterness souring her and everyone around her, so much so that Freddie had decided to ask her to leave the bureau and invited her in for that purpose.

Arriving late for the appointment, Anna Price was openly hostile as she sat down, her aggressive face defiant. 'So, why did you want to see me?'

'I wanted to have a talk with you,' Freddie began. 'I don't feel as though it's working out for you here.' She paused, but Anna said nothing. 'Maybe you have some ideas as to why that might be?'

The woman crossed her sturdy legs, her belligerence apparent. She knew about the woman in front of her and her jealousy boiled. Sleeping around! Having some bastard! she thought maliciously. It wasn't fair. *She* should have found someone. She was respectable, and a hard worker, not like this slut. Who was Freddie Wallace to give out advice? Who the hell was she to match people up?

'Anna?' Freddie prompted her. 'Did you hear what I said?'

'I heard,' she replied sharply. 'I was just thinking.' Her eyes were cold with spite. 'I think that I was misinformed about this place. I was told that this bureau could match people up, but you haven't found anyone for me – even though it's cost me a fortune.'

'Matchmaking is not an exact science, Anna,' Freddie said patiently. 'I can only introduce you to men and see what happens.'

'Perhaps I wasn't your type,' Anna said savagely, two high spots of colour flaming her cheeks. 'I wasn't good enough for you. I do realise that I'm only a lowly secretary, but I had to work hard to raise the fee ... '

'Anna,' Freddie said calmly, 'don't get so excited.' She was anxious to avoid a scene, but equally anxious to rid herself of this troublesome client. 'I'm not criticising you. I just thought that the bureau wasn't working for you and so I was going to offer to let you out of the contract.'

Anna Price's face set into a brittle bas-relief. It had taken her two years to save up the money for the fee, two long hard years of temping in jobs she hated, just so that she could get into this bureau and find herself a man. It had been all so carefully worked out. She would marry and then be secure for the rest of her life and freed from the responsibility of looking after her incontinent mother. But now this bitch was going to take it away from her. Now Freddie Wallace, who had taken her money, was going to take away her future.

'You can't do that!'

'Anna, I can,' Freddie said evenly. 'I don't want us to fight, but I am within my legal rights.'

The woman got to her feet uneasily. 'Your rights!' she hissed. 'What about my rights? You've got all this and it's still not enough. You're not fit to run this place, you're just a slut.'

The word ricocheted round the office. Freddie leaned forwards immediately and pressed the intercom buzzer.

'Chris, would you please see *Miss*,' she paused momentarily, 'Price out?'

The incident shattered Freddie's confidence and when the woman left, Freddie hurried upstairs to the flat above. Conrad was in the kitchen with Molly, eating egg on toast, his elbows poking out at his sides as he cut the bread. In silence, Freddie watched him from the doorway, noticing how his long school socks had worked their way down his calves, and how his hair grew low on the back of his neck. Oblivious to her scrutiny, Conrad continued to eat as Molly chatted easily to him, her eyes magnified behind her glasses, her arms folded on top of the kitchen table.

Freddie peered at her son's face carefully. 'Conrad, look at me. What's this?'

He shuffled his feet. 'I bumped into something.'

385

Freddie's fingers moved over the bruise and she glanced at Molly. 'Do you know anything about this?'

She shook her head. 'He said he'd fallen in the playground.'

'Is that true, Conrad?' she asked her son. He wouldn't meet her gaze. 'Is it true?'

'Yes, Mummy.'

Freddie smiled as though she was satisfied and then sat beside him at the table. Of course, he could have bumped into something – children did every day – but she wasn't completely convinced. She had kept him at home the day the news broke, but the following morning after Freddie had spoken to his teacher, Conrad had attended school. Aware that he could be subject to some taunting, Freddie had spent extra time with her son, coaxing him to tell her if there was anything wrong. But Conrad had denied all problems; instead he had taken his mother's anxiety on himself and comforted her.

Railings, five feet high, surrounded the playground, one discarded child's glove hanging from an iron spike. The sound of skipping, followed by the ringing of a school bell, swam on the cold air as Warren leaned against the wall and watched.

Conrad was unaware of him. He came out with the other children, but skirted the perimeters of the yard, keeping near to the school building and not venturing into the knots of playing children. His action was not cowardly, in fact he seemed merely aloof, wary, his eyes alert as he watched his peers. The cold made the child's skin pale and he frowned as a plane flew quickly overhead, his eyes following its flight and then returning to the playground, for one instant seeming to fix on Warren.

Warren's heart speeded, but then his son turned away, walking back into the school building. A solitary figure, watched by a solitary figure, waiting in the cold wind outside.

Three days later Freddie was startled to find Conrad screaming uncontrollably in a uncharacteristic temper tantrum and all her attempts to console him were rejected. A week after that, he returned home covered in scratches and bruises.

386

Frantically, Freddie called the school and spoke to his teacher again, Miss Walters suggesting that Freddie call round later that day. Freddie arrived early and waited in the chalk-smelling corridor for the teacher, Miss Walters coming towards her briskly, her hand outstretched. She didn't care what the papers had been saying, she told everyone in the staff room, she liked Freddie Wallace and she thought she was a good mother. You can't believe everything you read in print, she said protectively.

'Hello, Mrs Wallace, come and sit down.'

Freddie obeyed, smiling wanly. 'I'm worried about Conrad. I think he might be being bullied.'

'Oh … ' Miss Walters said, her own smile nervous. 'Well, that's not quite accurate. In fact, he's behaving rather oddly.'

'Oddly?' Freddie echoed.

'It all began with the newspaper articles about two weeks ago … ' Her embarrassment made her glance away. 'You know how children are, Mrs Wallace – we know that most of what gets in the paper isn't true, but their parents talk and the children pass things on … '

Freddie's face was ashen.

'Apparently some of the older children began to tease Conrad … '

'Tease him? About what?'

Miss Walters looked steadily into Freddie's eyes. 'About you, Mrs Wallace. They said some pretty nasty things … '

'Why didn't you tell me?' Freddie asked incredulously.

'I only found out myself yesterday. I'd kept an eye on Conrad but children sometimes work these things out for themselves, and he begged me not to tell you – '

'He's six years old!' Freddie said in exasperation. 'I am here to protect him, not the other way around.'

'But that's the point, Mrs Wallace. Your son feels very protective about you. He told me so. He said you were worried and that Molly had told him not to worry you any more at the moment. He loves you very much.' Miss Walters paused. 'I wanted to talk to you anyway,' she said. 'I was hoping that he would settle down, but when you phoned this morning, it seemed the right opportunity for us to have a chat.

Your son's behaviour has altered radically ... '

'How?'

'He's aggressive at times, and far from being bullied, he is often the instigator of fights.'

Freddie was baffled. 'Conrad? Are you talking about my son?'

The teacher nodded. 'Is he never violent at home?'

No, he's not violent, Freddie thought, he is gentle and loving. She remembered only the other night when he had padded into her room in the early hours and crept under the sheets. Laying his head on his mother's shoulder, he had fallen back to sleep, sandwiched between Freddie and his stuffed teddy bear. His hair had been damp, moist against her lips when she kissed him ...

'My son is not violent,' she said, but her voice lacked conviction. Children inherit their temperaments from their parents – Conrad was merely taking on his father's traits. She shook her head against the idea. 'I don't believe it.'

'As you know, he's always been quick and lively in class and has done well, but lately his concentration has been poor and he veers between withdrawal and aggression.'

Withdrawal and aggression – his father's son, the trauma in Freddie's life altering Conrad, as the trauma in Warren's life had changed him.

'What can we do?' Freddie asked, her voice low.

'Watch him. It might be a temporary phase,' she said. 'If he's showing none of these signs at home, he might simply grow out of it.' Her hand touched Freddie's. 'Don't worry too much, children go through these stages.'

'But not all children are violent.'

'No, but remember Mrs Wallace, that you and your son have been through – and are continuing to go through – a difficult time. Children who are very close to their parents pick up their parent's distress, and in Conrad's case, he not only worries for you, but wants to protect you.' She smiled warmly. 'You have a wonderful boy, Mrs Wallace, don't worry, he'll settle down. They generally do in the end.'

Freddie walked out of the school in a daze, climbing into

the car and taking Conrad's hand. His blue eyes – Warren's eyes – looked at her anxiously and he only relaxed when his mother began to tell him about Miss Walters, and what a nice woman she was. As George drove the car down Kensington Gore Conrad was happily chatting, all his anxiety forgotten, his little hand, still bearing a clutch of scratches, lying contentedly in Freddie's.

'I wondered if you wanted to go out,' she said. 'We could go to the cinema, if you like.'

'Love it!' Conrad said excitedly. 'When?'

For several hours Freddie lost herself in her son's company, talking to him and scrutinising him carefully. Together they watched a Disney film and then she took him to the Wimpey on Leicester Square, letting him indulge in a half pounder, a bag of chips, and a vanilla milk shake. She listened whilst he told her stories about school and was momentarily surprised when he confided that Molly was apparently smitten by one of his teachers. The news was delivered amidst a bout of giddy laughter, Conrad finding it uproariously funny that his nanny should wait at the gates and blush furiously when the maths teacher came into view.

'Molly's face was red, really red,' he said, sucking the milk shake up the straw noiselessly. 'Jimmy said that his mother told him Molly was keen on Mr Blake ... ' He stopped and frowned at the empty container.

'You mustn't tease her,' Freddie said. 'It's not kind, Conrad.'

'Oh, *I* don't,' he said easily, leaning over the table towards her, 'but everyone else does.'

They still hadn't arrived back at ten, Molly pacing around with her arms folded and a severe look on her face. It was not her place to criticise Freddie, she said to Mrs Allen downstairs as she watched her disinfect the outside drain, but it really was too late for a six-year-old boy to be out at night. Molly sniffed, her judgement on her employer more severe since the revelations of the past weeks had turned Freddie from angel to adulteress. Whilst Molly continued to grumble, Jean Allen listened half-heartedly and poured a liberal amount of Dettol down the grid, her rangey form hunched over, waiting for any misguided insect to make a run for it. Molly was reiterating her feelings for the third time when the doorbell rang. Jean Allen sighed noisily.

'I'll go,' Molly said eagerly. 'It's probably them now.'

Freddie walked in, hand in hand with her son, Conrad smiling happily.

'Did you have a good time?' Molly asked, still faintly embarrassed and avoiding Freddie's eyes.

'Great!' Conrad said enthusiastically. 'And we're going out again on Saturday.'

'Take him up to bed now, will you, Molly?' Freddie said. 'I've got a bit more work to do, but I'll pop up later.'

Deep in thought, Freddie made her way to the bureau. The exposure had been bad enough, then the confrontation with Warren – but Conrad! That her child should be affected and disturbed, that was a crippling blow. It was the one thing Freddie had wanted to avoid above everything. And now her son was altering, showing aggressive tendencies and sudden withdrawals and an obsessive need to protect her; displaying the exact pattern of behaviour of his father.

Pushing open the bureau doors, Freddie was surprised to find Chris still there, pouring over a sheaf of papers, her bespectacled eyes fixed on the rows of numbers.

'Oh, hello, Mrs Wallace,' she said, her tone preoccupied. 'I was wanting a word with you … ' She glanced at the papers again. 'Could you spare me a few minutes?'

Freddie nodded, taking a seat and listening carefully to what the woman had to say. Chris was worried, she said, having seen the recruitment fall off in Paris and many of the new clients going elsewhere. She had thought it a temporary blip, but when London began to follow suit, it was obvious that the business was in serious trouble. Besides, the bureau's reputation wasn't as good as it had been.

Freddie frowned. She had known that things were bad, but not this serious.

'We're in trouble,' Chris said shortly. 'The numbers are falling off and I'm hearing complaints all the time from people begging for reassurance and wanting to know if what they heard is true.'

'You know it is,' Freddie said evenly.

'*I* know, but they don't want to hear that,' Chris said impatiently.

Freddie sat motionless in her chair, her eyes fixed on the silent phones. She shivered suddenly, pulling her jacket around her. 'There is nothing I can do,' she said simply.

'But ... ' Chris's voice failed her momentarily. 'Mrs Wallace, you must realise the situation you're in. You can't keep running the business like this. You have to do something. Some of our clients are going to Mala Levinska's bureau instead of ours now.' She gestured impotently to the papers in front of her. 'We're losing money badly. You have to do something soon ... '

The old defiance came back into Freddie's eyes. 'What do you want me to do, Chris? Lie? Tell everyone that the story isn't true?' She shook her head. 'No, I can't do that.'

'But you have to do something.'

Freddie thought of Mala Levinska, then of her father and Bea, then of Warren, and lastly of her son. I made the decision never to be afraid again, she thought, and I will stand by that.

'There is a solution,' she said firmly, her mind made up. 'And I'm going to do the one thing no one expects, Chris.' She continued, 'I don't intend that the bureaux should fail. It's my achievement and Conrad's security.' Her face was lighted by a quick, sure smile. 'Don't worry, Chris. Both of us have put far too much into the business to let it go now.'

'So what are we going to do?' she asked.

'Watch me,' Freddie said simply, walking out.

Chapter Twenty-Nine

The following day Freddie flew over to the Paris bureau in the sumptuous surroundings off the Rue St Honoré. The consultants glanced up with a mixture of surprise and curiosity as their employer entered. Freddie had prepared herself carefully for the trip, dressing in a cream Chanel suit, her make-up immaculate, her nails varnished deep coral. As she strode into the bureau she looked composed and elegant, a handsome woman who could hold her own anywhere – and that was exactly what Freddie had meant to imply. She knew instinctively that if she showed any weakness now, she was ruined. There was to be no begging for understanding or forgiveness. She had decided on her course of action and was going to abide by it.

'Everything you've all been reading is true,' Freddie said in perfect French. Glances were exchanged rapidly. 'I won't insult any of you by lying. I made a mistake – but I admit it.' She paced in the reception area, her slim legs elegant in fine tights. 'Things might be a little ... bumpy ... for a while, until everyone forgets this scandal, but I wanted to come over and speak to you directly. I hope you will all stay with me, but if any of you feel you can't, I will, of course, understand.'

The assembled group were surprised, then impressed by her honesty. They had expected her to deny everything, but, they said afterwards, she showed a great deal of *chic* by owning up. Besides, they found themselves saying, with typical Gallic logic, people's love lives never ran smoothly. By the time Freddie left they were on her side and she knew it as she flew with wary optimism on to Rome.

Her words in the Rome bureau were almost identical, but the Italians' response was varied. Most of the counsellors liked Freddie Wallace and were willing to be sympathetic. The female consultants loyally commiserated with her but some of the men were judgmental and unforgiving, seeing in Freddie what they most feared in their own women.

'I can't stay,' one said flatly.

Freddie nodded, 'I'm sorry.'

'People talk … ' he went on, flinging out his hands to make the point. 'They talk! What are we supposed to say?'

'Nothing,' Freddie said calmly, her accent as perfectly manicured as her appearance. She strode over to the man and stood before him. 'I can't have anyone working for me who is going to talk, Bernardo. You see, what you must realise is that idle gossip could cost you your job.' She glanced round, to make the point to the others. 'If you continue to chatter about this scandal, you will not only help to ruin me, but you will ruin this business as well – and if the business goes, so do your lucrative jobs. I've always paid you very well – you would be lucky to find another employer as generous.'

The message went home to most of them, but some were determinedly against her.

'We have to fire Paola Castinelli in Rome,' she told Chris over the phone that night. 'That woman is trying to hurt me, and if I'm not mistaken she thinks she can move in and take over when I'm out of the picture.' Freddie sighed and threw down her coat, irritable with weariness. 'All this travelling is killing me. God, I'm so tired, and I haven't seen Conrad for days. Is he all right?'

Chris was quick to reassure her. 'He's fine. Your mother's come down for a few days, and Molly's spoiling him.' She changed the subject, knowing how exhausted Freddie was and trying to keep her spirits up although the business was still in a critical condition. 'You have to keep the pressure on for a while. It's helping, Mrs Wallace, believe me. People aren't gossiping as much as they were – by being honest you took the

393

wind out of their sails.' Chris glanced at the pitiful list of new clients lying on the desk next to her. 'I really think that before long we might recover most of the custom we've lost.'

Freddie leaned back against the hotel bedhead, slipping off her high-heeled shoes and rubbing her eyes. She wasn't convinced by Chris's reassurances. She knew that the damage was too deep to be repaired quickly. Mala Levinska's bureaux were now occupying the premier position, whilst Freddie's had been seriously undermined by scandal and the damaging gossip of people like Tony Shaw. Word was also out that Freddie Wallace was no longer too careful about who she took on as a client, and that some of her male customers were suspect. The rumour naturally scared off many potential female clients, and Freddie, no matter how hard she tried, could only staunch some of the flow of innuendo. Meanwhile, the pressure was still building dangerously behind the dam.

'Thanks for what you've done, Chris. You've been marvellous. Can you transfer me to the house phone? I want a word with Molly.'

Molly picked up the phone immediately, Conrad shrieking loudly in the background. 'Hi, how's things?' Freddie asked, with a jolt of homesickness.

'OK,' Molly replied. 'Conrad's just having his bath.' She called out to him and Freddie could hear the quick patter of his feet as he ran to the phone.

'Hello, darling,' she said gently. 'Are you being a good boy for Molly and Grandma?'

''Course I am, Mummy,' he assured her.

Her arms arched for him, and a real rush of longing made her anxious to be gone, to be home. 'What have you been doing?'

'Grandma read to me today, and Molly and I played with my train set.'

Freddie closed her eyes, hearing the sounds of the whistle blowing and the steady rat-tat of the wheels on the toy track. I will look after you and keep you safe, she swore, I will love you with all my heart, Conrad. 'And what are you going to do now?'

'He's going to bed.' Sarah's high voice said suddenly,

interrupting the conversation. 'Hello, sweetheart, when are you coming home? We all miss you, and although I'm sure you've got to do all this work, it's not really good for you – you'll be tired. You know all the stress you've been under. I think you and Conrad should come up to Yorkshire when you get back …'

'Mummy, I have to work at the moment,' Freddie explained patiently, struggling to keep the irritation out of her voice. 'I'll be back soon. Kiss Conrad for me and take care of yourself.'

Three days later Freddie returned to Rutland Gate after flying from Rome to New York and facing the counsellors there. They were hard-nosed, some resigning on the spot, others reluctantly loyal, giving her marks for her honesty and aware that their jobs were on the line if they didn't support her. Various tales of woe were passed on, as were a few malicious and inaccurate embellishments, but to all Freddie remained impassive, merely repeating, 'I did what I did, I don't deny it – now let's get the show back on the road.'

When she finally came back to London and climbed out of the taxi at Rutland Gate, Freddie was hazy with exhaustion, her hand shaking as she slipped the key into the lock and walked in. The house was silent for it was only five in the morning as Freddie slipped off her shoes and padded bare-foot and noise-less towards the stairs. Slowly she climbed, her vision blurring suddenly, one hand clasping the banister in panic. Heavily she slumped down on the stair, a thin film of sweat on her top lip. Her thoughts wandered, sudden confusion making her dizzy. Before her eyes the stairs shifted and figures appeared – Mike Kershaw and Harry, her mother holding Conrad, and Warren running … Moaning softly, Freddie tried to focus, her tongue running over her lips as she sank back to her childhood, and the hot smell of gravy on a summer's afternoon.

Seriously alarmed, Freddie tried to rise, but her legs slipped from under her and she fell heavily, knocking her head on the step. I'm home, she thought. I'm safe, it's all right. But she was unable to move and for an instant remained slumped there, before her hands reached out for the next stair and she began to haul herself up. First one stair, then the next, then the next, crawling up the beautiful staircase, her Chanel suit ruckled under her, her tights ripping. With every ounce of her will-power, Freddie climbed, and when she reached the top she dragged herself to her room and leaned her body back against the side of the bed, unable to go further. Her eyes closed, leaden with tiredness, yet still she couldn't rest. There is something I have to do, she thought blindly, there is something I still have to do. Exhausted and unable to think lucidly, Freddie sobbed with frustration – and then she remembered. Struggling round the bed she scrabbled hurriedly in the drawer beside her, at last finding what she wanted and sighing with relief. Only then did she stop. Only then did she sleep, whispering over and over, 'Sorry ... sorry ...' with Bart's burnt and broken watch in her hand.

'She's suffering from complete exhaustion,' the doctor said as Sarah followed him down the stairs.

'Oh dear, I did warn her. I kept saying that she should do less.' Her voice was thin with agitation. 'Will she be all right?'

'Your daughter is in very good health, Mrs Clements,' he replied evenly. 'Sleep is all she needs, sleep and relaxation.'

But Freddie couldn't rest. The business consumed her. She could see all that she had built up crumbling, and when she wasn't worrying about the bureaux she was fretting about Conrad. Insult followed insult, Mala Levinska spreading the rumour that Freddie had undergone a nervous breakdown, unable to cope with the strain.

Forced to stay in bed, Freddie asked Chris to bring up all her messages from the bureau and transfer the important calls. Delighted to see that her employer was not completely incapacitated, Chris brought up a stack of papers and sat beside Freddie's bed and passing her each message in turn. Without make-up, her employer's skin looked fiercely pale against her dark hair, her body wrapped in a pink satin bedjacket, with a matching coverlet drawn over her knees.

Unaware that she was being scrutinised, Freddie flicked through the sheets trying to concentrate. Apparently Beth Holland was seeing Daniel Haig again; Anna Price had been removed from the books and Harvey Reiner needed to talk to her.

'Do you know anything about this message concerning Dr Reiner?'

Chris glanced up and blushed. 'Only that he was told by one of our ladies that he was "a repellent little shit." '

'Oh God, who said that?'

'I can't remember, but it's on his file,' Chris replied, leaning back in her chair. 'Some of the old clients have left, I'm afraid,' she said cautiously. 'But others are right behind you.' Some were, but not that many, she thought with anger. Many were leaving the sinking ship just as fast as they could.

Freddie listened carefully. 'Beth Holland's been marvellous and Cleo Taylor ... '

Freddie studied Chris's face, knowing that she wasn't telling her everything. 'But?'

'The male clients are another story, I'm afraid. Daniel Haig is distant, Harvey Reiner is surprised but sympathetic, and Tony Shaw is cocky.'

'I never liked Tony Shaw from the day he joined the bureau,' Freddie said firmly, knowing that the man's good looks belied a weak nature inherited from his own father and exacerbated by his dominant socialite mother. For months Freddie had warned him about making passes at the clients, remembering the half-hearted proposition he had made to her, and for a while he had controlled himself – but not for long.

'He's made a pass at another client,' Chris said quietly.

Infuriated, Freddie picked up the phone.

'I want a word with Mr Shaw,' she said, dialling his number. 'It's Freddie Wallace, Tony. I've had another complaint about you. How many times do I have to tell you? Don't keep making passes at the clients. They don't like it.'

'If you're talking about the doctor, she was frigid.'

'She was entitled to be,' Freddie replied, her voice hard. 'Perhaps you should see it from a woman's point of view. How would you like it if someone forced themselves on you?'

'Is that an offer?' he responded evenly.

Frowning, Freddie tucked the receiver under her chin as she glanced at his file. Malcolm Prentice's report had been thorough, but gave little illumination. The graphology assessment had only stressed Tony Shaw's "insistence on having his own way". Freddie ringed the words with a red pen and said, 'I'll give you one last chance, or you're out. Don't keep trying to seduce the women.'

'She was leading me on … '

'Rubbish!' Freddie replied. 'And you know it.'

'They want you to make a play for them,' he continued insistently over the phone line, knowing how he would repeat the conversation later to Mala. 'They've all got the hots and they're all as randy as hell, or they wouldn't be here. All those pretty little notes you make in your files don't tell you the half of it!' he sneered. 'I've had nineteen women so far, and I didn't have to try hard either, they were only too glad that a man wanted them.' He smirked, certain he had shocked her. 'That Anna Price, for instance, I had her in the back of my car the second time we went out. She had her tights off before I could say "thanks for a nice evening" … '

Freddie's voice was sharp with rage. 'You're off the books, Mr Shaw. I won't have you at the bureau a moment longer.'

'Go screw yourself!' he replied coarsely. 'Yours isn't the only bureau. There are plenty of places like this around. Mala Levinska's for instance. Besides, you're hardly in a position to play the innocent, are you?' He paused to inflict the final wound. 'Just for the record, Mrs Wallace, I balanced every time I'd been laid against your enrolment fee, and it turned out that each screw cost me about twenty quid a time. Cheap at the price, I'd say, and at least I knew I wasn't going to get a dose of something.'

Shaken, Freddie slammed down the phone.

Throughout the spring, Freddie and Chris struggled to recover the business and by May it seemed as though they were beginning to make some headway. Having lost many customers, Freddie's frequent trips abroad to see new clients and hold introductory talks began to pay off and the future began to seem reasonably secure. Of Warren, Freddie saw and heard nothing. Rumour had it that he was back in his New York restaurant and several times, late at night, the phone rang and woke Freddie. When she picked up the receiver there was never anyone there, but she knew it was Warren, and she became more and more nervous, spending time checking the doors were locked and sorting anxiously through the post. Her unsteady emotional state was heightened as she watched her business rock and she wondered, constantly wondered, when and how the next blow would fall.

But nothing happened and as life settled back into a form of uneasy routine, Freddie found herself drawn back into her home life. Her relationship with her mother went on as it had always done, but Conrad continued to be troublesome at school, his temper flaring quickly, although when he was at home he was loving and endlessly affectionate with his mother, his moods restricted to his time away from her. Yet gradually he could not control himself at home either and after a few months he began to lose his temper with Molly.

'Now, Conrad,' Freddie said carefully. 'You must be nice to Molly, she loves you and you can't be cruel to her.'

He looked sullen and then smiled, his expression Warren's. Freddie paused and then caught hold of him. 'Is everything all right at school?' she asked for the hundredth time. 'I want you to tell me if you're unhappy, Conrad. I want you to talk to me.'

'Everything's fine,' Conrad said, with the composure of a child twice his age. 'Don't worry, Mummy.'

They knew that any further scandal could ruin Freddie and her business, so for months they lived in a state of unrelieved anticipation. But nothing happened. May dwindled down into June, the time of long days and slow nights. Freddie slept intermittently, the brandy decanter always by her bedside, although less frequently used.

Across London, the Wilkie women also slept, Bea always the last one home at night, Jao dozing fitfully in the room next door. And in Belgravia, Pennsylvania still worked on his book, his thoughts turning to Freddie often; whilst in York-shire, Harry stood by the Great Window in the Hall and looked out, the dogs beside him. All the lives Freddie's life had touched went on, and all breathed a sigh of relief as they readjusted to the calm.

Only one could not forget past traumas, and in silence the man across the Atlantic kept his pale eyes fixed on the future – and waited.

Jao stood by the bar, drinking a gin and tonic, the mixed clientele of the Altruist mingling around her. Twice she turned to leave, and twice turned back again, waiting for the tap on her shoulder, her body tense with anticipation. Bea would be incredulous if she found out, she thought, just as she herself would have been only a little while before. But things had changed, a series of abortive romances and unsatisfactory couplings had made Jao feel less sure of herself, the constant feminine company of the Wilkie women underlying her own anxiety.

Quickly Jao drained her glass and glanced round. She did not want to remain alone, it wasn't natural, and besides she had expected to meet someone through work years ago. But being a runner had relegated her to the lower echelons of the art world and her clients were all far too rich to be interested in the likes of her. Time was passing. She was now thirty-seven and scared enough to force the issue. Logic told her that she should have gone to see Freddie. After all, she was the ideal person to help, but she resisted the temptation violently, not wanting to admit her failings to anyone.

Sighing, Jao decided to wait for another five minutes and then if her date hadn't turned up, she would leave. The minutes dragged on and then, just as she picked up her bag to go, a small rotund man walked towards her with a look of intense pleasure on his face.

Jao swallowed and slid off her seat, making for the door as he caught up with her.

'Jao Wilkie?'

She affected a baffled look.

'Aren't you Jao Wilkie?' he repeated, his hand extended towards her, podgy and pink as a rubber glove. 'I'm – '

' – mistaken,' Jao said abruptly, turning towards the door and moving out into the suffocating summer night, St Paul's rising, doom ridden, behind her. She hurried along, shaking her head disbelievingly and remembering what the advertisement had said:

> 'I'm funny, excellent company, an attractive man with
> money and a good line in conversation, and I'm seeking
> a young woman with interesting looks for conversations
> about the arts – to be enjoyed over champagne.'

Jao snorted, cursing herself for having answered a lonely hearts advertisement placed in the back pages of *Time Out*. What a bloody liar he'd been, she thought, stunned. He had put in an advert which made him sound like a real high-flyer and he had turned out to be a little pink pig of a man. She crossed over, mouthing something obscene to a taxi which hooted as she passed. What a cheat, Jao thought furiously. What a damned, flaming, stinking nerve! For a while she was so angry that she forgot how disappointed she was. And how lonely.

In an office near to Ladbroke Grove a cleaner was just opening up, carrying her bucket and brush with her, her bottom pushing the door open as she tried to shuffle through the jammed door. Frowning she pushed against it, and then in irritation, put down what she was carrying and used her hands to press against the door. It moved slightly, allowing enough room for the cleaner to put her head around and see what was on the other side.

She screamed once, hoarsely, and stepped back, the door slamming shut on her, the weight of Beth Holland's body forcing it closed. Down the steps the cleaner ran, calling for help, her cries bringing several people out onto the street; a neighbour, watching the commotion, ringing for the police. It took only minutes for them to arrive, followed by an ambulance, the body of Beth Holland carried out in front of a growing audience, her face uncovered and turned up to the sure June sun.

At noon a startled Freddie was confronted by a red-haired detective, standing uncomfortably in reception with a notebook in his hand.

'Come through,' Freddie said, showing him to a seat in her office. 'What can I do to help you?'

401

The officer obviously felt out of place and was unusually uncomfortable. 'Do you have someone on your books called Beth Holland?'

'Why? Has anything happened to her?'

He sighed and glanced down at his notes. 'Do you have someone on your books of that name?'

Freddie nodded. 'Yes, why?'

'And do you have a man called Daniel Haig on your books?'

'Yes,' Freddie replied evenly. 'What's happened?'

'Should something have happened, Madam?' the detective asked suspiciously.

'I was only asking a question,' Freddie replied, surprised by his attitude.

The officer continued. 'What do you know about Daniel Haig?'

'He's a television producer who's been with us for ... ' Freddie stopped suddenly, 'I think I would like to know what's going on before I say any more.'

The man stiffened. 'Miss Beth Holland was found first thing this morning badly beaten, and we believe that Mr Daniel Haig might have had something to do with it.'

'Oh God ... ' The colour left Freddie's face so quickly that she gripped the sides of her chair for support. 'Why do you think Daniel Haig had something to do with it?' she asked quietly.

'Because Miss Holland told us so, Madam,' the detective replied evenly. 'So I would like to know if you know where he is now and if you do, I would like you to tell me.'

The questioning went on for over an hour, Freddie giving the officer a copy of Daniel Haig's file and assuring him repeatedly that all her clients were thoroughly vetted. He asked her if anything like this had happened before and when she said no, he asked her if she thought that her bureau investigated everyone properly.

'Of course I do,' Freddie replied, indignantly, knowing that this incident would be the death knell for the business. 'I insist on it.'

'I'm sure you do, Madam, but some of these places don't have a very good reputation.'

Freddie's voice was controlled. 'I couldn't be more careful

with the vetting procedure for anyone accepted by this bureau.'

The officer continued to write notes. 'I believe you have a psychiatrist working here?'

'Not full time. Dr Prentice just comes into interview the prospective clients.'

'Could I have his telephone number?' the policeman asked, adding. 'Oh, and the number of Dr Craig Benson too, please.'

Freddie wrote down both numbers and passed them across the desk, her hand shaking. 'Just tell me how Beth is, please.'

'Critical,' the detective replied coolly. 'Are there any other tests you have carried out?'

It took an instant for Freddie to compose herself. 'Yes, we do checks on the client's financial and work situations – to check that what they told us is correct – and we also do an astrology chart and a graphology test.'

He glanced up quickly. 'What's that?'

'It's a personality assessment made after judging a person's handwriting.'

The officer looked at Freddie for a long moment and then glanced away. 'Handwriting?'

'Yes,' Freddie replied, discomforted. 'When can I see Beth?'

'Soon, Madam, soon.'

When Freddie did arrive at the hospital, Beth Holland was in no condition to see anyone. Unconscious, she floated somewhere between living and dying, her injuries critical although her narrow face was unmarked. Having asked permission, Freddie went into Beth's room and stood silently by her bed, remembering her reluctance to become involved with Daniel Haig. *He's too possessive* she had said. *I don't feel comfortable with him*. Freddie touched Beth's hand and then cupped it in her own, trying to warm the damp skin.

Could I have checked the clients out more thoroughly, she wondered frantically. What other tests could have been done? Her mind drifted back to the first days of the bureau. She had been unqualified and untried, turning to Theo Gunther for help – but she hired good people to work for her, experienced people, and she had listened to them. Freddie breathed in quickly. I was careful, I tried to protect my clients, not like other bureaux. She sighed, already imagining the publicity. It was the end for her, she thought, peculiarly disinterested, her only real concern centered on the figure in the bed. Just get well, Beth, the rest can go to the devil.

'Come on,' a voice said gently, taking her arm, 'it's time to go.'

Freddie glanced up, shaking her head disbelievingly when she saw Harry. 'You always turn up when I need you most, don't you?'

'I should have come before, when the news broke in the papers ... '

'I thought you were angry with me.'

'No,' he said quietly. 'I just didn't know what to say.'

'No one did.'

He nodded, sitting down beside her.

'Chris phoned me this morning, just after it happened. I came as soon as I could. Remember, we're friends.'

'Allies,' she said softly.

'I suppose it's been tough for you?'

She nodded. 'Yes, but everything you heard is true, Harry.'

For several minutes she talked, sketching out the story behind the headlines and in the end he sighed and leaned back in the uncomfortable hospital chair.

'So who is Conrad's father?'

'Warren Roberts,' Freddie said simply. The confession was almost a relief.

'Does he know?'

She nodded. 'Yes, he found out somehow and came to see me ... and now I can't stop wondering about him. I get phone calls at odd times, and I know it's him. He's supposed to be back in New York, but I'm not sure. I have a feeling he's in London again, Harry. You see, I know he's watching me, keeping tabs somehow, and I know he'll do something. He'll never forgive me for taking his child. And now this ... she glanced towards the still figure of Beth Holland. 'It's over. You know that, don't you?'

'If you had been running another type of business, Freddie, the exposure wouldn't have mattered so much, but this coming on top of everything else ... '

'Don't you think I know that!' she snapped bitterly. 'I built

404

up the bureaux on my reputation, steering clear of anyone who wasn't respectable. I worked day and night ... Everyone knows how much I tried to make it work.'

'I know, Freddie, I know,' he said gently.

But she went on blindly. 'I lived down my past and I thought everyone had forgotten it. I had an affair, that was all. One stupid mistake. It shouldn't have happened, it shouldn't have mattered to anyone apart from Bart and me. God knows, he paid for it ... ' her voice fell. 'I thought Warren Roberts was in the past. I'd even hoped that after the news broke I could regain my reputation and save the bureaux. Oh God' she said savagely, 'What do I do now?'

'You could give it all up and move back to Yorkshire,' Harry said softly, wanting to ask her to return with him to the past, before any scandal. But he couldn't make the ultimate gesture and instead of offering marriage, offered Freddie friendship in its place.

'Things might be easier for you away from London.'

She shook her head. 'No, I'm not running away. What I did, I pay for. Besides, Beth needs me now. I owe her my support at least.'

'I admire your guts,' Harry replied hoarsely. 'You were always brave. I'm just so sorry that you've been so unlucky.'

'Not in everything,' Freddie said kindly, touching his hand. 'I was lucky with my friends.'

Mala could not believe the news brought to her hot foot by Tony Shaw. She even laughed when she heard about Beth Holland. Greedily, she looked around her office, seeing the rows of files, sensing the money she had made. Her revenge was sweet and tasted like sugar on her tongue. She had won at last. Yet the *coup de grâce* had not been executed by her. All her carefully laid plans had succeeded in undermining her rival, but fate had dealt the final blow. Now Freddie Wallace's business was as damaged and beaten as Beth Holland in her hospital bed.

It was over at last, Mala thought, and she had won. The reign of Freddie Wallace was ended. The Queen was dead, long live the Queen.

*

For another hour Freddie and Harry sat in the hospital room, then finally Harry said, 'I'll take you home.'

Freddie shook her head. 'No, I can't leave. You go if you want, Harry, but I want to stay here.'

'You can't do anything.'

'I don't know if I can, or can't, I just know that I have to be here.' She glanced at Harry, her eyes demanding reassurance. 'I keep wondering if I did enough. If I checked Daniel Haig out sufficiently.'

'There was nothing else you could have done,' Harry replied evenly. 'Nothing.'

'Surely Malcolm Prentice would have picked up anything violent when he examined him? Surely he would have uncovered something like that?' she asked, remembering how little Bart had valued psychiatric assessments.

'I'm sure he would.'

Freddie shook her head. 'No, you're not sure, Harry, and neither am I.'

'No, I'm not,' Harry agreed. 'But I do know that you did what you could.'

They waited throughout the long hours for news of Beth's condition but she remained unconscious, her personality suspended. Hurried nurses moved in and out of her room in the intensive care unit, the red-haired detective hovering constantly, drinking cups of tea from the machine in reception. Around three in the afternoon another detective joined him and they talked together in a corner of the reception area, the hospital intercom calling out patient's names over their heads whilst a pregnant woman struggled by with her arm in a plaster cast. Almost twenty feet away, Freddie sat with Harry, her thoughts with Beth Holland as the detectives glanced towards her.

'I've spoken to a few of her clients and the consultants who work at the bureau and they all confirm what she says about the selection process.' The newly arrived detective paused. 'I also heard a few interesting tidbits about her private life.'

The redhead glanced up, interested, 'Like what?'

'Like she's not got the right background for a matchmaker.' He passed some of the tabloid clippings to his colleague.

Frowning, the first detective looked back at Freddie. 'I'd never have thought it – she doesn't look the type.'

The information damned Freddie in their eyes and weakened her case. However much she insisted that she did her utmost to protect her clients, the detective remembered what they had just read about her and remained unconvinced. After a while Freddie realised that whatever she said they were going to remain hostile to her and her confidence faltered, her ears straining for sounds of activity from Beth's room.

Harry saw Freddie's anxiety and tried to reassure her. He sensed as Freddie did that the police were antagonistic and so remained with her during their bouts of questioning.

'So you honestly feel that you did everything you could to protect your client, Mrs Wallace?'

Freddie hung her head. 'Yes, yes … ' she repeated. 'I did everything I could.'

'We spoke to a woman called Anna Price just now … ' Freddie's head jerked up at the mention of her name. ' … and she said that she left because your male clients were always,' he glanced at his notes, ' "jumping on her." '

'That's nonsense!' Freddie snapped, then tempered her tone, afraid to antagonise them any further. 'Miss Price was asked to leave by *us*. She could not form a relationship with any of our clients and became disruptive, seeing it as our fault, rather than hers. I wouldn't take her word as gospel.'

'We spoke to Tony Shaw after that,' the detective continued evenly, consulting his notes again as Freddie glanced away in irritation. 'He said that you, Mrs Wallace, were not interested in your clients and spent most of your time abroad … '

'I have a child and a business in this country, so why would I want to be away from them?' Freddie asked, exasperated. 'And as for Tony Shaw, I had to ask him to leave too … '

'You don't have much luck with your customers, do you?' the redhead asked slyly.

'Only because you're asking the wrong ones for their opinions!' Freddie replied furiously. 'Why don't you talk to Harvey Reiner or Beth Holland … ' She stopped abruptly and the detective closed his notebook.

407

'Well, I think that's what we're all waiting for, Mrs Wallace, don't you?'

The afternoon limped on. Freddie phoned Rutland Gate to speak to Molly, but Jean Allen informed her that the nanny had gone to collect Conrad from school. Ringing off, Freddie leaned against the hospital wall, her eyes fixed on the silhouettes of the two detectives at the end of the corridor, their bodies black against the light coming in through the window.

Slowly she made her way back to her seat. Harry glanced up at her. 'So, how's things?'

'Fine. Molly's gone to pick Conrad up from school.' She replied, sitting down next to him. 'Do you think she'll be all right?'

They both knew who she meant. 'She'll be fine,' Harry said carefully.

'But what if ... ' Freddie stopped suddenly, glancing towards the opening door of Beth's room. For an instant she was about to rise and then hesitated, alerted by the look on the doctor's face. He glanced around and then moved towards Harry uncertainly and was about to speak when the red-haired detective interrupted him.

'How's Miss Holland?'

'I'm afraid she's dead.'

In his car Warren sat motionless. He had phoned Freddie the night before, putting down the receiver when she answered, not knowing what to say. He never knew what to say, or write any more. His thoughts were too huge to be caught with a pen, his emotions too intense for articulation. So now he watched his son through the school gates and tried to find reason in his over-heated brain – but there was none.

When he'd finally seen Freddie, she had rejected him again. That was fact. That was reality, bloody, unchanging reality. But by withholding his son and rejecting him, she had also tripped off a dangerous time bomb in Warren, a violent response which had festered and found no outlet. Conrad was his child, but the woman he loved had kept him away from him. Love and possession was denied. Only a bitter form of revenge remained.

And it was violent.

In the same moments that Warren sat plotting in his car, Freddie was told that Beth had died. Frantically she caught hold of Harry's arm as the detective continued to talk.

'I'll probably need to ask you some more questions later,' he said without any emotion. 'But you can go now.'

They followed the exit signs to reception, the pregnant woman with the plaster cast still sitting in the out patient's waiting room. Softly, the plastic inner doors slapped behind them as they left. Neither Harry nor Freddie spoke, and as Freddie climbed wearily into the car, she could hear Beth's voice and remembered her raucous laugh which bore no resemblance to the dead shape on the hospital bed.

In silence, Harry drove along, stopping at traffic lights, turning slowly round corners and working the gears automatically, his thoughts elsewhere. His feelings were in line with Freddie's. Both had seen death, too often and too closely, but whilst Freddie thought of Beth, Harry's mind ran on along angrier lines. The timing was wrong for Freddie again. It was unlucky and unfair, he thought, knowing with certainty that Beth Holland's death would be the end.

Having remained silent for most of the journey, Freddie suddenly turned to him and said anxiously. 'Harry, can we go past Conrad's school on the way back? We could pick him and Molly up and take them both home. I'll show you the way.'

Nodding absent-mindedly, Harry changed course, following all Freddie's directions, her voice rising as they hurried along. Her nerves, already overwrought, were taking their toll and when their progress was delayed by a parked lorry, Freddie began to fidget, her fingernails drumming on the dashboard, her anxiety obvious. Surprised, Harry glanced over to her and when the lorry finally moved he drove on quickly, parking outside the school gates and looking over to the playground.

He saw Molly first, as Freddie was still unfastening her seat belt. He saw her and, startled, struggled hurriedly out of his seat just as Freddie glanced up. Molly's face was swollen with crying, her eyes raw behind her glasses, her hair coming adrift from the pony tail at the base of her neck. She opened her mouth to speak and then glanced away nervously to the headmistress standing behind her.

'Molly?' Freddie said simply, walking towards her. 'What is it?' Then she knew. In that one instant, she knew and would never be the same again. 'Where's Conrad?'

'He was standing next to me,' Molly said frantically, her voice cracking, her tears huge under the magnifying lenses. 'I only turned away for a second to talk to Mr Blake ... '

Freddie took hold of her arms. *It's not true*, she thought disbelievingly. *It's not true. It can't be!* 'Where's my son ... where's my son?'

'He's gone,' Molly said dully, her head falling forwards.

Freddie repeated the words disbelievingly. 'Gone *where*? Where has he gone?'

Molly was hysterical. 'I don't know. I don't know.'

'What do you mean?' Freddie asked incredulously. 'What were you doing to let him go?' Her voice began to shake, the old echo of a stammer coming back. 'You've let someone take my son ... Molly, you can't have, you can't have.'

Harry interrupted her, walking in front of Freddie and looking directly into her unseeing eyes. 'I've just talked to the headmistress. She said that one of the other children saw a man pick Conrad up.'

'A man?' Freddie repeated hardly audible. 'Oh, God, he could be assaulted!' She said blindly, then paused, forcing herself not to panic; forcing herself to be rational. 'What did he look like?' she asked Harry.

'The child said it was a blond man,' he replied, mystified when he saw Freddie's panic fade and a slow look of realisation come into her eyes. Heavily, she leaned against him.

'We'll get Conrad back,' Harry said, putting his arm around Freddie and reassuring her repeatedly, his own shock making him garrulous. 'Don't worry, we'll get your son back. We'll bring Conrad home. We'll bring him home. He's your son.'

And Warren's, Freddie thought dully, and Warren's.

Chapter Thirty

Freddie, Harry and Molly returned together to Rutland Gate, Molly sitting in the back of the car, sobbing uncontrollably, Freddie silent, her eyes burning, her lips pressed together. I can't think of it, she said to herself repeatedly. I can't believe that my son won't come home … The loss hit her violently again, one hand going to her face as she tried not to cry out. Molly's distress pouring steadily over from the back seat.

'Molly, don't … please,' she begged, turning and taking the girl's hand.

'I'm so sorry … I'm so sorry,' Molly said brokenly, guilt making her inconsolable. She knew she should never have left Conrad even for a moment, but Mr Blake had waved to her and she just went over to talk to him. It wasn't a crime, was it, she thought. It was just so nice to see him and she hadn't thought it would matter for a moment. She swallowed with difficulty and looked into Freddie's white face. She had let her down, the one person she admired more than anyone else.

'We'll find him,' Freddie continued, comforting Molly and putting her own fervent hopes into words. 'We'll find him … '

'But you trusted me … ' Molly said, trailing off, her hand gripping Freddie's, her face swollen with misery.

'We're here,' Harry said quietly, parking outside Rutland Gate and getting out. The others followed him. Unlocking the front doors Freddie hurried in, Molly walking behind her, pausing, lost and bewildered, in the hall. She didn't know what to do, or say, her position was suddenly worthless – the child,

411

the reason for her life, had been taken and she was responsible.

'I'm so sorry ... ' she said, her voice breaking as she covered her face with her hands.

Numb with her own grief, Freddie turned and looked at her, then put her arms around the girl, repeating over and over. 'We'll find Conrad, we'll find him.' Her voice was steady as she spoke, her thoughts running on, her mind alert.

'I'll go upstairs,' Molly said finally. 'I'll go ... and tidy his room.'

Freddie nodded, watching as Molly walked away, her misery obvious in every movement, her footsteps quickening as she ran up the stairs and began crying again. Slowly Freddie laid down the door keys and walked into the drawing room, Harry following her. All her actions seemed unreal, unconnected – but her thoughts were clear.

'I'm glad your here, Harry,' she said, sitting down, an afternoon shaft of sunlight illuminating one side of her face. 'I know who took Conrad.'

He had expected as much, and yet the words still alarmed him. 'Who?'

'His father – Warren Roberts.'

Heavily, Harry sat down, his hands on his knees, his breathing rapid. He was stunned by his own feelings of shock. Stunned and faintly ashamed.

'I want to tell you something else, Harry,' Freddie went on, keeping her face turned in profile, avoiding his eyes. 'I did have an affair, which resulted in Conrad being born, but ... ' she glanced over, knowing that she owed him the courtesy of a full confession, '... it's not what you imagine. Warren Roberts was a friend of Bart's, and at that time Bart and I were struggling with our marriage ... ' She paused. How long ago it all seemed. ' ... I make no excuses, but one night Warren came for dinner. Bart was at work and he stayed on and Warren and I began to talk.' Her eyes looked into Harry's steadily. 'He was not an easy man to entertain, diffident, quiet, but for some reason he began speaking of his past and his family.' Freddie got to her feet, remembering the words as though she had heard them only yesterday. 'He had a wife

412

and child – a daughter – whom he loved very much. His little girl was called Alia, and she was six – the same age as Conrad is now – when she died.'

Harry flinched.

'Warren's wife and daughter were killed in New York in a hit and run accident. He had to identify his child ... ' Her eyes closed against the memory. She felt the same emptiness of loss that Warren had felt when his daughter died. 'It changed him, embittered him, and made him an intense, lonely man.' She paused for a long moment, and the moment expanded into a minute, the clock ticking, a door banging in another part of the house. Finally, Freddie spoke again. 'Warren told me about their deaths and he was so upset ... he was distraught ... ' Her hands clasped and unclasped. 'I just meant to comfort him – but we ended up making love.'

She stopped speaking then and sat down, her face once more turned towards the window, only her profile visible as she waited for Harry's verdict.

He sat motionless, the story taking shape in his mind and in his heart. It made perfect sense to him that Freddie would seek to comfort someone in distress by giving herself. After all, wasn't that what she had done for him? Without words, she had chosen to use herself to redeem the sufferer, bringing them back into the world with her own form of total and instinctive loving. Spontaneously, she had made love to Harry after the death of his father, and years later, she had repeated the act with another grieving man. Oh Freddie, Harry thought sadly, how harshly the world has judged you for your kindness.

'So why did Warren take Conrad now?' Harry asked finally, his voice without reproach.

Freddie breathed in a sigh of relief and turned to him. She knew Harry was not a man to discuss his feelings or articulate his thoughts but she could tell that he had not judged her and that he was going to help her.

'I didn't tell him that he was the father. I couldn't. Bart wanted a child so much, and I didn't think Warren would have made a good parent. Besides, I wanted to save my marriage and I loved Bart. I didn't – and I don't – love Warren.'

'But why did he take Conrad now?' Harry repeated, frowning.

Freddie shrugged listlessly. 'He only found out he was the father recently, and he came to see me. I rejected him. I wouldn't go back to him – maybe I should have! Maybe for the sake of my son I should have!' she said, getting to her feet and pacing around the room. 'Oh God, Harry, can you imagine how he must have felt? I was so *stupid* not to think of it before now – to think that Warren of all people would simply give up all rights to his child … ' Her actions became rapid and jerky. 'He lost his daughter, lost her, and his grief nearly killed him. Then I take his son away from him – dismiss him, keep his child – how could I do that?' she asked incredulously, as if seeing her actions for the first time. 'How could I have expected him to accept the separation from his son?'

'But kidnapping a child isn't a normal reaction for a father,' Harry said quietly.

'For Warren it is,' Freddie replied quickly. 'He's a complicated man, Harry. He will have thought all this out, and planned it, and brooded on it, and finally when I thought he had dropped out of our lives, then he would strike.' She shook her head, anger making her frantic. 'My son! I should have protected my son!'

'We'll have to contact the police,' Harry said softly. 'It's the only thing we can do.'

Immediately Freddie spun round, her frenzy replaced by sudden calm. 'No, that is exactly what we *don't* do,' she said, putting up her hands to prevent Harry interrupting. 'Warren might do anything if he is put under threat. He has to be left alone and not panicked. It is the only way I can be sure that I will get my son back.' She kept her voice clear. 'Warren will never, *never*, harm his son. He would give his life for Conrad, I know that,' she continued, working on her intuition, all logic suspended. This is the most important time of my life, she thought, I have to think from the heart, not the head – and I have to think like Warren.

'It's risky … '

'The risk would be not to trust him,' Freddie said firmly. 'I have to convince Warren to bring Conrad back home.'

'What!'

She nodded at the certainty of her words. 'He will, Harry, he will. Warren Roberts is not a bad man, he is a man who has suffered too much, whose whole life has been a series of battles against himself and the fates. He is not a bad man,' she repeated. 'He will treat his son well, I know.' She stopped, tears beginning. 'Oh God, I miss Conrad so much already ... '

The phone rang suddenly, interrupting her, and she hesitated, then extended her hand towards the receiver. Quickly she snatched it up, the sound of a crackling line scratching against her ear. It could have been a line from the northernmost tip of Scotland, or from over the Atlantic. A line miles away. A line which separated the winner from the loser, the father from the mother, and the mother from the child.

His voice said simply, 'Freddie.'

'Warren, how's Conrad? How's my son?' she said, her voice tensed with anxiety. Talk to him, don't alienate him – through him you will get your son back.

'Conrad is *our* son,' he replied quietly. A illogical man behaving logically.

Freddie swallowed. 'Yes ... our son,' she agreed. 'Where is he, Warren?'

He ignored the question. 'You were so wrong to separate me from my child, Freddie. Very wrong.'

His voice had the terrible composure of a fanatic.

'Warren, listen to me ... '

'No, I don't want to listen to you any longer. Conrad is my child and I intend to keep him.'

Freddie leaned back against the table to steady herself. 'You can't keep him, Warren,' she said, fighting hysterics. 'You have no right ... '

'He is my son. That's my right.'

'Yes, he is your son,' Freddie repeated, struggling with the words, trying to calm him and keep him on the line. I have to communicate with this man, Freddie thought, I have to learn to know him. 'We have to talk, I need to talk to you – and I have

415

to see my son.'

Warren laughed down the line. All affection suspended, suspicion in its place. Revenge before everything. 'But I don't want to talk to you any longer, Freddie. I have nothing to say to you any more. I tried to talk to you so often – it hurt so much, wanting to talk to you. But you didn't want to hear me. You ignored me and cut me out of your life and only now, now when I have Conrad, do you want to talk ... '

'I want my child back. Please, Warren, bring him back,' Freddie pleaded. 'You don't know how to care for him, you don't know how to feed or how to dress him. He hasn't got any warm clothes with him and he'll get cold. He could even get sick, Warren, and then what would you do? Don't keep him, please. He'll fret and he'll miss me. He's never been away from home before and he won't understand what's happened. Oh God, Warren, don't make my child suffer for what I've done. Please bring him, home, please.'

Warren listened, then responded evenly. 'I had a family once, Freddie. Don't forget that. I know what children wear and eat. Do you think I would let him suffer? Conrad will come to no harm with me.' He paused, suddenly compassionate. 'I would protect this child with my life,' he said, then added chillingly. 'But he stays with me.'

There was a momentary pause on the line before Freddie spoke again. When she did, she was steady and composed, all her thoughts centred on her son and how she would win him back. Through Warren, and through knowing him.

'Tell Conrad I love him,' she said evenly, although her eyes were blinded with tears. 'Be sure to tell him, and don't frighten him. Take care of him, Warren,' she said, spinning the first line of communication to him over the phone. It was fragile, tentative as a shadow, but he sensed it and caught it and a bond of understanding fluttered between them. 'Watch over our son, Warren, please – and phone me again, will you?' Freddie asked. 'Talk to me.'

On the other end, Warren faltered, feeling a half-forgotten sense of pity and compassion, and in that moment he answered her. 'We'll talk,' he said simply, and then rang off.

The phone slipped from Freddie's hand onto the floor as she moved blindly out of the drawing room and up the stairs. One by one she climbed upwards, walking into the nursery as Harry followed silently behind her. From the adjoining room came the sound of Molly's crying, although Freddie didn't hear it. All she could hear was an echo of her son's laugh and the sound of his voice calling her from the bathroom. In a state of shock she walked over to his empty bed and pulled back the counterpane, lifting the blankets to her face. They smelled of him, of the sweet, lost smell of childhood. One dark hair still clung to the blanket and Conrad's teddy bear lay against the pillow, a badge fixed haphazardly to it's chest. Behind her, Harry watched, then his throat constricted with grief as she leaned her face into the bedclothes and wept.

In a deserted warehouse by the abandoned end of one of the London dockyards, Conrad played happily, the hole in the roof above pouring a thin pool of sunlight onto the dirty floor below. Dressed in a new tracksuit and running shoes he was playing soldiers, running over the rubble and whooping with delight as he ran for cover making gunshot noises.

'BANG! BANG! BANG!' he went, holding up an expensive toy pistol and firing at imaginary villains.

'BANG! BANG! BANG!' he shouted, his attention suddenly caught by a figure who moved stealthily into the far end of the warehouse.

Alerted, Conrad crouched down, one foot landing in a puddle, the bottom of his trouser soaking up the wet as he waited silently, his heart banging. His eyes strained ahead into the empty warehouse, his palm sweating so much that the gun slipped in his hand, his tongue dry in his mouth. Carefully, Conrad lifted up the barrel of the pistol with his other hand, and waited, his fear mounting. I want to go home, he thought helplessly as he looked around the gigantic empty warehouse, I want to go home.

A noise exploded behind him and he spun round, losing his balance and falling backwards into the puddle.

'BANG! BANG! BANG! You're dead!' The voice shouted

417

as Conrad struggled to his feet and then ran, screaming delightedly, into Warren's outstretched arms.

In London the bureau was running itself, Freddie regaining her composure enough to make excuses, and cover up the abduction of her son with a false story. The Allens, her mother, Penn and the Wilkie women were all told that Conrad was staying with a friend for a while. Apparently his friend and his family had all contracted chicken pox and as Conrad had the same virus, it made sense for him to remain there with them. Smiling convincingly, Freddie told everyone that he was happier that way, and that it was better for him to be there than at Rutland Gate where he would infect all the clients. Anyway, she said cheerfully, he was glad to be off school. The story was believed and reiterated word for word by a stricken Molly.

Of course the school knew what had really happened, but the headmistress was sworn to secrecy on the grounds that any exposure might supposedly handicap the police in their investigations. The child who saw Warren abduct Conrad was also conditioned and told that the blond man was a friend of the Wallace family and that Conrad was temporarily suffering from chicken pox and would soon be back at school. One by one the participants in the drama were briefed and the real truth was known only to Molly, the school headmistress, Harry, and Freddie. No one else knew. Not even the police.

After much discussion with Harry, Freddie had decided that the police could never be informed. Since the murder of Beth Holland they were hardly likely to want to assist a woman to whom they were obviously antagonistic, and besides, as Freddie had explained to Harry, she would get her son back in her own way. The police might force Warren to do something rash – that was enough of a reason to keep them in ignorance.

'I won't have my child caught in a custody battle,' Freddie said to Harry. 'There is another way of solving this. There is a better way.'

'You're putting your own instincts before the police and the courts?' Harry asked incredulously.

Freddie turned to him with a look of bewilderment. 'I gave

birth to that child – Warren is his father. All my life I have obeyed my instincts, and I don't intend to change now. I know,' she said, pressing her heart, 'that only I can bring Conrad home. I have to convince Warren to return him of his own free will. If I get the police to bring him back, or the courts, then I will only have to face this agony again and again,' she said, her voice rising. 'Warren will *never* give up. The decision to return my son must be his, and his alone.'

'All right ... Whatever you say, I'll be behind you,' Harry said reluctantly, his thoughts running on. Perhaps Freddie was right, not only about Conrad, but in every other aspect of her life. If this kidnapping became public her business would never survive. The bureaux had only just weathered the last debacle. If it became common knowledge that Freddie Wallace's ex-lover had now abducted their son, it would be the last straw and the business would been destroyed overnight ...

A sigh juddered in Freddie's throat as she glanced over to the clock. The call from Warren had come the previous night, although it seemed a lifetime as she sat on the side of Conrad's bed and glanced around her. His toys were arranged in a tidy row on the table against the wall, his school books lying on a child-sized desk, a set of crayons neatly spaced out in a row. Not that Conrad would have left them like that. They had been arranged by Molly since, her hands shaking as she laid them out. Freddie's gaze wandered over the walls, across the wallpaper with trains printed on it, towards the punch ball on the stand in the corner. At the bottom of the door there were a few scratches where Conrad had caught the paintwork with his feet only the previous week and she had scolded him. Scratch all you like now, sweetheart, she thought hopelessly, just come home.

'Eat something, Freddie,' Harry said, cutting into her thoughts. She hadn't touched any food since Conrad had been taken over twenty-four hours ago. Nor had she slept. Instead she had spent the night pacing the floor, hysteria giving way to an intermittent blind calm.

'I'm not hungry,' Freddie answered simply. She glanced up at Harry wearily. Her eyes were heavy lidded. 'Do you think he might phone tonight?' she asked. 'I thought he would have rung by now, but ... ' Freddie glanced down at her hands. 'I mustn't panic. I must stay calm and think like Warren.' She touched her face with her hand absent-mindedly. 'It's the only way to find out where he's gone. He's got to take Conrad somewhere where no one will ask questions, or notice them.' She frowned, forcing herself to think logically, the effort agonising. Think, Freddie, think. Your son's life might depend on it. 'He's getting his own back and he's angry, so where is the first place he would he go?'

'Back to New York?'

'Maybe, but that's the first place he knows we'll look, so it's would be too obvious – and Warren was never that. Unless it's a double bluff ... ' She paused, reading the time on the nursery clock. 'Do you think he'll have fed Conrad yet?'

Harry's heart lurched uncomfortably even though his voice sounded light. 'Your son is very vocal, Freddie, I doubt if he'll let anyone starve him to death.'

Freddie smiled wanly, her thoughts wandering again. The only way to bring Conrad home was by logic. She would employ logic with an illogical man, because somewhere, underneath the anger and bitterness, Warren had goodness – it was hidden deep down, buried with Louise and Alia, but it was there. That little shudder of humanity would have to be unearthed, and when it was, Warren would be reached, and then, and only then, would he bring Conrad home.

The New York skyline yawned in front of both of them. Conrad was sitting on the bench with a baseball bat in his hand and a cap pulled low over his eyes although the sun had gone in and it was near to dusk. Across the East River, the first quick scattering of lights flicked on, the pointed spires and wedges of concrete darkening to black against the early evening sky. It was nine at night in New York and four o'clock in London, the birds singing the same song in both capitals.

Warren stretched his arms along the back of the wooden bench, watching as a stray dog sniffed along the wire netting and then cocked its leg against a sack of rubbish. The river

420

bobbed with seagulls, the metal struts of the bridge looking frail, seen from so far away. He stretched out his hand and closed one eye, pretending to grab hold of one of them and pull the whole bridge into the river below. Beside him, Conrad watched, fascinated, his child's legs swinging over the edge of the bench.

'What ya doing?'

Warren smiled easily. 'Pretending,' he said turning his gaze back to a dirty river tug which chuffed disagreeably along the dark water.

Warren's motive in abducting Conrad had been one of revenge. He had not considered the result or the final conclusion, he had just taken what was rightfully his. Instinctively he pulled the peak of the baseball cap over Conrad's eyes and grinned as the child struck out at him playfully. When he had first enticed the child into his car he had expected nothing, well, perhaps resistance, but nothing really. He hadn't thought deeply enough to plan for reactions. But there had been none anyway. Accepting Warren's story that his mother had told him to go with him, Conrad was either too surprised to fight or too frightened, but he had gone silently with his father into the unknown.

The child's courage was sobering. After all, Warren knew he was only six years old, but his composure was remarkable and his steady acceptance of all Warren said was almost eerie. In vain, Warren waited for the homesick reaction or the pleas to go home, knowing even then that he would have despised himself for inflicting such cruelty. But Conrad remained peculiarly accepting, his few questions drifting off into silence when he was given reasonable answers. Freddie had been a good mother, Warren realised with a jolt of admiration.

'When's Mummy joining us?' Conrad had asked on the plane, his excitement tempered with a nagging unease as he looked out of the window. He did not know that he was watching England disappear, only that he was leaving home. 'She never said anything this morning.'

Warren turned to face his son. Two pairs of blue eyes of exactly the same colour, matched each other. 'Don't worry.

She wanted to tell you but she didn't know about this earlier. She said that she'd join us very soon.'

'But she always said not to go with strangers,' Conrad explained carefully. 'What about my things?'

Warren frowned, momentarily caught off guard. 'She's bringing them later, and I've got plenty of new things for you,' he said, ordering them both a drink from the air hostess. 'She said not to worry.'

Conrad frowned as the orange juice was put before him. 'Mummy knows I hate orange,' he said simply, his excitement vanishing as a wave of homesickness washed over him. 'When did you say she was coming?'

'Soon,' Warren replied softly. 'Soon.'

Conrad slumped back into his plane seat, his English school uniform crumpled, a graze on his knee where he had fallen earlier that day on the school playground, looking raw. Suddenly his ears popped with the pressure and he swallowed, glancing over to Warren for reassurance. His eyes were closed, the crease between his eyebrows so dark that it looked like a crayon mark. Fascinated, Conrad studied him. He did not remember Bart and the only other men in his life were Penn and Harry, and neither looked like this man.

Warren shifted in his seat, the fingers of his hands interlaced, his fair hair combed back from his face, one leg stretched out into the aisle of the plane. Steadily Conrad continued his scrutiny, turning the man's name over and over – Warren, Warren – he frowned, trying to match the name to the man's face and as he did so, Warren opened his eyes. His gaze fell fully on Conrad and the child, although momentarily startled, did not glance away. Instead, with a genuine spontaneity, he smiled.

Warren stared at him, the smile jolting some memory of his own childhood, of his own dreams, and of Freddie – then slowly and tenderly, he smiled back. The bond between them was forged that instant.

Arriving in New York a few hours later, Warren collected his things from the apartment and then drove out to the dock area, stopping en route to get some food for both of them. He had already informed the restaurant that he was going to be travelling for a time and would be uncontactable, but had left specific instructions with Bob Rich as to how he should continue, knowing as he did so that the man looked upon his departure as his chance to take over the business himself.

Warren no longer cared. He had proved himself a success and had satisfied himself with money, possessions and power. None of these had bought him lasting peace. Inside, he continued to run from himself and had learned the dark fields of loneliness intimately. He had lost Freddie, then himself, bitterness clouding what goodness remained. The world had soured him and alone he moved down the dead, dark days into which no one penetrated.

Until Conrad. When Warren discovered that he had a son, his first reaction was one of exultation, followed by immediate anger. Freddie had lied to him. He had a son. A child, an heir. Something which belonged to him, something he could cherish, as he had cherished Alia. And Freddie had never told him. She of all people, who knew how much his daughter's death had affected him – she had kept his son away. His anger had been impossible to control, so that in the end he had convinced himself that no one could blame him for taking his child away. No one.

And it seemed as though luck played into his hands. The murder of Beth Holland had put Freddie in the most vulnerable position of her life. With her reputation both professionally and emotionally in ruins. Warren took the one thing she prized above everything – her son. It had been a monstrous act of revenge, planned without emotion, executed without mercy, and more successful than even he had thought possible.

Conrad was his flesh and blood, but he was his own person. The boy was his son by blood, but not yet in reality. The reality was a boy with a character of his own, who alternated between fear and curiosity, and whose bravery made Warren ashamed. As the anger faded, he remembered his own childhood and imagined how his son felt. His thoughts turned away from his own need for revenge and onto Conrad's need for comfort. Within twenty-four hours of abducting his son, he found himself automatically reverting to his previous role as father, repeating what he had done with Alia. When Conrad was hungry, he fed him; when he was tired, he made sure he slept; and when he was anxious, Warren reassured him.

'Your mother will be coming soon,' he said evenly. 'She's looking forward to the trip.'

Conrad laid his head down on the leather car seat, his eyes steady in the dim light. 'I miss her.'

Warren felt two emotions simultaneously – jealousy and pity, although the latter was far stronger. 'Didn't you have a good time today?'

Conrad nodded sleepily. 'Um ... but it's not like home,' he replied, closing his eyes. 'Mummy tells me a story sometimes ... Can you tell me a story?'

Warren stared out of the car window. Far above them, the moon provided a peep-hole into the darkness, a patch of luminescent stars trailing a bank of clouds. Evening slipped to night, hustling in the darkness, the clouds shifting from navy to indigo, to a final omnipotent black. Warren's eyes remained staring ahead of him, his body suddenly consumed with something beyond revenge – a sense of love coming like a warming to a frozen man. He breathed in deeply, his eyes fixed ahead, and then for an instant he saw a small boy playing alone, a child without friends. A child who was not Conrad, but himself, many years ago. A lost child.

I will not let the same thing happen to you, he thought. My life and my mistakes will not be yours. He sighed, aware of the responsibility of this other life, and relieved that he had the chance to repair the damage done. I will make amends he had sworn once, and now finally, and with total clarity, he knew how.

Then slowly and hesitantly, Warren began. 'Once upon a time ... '

Chapter Thirty-One

Bea shuffled the cards for the second time and then cut them, spreading the first pile out in front of her and then laying out the other remaining piles around the first. She frowned and leaned over, reaching for her reading glasses by the phone. Immediately the Tarot cards came into focus, a mass of coloured images looking up at her benignly. Well, they would seem benign to anyone who did not know how to read them. To her, they were not harmless, but a forerunner of something terrible. Unsettled, Bea gathered the cards together and put the pack back into its case, resting her glasses on top as she leaned back in her seat.

Beside her, Miku II snored on, his breathing rattling out of him as he dreamed, his legs twitching on the worn velvet covering of the settee. Absent-mindedly, Bea stroked him, her thoughts turning to her sisters, then to her daughter, and finally to Freddie. She frowned. Since discovering that Freddie had cheated on Bart, Bea had avoided contact with her, her sense of betrayal making her unusually stern. Yet she couldn't stop caring for her. Angry she might be, but indifferent, never.

The cards told her something, but the something was not specific. They spoke of a child, but whose? Her child, Jao? Or Freddie's? Or were they just symbolic, maybe meaning childlike, in which case they might refer to the endlessly juvenile Trisha.

Bea wished suddenly that Jao was there. Together they

could have talked it over, as they used to when she wasn't so busy. Bea thought of her daughter, of the paleness of her skin and hair and her breathtaking thinness. Was she beautiful? Bea wondered. Of course she was to her, but how did she appear to others, men, in particular? Bea wasn't sure, she was just surprised that her daughter remained unmarried. Perhaps it was because she was too busy, she thought, remembering how secretive Jao had become; or maybe it was because she was too immersed in her work and always travelling. One week in London, one week in Paris, constantly on the move, finding work where ever she could, although it was obviously wearing. And how proud Jao was, Bea thought, smiling, as she remembered how all Freddie's offers of help had been refused, Jao determined to set her own course ...

How likely was it that she would find a husband amongst rich art collectors and dealers? Not likely at all. Those were the kind of men who married into rich families, or married out into bimbo land. They didn't marry hard-working women like Jao Wilkie. Bea sighed and stretched her legs in front of her, her instinct telling her that Jao was unhappy, frustrated and perilously close to spinsterhood. No, she thought angrily, not Jao. Please, not Jao. As though to confirm her thoughts, Pam walked in through the front door.

'Hello,' she said flatly, as she walked into the sitting room and glanced round.

'Hi,' Bea replied, forcing interest. 'How was it at the clinic today?'

Pam glanced away, her mouth thin with self-pity. 'Two clients cancelled. I only had one person for a massage.' She looked over to her sister. 'I know you think my doing aromatherapy is a joke, but it happens to matter to me, and I was sure I could do well. I would have done, if everything hadn't gone against me. People are cutting back on luxuries now, what with the mortgage rates going up again. It's so unfair ... and it's not my fault.'

'I never said it was,' Bea replied wearily, grudgingly amused to find that the Government was now being held responsible for her sister's failure. She watched Pam with

426

curiosity. Time was sharpening it's cruel claws on both of them, she realised; time with nothing to offer but disappointment and old age. She could get used to it; Trisha would deny all knowledge of it; and Pam ... well, Pam had always been old.

'I'm sorry you weren't busy,' Bea said patiently, assuming the same tone of voice she had employed constantly throughout their lives. 'Things will be better next week.'

Pam sniffed disbelievingly as Bea glanced away, her gaze falling on the pack of Tarot cards. Some memory stirred uneasily as she thought back to the spread she had seen, her attention diverted when a pigeon landed heavily on the window ledge outside, its bright eyes peering in on her as Miku woke and exploded into a frenzy of irritated barking. Annoyed, Bea waved her hand at the bird and it flew off, away into the dull sky over Dorman Square. A bird of communication, she thought to herself, a bird employed to send messages. Bea sighed, unusually depressed. She had seen the message, but didn't know where to send it – or to whom it belonged.

' ... I was wrong,' Cleo said apologetically. 'Harvey is a really kind man.'

Freddie smiled half-heartedly, without thought, her mind working independently on the never-ending theme of Conrad. 'Good, I'm glad you like him.'

'Are you OK?' Cleo asked, leaning forwards, her heavy fringe held back with a hair band. No need to hide from anyone any more, Freddie thought.

'I'm fine. Just tired that's all.'

Cleo frowned, unimpressed. 'You're not still bothered about the bureaux, are you?' Freddie said nothing. There was nothing she could say. The figures said it all; clients leaving, membership dropping off, the news of Beth Holland's murder sending everyone scuttling away, back to the classified ads, to the back pages of *Time Out* – and to Mala Levinska. 'It was bad luck, but it could have happened to anyone,' Cleo continued. 'Beth could have been killed by anyone, it wasn't your fault.'

Freddie's gaze rested on Cleo for a moment. It *was* my fault, she thought, because I put her with Daniel Haig. I charged

427

money to introduce her to her murderer.

'You can't blame yourself, you have to look forward to the future.'

What future, Freddie thought dully. What was there in the future? The nursery was empty, there were no sounds of her son's feet on the stairs, no hurried confidences exchanged at bath time, and no moments in the day to plan for. No morning greeting, no lunch together, and no bedtime story and the all-consuming, forgiving caress before sleep.

Molly's grief was just as constant and without remission. As the first day of Conrad's abduction passed and then the second, she became steadily more desperate. Freddie found it hard to blame Molly entirely. Oh yes, Conrad had been in her care when he was taken, but it wasn't all Molly's fault, was it? No, Freddie thought suddenly, it was as much mine as hers. I had plenty of money, more than enough, so there was no reason for me to work so hard. So why did I? Freddie asked herself. Because I wanted to get my own back on the London social circle and on my father. I wanted to fill my days and escape. But escape from what? she thought, remembering how fast she had tried to run from the memory of Bart's death …

'Please don't worry. There's nothing to worry about any longer. They've caught Daniel Haig, and he's admitted that he killed Beth, so it's over,' Cleo said, alarmed by the blank look on Freddie's face. 'You will tell me if there is anything I can do, won't you?'

But no one could do anything and as the third day dawned Freddie found herself sinking into a state of suspended animation, her eyes constantly returning to the phone. Alarmed, Harry saw the deterioration in her and insisted on some action.

'We have to do something, we can't just wait.'

'He'll phone.'

'He won't!' Harry snapped, aware that Freddie was listless and close to defeat. 'We have to stop waiting for him to behave reasonably and start trying to find Conrad.'

Freddie blinked. 'They told me Warren was on holiday … '

'Who did?'

'A man at the New York restaurant. Bob Rich, I think he

said his name was.' Freddie said dully. 'I rang Maiden Lane too, but no one knows where he is.' Her eyes closed. 'But he'll call, he'll call ... '

'Oh, for God's Sake!' Harry shouted, suddenly angry. 'How do you know?'

The phone rang, severing the conversation. Harry glanced at it and leaned back in his seat, defeated, as Freddie got to her feet hurriedly and lifted the receiver. The muffled line took an instant to connect.

'Freddie, it's Warren.'

Her voice was high with relief. 'Warren ... How's Conrad?'

'He is well, very well.' Came back the reply. 'He's just eaten a steak.'

'Steak,' Freddie repeated enthusiastically. 'That's good, he likes meat. I always think it makes children strong ... Is he missing me?' she asked, hesitating. 'Is he?'

'He misses you,' Warren admitted, his voice more gentle. 'But he's not pining. He's OK, believe me.' Again a pause. 'He's been bullied at school, did you know that? He told me – only he said that the teacher thought he was in the wrong because the other boys made it look that way. He says some woman called Miss Walters thought he was a troublemaker.'

Freddie swallowed, unable to believe for a moment that her child had confided in Warren and not her. Why? Because Conrad had always tried to protect her, she realised, and now he could tell his side of the story to someone who was protecting him – someone stronger. Oh God, Conrad, she thought, oh God, why didn't you talk to me? Why couldn't you tell me?

'Freddie?'

'Yes, I'm still here.'

'Did you know?'

She nodded, even though he couldn't see her. 'I was told that he was troublesome ever since ... ever since the news broke in the papers. Apparently some of the other children were saying things about me – children can be so cruel. So I went to the school and talked to Miss Walters but she said it was Conrad who was causing trouble. I couldn't understand it at the time because he is always so loving at home.'

Freddie paused, astonished by the conversation. They were talking like a couple, discussing their child's problems as if it were the most natural thing in the world.

'Conrad needs to talk more,' Warren went on. 'And he needs to talk to a man. You did a good job with our son,' he said, pausing as he felt a rush of longing for her, 'but he needs a father, Freddie. He's got a temper that needs controlling.'

She laughed softly, like a nervous child. 'I know – but he's never taken it out on me.'

'I can help him,' Warren said.

The words reached out like an open hand. This is my offer, my gesture of love to you and to our child. I can help my son to be a better man than I am. I can turn him away from anger and violence because I know what it costs in terms of the dying of the heart and the slow going out of the soul.

'I can help him.' Warren repeated, his voice sliding over the ocean to London, his offer to make amends waiting, without breath, for the response which would dictate his actions.

Freddie paused, then took in a deep breath and said simply, 'I put my child in your keeping. I charge you to watch over him.'

And bring him home, she said silently, *and bring him home*.

The connection severed. Freddie laid down the phone and touched her face with her hand. The gesture was a nervous one which Harry had seen many times during the last three days, and as he watched her repeat it he could only marvel at her courage. There were no histrionics, no hysteria, just careful judgement.

I will bring my son home my way, she had said, taking a gamble on her own intuition to recover her child. She looked for no help from the law or the courts. The solution, she believed, was in her hands, and rightly or wrongly, she would stand by her decision.

'You are very brave,' Harry said suddenly.

Freddie turned, surprised. 'No.'

'Yes,' he insisted, contradicting her. 'I would never have had the courage to take all the responsibility on myself. I could never commit myself or make decisions – my life might have been happier if I had done so.'

430

'You committed yourself to your legacy, and to what you believed in,' Freddie said simply.

'As you committed yourself to your child,' he replied. 'I am a weak man, Freddie,' Harry continued, suddenly aware of his failings, 'but a constant one. Anything I can do for you, I will.'

Sarah Clements was fretting. She hadn't seen her husband for weeks and now her daughter was keeping her grandson from her. It was all too bad, she thought, snipping idly at some ivy in the conservatory, how no one cared about her any more. The leaves plopped onto the floor at her feet, green and juicy, too succulently healthy to be cut off from the main plant, but cut off nevertheless and left untidily on the tiled floor. Sarah laid down the secateurs, and walked out of the French doors onto the lawn, her thoughts going back to the time that Freddie had lived at home; the same time she had been envied as Mrs Clements, the woman married to Greville Clements, 'The Handsomest Man in England'.

And now he was pursuing the divorce, she thought incredulously, a small gasp of indignation escaping her lips. A divorce, why? It was too much to bear, Sarah thought helplessly, wondering whether or not to phone Freddie and tell her. The heels of her court shoes sank into the lawn, which stretched out like a slab of polished malachite before her, as she directed her steps towards the pavilion. She had always been fair, she thought, and even if she had sided with Greville a few times instead of with her daughter, that was what wives were supposed to do. A divorce, she thought miserably, sitting down, her expensive silk dress mottled by patches of sunlight falling through the trees overhead. She was his wife! And hadn't she always done what he wanted? Never asked too many questions? Kept his home nice? And never interfered in his business, even if it was her money which he enjoyed so much.

Sarah's bitterness ran up her spine like waves up a tuning fork. Oh yes, she had given him everything, hadn't she? Except a son, she thought dully. Her annoyance faded to disappointment instantly, a sudden breeze interrupting her thoughts and making the water rushes rustle in the lake, the noise evocative and damning, like the sound of children climbing through summer trees.

The fourth day of Conrad's abduction began with a rain storm, water pelting the windows and running down the office windows of the bureau at Rutland Gate. Having been instructed by Freddie to hold the fort, Chris fielded all the enquiries herself, passed over the interviews to Tina and Dot, and called in a temporary to do the filing. She had thought at first that the strain of Beth Holland's murder and the impending trial of Daniel Haig was the reason for her employer's anxiety, but she had been with Freddie too long not to realise that there was something more fundamentally wrong.

Perhaps Freddie was worried that the bureaux would not survive the scandal of the murder, and that this last blow would destroy the business completely? But it didn't seem likely, she decided, as she made coffee and glanced over to Freddie's office. Carrying the cup through, she laid it beside Freddie and left, half-expecting her employer to say something. But instead Freddie sipped the drink languidly, her eyes fixed straight ahead.

Oblivious to Chris's concern, Freddie sat perfectly still and felt only a terrible calm, as though some mechanism within her was faulted and she was receiving no messages and giving out no responses – other than one. Conrad, Conrad, Conrad – only Conrad mattered, him and nothing else. All that concerned her was his safety and the means by which she could convince Warren to bring him home. She knew it was going to be difficult, and that she had engaged in a mental duel with a man who was intelligent, complicated and unpredictable.

Yet Warren loved his son, and he would not hurt him. If Freddie could only find the key to Warren's personality, she could reason with him, and by reasoning, convince him to return Conrad to her. The signs were all there. The last conversation they had shared had showed a profound change in him. There was no tenderness, but there was no anger either. He had spoken of Conrad and his problems with genuine concern, as any good father would. *As any good father would,*

Freddie repeated to herself gently. *As any good father would.*

Of all the people in the world, Freddie's saviour was the old devil, her father. On the evening of the fourth day of Conrad's disappearance he telephoned Freddie.

'Frederica, this is your father.'

Her first impression was one of anxiety, then of relief. Her father did not know about Conrad. 'Hello, Father, how are you?'

'Fine,' he said. 'I'm afraid I have to talk to you. It seems a pity that we can't be close. A little while ago I believed we might be friends. I heard about the murder – I suppose everyone in the country did – and I can't say I was surprised. You have ceased to surprise me with your lunatic schemes and your complicated private life ... But aside from all that I have to talk to you.'

'About what?' Freddie replied, already dreading the words.

'I've asked your mother for a divorce ... '

Pain, quick and deep, infused Freddie's being.

'Madelaine is pregnant and I want to marry her. I'm not joking, this time I mean it.'

Sharp deep pain, cutting to the quick.

'And I have to tell you that I'm taking over the business now. It's mine, although I'll make provision for you and your mother ... '

Quick, savage pain, the ripping away of the skin.

'What the hell are you talking about?' Freddie said simply, her voice damningly cool and judgmental.

She made him feel uncomfortable and he lashed out. 'You are in no position to be angry with me. You're lucky I've made a point of telling you myself, I could have left it to my solicitor.' He paused, moderating his tone. 'Listen, Frederica, I've told you I'll make sure you and your mother are all right and that you have everything you need. I promise you that. I don't want a fight.'

'Oh, but I do!' she replied hotly, slamming down the phone.

All Freddie's old resentment reared up, full of fury and energy. *You want to take the business and all my mother's money,* Freddie thought; *the money you stole from my mother*

433

and now want to take from me and from my child. You're stealing my son's inheritance and after that, what else? Cambuscan? Freddie pushed back her chair sharply and stood up, her heart banging so loudly that it obliterated every other sound.

Slowly and resolutely she made her way upstairs, each step she took reiterating her thoughts. I will beat you, Father, once and for all, and I will do it for my child. Conrad will be the heir to Cambuscan, and I will secure his future and hold it in trust for him until he returns. Her anger, seldom fully expressed, uncurled dangerously as she pulled off her clothes and changed rapidly into a red and black suit before painting her mouth with vivid colour. Then, using an erasure stick, she smudged out the dark circles under her eyes and finally sprayed on her perfume, the one her son liked most. Conrad's favourite scent.

I am not afraid any more, she said to herself, as she slammed the front door behind her and walked across the late London streets, her heels tapping their way on the pavement like a blind man's stick. I know what I'm doing and no one on God's earth is taking anything else away from me or my child, Freddie thought grimly, as she turned into Eaton Mews North and stopped outside the little house where her father had kept his mistress for years. Without pausing, she rang the bell, hearing the sound of footsteps approaching before a women opened the door. You're hardly a beauty, Freddie thought, scrutinising the Swiss woman's face. You're getting older and pregnancy does nothing for you.

'Yes?' Madelaine Glauvert said, her accented voice faintly irritated. Perhaps she had been sleeping, Freddie thought, glancing at her stomach and judging her possibly seven months pregnant. A woman needed a lot of rest so far gone – just as she had done with Conrad.

'I want to see my father,' Freddie said evenly, pushing past the woman and walking into the lounge. Her gaze was scathing as she looked around. 'What a ... cosy ... little nook.'

'Just a minute!' Madelaine said uneasily. 'You can't just walk in here.'

'Oh, I think I can, as I have been paying your bills indirectly for years,' Freddie replied, sitting down and crossing her

434

elegant legs. 'Mind you, I really think that you should have made my father do more for you. After all, the pointing's not too good around the front door, is it? And frankly, this room is damp.'

Madelaine coloured, feeling suddenly threatened. 'He's not in,' she said, adding peevishly, 'although I suppose you thought I would deny that he was here.'

'I know what you are, so don't try to defend yourself,' Freddie responded coolly, before helping herself to a drink of brandy. 'But you're not what I expected. I thought he had more taste.'

'Get out!'

'Get lost!' Freddie replied, frighteningly calm as she sat down again. 'I've known about you for a long time. I came here once, about ten years ago, and watched you leave to go to some dance class.' She sipped her drink. 'You were younger then. But still, it's not your looks he's after, is it?' she said, glancing down at the woman's stomach again. 'I suppose you must be praying nightly that it'll be a boy. But who do mistresses pray to? I mean, you'd need to pick someone who'd be on your side – Mary Magdalene perhaps?'

'I want you to go.'

'I know,' Freddie said sympathetically. 'I've often felt the same way about you, especially when I knew my father was sleeping with you and lying to my mother. You made things very difficult for me, trying to make sure that my mother never found out about you.' She drained her glass and pulled a face. 'It's even cheap brandy. Still, if you have a boy you'll be in clover, and it'll be Courvoisier all the way ... If not, it'll be bye-bye, birdie.'

Freddie paused just as the door opened and her father walked in. She felt no fear of him any longer, just a violent determination to see justice done. 'Well, hello, Father. I was just – '

'What the hell are you doing here?' he bellowed.

At another time Freddie would have been intimidated, but not now. Now she was past fear. 'I thought we should continue our conversation ... '

435

'You were the one who put the phone down.'

'Because I wanted to talk to you here, where the crime was, or rather *is*, being committed.'

'My private life has nothing to do with you!' Greville shouted suddenly, expecting to see his daughter flinch as his wife and mistress did.

But Freddie was impassive, her eyes steady. She has such class, he thought wearily, such unflinching, unchanging class.

'Don't try and frighten me, Father, and don't take me for a fool either.' She refilled her glass with half an inch of brandy, her father watching her as she regained her seat. 'You can't just announce that you're taking over the company, it's not that simple and you know it. It's a family company, built up by the Clough family, my mother's family ... '

'I don't need a history lesson.'

'I rather think you do,' Freddie replied coldly. 'There are the shares to consider ... '

'I bought the shares off your mother, it was all done through my solicitor.'

Freddie frowned. 'I never knew that. Besides, you know that my mother isn't capable of understanding that kind of transaction and would simply do what you said. She trusts you. She always has, though God knows why. She even thinks you'll look after her.' Freddie regarded her father thoughtfully. 'I suppose you've been working up to this for a while, haven't you? Plotting away and getting more and more of my inheritance ... '

'What the hell does it matter to you?' Greville bellowed. 'You have more than enough money.'

'That's not the point,' Freddie countered. 'The business belongs to the family, not to you. You're trying to steal it from my mother and give it to your ... lady friend, who's about to give you the son and heir you want so badly. Although frankly, Father, I have a hunch that it'll be a girl, and then what will you do?' Her eyes narrowed; she was dangerous with anger. 'I want to see the papers you drew up and made my mother sign, because if my mother really wanted to sell those shares, she should have offered them up to other members of the family first ... '

'I am a member of the family.'

'And so am I, and I would have bought those shares rather than let you have control, and you know it.'

Greville said nothing. He was too surprised at his daughter's knowledge of the business to respond. In reality Freddie was not sure of her ground; she was just guessing and had only realised that she was right by the look on her father's face.

'You're too clever and too greedy, Father, and if I chose to take you to court your actions might well be seen as fraudulent.'

Madelaine took in her breath sharply. Freddie glanced over to her, her eyebrows raised. 'Did you really think for one minute that I'd let you have the company to give to your bastard when I have the rightful son and heir?'

Greville flinched and then caught his daughter by the arm and pulled her roughly out of her seat. 'Get out!'

She shook him off vigorously, her courage almost intimidating. I'm fighting for my son, she thought grimly, and I'll win. 'Let go of me! I'm not a child any more, and I won't be treated like one.'

'I've told you, I paid your mother a fair price for those shares and I'll look after both of you. I'm having a settlement drawn up now.'

'How kind of you,' Freddie said sarcastically, her thoughts running on. 'Do you know, I just had a very interesting notion. It couldn't be that your half-hearted attempt at a reconciliation the other month was just an attempt to soften me up?' she asked, smiling without humour.

'Get out!' her father shouted, pointing to the door. 'Get out, or I warn you – '

'No, Father, you can't warn me of anything. But I'll warn you. Give those shares back to my mother and I'll forget all this; but if you try to gain absolute control over the business I'll take you to court.' She smiled thinly. 'I'll take you to the highest court in the land and we'll see who wins then.'

'You wouldn't dare.'

'Oh God, Father, why don't you just try me.'

When Freddie returned to Rutland Gate, there was a fax on her private office machine, sent from New York, in Warren's handwriting. Quickly she ripped the paper sheet out of the machine and sat down to read it.

Dear Freddie,
Don't think you can try and find us in New
York – we're leaving today. I said I would
keep in touch, and so I'm writing to you as
well as phoning you. It seems so strange
that we never did this before – but we only
really talked once and that was briefly. Conrad
is well, and eating and sleeping as he should be.
I spray a little of your perfume on his
pillow at night to remind him of you …

Freddie moaned softly – the action was gentle, thoughtful, the action of a kind man, not Warren – at least, not the man she knew as Warren.

He has no bad dreams. But he has such
confusion in him. Did you know that, Freddie?
Or does he only show that to me? I recognise it
easily, because I see so much of myself in him, so much
frustration. I grew up too soon, and felt too
much – I don't want him to have to grow up as fast
as I did.
He talks, Freddie, about
London and you, about Molly and about Yorkshire.
When I took him, I wanted him because he was mine –
but now I want to help him, to teach him what no
one taught me. *Talk to me*, you said, well, I am …
I've been a bitter man, Freddie, and
a lonely one. I wanted you because in you I saw my
salvation. I never thought of what I could give you
in return. Oh yes, there was money and possessions –
but what else? You didn't want me and I couldn't
understand that. Now I do, oh yes, now I do.
Conrad is well, he is happy.
Warren
*

438

After sending Freddie the fax, Warren had left New York, driving overnight to Canada, arriving in Montreal as the dawn came up. Beside him, Conrad slept peacefully, his baseball cap pulled low over his face, his breathing regular. When he stopped at the traffic lights, Warren glanced over to his son and smiled, and then, catching sight of his own reflection, stared at the mirror in surprise. Gone was the man in the business suit, instead a younger man seemed to have taken his place. His dark blond hair was dishevelled by the wind which blew through the open window, and a casual shirt and trousers took him away from his past more certainly than the miles could.

He drove on, singing in time to the radio, hoping Conrad would wake, but the child continued to sleep, too tired from the constant travelling even to stir. The days passed and in park after park they played, in zoo after zoo, the shops mingling into one as Warren bought innumerable toys and books, then piled them all haphazardly into the car boot at the end of the day. Conrad still asked when his mother would be joining them, but the anxiety had gone from his voice and there was another emotion which Warren recognised. Was it love? he asked himself uncertainly, waiting for confirmation and knowing the answer when Conrad turned and laughed easily without a moment's hesitation. It was love, and it turned his heart.

And that was when Warren knew that he could never give his son up; that whatever happened there would never be anyone in the world who could take this child away from him.

They travelled constantly, on the run, settling nowhere, the days drifting into weeks. One morning they paused and spent some time sitting by a pond off a motorway in Quebec. Warren beginning to teach his son how to skim stones along the surface of the water.

Repeatedly Conrad tried and repeatedly he failed, until his temper snapped and a quick burst of fury made him strike out, hitting Warren's chest with his clenched fist.

Recognising the symptoms immediately, Warren caught hold of his arm, and the boy cried out.

'Don't!' Warren said simply.

439

Conrad winced and struggled to get free. 'Let me go!'

'Not until you promise not to hit people again.'

A flash of impatience flared up in Conrad's eyes as he struggled. 'I can do what I like!' he said childishly. 'Let me go! Let go! I want to go home now.' His fist lashed out again, and in response Warren hit him once, hard.

Conrad blinked, fighting to hold back tears as Warren took hold of his shoulders and knelt so that they were face to face. 'What good does it do, Conrad?' he asked quietly. 'You strike out at me, I hit you back – what good does it do? We just get more angry with each other.' He chose his words carefully, trying to articulate his feelings. 'I've lived with violence all my life. When I was a kid, the area I lived in was tough, so I had to be violent to survive, and when I grew up I kept thinking that striking out was the answer, but it wasn't.' He thought of the fight on his nineteenth birthday, and of the pent up violence within him all his life. An inability to communicate, frustration taking form in fists, not in words. And where had it lead him? To nothingness, to just more frustration. 'I don't want you to be like me.'

'You can't hit me!' Conrad wailed. 'Mummy never hits me. You're a bully.'

Warren nodded slowly.

'Yes, I've been a bully all my life. I've bullied people to get what I want, men and women, and it did me no good.' He touched Conrad's hair, frowning. 'I never knew until now that there was another way. You do know. You don't have to act like this. Cut it out, Conrad, get rid of all that anger – you don't hit people to get them to do what you want.' The words came to him almost effortlessly, as though he had wanted to say them for years and simply lacked the voice. Don't be like me, he was saying, don't start on the route to loneliness; let me save you from what I became.

'I want to go home,' Conrad said pitifully as he looked up at Warren, his chin jutting out belligerently. 'You can't tell me what to do! Who said you could tell me what to do?'

The words came out before he could stop them. Overdue and under used. 'I can tell you what to do because I'm your father.'

440

Conrad stopped sulking and stared at Warren, his gaze so intense that it seemed for a moment that he assessed him.

'My father?'

Warren nodded. Now that the words had been spoken a kind of understanding overtook both of them as Conrad put his head on one side and said simply. 'Does Mummy know?'

It was the first time Warren had laughed for months.

That night, as Freddie paced the floor, Warren rang. His voice came over the ocean to Rutland Gate and as she picked up the phone she had an unfamiliar sensation of excitement which surprised her. She actually *wanted* to talk to him – not just to know how her son was, but to talk to *him* – to Warren Roberts. The thought left her reeling for an instant.

'Conrad knows I'm his father,' he said softly. 'I had to tell him, Freddie. It was the right time for him to know. He's well and safe. Are you all right?'

'I miss him,' she said simply. 'When are you bringing him home?' Her anxiety made her clumsy, for once pushing the issue, demanding reassurance.

Warren drew back immediately. 'Don't ask, Freddie. I've told you, don't ask.'

'My father is trying to steal my inheritance from me and from my child – he is trying to take the business because his mistress is pregnant.' Her voice faltered. 'Everyone is stealing everything I value and you ask me not to ask for my son's return.' All fear had left Freddie, her anger was now formidable.

Warren's shock was palpable. His action seemed suddenly indefensible when he saw Freddie threatened by someone else. 'Why would your father do that to you?'

'My father dislikes me,' she replied without any emotion at all. 'He wanted a boy and I was a disappointment to him.'

'You were a disappointment?' he asked, incredulously.

'He's a strange man, and I think he's also a sick one now. When I was little he behaved abominably to me,' she explained slowly, wondering how it was so easy to confide now, when she had kept the matter secret for so long. The words tumbled out, the stories of petty injuries and deep fears – and finally the tale of Mrs Gilly. At the other end, Warren listened avidly, experiencing her childhood as she took him back down the years. Then, when she finished, she began to ask him questions as though they were friends – and he told her about his upbringing and about his parents.

'I went back to try and find them, but they were both dead.' In her mind, Freddie saw the piece of paper on the door outside the furrier's workshop and felt the sense of loss, sharing it with Warren. 'I thought ... you know ... that I could make them proud of me.'

'I thought so too,' Freddie said gently, thinking of her father. 'But you can't. He was "The Handsomest Man In England," ' she said suddenly, oddly amused. 'That's what *Tatler* called him once. I remember Avery being so irritated by it.'

Over the phone line the question came quickly. 'Who's Avery?'

'Harry's father,' Freddie replied, sitting down, her energy gone suddenly. She wanted to talk and to listen. *Talk to me* ... 'People expected me to get married to Harry. He was the heir to Lord Avery, and had the estate next to Cambuscan in Yorkshire. My father was very keen that I should marry well, you see. He wanted the title to make himself respectable.'

Warren felt a deep pain and primed himself for the next question. 'Did you love Harry?'

'Yes,' she said simply.

'So why didn't you marry him?'

'He was not a man anyone could marry; he was too wedded to his inheritance. It always came first – and maybe that was right. The Hall was inherited by his father and then passed down to him when Avery died ... ' She trailed off, the memory of smoke and fire coming down the years to her.

Warren picked up on her hesitation immediately. 'What happened? How did he die?'

'In a fire,' she said, her voice breaking suddenly. 'He died when the Hall caught fire. He had arthritis and there was an accident with a gas heater – we went in to get him. ' She carried on, her eyes filling, thinking back to the night. 'But we couldn't get him out in time. He was already dead, you see. We were too late.'

'Oh God,' Warren said, closing his eyes. *How little I know you, Freddie, and how I misjudged you. I thought you had lead a charmed life. Rich and spoiled, a woman who had never really suffered. I never knew your past – and I never thought to ask.*

'Do you still see Harry?'

Freddie sighed. 'Yes, he's the only one who knows about Conrad,' she admitted. 'He's been a great help, and a good friend, Warren.' *The words swung across the wide sea. He has been a friend, that most precious of people. A friend.*

'Warren?'

He remained silent. *His thoughts were divided – his need to get to know his child, against his need to comfort Freddie. Bewildered, he hovered.*

'Talk to me.'

The words were almost a command and he responded. 'I have hurt you very much, haven't I?' he asked suddenly.

'Yes,' she replied.

'I don't want to hurt you any more.' He said, trailing off. 'What are you going to do about your father?'

Freddie sighed, frustrated that he had changed the subject. *She had thought for an instant that he was about to weaken and bring Conrad home, but not yet, she realised. It was too soon, there was still some way to go. God grant me strength, she thought, fighting exhaustion.*

'I'm going to take him to court and when I win I'm going to take Conrad up to Cambuscan,' she said quietly, testing the man on the other end of the phone. 'It's his home.' Smiling, *Freddie thought back and remembered the time she had taken Conrad there as a child and held him up in her arms in front of the house, in a pledge, an offering of sorts. 'This is your home,' she had said to her son, and she had meant it. 'Your home, for ever, for keeps.'*

'Go and fight your father,' Warren said, his firm voice filling her with an unexpected rush of courage. 'Go and win, Freddie, go in there and win.'

'Then will you bring Conrad home?' she asked.

443

But the phone went dead, the connection severed. Gone was her son from her and also something else, some flicker of a man she had glimpsed and liked, a changed man as yet not fully known to her – a man taking shape as he talked.

Mr Godfrey Hudson's chambers in Lincoln's Inn were already busy at nine-fifteen. Several phones rang at once; a secretary hurried by with a sheaf of papers; a clerk took orders from the burly counsel who had just arrived and stood puffing out his cheeks after climbing the stairs two at a time. His dark grey three piece suit was well used, his shoes polished but old, the cracks across the front deep as knife slashes. A mass of thick grey hair, liberally coated with oil, lay against the domed contours of his head, his eyes a nondescript colour behind gold-rimmed glasses.

He was still puffing impressively as he caught sight of Freddie waiting in the crowded reception area. He turned back to his clerk. 'The trick is to take the stairs two at a time, breathing *out*. That way you don't get short of breath.'

The clerk nodded, without making any reference to Mr Hudson's hyperventilating, and said quietly. 'Mrs Wallace is here to see you, sir. She has an appointment.'

The barrister turned, took a long look at Freddie and her solicitor, Andrew Rose, and then, smiling wanly walked into his room, intimating with his hand that the visitors should follow him. The room was functional, not at all what Freddie had expected, and curiously impersonal for a barrister's chambers. There were few references to the law, apart from a couple of indifferent cartoons of Marshall Hall, and the worn antique furniture would not have been out of place in a surgery on Wimpole Street.

Godfrey Hudson sat down, wheezing. 'So, what can I do to help?'

Andrew Rose was forthright. 'We want to know what our chances are.'

'Good.'

' "Good" that we want to know? Or we have a "good" chance of winning?'

444

Godfrey Hudson regarded Andrew Rose critically, seeing a small Jewish man who was known to be shrewd and who was also known to hate wasting time. In the legal profession, such an eccentricity was enough to earn him a speedy reputation.

'Mr Rose, having thought the matter over at length, I would seriously consider our chances of winning this case are good,' Godfrey Hudson replied, pausing for effect. 'In fact, I'm sure that if we wrote a firm letter to Mr …,' he glanced at his notes, ' … Greville Clements, he might well settle out of court and thereby leave Her Majesty's judicial buildings free to pursue justice and allow you the opportunity of perfecting your golfing skills.' He smiled broadly at his humour and glanced over to Andrew Rose.

'That was my thought too, but regretably Mr Clements replied to my letter this morning,' he passed some papers across the desk, 'saying that he wasn't interested in settling and that he was prepared to take the matter to court.'

Godfrey Hudson read the letter slowly, one hand smoothing the top of his oiled hair, his chair creaking violently as he rocked backwards and forwards. 'Would Mrs Clements be willing to testify?'

Freddie leaned forwards. 'My mother is not the best person to give evidence … ' Godfrey Hudson glanced at her in surprise, almost as though he hadn't realised she was there.

'She gets easily confused.'

'But your father bought the shares from her?'

'For a million and a half.' Freddie replied nodding. 'But they're worth twice that and he knows it. The business is a family one and there are articles and clauses in the company rules which state that anyone in the family who wishes to sell their shares has to offer them up to all the other members of the company first – '

'But your mother never offered them up to you?'

Freddie shook her head. 'No.'

'Why not?'

'Because she wouldn't understand or even realise that was what she had to do. She trusts my father. She always has,' Freddie replied, trying to keep the animosity out of her voice.

'My father has been trying to gain control of the company for a long time. He deceived my mother into … '

' "Deceived"?' Godfrey Hudson queried.

Andrew Rose interrupted. 'He convinced Mrs Clements to sign over various properties to him. We cannot prove that he did it as an act of deception, only that she appears to have gone along with his wishes willingly and without coercion.'

'She's not fit to make such decisions herself!' Freddie said heatedly. 'She's never been fit to understand business matters.'

'So why didn't she ask your advice?' Godfrey Hudson queried.

'I was never told anything about the business when I was a child, or when I grew up,' Freddie replied evenly. 'My father didn't think it was anything to do with me, even though it was not his business, but was a family business which should, by rights, be passed down to me, and then to my son.' She paused, and swallowed, remembering Conrad. Get on with it, Freddie, she said to herself, you're doing this for your son. 'I was kept in the dark about all the family's business affairs. He prefered it that way. After all, he is a solicitor.'

The chair creaked loudly as Godfrey Hudson looked up, surprised. 'Your father is a member of the legal profession?'

'Yes,' Freddie replied calmly. 'So you can see why my mother trusted his advice. She thought he would look after the business, but instead he got her to sign over more and more control – she doesn't even have her own bank account – and now he wants the business for himself.'

'Why? There must be a reason.'

Andrew Rose glanced over to Freddie as she replied. 'My father has a mistress and he wants to divorce my mother and marry this woman, especially now that she's pregnant … '

Godfrey Hudson sighed … more complications.

'You see, he always wanted a son and heir and so now he's about to become a father he wants to take the business away from me and my son, to give it to his … '

'Offspring?' the barrister offered helpfully.

Freddie nodded. 'I didn't realise how far all of this had gone until the other day when my father informed me of his intentions. Unfortunately, my mother and I are not that close, and after I married, naturally she turned to my father even more in my absence. Apparently my father took advantage of her more and more and she wanted to hold onto him ... so she agreed to everything he said.'

'Dangerous,' Godfrey Hudson remarked phlegmatically.

'Yes, it was,' Freddie agreed. 'I went up to see her in Yorkshire yesterday and tried to find out exactly what she had signed, but she had no idea.' She passed some more papers over the desk. 'However, I did get these. They're the legal documents to cover the transaction of the share sale.'

Hudson read them carefully, wheezing and clearing his throat before turning his attention back to Freddie. 'You had one-third of the shares, and your mother had two-thirds?' he asked. Freddie nodded. 'And now your mother has no shares and your father has her two-thirds?'

'So he has control.'

'No, he doesn't, because it's not valid. The company articles state categorically that the shares have to be offered up to the other directors – you, in this case – and then if you don't want them, he can buy them. But you have to be offered them first.' Godfrey Hudson glanced over to Andrew Rose. 'Get him to settle out of court. Clements is a solicitor. He must know that he hasn't a leg to stand on.'

'It's a matter of principle,' Freddie said simply.

'Then it's going to turn out to be a very expensive principle,' the barrister replied with amusement. 'He'll lose if he goes to court and then he'll have to give the shares back and pay the costs.'

'You don't understand,' Freddie said wearily. 'He thinks I'm bluffing. He thinks I'll never dare to go through with it and that I'll back off at the last moment. Believe me, my father doesn't think I'll take him to court,' she concluded, watching Godfrey Hudson's face as he blew out his cheeks in irritation.

'Well, it's going to come as quite a shock to him then, isn't it?'

It did. When Greville heard that his daughter intended to

447

take him to the High Court he hardly paused for breath before racing up to Yorkshire and arriving at Cambuscan late that evening, tingling with fury. Struggling to put his key in the lock, he swore violently, and when the door did open, he pushed back so hard that it banged into the wall behind, a flake of plaster dropping to the ground like the last petal of summer.

Taking the stairs at a run he threw open the bedroom door and snapped on the light. Sarah immediately jumped up in bed, her hair dishevelled, her face pink with shock.

'Greville,' she said, her voice more highly pitched than usual. 'Darling, how lovely to see you.' She got out of bed and put on her dressing gown, struggling to get her left arm into the sleeve. 'Oh dear, I seem to be stuck ... how silly of me.'

He ignored her and asked simply, 'Sarah, what the fucking hell is going on?'

'Going on?' she repeated, finally getting her arm into the sleeve. 'I don't understand, dear. What are you talking about?'

'Your bloody daughter!'

'Freddie?'

His temper flared. 'Frederica.' He said coldly. 'Who the hell else is your daughter?'

'Our daughter, Greville,' she said calmly. 'She is *our* daughter.'

'Who ever's daughter she is, I want to know what's going on. She put you up to this, didn't she?'

'Up to what?' Sarah asked, walking over to her husband and touching his sleeve pathetically. 'Let me make you something to eat, darling. Then we can talk.'

'You stupid bitch!' he shouted, pushing her away. 'I don't want to talk to you, I just want to know what's going on.'

'I don't know,' Sarah wailed, rubbing her arm absent-mindedly. 'I really don't. She just came to see me the other day and asked me about the business and what I had signed for you. I didn't know I did wrong to tell her, Greville. You must believe me.'

His eyes were suspicious. 'Did you show her anything?'

'No ...' Sarah paused. 'Only those papers about the shares.'

His voice was strained. 'But you didn't let her keep them, did you?'

Sarah didn't dare answer for a moment, because suddenly she knew how serious it was. 'I ... '

'What!'

'She took them,' she cried pathetically. 'I didn't know it was wrong, I swear it,' she said, catching hold of his hand. 'I would never have done it if I'd known. Oh, Greville, let's talk... '

'She's taking me to court,' he replied, looking at his wife in disbelief. 'Your bloody daughter is taking me to court because she wants the shares for herself.'

'Well, she can't have them!' Sarah said blindly. 'If you want them, you can have them. I'll talk to her, Greville, and make her see sense. You're her father, she mustn't do anything to hurt you, not when you've been so good to her.'

For an instant Greville Clements loathed his wife. All his last vestiges of pity for her were gone. He looked down at Sarah's sagging face and figure and at the plump hands which clutched at his jacket and he wanted to be rid of her.

'I *have* been good to her, haven't I?'

'Oh, yes,' Sarah agreed, relieved that his anger seemed to be fading. 'Very good. You've always been good to me too, Greville, and you know how much I love you.' She paused, then tried to smile flirtatiously at him, but the result was grotesque. 'Come back to me, darling, and forget this silly nonsense about a divorce. I'll persuade Freddie to stop if you come back ... '

'Why should I? What is there here for me?'

'I love you, I can make you happy.' Sarah said blindly. 'What else is there?'

'My mistress,' he said bluntly. 'She loves me too. So how can you say I'd be better off with you?'

'She doesn't know you like I do,' Sarah pleaded hopelessly. 'I can give anything you want. Money and power, anything. She can't do that. In fact, she can't give you anything more than I can – '

'Except a son,' he said, satisfying his own fury as the words struck out at his wife.

449

Sarah's hands fell away from his jacket as her eyes fixed on her husband until she could see nothing other than his remarkable, unchanging eyes, and in them, her last chance of happiness. No sound came from her lips. She seemed almost rigid with shock, as the memory of her own failed pregnancies came back, one after the other, together with the months spent resting to provide this man with his son. Day after day of sickness, weariness, dragging her body through physical torment, her legs swollen with fluid, her breasts heavy and raw, her stomach distended with a child who was never born to breathe ... And for what? For what did she torture herself and ruin herself and belittle herself, spoiling her own body and life? For him. For Greville Clements – the man who was now openly enjoying her distress.

Greville walked to the door without turning. Having said what he wanted to say, there was nothing else left. His anger was appeased for a while, at least with his wife, and as for his daughter ... he smiled bitterly. No, Frederica would never really take him to court, she was too afraid of him. She would call it off at the last minute. Climbing back into his car, he started the engine, slamming his foot down on the accelerator, the dark roar throbbing under him and exciting him. Then his focus blurred for an instant, and he felt conspicuously unwell, his head falling forwards. Then, almost as quickly as it had occurred, the sensation passed and he drove off hurriedly.

Frederica would never go through with the court case, he assured himself as he made his way along the dark road. She hadn't the guts to do it alone – and there was no one around to back her up.

Chapter Thirty-Two

Paris

Notre Dame cathedral soared in front of them, the gargoyles peering down, the bells ringing out over the hustling streets, filled with meddling tourists. The sun blistered down on the pavement cafés and peered over the shoulders of street artists, the innumerable reproductions of the Mona Lisa glaring woodenly at the soles of passing Reeboks.

Warren screwed his eyes up against the sun whilst Conrad trotted beside him, happily eating an ice cream. For two weeks they had travelled, taking plane journeys or hiring cars, but constantly moving, Warren sending only the one fax, but phoning Freddie repeatedly. Indeed, over the last three days he had phoned her every evening and once during the day. They talked as neither of them had ever talked to another living person. Warren found for the first time in his life that he could be tender, without being afraid of incurring ridicule; and Freddie found herself confiding in Warren, taking from him some of the huge strength he possessed. All his intelligence and formidable will he offered to her, and spurred her on when she faltered about the court case – pushing her in a way that Bart had never done. He wanted her to achieve and to be brave. Where Bart would have protected her and asked nothing of her, Warren expected her to be remarkable.

And yet he would not return Conrad to her. Instead Warren tended their child and listened to his son as he had once listened to his daughter – seeing in Conrad a continuation of Alia, one life cut short and extended in another. The bond between them grew quickly as Conrad tested Warren constantly. Frequently difficult and moody, he displayed all the symptoms of an unstable child; and fortunately Warren dealt with all the disturbances, expecting them, for he had already experienced them himself. He loved his son with total commitment, just as he loved Freddie.

For it *was* love. Over the phone line and through all the distance of separation, they talked openly, and Warren felt himself consumed by Freddie. He felt for her as he had never felt for anyone. Her anxieties and memories became his, and any weakness she showed was accepted then turned into strength by him. He passed to her his fierce will, and she responded by passing to him her kindness and her own brand of courage. Before very long, each waited to speak to the other daily. Each longed for the other. In a love affair conducted without touch, but through the power of the voice and the heart, they moved towards each other inexorably.

Yet at that moment Warren was strolling along the Paris pavement with Conrad, glancing at the groups of women sitting drinking coffee and sometimes thinking he saw Freddie's face behind a pair of sun-glasses or recognised her legs as a woman sat down. Her hair seemed to be everywhere, dark under the sunlight; her skin repeated in the skin of every French woman; her eyes meeting his in every glance; and her body echoed in the bodies walking around him. He longed for her again. He no longer felt angry that Freddie had kept Conrad from him – he could finally understand her reasons. All the bitterness was being dissolved in their conversations and through their child; all Warren's anger was expunged by the boy who walked beside him. Inseparable, they travelled and at night Conrad slept beside his father, his small sturdy body curled up, his sleep undisturbed and placid. The legacy Warren had passed down to his son was not apparent in sleep, the temper gone from him as he dreamed, and soon the tantrums became less frequent as Warren enforced his own brand of firm, yet understanding discipline.

Under such guidance, Conrad flourished. He did not forget his mother and thought of her frequently, but she became a more distant memory as he turned to his father, wanting to please the man who had come into his life and who so

452

obviously cared for him. Only occasionally would Conrad feel the intense pain of homesickness when something triggered a memory – as it did that afternoon in Paris. He had been walking along happily when he smelt a perfume and recognising it as the one Warren sprinkled onto his pillow at night, turned and looked for Freddie. But she wasn't there and he stood helplessly, the sun melting his ice cream, the cold whiteness pouring down the palm of his hand.

'What is it?' Warren asked.

'I miss Mummy,' Conrad replied simply, wretchedly. A child remembering.

There was no annoyance or jealousy in Warren any more, and as he touched his son's hair lightly, he said, 'I know, I miss her too.'

'When will she come?'

The sun struck them full in the face, their shadows falling sadly on the pavement behind them. 'Soon.'

'You said that before.'

'I know,' Warren replied.

'So when *is* she coming?' Conrad repeated, the ice cream still trickling between his fingers, the urgency in his voice tearing at Warren.

'Do you want to go home?'

'Yes,' Conrad replied suddenly, looking up at his father. 'Can we go now?'

'You can – but I can't,' Warren answered carefully. He had been preparing himself for this moment for days. What he had set out to do – to steal his child – he had accomplished. But he had not been prepared for what followed. He had never anticipated the changing of his soul, or the breakdown of years of anguish. Through Conrad, Warren had found he could feel affection and inspire it, and by talking to Freddie, he had exposed his real self and fallen so soundly in love that no trace of his original self remained. *If I lose you now*, he thought looking at Conrad with a composure which astonished him, *it will almost be enough. I can't hope to keep you, or to have Freddie, but through both of you I found myself again – and maybe that will have to be enough.*

453

'Conrad, I'll take you home, but I can't go with you.'

For a moment his son said nothing. He merely looked at Warren and tried to imagine leaving him. For so long they had been together and he had had such a good time. He'd been really happy, he thought, going places and playing games ... The perfume drifted across to him again and he blinked in the blinding sunlight, thinking of his mother and his toys and his school friends.

'Are you sure you can't come back with me?' he asked quietly.

'I'm sure,' Warren replied, his heart shifting, his chest tight with agony.

Then with a gesture of childish impatience Conrad tossed the soggy ice cream cone into the gutter and shrugged. 'Oh well, where are we going this afternoon?'

Sitting on the window seat in the drawing room, Harry glanced over to Freddie and wondered about her. He had spent as much time as he could with her, leaving his beloved Hall, and travelling down to London where he stayed in Dione's flat, calling over to Rutland Gate regularly. At first he had found conversation easy, most of it restricted to Conrad, but as time passed a peculiar change came over Freddie, and an unearthly calm descended on her. He had known, as had Mike Kershaw when she was a child, that Freddie had some form of insight. After all, she had sensed the fire long before Avery's death, but her stillness puzzled him. Such peace, such acceptance couldn't be normal, could it? Her son was kidnapped – of course she knew that it was his father who had Conrad, and that he was well – but how could she accept the situation?

And the phone calls ... Harry glanced out of the window. The first few had been frantic, almost desperate, but now when he overheard her talking it was as though he was an eavesdropper, their tone was so private. He has your son, Harry wanted to shout, you should hate him. Oh, but you don't, Freddie, do you? You don't. Almost as though she realised he was thinking about her, Freddie glanced up and smiled. The expression jolted Harry and made him momentarily light headed. Oh God, he thought with bewilderment. I still love you.

'How are things at the bureaux?'

There was a slight pause. 'Not bad. I think we might be holding our own,' she replied, as though it mattered to her; as though the business was still important. 'Are you all right, Harry? You look tired.'

'I'm fine,' he answered. 'I just feel I should be doing more.'

'There's nothing more you can do,' Freddie replied evenly. 'By just being here, you've helped me so much. I can't tell you how grateful I am, Harry.' Her thoughts turned back to her childhood suddenly. 'Do you remember the green bay tree in the garden at Cambuscan?'

Harry nodded.

'When I was a child it used to frighten me. I thought of it as being unbending, unforgiving and yet lonely, almost as lonely as I was. But last night I dreamed of that green bay tree and I realised that it had been standing there for generations, strong and unmoving. It has seen all our tragedies and absorbed them all … Well, that tree is now a symbol for me, Harry, and for Conrad. We will endure.'

Harry could find no words to answer her and after another moment, Freddie continued.

'Do you think Conrad is well?' She trailed off. 'Oh, God, it's not that I don't want him to love his father – I just don't want him to forget me.'

'He won't,' Harry replied carefully. 'But if he does love Warren, it means that he's treating him well.'

'I know … ' she said quietly. 'I know … it just hurts, that's all. Every day that passes I feel Conrad drifting away from me. In the mornings I go into the nursery and look at his things and remember what he used to eat and I wonder … if he's changed.' She stopped, struggling to control herself. 'All those little things we used to do, like saying good-night to each of his toys – Warren can't do that, and I thought Conrad would miss it … but perhaps he's forgotten already.'

'He's with his father, Freddie, everything's different for him.'

Freddie pushed back her hair. 'I'm ashamed, but,' she

spoke so softly that Harry had to strain to hear her, 'I keep wanting Conrad to run away to prove that he loves me. Isn't that selfish? I want him to choose *me*.' Her voice broke. 'But if he did run away something dreadful might happen to him, so I pray that he stays with Warren because I know with him he'll be safe. I know he won't hurt him ... and that's the most important thing, isn't it, Harry? That Conrad should be safe ...' A sudden rush of pity welled up in her. 'I don't feel anger towards Warren any longer,' she said, frowning. 'I don't want him punished ...'

'He took your son!' Harry said, furiously.

Freddie's eyes were impassive as she glanced over to him. 'He took his son away from me – as I kept Conrad away from him. The scores are about even, actually.'

As the third week of Conrad's disappearance began, Freddie again visited Godfrey Hudson with Andrew Rose, and she gave them instructions to take out a legal injunction against her father which forbade him to deal in the shares he had fraudulently obtained. In effect, she tied his hands, and believed that the action would finally force him to take her seriously and return the shares to her mother and thereby avoid a court case.

But Greville made no response and for once remained silent, Freddie phoning her mother the same evening to advise her of what she had done. Sarah seemed distant, even more desultory than usual. Knowing nothing of their argument, Freddie was surprised by her mother's lack of interest and forced the matter.

'What's going on? You sound strange, Mummy.'

'I'm OK, darling,' Sarah replied half-heartedly. 'But I can't give you any advice. You must do what you think is right.'

'I will, but I wanted to explain why I was taking father to court.' Freddie paused. 'Are you sure you're all right?'

Sarah nodded, smiling languidly as Meg came into clear away the dinner things from the table in the dining room. 'I'm lonely, that's all. You never come to see me any more and I haven't seen Conrad for weeks.'

Neither have I, Freddie thought helplessly. 'I'm busy at the

456

moment, and you know that Conrad's got chicken pox, so he isn't seeing anyone for a while. I have a lot on my plate just now, please try and understand that.'

'I do, sweetheart, I do,' Sarah said, without conviction. 'I just can't follow what's going on. It's all so complicated.'

'Father was trying to get complete control over the business by having the majority of shares,' Freddie explained patiently. 'I had to stop him because the firm is not his to do with as he pleases. It's yours, ours, and Conrad's one day. You must realise that I have to prevent his getting ... '

'I don't want to talk about your father!' Sarah snapped suddenly, taking her daughter by surprise.

'OK! OK! If you don't want to talk about him, we won't,' Freddie said soothingly, her mind running on. 'The case comes up at the end of this week, in the High Court. I have to give evidence.' She paused, but there was no comment from her mother. 'Hopefully it will all be over then. You'll get your shares back and I'll – '

'No more!' Sarah shouted, her voice piercing. 'I don't want to know any more. You just do what you have to, sweetheart, and I'll talk to you soon.'

With that, Sarah put the phone down.

Freddie never expected support from her mother, but she had expected some gratitude. She knew that Sarah loved her father to distraction and would do anything for him, but why protect him now, when he was going to divorce her? Leaving her for a younger woman who was having his child? Freddie shook her head disbelievingly. She knew that if her mother thought that she could get her husband back, she would sign over her money, her home, and her grandchild's future without a second's thought.

Freddie suddenly felt isolated. Harry, for all his careful attention, could never really understand; Bea had never forgiven her; Jao was travelling; and her mother ... well, her mother loved her father, so there was no support there. *I am on my own*, she thought, surprised that the realisation did not frighten her as much as she expected it to. Sighing, she rose to her feet in the drawing room, picked up Bart's photograph

457

and studied his face, her fingers running over the glass tenderly. The room was quiet, the night drawing in outside, a soft indolent wind brushing against the curtained windows. But as she looked at Bart's face the wind blew up more fiercely. The magnolia tree outside scratched the window suddenly and the feeling of fear from her childhood came back like the Ice Saints from over the moors.

'It's not over yet,' she said bleakly. 'It's not over yet.'

'We've got a lovely new client,' Chris said happily as Freddie walked into the bureau. 'He's really nice.'

Smiling, Freddie moved into her office to be greeted by a tall, young man with long, brown hair and a boyish expression. He was dressed in an overlarge corduroy jacket and tweed trousers.

'Sim Bennings,' he said, offering his hand.

Freddie liked him on sight and accepted his handshake, offering him a seat and sitting down herself.

'So you want to join the bureau?' Freddie asked, glancing at his notes, all of which were in order, as were his psychiatric report and medical assessment. Apparently Sim was a commercial artist, poor but imaginative, with a degree from Newcastle University and a very sharp line in humour.

'I'm forty – I know I don't look it, so don't be embarrassed to say so,' he joked, 'and I haven't found the woman I want. Well, one that wants me too. I need someone who can have a good laugh, and who wants to poke fun at things a bit. You know the type. Someone who doesn't take themselves seriously.' He tugged at his old jacket. 'I'm strapped for cash – which just goes to show how successful I am at my job – but I've got the money for the enrollment fee. Took me nearly a year to save up.' He smiled, and Freddie smiled back, a sudden thought occurring to her. This man was perfect – utterly, completely, and totally perfect.

She had promised Jao once that she would return a favour to Bea. She had promised it because she knew that one day she would be in the position to keep that oath. Over the last year, Bea had been struggling to support the house in Dorman

Square, and although Freddie had offered help via Jao, she had refused any assistance. I know why you're angry with me, Freddie thought, because I betrayed Bart. Well, now I have a way to repay you.

For years Freddie had known that Bea's one wish, above everything, was for Jao to be happy and married. That was the most important consideration in her life and the one wish she wanted granted. Well, Freddie thought, maybe I can grant it for you at last.

'Sim,' she said carefully. 'I have a little suggestion to make – it's unorthodox – but hear me out.'

He grinned, already interested.

'How would you like to meet your ideal woman?'

'Of course! That's what I saved up the money for.'

Freddie shook her head. 'No fee.'

His eyebrows shot up.

Quickly Freddie scribbled the Dorman Square address on a piece of paper and pushed it over to him. 'Go there and tell the woman called Bea Wilkie that you want to rent her top flat – she has a daughter called Jao … '

Realisation dawned in his eyes and he grinned hugely. 'But why are you doing this? What about the money?'

'No money,' Freddie said, getting to her feet. 'This is an old debt that's needed paying for a long time.' Firmly, she guided him to the door. 'Never tell Bea or Jao that I sent you, just go there and let nature take its course.'

Sim took her hand and kissed it like a knight of old. Then he looked at her face carefully. 'Thank you,' he said, laughing with pleasure. 'I don't know what to say.'

Freddie shook her head. 'Don't say anything – just be happy.'

Sim turned as he left, his hand on the glass doors of The 107 Club. 'I'll never forget this – or you.'

'Too damn right you won't,' Freddie replied laughing. 'I'll dance at your wedding.'

Chapter Thirty-Three

The court was half empty, the case not well attended, apart from the major participants: the two counsel, the judge, solicitors, and Freddie and Greville Clements. Greville had contested the injunction, pursuing the matter recklessly to the High Court, dragging his solicitor and barrister behind him. At the back of the court Madelaine Glauvert sat with her hands over her pregnant stomach, her skin dry, her clothes expensive but hardly flattering to her condition.

The case had been arranged to be heard that Friday morning at eleven. Freddie performing automatically through an exhausting week at the bureau, her mind constantly returning to Conrad as she tried to keep the secret of his disappearance and also to cope with the day to day work at 107 Rutland Gate. The business was teetering on the brink, and only the combined efforts of Tina, Dot and Chris helped to keep it from toppling into the abyss, although when Tony Shaw appeared in the gossip column of a glossy magazine to make thinly veiled references to the bureau, the phones were busy for days. Freddie could only pray that no one would discover Conrad's abduction by accident.

After the shock of Beth Holland's murder, some of the consultants had sought work elsewhere at other bureaux in London or Europe. Some even joined up with a jubilant Mala Levinska who was delighted to see that the misfortune she had set on course was rolling on nicely without hindrance. Yet as the The 107 Club struggled to survive, those who remained were even more determined to outlast the crisis.

Dot was immovable. 'I'm not happy about the way things are here, and as you know, I shoot from the hip ... '

'Or is that the lip?' Tina said, laughing lightly. 'Oh come on, cheer up, we've gone through worse.' She went on, 'Anyway, we've got some new clients and I know they're going to be lucky.'

Chris looked up from the account books. 'It's not good, but we'll get through,' she said, although the figures had shaken her and she was surprised that Freddie was spending so little time in the bureau. She didn't know about Conrad, or the imminent court case with Greville Clements. 'Mrs Wallace needs all the support she can get at the moment.'

'She's getting it,' Dot said firmly. 'I read a nice piece about her in the *Mail* the other day, so perhaps the tide's turning.'

'It needed to,' Chris said quietly. 'It certainly needed to.'

And whilst they remained at their posts downstairs, determined that none of them would give in or desert, upstairs, Molly also hung on. Her guilt was all-consuming and Freddie's reassurances made no difference to her wretchedness. Freddie might say that Conrad's abduction was not her fault, but Molly knew better. Every day reminded her of Conrad's absence and her guilt; every afternoon at four the clock chimed the damning time that Conrad was taken, the hour which, for the remainder of Molly's life, would never cease to make her stomach lurch in remembrance.

Throughout the day, Molly did not cease from restless activity and at night she did not sleep, lying open-eyed, listening to Freddie walking about in her room below. The strain became something palpable, like a cord between them. When one of them referred to Conrad, the cord tugged, pulled, inflicting pain on each of them. Both women loved the child and both worried for him, missed him, and waited hopefully for the phone calls from Warren. Yet as time passed, Molly found it extraordinarily difficult to keep the abduction a secret and made constant references to Conrad, nearly confessing all to Jean Allen one morning when she enquired how Conrad's 'chicken pox' was getting on. It was even more difficult when Sarah rang and asked how Conrad was, re-questing news of a child who was missing, Molly fumbling her excuses and making nervous jokes to cover up.

Yet gradually the lying became easier, even though Molly wondered how the story would change if Conrad never re-turned ... The thought shocked her and she cried out, turning over and burying her face in her pillow, her eyes red rimmed the following morning. How long would they wait, she wanted to ask. How long?

But with a calm which was awe inspiring, Freddie contin-ued to work and wait, to talk and coax and wait again. She answered the phone and held conversations and believed that somehow, some day, Conrad would come home, and the bureaux and their lives would be restored. Even when Warren didn't phone one night in the third week of Conrad's absence, she held on, using perception rather than logic and believing instinctively that all would be well.

Yet the Friday court case came up on Freddie quickly, her composure threatened as she arrived alone, for Harry had been called back unexpectedly to Yorkshire. Anxiously, she glanced around the court room before leaning towards An-drew Rose.

'That's him,' she said, pointing to Greville. 'That's my father.'

The solicitor glanced over, nodding briefly to his colleague representing Greville Clements and then turned back to Fred-die. 'This is ridiculous, he hasn't a chance of overthrowing the injunction.'

'Then why would he try it on?' Freddie asked anxiously. 'My father's not a fool. He must have some motive behind all of this.'

Andrew Rose shrugged. 'God knows. I never thought it would get this far. I'm sure he didn't either.'

'He was mistaken then, wasn't he?' Freddie remarked wryly.

The judge came in hurriedly, glancing round to the clerk of the court and then at the assembly in front of him, before casting his eyes quickly over the notes of the case and talking

462

to both counsel. Their conversation was animated and laborious, the judge listening carefully as Godfrey Hudson wheezily outlined several issues, his hands extended theatrically when he wanted to make a point. Without being able to hear what they said, Freddie watched from her seat, her hands tightly clasped together, her head banging with the beginnings of a headache.

'Why don't they get on with it?' she hissed to Andrew Rose.

He shrugged. 'I'm not sure.'

Sighing, Freddie leaned back in her seat and then sat forwards again when the judge called everyone to attention.

'I have been advised by counsel acting on the behalf of Mr Greville Clements that there is some further evidence to be considered, so the case will be heard on Monday at nine-thirty instead. Case dismissed.'

It was then that Freddie nearly lost control, and slumped back dejectedly in her seat as her father and Madelaine Glauvert left the court without even glancing in her direction. Slowly she rose to her feet, her head buzzing as she walked out into the Strand, Andrew Rose following.

'It's a flaming nuisance,' He said. 'Still, it'll be heard on Monday, that's not too long to wait.'

It's a lifetime, Freddie thought, a lifetime. Everything on hold again. Waiting for news, for Conrad.

'I'll get you a taxi.'

Freddie shook her head and began to walk slowly away, down Bedford Street towards Covent Garden. Her mind functioned laboriously, her feet dragging over the pavement, the constant question running over and over in her head – Where was her son? Where? Call me, Warren, *talk to me*.

Without knowing where she walked, Freddie crossed London and entered St Martin's Lane, turning her steps towards Cecil Court. Blindly she peered into the booksellers' windows, the dull bindings of old, out of print volumes turning their dry spines to her view. Everything Warren had said began to blur, the words jumbling. A gaudy hanging basket creaked as she passed and made her jump, and unsettled, she hailed a taxi and returned home. A long weekend stretched

463

out before her, two days and two nights to fill; two days and two nights to nag at her, worry her, and tease her. Why hadn't Warren rung? Why? I might have lost my son for ever, she thought suddenly, a roar of panic making her heart beat too fast, her palms sweaty. No, she said to herself, no, he'll come home, I know he will. I'll win this case on Monday and he'll come home. I won't be beaten, she thought, rousing herself. Not by anyone. I've paid for what I've done and I'll have my son back. She folded her arms, her nails digging into her skin as she paced around her study. There is nothing that can't be saved. Nothing, not my son or my business. I just have to believe, that's all. I just have to believe in myself. Nervously she glanced at the phone and willed it to ring, but it remained maliciously silent throughout the evening and later stayed quiet beside her bed. At three in the morning she flicked on the light and reached for the brandy decanter, her hand hesitating then falling away. No, Freddie, she thought, better to remain clear headed. She glanced over to the phone again and it seemed to swell before her eyes, suddenly the largest piece of furniture in the room. A gigantic object, filling every corner as it sat like a huge cream toad – but it remained silent.

'Can I come in?' Molly said, entering timidly, her head hung low, her hair still tied back in a pony tail, her glasses slipping down her nose. 'I wanted to ... '

'Talk?' Freddie said, finishing the sentence for her.

Molly nodded, standing awkwardly, her face grey with pallor, her eyes swollen.' I wanted to say ... ' Her voice trailed off, her fingers clutching the sides of her dressing gown, her misery filling the bedroom.

Freddie put her arms out to the girl and Molly rushed forwards, her face pressed against Freddie's shoulder, her tears already old ones as she repeated over and over again, 'I'm sorry ... Oh, God, I'm sorry ... I'm so sorry.'

'Hssh,' Freddie said simply, rocking her on the side of the bed. 'Hssh.'

'It was my fault.'

'It was no one's fault.' Freddie insisted, lifting Molly's chin and looking into her eyes. 'The only fault you have is that you love Conrad too much.' She smiled gently, as though she knew something, and for the first time in weeks, Molly relaxed. 'When I was little,' Freddie began, 'I used to have a rabbit, a pet rabbit.' She thought of Mrs Gilly and of the Kershaws, drifting back to her own childhood. 'I was thinking that when Conrad comes home we'll get him a pet. A puppy.' She looked at Molly. 'Do you think you could cope with a puppy too?'

The girl could hardly speak.

'It would be a lot to look after, I know, especially with Conrad being such a handful.' She continued to rock Molly as she had rocked her son so often. 'But you can cope, can't you, Molly?'

'I can do it, Mrs Wallace, I can,' the girl said, desperate to prove that she was worth this second chance.

Freddie nodded, her thoughts fixed ahead, planning the future for herself and for those she loved. 'Of course you can do it, Molly,' she went on dreamily. 'We'll get Conrad a puppy, ready for when he comes home.'

The following morning, Warren phoned. Sick with relief, Freddie answered.

'Thank God, I thought something had happened to you.' They both paused – was her concern just for Conrad? Or for him too?

'I'm sorry, I couldn't get to a phone yesterday – I should have called. I was so anxious that you'd be upset,' he went on hurriedly, his voice unlike his own, altered by responsibility. 'Conrad's well, and happy. How did the case go?'

'It didn't,' Freddie said flatly. 'It's been put off until Monday. It's hard, Warren ... it's so hard.'

'Come on, keep fighting,' he urged her. 'You'll win, I've told you, you'll win.' He changed the subject. 'I took Conrad roller skating, he's good.'

'He could have fallen – '

'But he didn't,' Warren said quickly. 'Do you think I would let anything happen to our son?'

'No, Warren, I don't,' she replied honestly. 'And I don't understand why I don't hate you any more.' Her voice was

465

steady. 'I miss my child, and yet I feel as though he should be with you – not all the time, but some of the time.' She offered him her trust and he took it gently, as though it was liable to break and shatter for ever if he wasn't careful with it. 'I think of you both.'

'I think of you every moment,' Warren said, his voice low. 'Each second of my life is yours.'

Freddie sighed, almost having expected the words. 'Tell me, Warren, does Conrad love you?' Freddie asked.

'Yes ... not as he loves you, but he does love me.'

Freddie nodded, anguish mixing with relief. 'I'm glad ... I want to see you,' she said, then paused. 'This is not a trap – I really do want to see you both. Conrad, and you.'

The line crackled then cleared again.

'I didn't hear what you said!' Freddie called out, but Warren's voice was already fading.

'I'll call Monday,' he said simply, before the connection was cut.

Sunday came in sullen and heavy with bells, the evening clinging on like a child reluctant to go back to school. At seven, Harry came back to London, already anxious about the court case in the morning. He had seen Sarah Clements briefly the day before in Yorkshire and had been surprised by her attitude, her high voice almost squeaky with annoyance. As courteous as ever, she had invited Harry in for tea, regaling him at long length about Greville's myriad unkindnesses, her loyalty finally washing out like a spring tide. Patiently he had listened and avoided questions about Conrad, his own thoughts with Freddie, as they were now.

'I'll call round to collect you in the morning,' he said to Freddie, full of concern.

She smiled, the enigmatic smile, the smile of her childhood when she was certain of something others only guessed at. 'Fine, I'll be ready at nine, Harry. Thank you.'

As the first light of Monday morning heralded in the new day, Freddie rose, her mind obsessed with the day to come, her face impassive. I must be strong, she told herself, now is not the time for weakness. Quietly she made her way downstairs.

Molly, already in the kitchen, glanced up and smiled as Freddie came in.

'I know today's important, so I've made you breakfast,' she said simply, laying the tray down on the kitchen table.

Freddie smiled but ate with little appetite, her whole attention on the court case to come. She would win and then when her son's future was secure, Conrad would come home. Yes, she thought, her hands toying with a piece of toast, *then* he would come home.

'Eat it all up,' Molly said. 'I always tell Conrad that he needs a good breakfast … ' She stopped, mortified.

'It's all right,' Freddie said quickly. 'I want to talk about him too … especially today.'

Back to the court Freddie went at nine-fifteen, catching sight of Madelaine Glauvert and then her father. They looked almost smug, Freddie thought, as she noticed with pleasure her father's flicker of surprise when Harry sat down next to her. You thought I would be alone. You wanted me to be alone, as I was when I was a child, all the easier to intimidate.

As though she was watching a replay, Freddie saw the counsel approach the bench and a long exchange take place, her father leaning down and kissing his mistress's hand as Freddie turned away, her head banging. Get on with it, she thought impatiently, get on with it.

The case began slowly, picking up speed as Godfrey Hudson attacked Greville's counsel for even allowing the case to come to court, the man replying that his client was only protecting his own interests. Indignantly, Hudson pursued the matter. Freddie leaned forwards to listen but was so preoccupied that she was startled to find herself suddenly called into the witness box to give evidence.

Trying to collect her thoughts, she rose to her feet and walked across the courtroom, her eyes fixed straight ahead although she was aware of her father's stare. The faint dizziness she had experienced on waking began to increase, her heart beating fiercely as she gripped the rail of the witness box. Carefully she gave her evidence, the long memory of her childhood coming back to her as she faltered once and knew, without looking, that her father smiled. Swallowing, she struggled to compose herself, her eyes blurring before her as she fought to keep control.

But all the anxiety had finally done its damage and her attention wandered. Losing her grasp on reality, Freddie could only watch helplessly as the people in the court drifted into shadows, others taking their place. In front of her she could no longer see her counsel, but Conrad calling to her, and then Warren standing where Godfrey Hudson had been. She remembered the smell of the stables at Cambuscan and the fear she had felt looking out from the top window as her father came home.

The court juddered before her. It shivered in a heat haze, her mind jamming and constantly re-running the face of her child and the sound of Warren's voice. Then Bart appeared before her, kind, loving, affectionate – but suddenly his face changed to assume the look with which she knew he had died. The look of anger which had followed her down the years, together with the last question he ever asked anyone.

'Is he my son? Is he my son?'

But as Freddie struggled to answer Bart, his image faded. Stay with me, she called out to him, stay with me, Bart, stay with me ...

Watching her in the court, Andrew Rose turned to Godfrey Hudson and said something as Freddie tried to reply to the barrister's previous question, a look of desperation on her face. Then, just as she felt herself about to faint, she heard a noise behind her and thought she saw the courtroom door opening. Agonisingly slowly, she watched as her mother walked in dressed as though for a garden party, her outfit ludicrously frivolous and out of place. Transfixed by the mirage, Freddie wanted to laugh out loud, until she realised that it *was* her mother there, not a hallucination, but Sarah Clements, come to give her daughter support.

Galvanised by the sight, Freddie's head cleared immediately and she rallied, continuing to give evidence, her voice clear and firm in the court, her mother's eyes watching her, willing her on. It was not difficult for Freddie to imagine what it had cost her mother to defy her husband, so she fought for them both, for her mother and her child, and when she had finished she returned to her seat and grasped Sarah's out-stretched hand in her own.

The judge paused and then called both counsel over, dis-missing the court as he retired to his chambers. As everyone filed out, Freddie turned to Andrew Rose. 'What's going on?'

'The judge refused to lift the injunction and he wants us to settle out of court.'

She frowned. 'What does that mean?'

'Basically that your father has got his comeuppance,' he replied, getting to his feet. 'Godfrey Hudson's talking with your father's counsel now, so the whole thing should be settled soon.'

Impatiently, Freddie glanced through the doors of the court, watching as the two barristers argued, her father deep in conversation with Madelaine Glauvert further down the corridor. Smiling encouragingly, Freddie turned to her mother. Sarah was sitting on one of the benches, her plump legs crossed, resolutely ignoring her husband only yards away.

'Oh God, I was so glad to see you,' Freddie said, sitting beside her.

'I don't know what all the fuss is about,' her mother replied, touching her hair self-consciously. 'Your father's mistress is such a plain woman.' Freddie bit her lip, trying not to laugh. 'To think that he wanted to give her my money!' she said disbelievingly, her voice shrill. 'Over my dead body. My family worked for that and it's not going to the likes of that cheap tart. It's yours, sweetheart, and Conrad's, when the time comes.'

Freddie said nothing, she just clung to her mother's hand.

The verdict was a triumph. Greville Clements was ordered to return the shares to Sarah or to buy them legally, paying their true price. As the shares had been proved to be worth three million and not one and a half million, even if Sarah were willing to sell them, he would have to find the remaining million and a half and the news was not welcome to him. On top of this he was to pay ten per cent of the total share value to his wife in recompense. With a grim sense of justice having been done, Freddie watched as her father rocked at the verdict and her eyes remained fixed on him as he was informed by the judge that he would also have to pay his daughter's legal costs.

The judge glared irritably at Greville. 'You are a solicitor, I believe, and as such you must have known that your actions could be interpreted as fraudulent.' He paused. 'As this is a family squabble, it has been settled without too much trouble, but I advise you to be more scrupulous in your dealings in future and to stop wasting the court's time.'

Greville nodded abruptly, his stiff neck bending under the yoke of the law, his greed turning out to be more expensive than he had imagined. Beside him, Madelaine Glauvert looked stunned, her careful make-up failing to disguise her pallor as she heard the verdict. For someone who loved money so much the news was devastating, Freddie thought, almost seeing the Swiss woman age before her. But when her gaze turned back to her father her triumph was short lived. His glorious face was waxen, signs of illness and disappointment marring the fabulous features – he looked unreal, like a perfect shop dummy without life or reality, and with a jolt of pity, Freddie turned away.

Outside the court, the morning was a kind one, the sun peeling back the clouds as Sarah glanced at her daughter. 'We did well, didn't we?' she asked, childish with glee.

'We did well,' Freddie agreed. 'Are you going to come home with me?'

'No, I'll get back to Yorkshire,' her mother replied, almost flirting with her freedom and her new found independence. 'I want to go home now – and I hired a car so there's no problem about transport.' She touched Freddie's arm gently. 'What about you, why don't you come back to Cambuscan with me, sweetheart?'

'I have work to do,' Freddie said, glancing away. 'I have to stay here for a while, but I'll come home soon, I promise.'

Sarah nodded, her thoughts already drifting off. 'Well,

make sure you do. I want to see you and Conrad. Promise me?'

'I promise,' Freddie answered, watching as a car drove up at the kerb to collect her mother. The silly mass of her chiffon dress fluffing around her on the back seat as Sarah sat down. Waving, Freddie watched until the car wound its way out of sight and then she leaned against the entrance doors of the court and took in a deep breath.

'Do you want a drink?' Harry asked, materialising beside her, his hands deep in his pockets.

Freddie turned slowly. Harry's back was against the light and for an instant she couldn't make out his features – he could have been anyone.

'No ... No, thanks, Harry.'

He nodded, his voice subdued. 'I care a great deal for you, Freddie,' he said. 'More than you know. I should have told you a long time ago, but ... ' He shrugged and she touched his arm.

'I love you too,' she said softly.

His face brightened. 'Then will you ... '

Repeating the same action she had used years earlier when they were very young, Freddie laid her hand gently over his mouth. 'Don't say anything now, Harry ... not now.'

He hesitated, then smiled with that midsummer smile she remembered from the first day they met, when he had cleared the high gate to come to her.

'I'll see you tomorrow!' he said cheerfully, using the very same words as he ran down the court steps and out into the throng of the busy streets.

Freddie watched him go and heard the noises behind her, the corridors echoing with voices and footsteps, the sound of a telephone ringing in the distance. Then, as she hesitated at the exit, she was suddenly uncertain of what to do next. Under the kind sun, she stood trying to plan her future. Conrad would come home and then she would spend more time with him, taking him with her on her travels to the foreign bureaux. Yes, she thought, I can build up my reputation again, there are always people who need matchmakers and always other

471

cities to explore. We can see Dione and I'll take Conrad to the galleries – and besides, I have to even the score with Mala Levinska. My name means something, Freddie thought, for all the scandal and the gossip, it means something and so does my money. Her thoughts ran on. I can make people happy and …

Freddie stopped thinking suddenly, standing on the pavement, hopelessly bewildered and wondering what to do, and where to go next. She was fooling herself. It wasn't enough, she knew that. There was something lacking in her life that work and even Conrad couldn't fill. I have tried to ignore it, but it won't go away, Freddie thought blindly, making her slow way down the steps. Her momentum had gone, and she felt suddenly as lost as a child. Where was her composure now? she asked herself. She had been so certain that somehow Conrad would materialise as soon as she settled his future, as soon as she had had her day in court – but how would he come back to her? How? And why had she thought that? What had made her so certain? Blindly, Freddie gestured to her car and climbed into the back seat, her confidence crumbling. It was all a sham, a hoax, she thought desperately. My son is missing, gone. There is nothing else. No other reality, my son is gone …

They drove out into the traffic, Freddie blind with anguish and jumping with alarm when the car phone rang suddenly. Immediately George answered it, and transferred the call into the back seat.

The line hissed for an instant then cleared. 'Freddie – you won! Well done.'

She smiled, feeling such relief at hearing his voice that she could hardly speak. 'Yes, I won, Warren – I won for Conrad.'

'I know,' he said, with a rush of real pride. 'I told you that you would – I knew you would. It was justice, and you deserved that.' He hesitated, then continued. 'Was Harry with you?'

'Yes.'

'Do you still love him?'

A long moment pulled them apart. 'Yes,' Freddie replied.

'But not in the way you think. I love him as a good and gentle man ... and as a friend.'

'And me?' Warren asked. 'How do you love me?'

Freddie closed her eyes, the buildings sliding past the car windows as they drove on. 'I love you now for what you are – and for what I hoped you were when we made love.' Her voice was clear with certainty. 'You are my heart.'

The words echoed between them as Freddie waited for his reply, but there was nothing, simply a dead phone line. In shock, she dropped the receiver. So this was to be his final revenge, she thought bitterly. He had made her love him and then, when she had admitted it – finally putting the feelings into words, then he had rejected her as she had once rejected him. No, Freddie thought stubbornly, no, you are a good man now, Warren. I don't believe it of you. I won't.

The roads slipped past. London was lovely on this warm morning, newspaper sellers calling out on the sides of the streets, a flock of pigeons flying suddenly into the noon trees. Almost as though they walked before her, Freddie saw all the people who had been precious to her throughout her life – her mother, the Kershaws, emotional Penn, the gentle Harry, the elegant Dione, Bea and her sisters, and Jao with her sharp wit. All of them paraded in front of her eyes and then she remembered Bart – she saw him and recalled how much she had loved him and how much his death had tortured her. No, Freddie thought, shaking her head. No, I could not have fallen in love with a worthless man. I could not, Bart. Warren has changed, as I have. You always liked him and you would forgive us both now.

Yet still Freddie felt hollow and saw nothing as they drove along. The fear she had controlled for weeks uncurled and threatened to consume her. No, Warren, she assured herself repeatedly, I don't believe it of you. The cruel part of you is gone now, it's dead. I won't, I *can't* believe otherwise. No. You are a good man, I know it. I would stake my life on it – as I staked the life of my child.

The car sped on, finally arriving outside Rutland Gate. Freddie rose wearily to her feet and fighting back tears, stood on the pavement with the door key in her hand.

She heard the footsteps first, then the voice came echoing down the street, loud and certain.

'Freddie, wait!' he shouted. 'Wait!'

Instantly she spun round, dropping the keys, her arms extended as Warren ran the remaining yards towards her – whilst beside him Conrad whooped with laughter, his hands waving frantically under the watching sun.